PRAISE FOR LAUREN KUNG JESSEN

YIN YANG LOVE SONG

"Finished in one sitting. I absolutely adored it!"
—Christina Lauren, *New York Times* bestselling author

"The perfect balance of comforting and wildly romantic."
—Abby Jimenez, #1 *New York Times* bestselling author of *Say You'll Remember Me*

"With fluid writing and an unputdownable story, Jessen's witty rom-com leans hard into the fakedating trope with great success."
—*Library Journal*, Starred Review

"With a cast of loveable aunties, a generations-old curse, and the fascinating inclusion of traditional Chinese medicine, this uplifting story is truly special." —Melissa Wiesner, author of *Wish I Were Here*

"Jessen has crafted another charming, heartwarming romance that highlights Chinese culture as well as finding true love." —*Kirkus*

RED STRING THEORY

"I devoured this! Beautifully written, DEEPLY romantic, real, funny, heartfelt." —Christina Lauren, *New York Times* bestselling author

"Jessen impresses with this surprising and sophisticated contemporary romance. It's unusually cerebral for a romance, marrying a believable love connection with a thoughtful meditation on how humans make meaning in life. The result is smart, sensitive, and striking." —*Publishers Weekly*

"A lighthearted slow burn that's full of hope and heart. Delightful, inducing squeals and sighs in equal measure."
—*Kirkus*

"There's nothing I love in romance more than fated mates, and Lauren executes it beautifully in *Red String Theory*!"
—Sarah Adams, *New York Times* bestselling author

"A love story to Manhattan…Lauren Kung Jessen keeps getting better, and I can't wait to see what she delivers next!"
—Meredith Schorr, author of *Roommating*

LUNAR LOVE

"Tradition meets modern progress, and it's a delicious combination!"
—Abby Jimenez, #1 *New York Times* bestselling author of *Say You'll Remember Me*

"Debut author Kung Jessen does an impeccable job helping two adversarial lovers find common ground in their Chinese American heritage and creating a slow-burn romance with lots of humor, family, and food."
—*Library Journal*, Starred Review

"Jessen's debut rom-com hits all the beats of a tried-and-true rivals-to-lovers narrative."
—*Publishers Weekly*

"A refreshing and unexpected take on matchmaking! This will be a perfect match for any reader looking for a heartwarming romance steeped in cultural traditions."
—Jesse Sutanto, national bestselling author of *Dial A for Aunties*

"Lauren Kung Jessen writes supremely satisfying slow burn and rivals-to-lovers. There's heat, friction, sparks—it's a lit match."
—Sarah Hogle, author of *Old Flames and New Fortunes*

THE FORTUNE FLIP

Also by Lauren Kung Jessen

Lunar Love

Red String Theory

Yin Yang Love Song

THE FORTUNE FLIP

LAUREN KUNG JESSEN

FOREVER

NEW YORK BOSTON

This book is a work of fiction. Names, characters, places, and incidents are the product of the author's imagination or are used fictitiously. Any resemblance to actual events, locales, or persons, living or dead, is coincidental.

Copyright © 2026 by Lauren Kung Jessen

Reading group guide copyright © 2026 by Lauren Kung Jessen and Hachette Book Group, Inc.

Cover design and illustration by Sandra Chiu
Cover copyright © 2026 by Hachette Book Group, Inc.

Hachette Book Group supports the right to free expression and the value of copyright. The purpose of copyright is to encourage writers and artists to produce the creative works that enrich our culture.

The scanning, uploading, and distribution of this book without permission is a theft of the author's intellectual property. If you would like permission to use material from the book (other than for review purposes), please contact permissions@hbgusa.com. Thank you for your support of the author's rights.

Forever
Hachette Book Group
1290 Avenue of the Americas, New York, NY 10104
read-forever.com
@readforeverpub

First Edition: March 2026

Forever is an imprint of Grand Central Publishing. The Forever name and logo are registered trademarks of Hachette Book Group, Inc.

The publisher is not responsible for websites (or their content) that are not owned by the publisher.

Forever books may be purchased in bulk for business, educational, or promotional use. For information, please contact your local bookseller or the Hachette Book Group Special Markets Department at special.markets@hbgusa.com.

Print book interior design by Marie Mundaca

Library of Congress Cataloging-in-Publication Data has been applied for.

ISBN: 9781538772348 (trade paperback), 9781538772355 (ebook)

Printed in the United States of America

LSC

Printing 1, 2025

For my mom and dad, who I'm so lucky to have as parents and who taught me that success is a mix of a little luck and a lot of hard work.

CONTENT GUIDANCE

Dear Reader,

Thanks for picking up *The Fortune Flip*. I'm excited for you to go on this journey with Hazel and Logan! While this book is a rom-com and you can expect a happily ever after, I do want to let you know about some of the sensitive topics explored in this novel in case you're the type of reader who prefers that. If you think of content warnings as spoilers, skip the next paragraph.

Please be aware that job loss, death of a parent (in the past, off page), parental gambling addiction, and references to drunk driving (in the past, off page) are integrated into this story. I've done my best to handle these topics with compassion and thoughtfulness. Please read with care.

With love,
Lauren

Chapter 1

HAZEL

It's the fortune teller's bird that first catches my eye.

It looks like a sparrow, its coloring so white it practically glows. A second bird sits behind the first as they wait in their wooden cage.

"I need my fortune read, please," I say to the fortune teller sitting behind her table.

As soon as the words come out, the dark sky cracks open, releasing a heavy sheet of rain. With a newly burst pipe in my apartment building, I should take advantage of the free water. This rainstorm is probably my only chance for a shower for the night. Or the week.

Instead of walking the fifteen minutes home from Chinatown to the Lower East Side, I duck under the fortune teller's tent illuminated by bistro string lights. I sit in one of the chairs opposite her and place my purse, leftovers, and folder on the table.

The fortune teller introduces herself as Wendy. She has curly, chin-length gray hair, bright red lips, and a calm demeanor. She points to the sign behind her. "Fluent English. Fortune Reading. $10/reading. Cash only."

Conveniently, I carry cash. Credit cards aren't always reliable, and paying with cash sometimes means discounts. I give her my last twenty-dollar bill. Wendy hands ten dollars back and redirects me to the birds.

This close, I notice the faint red rings around their eyes. I'm both intrigued and intimidated by the alleged power they hold. They're like small, bird-shaped snowballs, their bodies measuring no more than five inches in length.

They remind me of the time a bird flew into our house when I was in first grade. It was round and soft-looking, with light brown on its feathers and a splash of yellow right between its eyes. I only remember because then, just like now, the bird looked right at me.

"A sparrow," Dad had said excitedly to Mom. "How auspicious. We should keep going. Happiness is just around the corner. This is our sign."

"Keep going" didn't apply to all of us. Mom died later that year. The "happiness" that was supposed to be around the corner? Well. It was less of a corner and more of a wall.

So much for auspicious.

"Do I look at you, or...?" I ask Wendy, wanting to make sure I don't mess up my first-ever fortune reading.

"Everything should pass through the sparrows," Wendy says, confirming my assumption. She explains that I'm supposed to ask the birds a question and that they'll pull three cards from the two boxes on the table. She'll interpret what the cards mean. "The first card represents our past, which influences our present. The second represents your current state. The third card gives us an idea of what lies ahead."

What my future holds.

Instinctively, I reach for Mom's charm bracelet on my left arm. The one I never intentionally remove. The one that somehow broke off without me realizing. Gone is the bracelet with the strawberry charm (her favorite fruit), her July birthstone (ruby), a dove (Dad's nickname for her), and a croissant (her childhood dog's name).

I swallow thickly at having lost what feels like a piece of her. At least there's still the lake house.

THE FORTUNE FLIP 3

I eye the red and orange cards tucked away neatly in their individual boxes.

"What are you wondering about right now?" Wendy asks.

"I'd like to know my future."

She eyes me. "Anything in particular you want to know?"

"Everything. I want to know all of it." I fold up the sleeves of my sweater just so I can give my hands something to do.

Wendy simply nods and points to each bird. "This one's Doc, and that's Marty, if you'd like to personalize your ask. Make sure to include your name and birthdate."

"My birthday? Why?" I ask, knowing this personally identifiable information isn't for these two innocent-looking, warm-blooded vertebrates but for Wendy, who will use the information to guide her fortunes. Or who knows what else.

"It helps me calculate your future," she states plainly. "I want to give you the most accurate reading."

Today was already bad enough. Do I really need to know how tomorrow and the next day—and every day after that—are going to be worse?

This impromptu reading was probably a mistake. And impulses have gotten me nothing but regret.

I glance around nervously, looking for an out from being yet another Yen family member about to make a reckless decision. The slick street is lit up by glowing store signs and food stall lights. Round red, pink, and orange lanterns dangle from one side of the street to the other. Through the downpour just outside the tent, I spot others huddled under stalls with signs advertising dumplings and mooncakes and with gold-painted trinkets for sale. Above all that, a large sign reads in blocky font "Good Fortune Fair."

Oh, right. Mid-Autumn Festival is next Friday. How is it already almost the end of September?

The sign looks more like an invitation instead of the warning that it is. But that's exactly what I want. No, *need*. Good fortune.

This is what happens when very bad days strike. It's impossible to resist anything that might make me feel better. After a quick, soul-crushing trip to the New York City Clerk's Office, I went to Sweet Escape, my favorite candy store. Then I went to dim sum to satisfy my sudden cravings for BBQ pork steamed buns. The restaurant had just sold out of char siu bao, the only thing I wanted in the first place. I overcompensated by ordering ten dishes off the cart. After all, I did wait two hours for a table, so I was getting my money's worth. I paid sixty-five dollars for an assortment of fried, steamed, boiled, and baked dishes and treats—taking most of it to go—not worrying about it until after. I haven't splurged on dining out in, well, who knows how long.

The good news is that I now have leftovers. Red bean sesame balls and shrimp rice noodle rolls may just be my saving grace later.

I take a steadying breath. I'm already here, and the birds are waiting. "Okay. Sure. Doc and Marty, I'm Hazel Yen. I was born on October 13, 1996, and I'd like to know…what does my future look like? Please. And thank you."

I don't know how to talk to birds, exactly, but I figure good manners couldn't hurt.

Under the orange glow of the lights, Wendy lifts both cage doors open.

Doc, the bird in front of the box with the red cards, hops out first. Marty steps forward onto the box with the orange cards. Doc moves his beak along several of the cards, taking his time with each one. My heart beats in anxious response.

Please pick good fortunes, please pick good fortunes.

I catch myself as a flicker of hesitation pulses through me. This is self-sabotaging at its finest. In an instant, this all becomes too real.

I pick up my stuff and wait for the right time to make my escape. But then Doc makes his selection from the back of the box. A few cards are dragged up together, but Wendy picks the highest one before giving Doc a grain of rice as a reward for a job well done.

My heart lurches. There, lying right in front of me, is an actual card with a prediction about what my life might look like.

Who knows? Maybe that card will be calming instead of cautionary. Maybe the cards will shed light on why, just hours ago, I was laid off without any explanation. And maybe, on the day of signing my divorce papers, I'll get reassurance that there's love—a lasting love that I can count on—out there for me.

Maybe I'll learn that today wasn't actually a very bad day, but instead a very lucky day.

Oh god. I sound like Dad.

Worst-case scenario, it's all bad, and life will be exactly as it has been.

Doc repeats his steps as Marty takes a couple of hops forward and lifts a card from the front. This time, only two cards are dragged up. The most prominent one in the stack is what Wendy begins to reach for.

I lean in closer, 100 percent of my attention on the cards and what they'll reveal.

Possibilities swirl around my mind. Like a life buoy, I cling to potential answers about my future like maybe these cards just might save me. Like maybe—

"Toffee!" someone shouts behind me.

What happens next is a blur.

There's a smear of white, black, and red, the sounds of bird wings flapping, paper shuffling, and... meowing?

In reaction, I hold my arms up over my face and shut my eyes. My bag of leftovers swings out of my hand.

A few seconds later, it's quiet.

"Are you okay? I'm so, so sorry," a man's voice says.

I slowly lower my arms and open one eye to find a frazzled Wendy, with Doc and Marty back in their cage with slightly ruffled feathers, and a white guy in a tie-dye, long-sleeve Henley holding a black-and-white cat in a harness. He and his cat are drenched.

I blink, my eyes adjusting to the neon tie-dye like I'm seeing sunshine after stepping out of a dark movie theater. It's as though a pack of highlighters leaked all over his clothes. The man—who looks slightly older than me, thirty maybe?—comes into clearer focus. As he steps toward me, I have to tilt my head back because he takes up so much vertical space, his blue baseball cap a shade darker from the rain.

The man apologizes profusely. To his credit, he does look sorry. Under the bistro lights, the cat's tea-green eyes seem to match his. On second glance, this guy's pupils are rimmed in teal, warmed by the outline of thick brown lashes.

I follow his mesmerizing blue-green gaze as it drifts from me to the ground.

All my stuff has been knocked over, my bag of leftovers split open. Now the siu mai and lo bak gao are covered in...street. There goes my midnight snack.

Tie-Dye Guy steps under our tent and bends down just as I do, our foreheads knocking against each other. We both grunt.

He kneels beside me and sets his cat down next to him.

"It's fine. I got this," I say, shooing him away.

The man lifts my now-empty folder. Beside it are my divorce papers, the ink practically still wet. Well, now it's literally wet. And smudged. Which doesn't matter, really, now that it's all over and done with. Even with it being a straightforward, no-fault divorce, it still cost hundreds of dollars. It was my most expensive mistake to date.

"Uh, here," the man says, stuffing the papers back into the folder and handing it to me. There's a micro lift in his eyebrows, telling me all I need to know. "Please, let me help."

I let out a pathetic laugh. "Nothing about *this*"—I gesture to myself while holding a piece of turnip cake—"can be helped."

He lifts one of the fallen-apart dumplings, the shrimp dangling precariously. "I don't think it's our fault. They don't make dim sum like they used to." As he says this, the shrimp gives up and falls.

The cat comes up and licks it. At least one of us gets to enjoy it.

All of this makes me laugh because it's exactly how I feel. Like shrimp that's fallen on the dirty ground, and there's nothing to be done about it.

My reaction surprises us both. Tie-Dye Guy joins in, and for a second, it's nice to be laughing with someone, our sounds blending into one. His laugh feels like being covered in a dry, warm towel after coming in from the rain. It seemed impossible, but I think a fraction of my stress melts away.

Our eyes lock as I'm catching my breath. Up close, he's even more beautiful than any person has a right to be. It's a weird thought to be having while sitting on the street in the middle of Chinatown.

Then I remember the fortune teller. The reading.

Any gains from our nice moment disappear when Tie-Dye Guy's smile falls, and he says, "You're bleeding."

I press the back of my hand to my forehead, the turnip cake wobbling between my fingers.

"No, your arm," he says.

Spanning the underside of my right forearm are long scratches. As soon as I notice it, the area begins to sting.

"Perfect," I mumble, tossing the food back into its container.

"We need to get you cleaned up," Tie-Dye Guy says, helping me up.

"*We* don't need to do anything."

He holds his arm out. "At least wipe your hands on my shirt. I have to wash it anyway."

I eye him. "Your shirt's bad enough. I don't want to make it worse."

Tie-Dye Guy laughs. "Wow. Haven't heard that one before." He straightens his arm. "Come on."

It's tempting. I hate the feeling of having dirty hands. But also, he's a stranger. "Absolutely not."

"Really, it's fine," he insists. "Of all my bad shirts, this one's my least favorite."

I don't want sticky fingers or for my clothes to smell like dim sum. Especially when there's no water for laundry.

I give in and use his arm sleeve as my napkin. "Thanks."

It's not like I'm embarrassed about taking him up on his offer. I just can't look at him directly as I do it. The fact that his gesture seems chivalrous says a lot about my day.

My attention drifts back to Wendy, who's been busy tending to her birds. I look down at the table. It takes me a second to process what's happened.

Once I do, I feel my heart drop to my stomach. My hands fall from Tie-Dye Guy's sleeve, grazing his knuckles on the way down. I inhale sharply, choosing to believe that this sudden intake of air is a reaction *not* to the short-lived skin-on-skin contact, but because of what I'm witnessing.

I was wrong about my worst-case scenario.

A bad fortune is better than a fortune that was never supposed to be yours.

Because after all that commotion, I now find myself with not three fortunes, but six.

Chapter 2

HAZEL

"No one move!" I say, holding my arms out.

I squeeze my eyes shut, trying to remember where Wendy placed the first card. It's too hard to know now that there are six cards on the table.

"It was that one, right?" I ask Wendy. "I remember Doc picking that one and you flipping it over there. Or was it Marty?" I lean closer to the birds. "Do you remember what fortunes you picked?"

"Fortunes?" Tie-Dye Guy asks, looking over at Wendy's booth sign. "Tell me I did not just mess up your future."

"There's a very good chance you did." I hate how panicked my voice sounds. I'm not freaking out over a fortune-telling reading, am I? It all becomes too overwhelming. I feel myself detach a little.

"Let's look for little beak marks," Tie-Dye Guy proposes.

The three of us scan along the sides of the cards, looking for evidence of having been freshly plucked.

According to Dad, bad things happen in fours. In Chinese culture, the number itself is considered unlucky. It sounds too much like "death."

I think the same logic applies to mistakes.

Mistake #1 was not making myself indispensable at work. I spent practically the entirety of my twenties at that place. I was loyal. That's rare these days. Was I the muscle behind their best reports? Yes. Did I have the most historical context, having been at the company for nearly eight years? Also, yes. But clearly, I was not essential enough to keep when my company merged with a bigger one.

Now I no longer have a job. The same job that not just supported me but also Dad and my brother. Plus, I liked being a data analyst. It suited me. And I worked hard for it.

It took my manager no more than a minute to sledgehammer the foundation of my life. *It isn't personal*, he had said at the end of a full day of work. And he's right. It isn't. Because that would mean I'm more than just a cog in a machine, a line item on a spreadsheet.

Mistake #2 was coming to a fortune teller. How, exactly, was this supposed to make me feel better?

Which brings me to Mistake #3: running into Tie-Dye Guy. Or no. Him running into *me*.

"Again, I'm really sorry. Toffee wasn't trying to hurt the birds," he says once we find that, unfortunately, there are small indents on every card. "Toffee just—he has this stuffed toy that he loves...it's a bird." He grimaces. "I can see where this all went wrong."

Wendy looks unamused by this.

The cards are a mess. A physical representation of my life, it seems. Money, a job, love, my future. It was all too much to hope for, clearly.

"Can we get the birds back out here? Do they have muscle memory or something?" I ask Wendy.

"The fortunes have been selected," she says definitively.

I shake my head. "They picked two very specific cards for me before this guy and Coffee even got here." I try very hard to suppress the fact that a black cat has crossed my path. I do not need any more bad luck today.

"His name is Toffee, and technically, he isn't my cat," Tie-Dye Guy says, like this might absolve him.

Toffee sniffs the air and lies down like this entire ordeal has exhausted him. Now that the damage has been done, he couldn't care less about the birds.

I stretch my neck up to look at Tie-Dye Guy. It's hard not to notice his height. He's got to be at least a foot taller than my five foot three.

"You're the one walking him," I press, the edge in my voice sharper than necessary. I rub my temples. "That makes you responsible for this."

"Well, yes," he says guiltily. "Toffee's muscle strength usually isn't that... forceful. Or sudden. He requires his daily walk or else he gets grouchy and tired. He'll keep Mrs. Walker up all night, so I need to maintain his routine." He tilts his head. "Though the rain didn't help."

"You," Wendy says, pointing from Tie-Dye Guy to the empty seat next to mine. "There."

I turn to face him. "No there. No sitting."

Tie-Dye Guy freezes in place, now half squatting over the chair.

"But she told me to," he says.

My mouth drops open in silent protest until I can find the words. "But what if you get good fortunes and they were actually supposed to be mine?" I ask.

The man seems to consider this. "Or they could've been bad and I'm sparing you from an unlucky life."

"Too late for that," I mumble.

"What's your name?" Wendy asks him.

"Logan," he responds. "Logan Wells."

Wendy nods curtly. "Good. Let's finish this reading. Just ten dollars more for the extra three cards."

Logan glances at the sign and pats himself down as he remains in his bent position. "I don't carry cash."

"What about the cat?" I ask dryly.

"I'm sure he'd be more than happy to share his catnip," he says, opening his wallet. "Would you accept a MetroCard? Now that they've been phased out, one day they might be valuable."

Wendy shakes her head. "Cash only."

Logan looks at me for permission to sit. "I like to think that I could do this all night, but I helped a friend move earlier this week. Five-story walk-up. I don't think I have much longer."

"My birds did draw these cards for a reason," Wendy says, putting the pressure on.

I steal a glance down at The Reason sitting contentedly next to Logan's leg, which is where I look next. Even soaked, his jeans look soft and well worn, like they might be his favorite pair. They're plastered against his thighs, accentuating his well-defined—and probably now burning—quad muscles.

I ignore the explosion of heat in my chest and nod to the chair. "Please. Stay a while. And you know what? My treat," I say with forced pep. Paying it forward is supposed to help, right? Maybe this good deed will stop anything else bad that's coming my way.

Or maybe I'm desperate to see what each of those cards says. But really, maybe it's because today I want to be right about something: that my fortune isn't so good. Not before, not now, and not in the future.

"But are you really prepared to know what your future holds?" I ask Logan.

He lets out a sigh of relief as he sits and smiles at me. A double parentheses brackets his mouth on both sides. It's like his smile has caused a ripple effect across his cheeks. Every physical part of him screams *man*, but this? This feature of his is boyishly charming.

"It's not how I saw this walk going, but why not?" Logan says.

He even sounds...excited? "I'm open to seeing what happens." Our eyes linger on each other's for a beat too long. God, he really does have pretty eyes. "Only if it's alright with you, though. Would you be okay doing this together?"

Together. This all started because of my bad decision. Now I'm in it with a perfect stranger.

I slide my last ten-dollar bill out of my wallet and reluctantly hand it over to Wendy. First candy and dim sum. Now fortune-telling. My budget is going to hate me.

"That's really nice of you," Logan says. "Thank you. I owe you."

Wendy slips the bill into a soft pouch and points to the three cards. "Just like in life, we'll have to work with what we've got. Those fell closest to you, Hazel. Let's call them yours." She gestures to me. "Please state your name and birthday, and ask your question again to Doc and Marty."

"Like *Back to the Future* Doc and Marty?" Logan asks. "That's clever."

Wendy smiles, waving toward her setup. "How could I not?"

Is Logan...befriending the fortune teller? He's definitely getting the good fortunes now.

I turn away from him. "I'm Hazel Yen," I whisper to the birds.

Behind me, Logan laughs.

I give him a look over my shoulder, and his laughter subsides, a residual smile on his face. He just sits there with his well-worn jeans and his bracketed mouth and looks at me. Really looks at me. It's not a face-off, but I treat it like one, and for the next couple of seconds, we're just regarding each other.

And then I remember the situation we're in.

Who cares if Logan's hot, even in that eyesore of a tie-dye shirt? The man ruined—and then joined—my desperate attempt for answers. It does feel slightly reassuring, though, to know that I'm not the only one making mistakes today.

"What? You don't want me to know your name and birthday?" Logan asks.

I furrow my eyebrows and glance away. "Of course I don't. I don't know you."

My colleagues at work don't—didn't—even know my birthday.

Logan dips his head to meet my eyes. When he does this, it's like he's trying to show me that I'm all he's focusing on. There's nothing, and no one, else.

"Fine." He runs his hands down his thighs, his forearms flexing. "But then you don't get to know mine."

There's a charge in the air surrounding me and Logan.

I feel my body spin in his direction. "And here I was hoping to get you something nice," I say.

A bigger smile stretches across Logan's face. "Well, you missed my last thirty-one birthdays, so I wasn't expecting much."

Wendy clears her throat, and I startle. The last thing I want is a connection with another good-looking guy. I've got the proof in the folder in my bag to see how that would end. "As I was *saying*…" I angle back toward the birds, lean in, and whisper, "I was born on October 13, 1996. What does my future look like?"

I sit back against the seat, my cheeks heating. I have no reason to be embarrassed. Knowing more about the future is the entire point of this. Still, I feel too exposed. Too impulsive.

An impulsive fortune-telling. An impulsive marriage. Why do I do this to myself when it all leads to nothing good?

"Great question," Logan says, rubbing his hands together. Veins run like little streams along the back of them, trickling out toward his long fingers. His hands look strong, like he could carry heavy things all day long and not even be tired at the end of it. "I'm going to ask the same."

I try to focus on what's important here: the cards. My fortune. My future.

Wendy unfolds the first card and smooths it over the table. "We'll begin with your past, then analyze your present and future," she says.

The cards are intricately painted in vibrant colors, depicting scenes with characters who look otherworldly. On this first card, a smiling woman in gold gestures toward a child. They're surrounded by six vases filled with flowers.

"You carry a lot of responsibility," Wendy says, her mouth turned down. Is that a frown? "You have for a long time." She holds my gaze for a few long seconds. "You're living too much in the past. You were happy then, but you were also sad. You're missing out on the present. Get in touch with your inner child. Play. Have fun."

My throat goes dry. I don't attempt to speak. Everything Wendy just said was eerily accurate. I cross my legs and my arms like I'm folding myself up. Usually, it comforts me, but right now, I can't hide.

My responsibilities practically roll out in front of me, like a mental news ticker. They're in no particular order because order would imply control, of which there is none. Bills. Student loans. Mortgage. Rent. Food. Health care. Money for Dad and Jerry.

Wendy analyzes the second card, which shows an older woman in flowing robes lifting her hands to a cobalt sky. Multiple swords fly above her, pointing somewhere off the card. I can't tell if she's defending herself, taking action against someone else, or practicing her skills.

"You'll experience a loss soon," Wendy states.

I huff out the last of the air in my lungs. Literally? Or does she mean that theoretically? This card is supposed to represent the present. I've already lost my bracelet, job, self-respect, hot water, and dim sum. I'd say I've lost enough today as it is.

"A loss? What loss?" I ask.

"It's going to be a difficult time with the suddenness of it," Wendy explains, her face neutral. "You may not understand or be ready to face your deeply buried wounds, but dealing with them will set you free."

"Maybe it's the dim sum, and it's behind you now," Logan says so genuinely I think he's trying to help.

"It's actually underneath me," I retort. To Wendy, I say, "*Going to be* sounds like a future thing."

"It's a fluid timeframe. These cards are responses to your question, but this entire reading only lasts three to four months," Wendy explains. She unfolds my third card before I can ask more clarifying questions. On it is a flying woman in a navy gown sending down what looks like lightning strikes at a building. The scene looks bad. Like something is falling apart.

My life, obviously.

Wendy watches me closely. "There's an event that will shake you."

My heart races. "Didn't that already happen? Isn't that what the last card was?"

"This has yet to happen to you," Wendy says, tapping her finger on the dark storm clouds before sliding over to the split-in-half structure. "It will be painful."

"Painful?" I shriek, my voice climbing three octaves. So much for numbing myself. This is what I get for demanding answers. "I need more details than that. Why is there lightning?"

"That's not always a bad thing. Nor is pain," Wendy simply states. Easy for someone who isn't about to experience pain to say. "Lightning can represent a breakthrough, a surge of insight, or a new perspective."

"Yeah, like Zeus," Logan contributes. "Maybe it means you'll be coming into authority or power."

I want to both laugh and cry at that. "Wasn't lightning used as a weapon of punishment?" I ask. I'm getting distracted. "That's not the point."

The point is: I never should have come here. What's worse, Logan is a witness to what my life has in store. Without him here, I could've played off these fortunes as a post-job loss overreaction. Now this moment is part of someone else's memory.

The solution here is simple. I'll just have to never see this guy again.

I'm lost in my thoughts for too long, and Wendy turns to Logan. She asks him to state his name and birthdate. As they move on to his fortunes, I can't move on from mine. Everything around me fades away as my head throbs. All I hear, ringing clearly in my mind's ear, are the fortunes I paid for with the last cash that I had:

I'm living too much in the past.
I'll experience a loss soon.
There's a painful event that will shake me.

A buzz from my phone distracts me from fully spiraling.

> **Aunt Alexis (9:31 PM):** Hiya, Hazel. Sorry to bother you. Trying to get in touch with your dad. Did he get a new phone number again? I need him to call me back. Can you help?

Last time Aunt Alexis got in touch, Dad owed her money. I don't get into the details with her. I pull up my thread with Dad and ask him to call his sister back. I toss my phone into my bag before I'm alerted to any new messages.

Outside the tent, the rain slows and then stops, leaving puddles behind. In them, I can see the strung lanterns, their colors brighter in the reflection.

I sense Logan shift in his seat next to me as Wendy taps on the last card, wrapping up whatever it is she's saying. They're done already? I missed everything she said.

Before I can ask Wendy to repeat Logan's fortunes, she randomly stuffs the cards back into the boxes and gives her birds more rice. A line has formed. Wendy looks eager for us to leave.

We thank Wendy, Doc, and Marty. In one swooping, seamless hand motion, our fortune teller waves goodbye and welcomes the next customer willing to pay for a little bit of hope.

If only they knew. I'd warn the rest of them, but Wendy was nice enough. She has bills to pay, too.

"Well, bye," I say to Logan and Toffee, taking a hard left down the sidewalk.

"Hey, wait up!" Logan calls out, catching up to me. Toffee trots quickly beside him.

"Let me pay you back for that," he says. "Please. It's the least I can do."

I raise an eyebrow at him. "I thought you didn't have cash."

"I don't, but I have credit and debit cards. There's a bodega on the corner. How about I buy you ten dollars' worth of Band-Aids?" He nods at my scratched arm, where Toffee's made his lasting mark.

I wave Logan off. "I'm fine, thanks. I can clean up when I get home."

Then I remember there won't be water to wash with.

"Seriously, I'd like to treat you to a first aid kit before that gets infected. Cat scratches can contain a lot of bacteria, and Toffee gets daily walks. It's best not to think about what's on these city streets," Logan urges.

Something about him draws me in. Just like the damn birds.

He takes off his baseball cap and runs his hand through his sandy-blond hair, the damp strands brighter under an illuminated shop sign. Doesn't he want to get home to dry off? Get warm? I don't understand why this is so important to him.

But if Logan wants to pay me back in expensive New York City bodega medical supplies, so be it.

"Can we make it quick?" I ask, tossing the now-contaminated bag of leftovers in a trash can. "It's been a day."

The three of us head down the street together. It's the opposite direction of home, but today has already gone off the rails.

Might as well get Mistake #4 out of the way.

Chapter 3

LOGAN

You're someone who likes to press his luck, aren't you?" Hazel asks as she pulls a packet of cherry gummies from a shelf below the checkout counter. Her question sounds more like a frustrated comment.

"What makes you say that?" I ask, grabbing a box of cotton swabs. The bodega's heat has finally started to permeate my cold, damp shirt and pants. Going home to change would've been the sensible thing to do, probably, but after everything that happened earlier, I'm not ready to say goodbye to Hazel quite yet.

"I can just tell," she says. "For one, you wear that shirt out in public. And you probably carry too many plates and bowls from the kitchen to the living room."

"Sometimes I even carry too many plates and bowls *while* wearing this shirt."

She doesn't laugh.

"Swing and a miss," I mumble.

Hazel's eyes flick up at me. "No, that was funny. But also, you were walking a cat on a leash. Feels a little luck press-y."

She resumes browsing, passing the island of ready-to-go food. She turns halfway back to me. The depth of her dark-brown eyes draws me in. There's an entire forest in them with a warmth that feels reserved for special occasions. Maybe even for special people.

I peer over the food island at her as she skims the items, seemingly distracted. Her face is illuminated from below, the light accentuating her cheekbones and full bottom lip, the dip of her Cupid's bow. When she glances up at me again with something playful in her eyes, it nearly takes my breath away.

She's gorgeous.

"In my defense, I'm pretty sure the smell of chicken lured him in," I say. "Like his namesake, he can't fully control himself."

"Caramelized sugar can't control itself?"

I laugh at this. "Mr. Mistoffelees is his full name," I clarify. "His owner, Mrs. Walker, was in the original production of *Cats*, and because Toffee's a tuxedo cat, she couldn't help herself." Hazel looks confused so I add, "Mr. Mistoffelees couldn't fully control his magic?"

Her expression doesn't change. "I don't know what any of that means," she says, walking away from me and scanning the fridge filled with beers and sodas.

I move over to the register and offload everything in my arms except Toffee. I take in the "No Smoking" and "Smile, You're on Camera" signs next to the bodega's social media handle advertising a chance to win a free king-size candy bar for each follow. I browse the shelving containing impulse buys. Anything to distract me from her.

"Add your cherries to the pile," I tell Hazel when she meets me at the front. Her eyebrows shoot up skeptically when she sees the pile of items on the counter. "This is all part of fixing you up. When hydrogen peroxide touches that"—I nod at her arm—"you're going to want something to bite down on."

Hazel doesn't fight this and sets the candy on the counter. As she does, she glances over the clerk's head at the wall of medicine and pain relievers. I follow her line of sight to a sign for Advil, but there aren't any boxes left.

"Anything I can grab you?" the clerk asks her.

Hazel shakes her head. "Oh, uh, I'm good."

The young clerk nods to me. "Ready?" he asks as he begins scanning everything.

"One box of antiseptic ointment, please. And actually...any chance you have more Advil back there?"

"I just sold my last one," the clerk says.

"Nothing in those boxes?" I push. "Would you mind taking a quick look? I'd really appreciate it."

"Uh...yeah, sure. One sec," the clerk finally agrees. He opens the flaps on a few boxes behind the counter.

"They probably don't have any more," Hazel says.

"Let's just see," I say.

"Ah-ha! You're in luck. Didn't realize this was back here," the clerk says, placing the box next to the other items. He nods at my wrist. "Cool bracelet."

Peeking out from under my long sleeve is my red, woven bracelet. "Oh yeah, thanks. It's by a string artist from the city. She had an installation in Times Square. Once it was over, they reused the material for these." I glance at his *Indiana Jones* T-shirt with a vintage-looking airplane flying through the clouds on it. "Nice shirt."

"Harrison Ford's the greatest," he says.

"Did you know he was a carpenter before hitting it big?" I ask, setting Toffee on the ground to grab my wallet. I tap my credit card on the card reader.

"Oh yeah? He came in here once. Great guy," the clerk says as he moves the last item into a paper bag, clearing off the counter. The bright blue of the New York Lottery mat draws my focus.

"What's the Powerball at?" I ask.

"Thirty million," the clerk says.

I grab a play slip from a holder on the wall, along with a pen.

The clerk hands me the bag. "Quick Pick?"

"I'll pick my own." To Hazel, I say, "I'll split whatever I win with you."

Hazel's head snaps up in my direction. "Do you do this a lot?" she asks.

"Pay for goods? Most of the time, yeah," I joke.

"No. Play games you know you'll lose," she says, crossing her arms. "Join random peoples' fortune readings. Offer half your lottery winnings to someone you don't know. Which you don't need to do. Obviously."

Hazel follows me and Toffee outside to an empty bench. Next to us, the bodega's flower stand is lit up, showcasing colorful roses, baby's breath, and mums wrapped in cellophane.

"Do you like any of those?" I ask.

Hazel glances over her shoulder. "They don't last long enough to enjoy them." She looks back at me. "Please don't get me any. You already got me enough."

"You sure? Those lilies look nice."

"They do, but I don't have water to put them in," she says. "Pipe broke."

"That's rough, sorry." I lift Toffee onto the bench and sit next to him. I pat the space beside me, but Hazel doesn't join us.

Instead, she asks, "Hey, what did the fortune teller say to you?"

"She said a lot of things. If I remember correctly, you were there, too."

"Nothing gets you disassociating faster than three bad fortunes," she says. I can tell that she's trying to make this sound lighthearted.

I pat the bench again. "You can trust me to help you with this," I try to reassure her.

She frowns, staying where she is. "You don't need to do that. I can take it from here."

"In my line of work, there are a lot of cuts. I'm pretty good at cleaning them up."

"Where is it you work that you get a lot of cuts?" she asks.

"I'm a carpenter. Well, now I work in a theater."

"Like on Broadway?"

"As of a few months ago, yes," I say as she makes a *huh* sound. "Now sit. Please. No one should have to bandage themselves up."

Toffee hisses at a dog walking by, prompting Hazel to sit between us and drape her unscathed arm over him protectively. The other arm she holds out toward me.

I rip open the bag of cherry gummies and hand it to her. "We can talk about whatever will take your mind off this," I say, setting her arm on my knee. Her hand is freezing, which makes me wonder if she's nervous.

I hold underneath her arm to keep it steady as I analyze her scratch in the light of the bodega's storefront window. It's worse than I thought. There are two six-inch-long parallel scratches. Just below her inner elbow is a miniature tattoo of the outline of Mickey Mouse's head. It surprises me, this particular permanent choice she's made.

"I want to talk about your fortunes," she says again, keeping her eyes on me. I feel her arm flex in my hand. "She must've said something really good for you to buy a lottery ticket."

I open the canister of hydrogen peroxide wipes. "She did say good things." My smile drops after I hear myself. "Oh. Shit. Did I take your good fortune?"

Hazel looks back at me, her eyes widening. "I don't know, did you?"

"I don't know! Do you want mine? Seriously, you can have them."

"Pretty sure that's not how it works. And besides, I don't want your pity fortune." She gasps. "Wait, is this why you're offering to split your winnings? To assuage your guilt of fortune-stealing?"

"Gummy," I prompt, and with her free hand, Hazel quickly reaches into the bag and stuffs a handful of cherries into her mouth.

I make quick work of dabbing across the scratches with the wipes. She doesn't react.

"Wow, I'm better at this than I thought. Did that not hurt?"

"It was es-croosh-ting." She swallows the candy down. Her watery eyes find mine as she licks her upper lip. That lick does something to me. "Excruciating."

I track her eyes sliding down my face to my lips. It's quick, but I'm quicker. She catches me catch her. Hazel turns her head away as her cheeks pinken. She's so fucking cute when she blushes.

Hazel closes her eyes and rubs her temple with her free hand. "Can you please just tell me what your cards were? Do it quickly, while everything already hurts. Get it over with at once."

I open the boxes of Neosporin and cotton swabs. "First of all, no, I'm not trying to ease my conscience," I say, responding to her earlier question. "I don't like having debts. This is me paying you back. Wendy said abundance is coming my way in my job or finances. That was from the present card, so it could happen any day now."

"I can relate to the debt thing, but the reading cost ten dollars," Hazel says, peering into the bag. "This more than covers it."

I squeeze ointment onto the cotton swab and run it over the long red lines.

"What about the future?" she asks. "What did your third card look like?"

I dump the box of Band-Aids into my lap, dozens of miniature Hello Kitty faces smiling up at us. I peel off the backing to the bandages. "Wendy said I have everything I need to make my dreams a reality and that next month is a good time to execute on any ideas or goals I've wanted to achieve." I shrug, pressing down gently on the sticky strips. I use up the entire box. "You're good to go."

She looks down at the clowder of cats on her forearm. "Thank you. After everything today, that was the least painful part about it." She runs her finger along the row of bandages. "Why are you being so nice to me?"

"Why wouldn't I be?"

"Because I've been, I don't know..." She avoids direct eye contact. "I'm in a bad mood. And you helped me. With wet clothes on."

Hazel doesn't play games. She's straightforward and blunt, and when she's mad, it's clear.

Her honesty is refreshing and attractive as hell.

I dip my head to meet her eyes. "I guess I didn't want to say goodbye yet," I confess. "And it's my fault you were all scratched up, so it didn't feel right to leave you like that."

This is the moment we both realize her arm is still in my hand. By the looks of it, she's surprised, too. There's an energy in the air around us. That's the best way I can describe it. A spark, a pulse.

She doesn't jerk her arm away. Instead, she lingers, drawing out this physical connection between us. She turns her arm so that her fingers graze my forearm, the texture of her Band-Aids brushing against the pads of my fingertips. Hazel's lips part briefly before she presses them together and sits back, pulling her arm away with the movement.

"So, October is your month, huh? Is something big happening?" she asks.

I squeeze my hand into a fist. "I do happen to have a huge event next month. Opening night," I say. "It's my first show as head carpenter. Wendy said I need to act on my goals. They won't just happen. And it can't be about money or fame. I need to have a deeper connection with my ideas." I toss all the extra supplies and garbage into the bag.

Hazel sits back against the bench. "Wow. That's...great." She goes quiet for a few long seconds, and I think that's the end of it.

Then she adds, "I don't really know you, but it sounds like you need that luck as much as I do." Her tone is softer toward me than it's been all afternoon.

"I know what you're thinking. Us white men in America need all the luck we can get," I say sarcastically.

I get a single laugh—and an eye roll—at that. "What was the first card?" she asks. "The past."

I toss a handful of candy into my mouth while I recall Wendy's interpretation of the card that had a peaceful-looking person sitting next to incense, the smoke a wavy river floating overhead.

"She said I was fortunate, but that I've also had hardships that I've overcome," I share. It was too vague to know for sure what she might've been referencing, but her words stirred up memories of the accident eleven years ago. The turn of events. Rejecting life as I knew it. The luck. So much luck. "I kind of want to see if she's right." I wave the lottery play slip in the air. "And then I'm going to split whatever I win with you."

"Yeah, okay. Give me half. Really excited for that," Hazel says with a teasing smile. "You know, it'd be easier for you to withdraw cash from the ATM."

I grin. "But where's the fun in that? Isn't this what people do? Go to a fortune teller, get told something fortuitous, buy a lotto ticket?"

Hazel scoffs. "Yeah. You're right. They do."

"I know we have a better chance of waking up tomorrow having like, body swapped or something, but—" I shrug. "I'm curious, is all. Let's just see."

"What'd I say?" she says with a hint of laughter in her voice. "Pressing your luck."

"Go big or go home, right?"

"I'll take going home," Hazel says, but she doesn't make a move to leave.

I think maybe her curiosity has won out. I uncap the blue pen. "We can choose five numbers between one and sixty-nine. Then one number will be our Powerball. It can be one to twenty-six. I know you don't gamble, but would you be willing to pick the Powerball number?"

Hazel starts to shake her head, seemingly changing her mind halfway through. "Okay. For you, I will," she says, her eyes lingering on mine. "Six."

I fill in my numbers and then go pay for the ticket, taking the play slip and pen with me while Hazel watches Toffee. When I return, I hold out the ticket. "I've thought about it, and I think you should hang on to this."

Hazel's eyebrows furrow into a V-shape. "You thought about it on your walk from here to there and back again? You should take more time with that idea."

"Maybe my fortune will rub off on you," I say. "I want you to have some luck, too."

She flashes a look at me as if to communicate *you're not serious*.

"Luck isn't contagious," she says, standing to meet me. She sets Toffee on the ground. "You can't just... transfer it."

"Not with that attitude, you can't." Again, I try handing her the ticket.

Hazel holds her hands behind her back. "I'm serious. You don't want me touching that thing. Didn't you hear my bad fortunes?"

"You think your luck is so bad that, if you touch this ticket, it won't, what? Win millions?"

"That's exactly what I'm saying," she says, her mouth a hard line.

Just like before, under the tent, we're in a standstill, our eyes locked on each other. And just like the first time, Hazel's not smiling, but this time, her eyes are. There's that warmth shining through, directed right at me. It's overwhelming in the best way.

"Okay. What about this?" I continue when Hazel doesn't budge. "According to my Welsh grandparents, black cats bring good luck." I rub both sides of the ticket on Toffee's black fur. He looks up at me, annoyed. I try to hand her the ticket. "Here."

I so badly want to prove her wrong. It's also possible I want to alleviate some guilt. Who's to say my good fortunes weren't originally hers? But given my history of good luck, I doubt it.

Hazel looks at me reluctantly, ultimately giving in. "Fine." Our fingers collide in the ticket exchange, the static electricity from Toffee's fur giving us both a little shock. "Nope," she says immediately, trying to hand the ticket back to me. "We almost set the thing on fire."

A deep laugh escapes me. "Or maybe that was the lightning Wendy was talking about."

"I think it was a mistake to let me touch it. It's a loser now."

"Okay, hang on to it for a sec. Let me just look this up," I say, typing into my phone. "The next draw is…" I look at the time: 11:01 p.m. "Now."

And then right there on the screen, the numbers come into focus. Below today's date are six all-too-familiar numbers.

10. 13. 30. 31. 23. 6.

A garbled noise crawls its way out of my throat.

"Knew I shouldn't have touched it," Hazel says, pushing the ticket back into my hand.

I confirm the numbers.

"No, Hazel…" I stand and pace in front of the bench. "We won."

She lets out a small laugh. "Oh yeah? What'd we win? A gazillion dollars?" She's saying this to Toffee in a funny voice as she scratches his chin.

"Hazel. I'm serious. We won." I turn my phone toward her and hold up the ticket next to it.

Hazel's eyebrows shoot up. "I— We—"

For a few seconds, we just stare at each other. Then the shock erupts into excitement.

"We—we won the lottery!" Hazel says as she leaps off the bench and launches toward me in a hug. We jump up and down together, our laughs and *oh my god*s and *holy shit*s blending.

"Oh my shit," I blurt out. Nothing makes sense right now.

"Holy god," she says breathlessly as she presses her hand over her chest. "Thirty million dollars?"

I nod rapidly. "We won't get the whole amount, with taxes and everything. Millions still, probably."

The death of Hazel's smile is quick and sudden. Now she's just standing there...blinking.

"Wow. This is—I don't even know. Wild. Surreal," I say, checking the numbers again. "Unusual."

Her eyes lock with mine. "Unusual?" she says, looking a little pale and a lot panicked. "This is more like impossible. Inconceivable. It doesn't happen. And it definitely doesn't happen to someone on their first time playing the lottery. No." She looks around. "This isn't happening right now."

"I know, I can't believe it either," I agree. "We need to claim it somehow. Put our names on the back."

Hazel puts her hands up. "No. Wait." She raises her eyes to meet mine. "Don't put my name on it. I—I don't want any of the money. It's all yours."

A surprised laugh tumbles out. "Hold on. We win the lottery, and you...don't want a single dime?"

Maybe this is what shock looks like on her. If she's feeling anything like what I am, this is...a lot.

"I don't," she says, quickly shaking her head. "Money like that just brings problems."

"But I promised you. Half of this is yours."

Her expression softens. "That's really good of you. But you can break your promise. I won't be mad," she says casually, like she's used to promises not being kept. She gathers up her things, tossing one last candy cherry into her mouth.

"We don't have to decide on anything right now. Let's just..." I try to think of something useful. "Let me take you out to dinner."

Hazel, half turned, spins to face me. The stunned look from seconds ago dissolves into something more amused. I feel the same jolt of electricity from earlier when she licked her lips.

"We're way past dinnertime," she says.

"A midnight snack, then?" I try. "I need to make up for the dim sum. And to celebrate, you know, this."

She takes a step closer to me. "You just can't stop pressing, can you?"

I move toward her, dipping my head to look into her eyes that won't leave mine. "I'm going to press one more time."

Hazel swallows. She's so close I can smell the cherry on her lips. Then, before either of us says anything else, she puts her mouth on mine.

The kiss takes my breath away. It feels like it isn't the first one between us—and that it won't be our last. If the air wasn't charged before, it's full-on vibrating now.

But then Hazel pulls back, and I immediately miss her mouth.

She steps away. "Oh my—I'm so sorry," she mumbles, pressing her knuckles to her lips.

I move forward to meet her. "I'm not."

Her cheeks flood with pink. "I don't know why I did that."

"Why *we* did that." Because I undeniably kissed her right back. I swear I see a sparkle in her eye.

In an instant, the sparkle turns to sadness. "On any other night, this might've had a future," she says. "We'd get pizza. Maybe gelato. But I just...I need to leave tonight in the past."

I hope she doesn't mean permanently. A pang of disappointment hits me, but I understand where she's coming from. I've had those days, too. "Being with you in the present was enough," I manage.

She bites down a smile. "That's so cheesy."

"Just like the pizza we'll never have. Or we can rain check it," I offer.

Hazel looks down at the ground.

"You don't have to explain anything. Just...here." I locate the Advil box in the bag. "Don't forget this." I drop the pain reliever into her bag and slip the lottery ticket in with it.

"Thanks for the medical attention," she says, shouldering her bag. "See you at the next fortune-crashing."

And with that, she's gone.

Chapter 4

HAZEL

I wake up the next morning with a throbbing headache.

I need to leave tonight in the past?

I groan into my pillow. Why did I have to say that to the one good thing about yesterday?

And because my brain can't help itself, I run through my other mistakes like a mantra. The layoff. My lost bracelet. The fortune reading. Kissing a stranger.

But if I'm honest with myself, kissing Logan didn't feel like a slipup. I'm just going to chalk it up to the way he gently took care of me in my weakened state. He was a spot of sunshine in a shitty day. I wanted to bask in that warmth for as long as I could. I wanted one good thing.

I mentally edit my list. Kissing Logan wasn't a mistake. Leaving him at that bodega was.

And okay, maybe walking away from millions of dollars was, too.

It's that last part that makes me doubt any of it happened at all. Winning the lottery? Yeah, right.

If not for the Hello Kitty Band-Aids on my arm, I'd think yesterday was one big disaster of a dream. One that could do without analyzing. I trace my fingers along the outline of Kitty's face, remembering how Logan's rough fingers felt against my skin.

The fact of the matter is that I should not know how strangers taste. Or how this particular one's mouth feels on mine. I also should not know that he has exactly three crinkles next to each eye when he smiles or laughs. Which is often.

And I really should not know that he's someone who can quickly unnerve me in a way no one ever has.

Maybe I was low enough to think I could change the prophecy by doing the opposite of what I should do. Or I was trying to throw what's written in my future off its tracks.

I glance at the clock on my nightstand: 9:46 a.m.

Shit! I'm late.

I jump out of bed in a panic and realize halfway through washing my face that I, in fact, actually have nowhere I need to be. That the routine I've been following all these years is no longer relevant—Wait. Wasn't the pipe broken yesterday?

As I towel my skin dry, I walk out to my bedroom–slash–living room–slash–kitchen. A room divider between my bed and couch helps break up my studio apartment. It's a tight fit in here, but it's rent controlled. Which means I can afford to live alone.

I test the kitchen sink. That works, too. Then I see it: a white slip poking under my door. I freeze. A rent increase? Something else that's broken?

I grab the slip. Building management brought someone out early this morning to fix the pipe.

Huh.

That's shockingly fast. Last winter, I went for a whole month without heat because the superintendent was on an extended vacation and refused to check emails or phone calls.

That's one problem solved. Now I need to fix another. It's time to job hunt. Applying is all I can control right now.

But first, I need fuel. I finish washing up, get dressed, and head back to Sweet Escape.

The woman- and Asian-owned candy shop is a gem on the Lower East Side, close to where I live. Too close. Ever since the shop opened, I've been here every week, stocking up on candy for myself, usually after work. I have to imagine I've been their most loyal customer.

The outside door and window frames are painted a tangerine color. This place looks like a treasure box with souvenirs from international travels lining the mandarin-orange walls. Glass biscotti jars hold candy from all around the world. Small silver scoops and tongs are placed neatly on hand-painted ceramic dishes next to each jar.

"Back again?" Emma Chen says as the silver bells above the door tinkle. According to the shop's website, Emma quit her job as a lawyer at forty-two to open this place.

I offer a tight-lipped smile. "Didn't get enough yesterday."

I grab a clear bag with the shop's name printed on it and do my usual loop to see what calls out to me. I pass by salted butter caramels from France, sour kiwi gummies from Spain, and Crown Churroz from South Korea. I stop at the jar filled with White Rabbit candy, grabbing a few.

A door to the back room opens, and Gloria comes out with a box with *black licorice laces* written on the side.

Gloria Van Asten is the spitting image of Helen Mirren but without the accent. From conversations I've overheard, she's a seventy-one-year-old purse designer who lost her Upper East Side apartment in her highly contested divorce. Apparently, she still got a good amount of money from her ex-husband right before he died two months later.

"He was already dead to me," Gloria once told a customer.

"We're almost out of licorice," Gloria tells Emma now. "It'd be good to have for Halloween."

Emma smooths a strand of hair back into her blunt bob. "Already? Shoot." She makes a note on a Post-it and sticks it on the whiteboard behind her. I hope that's not her inventory system. "We sold through those fast."

Gloria points the box in my direction. "You, again!" she says cheerily. I don't think she actually works here, based on previous conversations I've overheard. Yet she's always around. Gloria joins Emma behind the checkout counter and removes a tray. "Darling?"

I look around, confused. There's no one else here right now so she must be talking to me. She waves me over.

"Hi?" I say, making my way to her slowly.

"What's your name?" Gloria asks.

"I'm...Hazel," I say. "Why?"

Gloria drops one of the licorices into her mouth, the black spaghetti-like string dangling over her chin. "Because we'd like to greet you with something other than, *Darling!*" she says around the candy. "As nice as that sounds."

"You're in here all the time," Emma says. "Might as well know each other. I'm Emma."

"It's nice to see you outside of your typical after-work pop-by. Almost didn't recognize you in the daylight," Helen Mirren's doppelgänger says. "I'm Gloria, but you can call me Glo." This is information I already know from my research. She gives me another smile before going to refill more jars.

My gaze darts from her to a "We're Hiring" sign placed beside the window display.

Emma watches me for a few seconds. "Are you on lunch break or something? Taking the day off?"

"I...no. I'm just changing things up," I say, avoiding eye contact with her. I don't want to get into this right now. Especially not with two people I hardly know.

Emma hums under her breath. "Well, *if* you were ever looking for work, I'm happy to see what we can do."

This surprises me.

"That's... very nice of you," I say. "But I'm just on a break." Or I'm in denial. Shock, maybe?

Emma hands me her card. "In case you change your mind."

I'm confused. How does she know I'm not on my way back to work right now? I glance down at my dark grey sweatpants and crewneck with "Asian American Girl Club" embroidered on it. It's a far cry from my typical work attire: dark jeans and blazers.

I set the bag of candy down. I need to get out of here. "I'll just take this." I remove my wallet from my purse, pulling off a piece of paper that's stuck to it.

What is this—oh my god. The top of the ticket reads "New York Powerball" with yesterday's date time-stamped on it.

I flip the ticket over. On the back is a phone number scribbled in blue ink. Logan must've written this when he went in to see the clerk.

I hate that this makes me grin. Even before the kiss, he must've felt enough of a spark like I did to want to give me his number.

As unbelievable as it sounds, I still can't keep this ticket or accept half of the money. My stomach knots with anxiety and I'm... relieved? It's a reassuring reminder that I'm still human.

Big money like that creates too much change. It draws the wrong kind of attention. In the rare times Dad won money, people I'd never even heard of would come knocking. It's literally how I learned I had a great uncle who was still alive. Old debts need to be settled.

You have to get good at saying no. To gambling, to money, to the people asking for it. Dad never mastered the art of no, always losing more than he gained. I'm trying to learn this lesson for the both of us. The pendulum swung enough when I was a kid. I don't want that kind of life now. Once I get another job, I'll be back on track.

I toss the ticket and Emma's card into my purse with a frustrated sigh and hand her my credit card.

"Let me give you some extra, on the house," she says. The expression she's directing at me is one I'd define as *concerned*. "We just got sour peach fish from Sweden. Maybe it'll bring you some good luck."

I had forgotten that fish symbolize abundance in Chinese culture. That was the candy I got last night. Maybe I should've visited *before* work.

"I already had those—" I start to say when Emma gasps. With the little tongs, she lifts something shiny from the jar.

Now it's my turn to be surprised. "That's...my mom's bracelet!"

Emma drops it into my hand. The latch is broken, which is how it must've fallen off. I can go get that fixed today. As for the charms, all but the bird is missing. I dig through the jar for them, but they're not in there. At least I have the chain back.

Any good endorphins I gained from the returned bracelet vanish when my older brother calls.

I swallow, hesitating. What does Jerry want now?

"Sorry, I need to take this," I say to Emma, who nods as she packages up the remaining fish.

I take a long, slow inhale through my nose in preparation. On the fourth ring, I answer.

"Have a sec?" Jerry asks.

Probably, he needs more money. Being a van life influencer traveling around the country may be lucrative for some, but it's not for my brother. Every month he texts in need of cash, so what can I do but send what I can? For most of my life I've taken care of him. I can't stop now. It's a little hard to find yourself when your van is broken down on the side of the road. "It's only a matter of time," Jerry tells me every time I check in on the status of my reimbursements. If he can just build up his following, he tells me, the bigger sponsors will come.

But now, his tone of voice tells me that this is something different. And the fact that this is a call, not a text.

"What is it?" I ask.

"I had an accident."

He says it like he's updating me on trip progress. *I've made it to Montana. The weather's great.*

"I'm in the hospital," he adds.

"Were you rear-ended or...?" I ask, trying to sort out the details.

"Frogger's fine," Jerry assures me, like I cared at all about his van. "It's me. I broke my legs."

I move to the corner of the shop for privacy. "Plural?"

"Both, yeah," he says. "Jumping off a waterfall. I miscalculated how far I'd need to jump. Hit the rocks on the way down."

"Jesus," I mutter as I watch people outside the storefront window going about their days.

"Pretty sure I saw him," Jerry says. "When I hit the water. The pain was unbearable. Swear I saw the light for a second."

I sigh under my breath. "I'm glad your sense of humor is still intact. What hospital are you in?"

"I'm still in St. George. Danielle's with me. They airlifted us to the nearest hospital." A sliver of exhaustion is layered into his voice. "You won't see it since you don't have social media, but I'll have to send you a photo of the waterfall. It was breathtaking. Literally. It took my breath away."

This gives me pause. "Can you send a photo? Of your legs?"

"Of my *legs*? Hazel, that's so weird."

"Or of your hospital setup," I say, suspicion sweeping through me. "I want to see how bad this is."

"I'm literally suffering, and you want documentation of it?" Jerry asks. "That's beyond messed up."

"You're right. That was a weird thing to ask. When did this happen?"

"A couple days ago."

"And you broke both of your legs."

"Oh my god, yes," Jerry mutters. "Why are you repeating it?"

Because I don't believe you. "Because I want to make sure I understand," I say.

"I needed emergency surgery," he says, rushed. "They had to put in screws. Something about helping the bones heal properly. The doctor said I got lucky. This could've been even worse if I had hit the rock differently."

Nothing about this feels lucky.

"I'm sorry. That's awful, Jerry," I say, focusing on a jar of clotted cream fudge from the UK so I don't have to feel the flood of guilt that rushes in. They're so smooth and shiny in their individual clear wrapping—

"Hazel? You there?"

"What? Yeah," I say, turning my back to the sweets. "I'm glad you're okay. You'll be groggy for a bit, I'm sure. Have you talked to Dad? I can fly out—"

"No and no," he says quickly. "I don't want to trouble anyone."

"It wouldn't be any trouble to come visit my severely injured brother."

"Thanks, but I'm just…while I'm recovering, I'd rather not see anyone," he says, "And can you not tell Dad? I want to tell him myself when the time is right. Once I figure things out. Otherwise, who knows what he'll do to get the money. I don't know if he can get another loan at this point."

Obviously, telling Dad would not be good for anyone.

I'm quiet for a moment. "You think he'd need to get a loan for this?"

"This is going to be expensive," Jerry groans. The exhaustion has turned to tentativeness. "I was at the waterfall in the first place to get pictures for a swimsuit brand I'm working with. It was the biggest deal I had in the works. They won't pay me until I send over the deliverables, which isn't gonna happen."

Jerry always has something in the works. The initial Van Life Plan was for him to pay me back with the money he made from his marketing job, which had gone remote during the pandemic. Being a digital nomad lasted two years until Jerry's company wanted everyone back in the office. Jerry did not return to the office.

By the end of our conversations, a little part of me always believes that he's going to make it work. He learned how to be convincing from Dad.

The one time Dad hit a $30,000 jackpot, he just had to go and buy Jerry a used Volkswagen Westfalia camper. It was all Jerry needed to give up his apartment and go "find himself." He promptly named it Frogger and poured his life savings—and a portion of mine, to invest in what he sold to me as a "startup loan"—into renovations, a lime-green paint job, maintenance, and photography equipment.

I tidy the tongs and scoops to distract myself with a task. "How much will insurance cover?" I look at my phone screen after a too-long silence. Still connected. "I didn't hear what you said."

More silence.

"Then you heard me," Jerry finally says.

"You don't have insurance?"

It's pointless asking. Of course he doesn't. Health insurance requires a job or money.

On the other end of the phone, I hear sheets rustling and the beeping of machines. Probably what Jerry's hooked up to. It's an awful image in my mind.

"I was on Danielle's, but then she quit her job last month when we had a few leads," Jerry says.

Leads. Not even sure things. No contracts in place. They gave up health insurance because a brand might be interested in them.

"Jerry, how much is your accident going to cost?" I ask.

"Nothing firm yet, but I think it might be forty-five thousand dollars based on some discussions and Googling. Because I know you're going to ask, yes, I looked into the hospital's payment plans. I requested hardship assistance, and because I did have some earnings last year, they should cover half," he explains.

Jerry has looked into this already? That's new.

Before I can say anything, he adds, "I know you just sent money last week, but I don't know what to do about the ten-thousand-dollar down payment. Can you please just tell me what to do? You have good credit, right?"

This wasn't a call for comfort. It was—as expected—a call for cash. Does he think I have that kind of money lying around? I mentally add up what I have in my savings and the two-week payout I'll get from my company. I should also be getting paid out for all the PTO days I didn't take, which was most of them, give or take a sick day or two. This down payment alone would wipe out three-fourths of my bank account.

I feel like a body floating, and I'm just watching myself move around Sweet Escape. I'm a husk of myself. I hear the words he's saying, but I don't feel the weight of them.

"I...yeah?" I decide not to pile on to his situation by sharing that

I've been laid off, but I do say, "I already have all my bills and the house—"

"Grandma and Grandpa's lake house?" Jerry asks. "You're still paying that off?"

"Dad can't afford the mortgage on his own, so, yeah. And once it's paid off, we agreed that it would be mine."

"I didn't realize you still wanted it."

Jerry and I used to spend our summers with my grandparents at their lake house, just the four of us. Dad would get a break from us. We'd get a break from him. My happiest childhood memories all happened there. It was where I could breathe. Relax a little. Be a kid.

My grandparents had a pontoon named *Wishful Sinking* that we'd take out every night to watch the sunset while we drank pink lemonade. Then, in an ironic twist of fate, in the summer of '09 we lost *Wishful Sinking* when it sank after a heavy rain. The loss didn't deter us. Our nightly boating turned to sunset swims.

The lake was where I learned how to swim. It made me realize we didn't need anything fancy to enjoy the water. And when the waves were rough, Jerry and I sat on the dock playing cards while our grandma grilled and Grandpa made his famous blackberry pie with homemade whipped cream.

But then my grandparents died within a year of each other. Dad inherited the house, and we moved out of our apartment rental and into my grandparents' home, which was fully paid off. Moving in after such a painful loss was like pressing on a fresh bruise with all the strength I had.

It drudged up losing Mom, too. Dad grieved her death by gambling, chasing losses and dopamine hits. He's still grieving.

At sixteen, I only had a couple of years there before heading off to college on a swimming scholarship. I found moments of peace in my daily swims, this time at sunrise. On very quiet mornings when

I had the lake to myself, I could hear the motor of the pontoon, feel my grandparents' laughter, and taste the blackberry pie. Being in that house, it reminds me of Mom and her parents. It reminds me of what it felt like to be carefree. I want that feeling again.

My rational thinking stops my memories from taking on a too-vibrant hue. Dad owned the home free and clear, until he didn't. After one too many bad bets, he took out a mortgage on the house a few years after moving in. I worked my way through college, setting money aside for tuition, textbooks, and the house, pocketing whatever remained. For years, this is how it's been.

"Yeah. I want the house," I say quietly.

"Okay, well, it sounds like the remaining amount will be a payment plan. If you can get a loan, I'll pay you back. I swear. With interest! Easiest money you ever made," Jerry says with the casualness of that time he happened to be driving through Chicago during Lollapalooza. Though asking for leg surgery money is not the same as asking for concert tickets.

I let out a thinking noise because I don't know what else to say.

"I didn't know who else to turn to," Jerry says. "Did I ever tell you you're my favorite sister?"

And this is how it goes. Jerry comes to me when he doesn't know what to do. It could be van troubles or festival passes or broken legs. In the end, I always show up for him. I always will. He knows this. I know this.

"Let me figure out some things on my end," I say. "Do you have a contact at the hospital? Give me the name. I'll call—"

"Don't make any calls," Jerry pleads. "You're already helping me enough."

"I want daily updates."

"I'm not calling every day."

"Text, then," I insist. "I'm serious. Or I'm coming out there."

Jerry groans. "I regret this." There's a seconds-long silence. "Fine, I'll text."

We hang up. Right away, as if done out of spite, Jerry sends a photo of his cast-covered legs on a hospital bed.

LMK if you need any more proof, his text reads.

Shame shoots through me. I have the data to prove Jerry isn't to be trusted. There's always something wrong, and he's never paid me back, to start. But this looks bad.

I envision the dark-blue sky and swords of the fortune teller's card.

Lightning strikes. Storm clouds. Painful.

"Hey, everything okay?" Emma asks. She hands me a bag tied off with orange ribbon when I meet her at the counter.

"Oh, here," I say, handing her my credit card.

"You already paid," she says nicely. "I added some extra sour strawberries. I know you like those."

I blink. "Right. Sorry. Thank you."

I head back home, itching to get my job hunt started. As I walk, I research broken legs and surgeries. Depending on how long Jerry stays at the hospital, this might be a lot more expensive than he thinks.

I'm clutching the charm bracelet in my hand. The little gold dove with its black gem eye stares back at me.

Now birds make me think of the fortune-telling reading...and Logan. If birds as a collective whole are going to remind me of him, that will be very inconvenient.

Without thinking, I take the lottery ticket out of my bag and flip it over to Logan's phone number.

Maybe I need a little sunshine.

Chapter 5

LOGAN

On the second day of load-in at the theater, I start a fire.

The smoke units were running fine at first, but the carpet wasn't flameproofed and the whole thing turned to ashes.

And yesterday, the numbers that get attached to each set piece, the ones we use to guide us when we're assembling them, were all mixed up. That was just the beginning of all the unusual things that have been happening—

Thump!

"Not the canoe!" Richie Berrío, the head of Props, groans.

We both run over.

"I got it." I lift the now-cracked canoe. It's not heavy, but it's the type of weight I've missed ever since becoming head carpenter on this production. Before my title upgrade three months ago, when I was still a production carpenter building sets, I was the one measuring, sawing, hammering, drilling, building, and repairing. Now my days are filled with managing my crew and keeping them happy, approving payroll, and making sure the theater we're moving sets into doesn't fall apart. Still, I get to work on Broadway and be a small part of making imagined worlds come to life in the most literal way possible. It doesn't get better than that.

"Glue's not gonna fix this," Richie says, irritated.

THE FORTUNE FLIP 47

I set the canoe out of the way. "It's worth a try."

Richie grunts. "I had your confidence once. Then you turn sixty and start thinking twice before walking up stairs without rails."

"Hey. That was my first staircase," I say, smirking at his reference to the first show we did together seven years ago when I was starting out. Every now and then, I'd pick up jobs helping with load-ins, which is how I met Richie.

"You figure out the set piece numbers yet?" he asks.

"Not yet, but it's going to be great," I say with an upbeat attitude. "It'll be like a puzzle. I love those."

Putting the sets together takes hours and a lot of coordination. We did not need this hold-up.

Richie barks a laugh. "I'd put it on the team that messed this up. You're very good at saying yes to things you maybe shouldn't. Hey, you still in for Fantasy Soccer? I assume so, Mr. Winning Streak."

"Sure. Yeah. Count me in," I say.

"You got it. Have fun," he says, clapping me on the back as he leaves.

"This is no big deal," I mumble to myself.

I flip through the set of blueprints, cataloging what should be here. For this show, there's the log cabin mansion's suite, the hotel lobby, the main hall for a dance-off, the dock where the two leads kiss, the campfire and log benches, and the canoe for their romantic sunset paddle. And then there are a variety of drops: stars, sunrises, sunsets, and the lake the resort is built on.

Before I can figure this out, one of my stagehands informs me that some of the mechanical pieces that need to get rolled onstage keep getting caught in the tracks. I take a break from the set pieces to address that issue.

Everything seems to pop up at once, and I lose track of time and send everyone to lunch late. It's not the smoothest start, but hey, that's showbiz. I'll use the next thirty minutes to come up with an action plan. It's all going to be great.

And then something actually great happens.

This is Hazel. Rain check pizza? the text from an unknown number reads.

I respond right away. **I'll take the pizza, but not the rain.**

"You're soaked. Again," Hazel says, looking me up and down. "You know, I said 'rain check pizza' metaphorically."

Her cheeks are pink from the cold, her eyes bright. She's in a gray wool sweater, light jeans that fray at the bottoms, and black combat boots. I can't believe she's standing in front of me. I thought I had lost her for good a couple of nights ago.

I raise my hat and push my hair off my forehead. "I'm now convinced that I have my very own storm cloud following me around."

Hazel nods. "A stranger gave me their umbrella. Odd, right?"

Something odd has been going on, but I don't know that it has to do with umbrellas.

I open the door to Curtain Call Pizzeria and follow Hazel in as the scent of tomatoes, cheese, and spicy pepperoni welcomes us. When she texted yesterday, I figured there was no better place than the best pizza shop in all of Manhattan. What would typically be booths are old theater seats. The walls are plastered in Broadway posters and *Playbill*s. Above us, hundreds of props dangle from the ceiling: lamp shades, brooms, signed casts, pies, newspapers, cameras.

"Your usual spot's taken, Logan, but help yourself to wherever you want," Suze says to us, adjusting the black vest all the servers wear, as though they're theater ushers.

"Thanks, Suze," I say, introducing her and Hazel to each other.

THE FORTUNE FLIP

Drake, another regular here, waves to me from his preferred seat at the counter. He's doing the crossword puzzle, like always. As Hazel and I walk to an open table near the window, I say, "I know the location's touristy, but between the food and the vibes, this place is an underrated gem."

I gesture for Hazel to take the seat closest to the window so she can get the best view of the place. Triple-pocket menus made to look like oversize *Playbill*s are waiting for us on the table.

"It's really nice to see you. I'm happy you texted," I tell her once we're settled. "It was because you needed more tie-dye in your life, wasn't it?"

"Exactly. I ran out of napkins," she jokes. "In your texts, you said you needed to talk to me about something, and I think I know what it's about." She removes the lottery ticket from her bag and sets it on the table. "This is yours."

"Ohhh, so that's where it went," I say, playing coy.

She narrows her eyes. "You shouldn't have put the ticket in my bag, Logan."

"How else were you going to experience a little luck?" I ask. "Or get in touch with me?"

The corner of her mouth curves. "I wasn't planning on getting in touch. And if I hadn't texted, you would've missed out on millions. With that much money, you could, I don't know, buy a DeLorean and go back in time or get yourself an Ecto-1 and bust ghosts."

"Well, that would've been the biggest loss," I say. "You not texting."

This brings back the pink in her cheeks. It's still just as cute as the day I first met her.

Wordlessly, she slides the ticket toward me. She picks up her menu, her eyes drifting over the offerings. "So, what's good here? I'm thinking eggplant. These prices aren't terrible, actually. The BBQ one looks good. A whole dollar more, though? Geez."

I don't move on as quickly. I lean closer to her, my forearms crossed on the table, the ticket still where she left it. A cool thirty million casually resting right there between us. "The other day, when you said *money like that just brings problems*, can I ask what you meant?"

She blows out a breath and looks at me like, *isn't it obvious?* "Besides people wanting something from you, lottery winners have historically had it rough. It typically doesn't end well. Within three to five years, almost one-third of winners go bankrupt. They become targets. Winners struggle with anxiety, guilt, broken relationships, paranoia."

"How do you know so much about it?"

"I looked into it after we—" She pauses. "It just sounds like a burden, is all."

"Yeah. I've heard those stories, too," I say. "Which is why I'm going to follow your lead. I don't want the money either. Because I get it. Money can bring problems." I tap the ticket. "I am glad this brought you back into my life, though."

Hazel drops the menu onto the table. "Wait, hold on. How can you not want the money? You can't turn down millions of dollars," she says as though I've just told her I don't believe in the moon.

Suze comes over to take our order. "Three pepperoni slices, as usual?" she asks, pre-empting my order. "Oh, milkshake machine's down. Sorry."

"Seriously?" I eye Hazel, whose chest rises and falls in perfect sync with Dean Martin's "Ain't That a Kick in the Head" pouring out of the speakers.

"It finally gave out," Suze says with a shrug. She runs her hand through her silver hair. "Died making a mint cookies and cream."

"May it rest in pieces," I mumble.

"Two slices of eggplant, please," Hazel tells Suze. "Is it possible to do half grapefruit, half orange juice?"

"Actually, yes!" Suze says. "We got a fresh box of grapefruits in a few minutes ago. Haven't had any in all month."

When Suze leaves, Hazel places two fingers on the ticket and slides it even closer to me. "Don't reverse psychology me."

"I wouldn't dare. Look, this is how serious I am." I lift the ticket and am about to rip it in half when Hazel huffs out, "Wait!"

A low whine-groan escapes her throat. "Logan," she says, squeezing her eyes shut, "I actually...I need this money."

"You want it? What about all the stuff you just said?" I ask. "You could've just led with that, you know."

Her eyes blink open as she shakes her head. "No, I don't *want* it. I *need* it," she clarifies. "And I meant everything I said earlier."

"Okay, well, if you want the money, it's yours," I tell her. "I promised you."

"You don't have to split it, of course. I don't even need my entire half—"

"The entire half is yours."

Somehow, Hazel looks more miserable.

"Thank you," she says. "I owe you."

"You don't owe me anything. If you're worried about people knowing you've come into a fortune, I may have an idea." I hold a hand in front of my face. "Disguises."

"Like...we wear masks?" she asks.

"It can't be that obvious, but I work with the best wig and makeup people in show business. They might be able to help," I offer. "Our names will still be out there, but I don't know if we can get around that. New York requires people to disclose their identities."

"If I don't look like myself, that would help," Hazel says before quickly adding, "I'm not hiding from the law or anything." She twists a long strand of her hair. "And it's not that I'm worried about the world knowing. I just don't want *my* world to know." She releases a deep breath. "So, okay. Disguises it is."

I tap the ticket against my palm. It makes me think of the kiss, which reminds me...

"So, the thing I wanted to talk to you about," I start. "I don't know if I'm being irrational, but something strange has been going on. I think our luck flipped or something." I suck in a sharp breath as I hear how this sounds. Is that even a thing? Luck flipping? "It must've been when the fortunes got mixed up."

"You think...our fortunes...flipped," she repeats slowly.

"Something like that, yes," I say. "I don't know how else to explain it. I've been having bad luck."

She pauses mid–temple rub. "Is that new for you?"

"Yes, actually," I say.

"Seriously?" Hazel side-eyes me. "Bad things don't happen to you?"

"No one gets through life unscathed, but luck is always on my side. Even the worst things could've been worse."

"So you took all my good fortunes when you didn't even need them," she says, mostly to herself.

"In the past few days, it's like everything's going wrong at my job." I tell her about the set number mix-up and the fire. "Then we were given the wrong installation points, and automation rigging is already complicated. And a set wall fell, even after being secured, right onto the lake backdrop, which now needs repair and repainting. Not one show I've worked on has ever gone *this* wrong, but now that I'm head carpenter, it's all going to shit."

"Wow. I'm sorry," Hazel says. "All that happened in the last, what, two days?"

"Uh-huh." I adjust my baseball hat, the strands still damp underneath it.

"That's awful."

"Yes, and—" I cut myself off, hearing how negative I sound. I take a breath. "I'm complaining, and I shouldn't. Everything that's happened comes with the job. I'm probably just tired. It'll come together, and thankfully, no one got hurt. It's just weird. Everything went so smoothly during spotting and rigging. It was all laid out, we altered the stage correctly, everything on deck lined up with the grid," I reflect. "And then load-in happened."

"I'm not saying I don't believe you," Hazel says. "But two days isn't a lot of data to work with."

"You want more proof?" I glance around the pizzeria. "Okay. Follow me."

Hazel slides out of her seat and traces my steps to the crane machine in the corner.

"This machine hates me now," I tell her.

"These machines hate everyone. They're rigged," she says. "It's practically a slot machine. No one ever wins."

"Yeah, well. I win every time."

"Seriously, he does. It doesn't make sense," Suze says as she delivers drinks to a nearby table.

In the machine is a jumble of hundreds of small, New York City–themed stuffed toys: apples, hot dogs, taxi cabs, pigeons, and landmarks.

I remove a couple of quarters from the honesty jar that Curtain Call Pizzeria offers for customers. We're supposed to add what we take back into the tip. I steady myself as I grip the handle.

"If you're so lucky, does that mean you have millions of dollars? Shouldn't you have already won the lottery?" Hazel asks. I must make a face because she follows up with, "Have you? Won the lottery before?"

"No, it was my first time playing," I say, nodding to the pile of stuffed toys. "Which one do you want?"

"The soft pretzel, I guess," Hazel says on an exhale. "What's your strategy? You jiggle the handle? Bounce the toy off the other plushies?"

I maneuver the claw over the knitted brown pretzel sprinkled with beaded salt. "No strategy. Luck," I say, tapping the button to initiate the grab. The claw lowers, its prong slipping through the pretzel loop. As it's lifted into the air, the Empire State Building and everything bagel it was tucked between go tumbling. On its way back toward the drop-off, the claw abruptly stops. The pretzel unhooks from the claw, falling back onto the pile as the claw resumes motion, the arm folding back in on itself in completion.

"There. See?" I say, waving toward the glass. "Also, sorry. I wanted to win that for you."

"That claw is flimsy at best," Hazel says, crossing her arms. "It jerks back on purpose."

I tap on a sheet of paper taped to the side of the machine. "See those eighteen tally marks? Mine."

"That's a lot of plushies."

"You heard Suze. I've never lost once," I say. "Now you try."

"I never win those things," she says with a shake of her head.

"That's the point. If you win, something's up."

"Me playing will convince you either way?"

I nod. "But you need to actually try to win."

She considers it for a few seconds before adding quarters into the machine. It beeps back to life. Hazel pushes the handle forward until the claw is centered over the soft pretzel. She presses down on the button. The claw descends, gripping the pretzel through the loop. It stays put, even when the jerking motion happens.

Hazel's clearly shocked by her win as she claims her reward. "But—but I'm the person who somehow gets quarters stuck inside pinball machines. And not the money slot part. The actual game."

"Must be beginner's luck," I say, writing her name on the paper and adding a tally mark next to it. "Or...flipped fortunes."

Hazel still looks skeptical. She tries again, this time winning a stuffed rat. After racking up five tally marks in a row, she seems slightly more convinced...or confused.

"Come with me," I say, heading back to the table just as Suze brings our food. She drops off fries as an apology for the milkshake machine being out of commission. "First, it was the milkshake, which is the best in the city, by the way."

Hazel sets her mound of plushies on the chair next to her. "I guess I can't corroborate your statement without that machine."

"Watch. Normally, this pizza is perfectly crisp on the outside with a soft and doughy crust." I lift the slices. The bottoms are burned while the middle is still raw.

Hazel gestures with the soft pretzel toward her plate. "Check my slices! It's probably not just yours."

Both sides of her pizza are golden and crisp, the middle perfectly baked. She pulls her slices apart, the cheese stretching from one half to the other, the way it does in commercials.

"And these fries?" I add. "Crisp. I don't know when they switched to waffle fries, but the crinkle fries were"—I shudder—"not good."

Hazel crunches into one. "These are tasty." She thinks for a moment. "I'm not saying you're right, but a pipe had burst in my apartment building."

"I remember."

"It was fixed the next day. Repairs with that kind of speed are unheard of."

"But?"

"But for all the good things that happened, there have been worse things," Hazel says as she seems to debate something. "My brother broke his legs."

I set the fry down. "Did you say legs, plural? Is he okay?"

"He's recovering. But it's why I need the money. There will be a lot more bills coming on top of...everything else."

"I'm sorry. That's stressful." The words "break" and "legs" bring forward something else to mind. "Oh my god. I told an actor before one of his performance rehearsals to break a leg earlier this week," I recall. "Do you think that somehow transferred to your brother?"

She scrunches her forehead. "What's with that saying? I never understood it."

"It's theater superstition," I say. "There are actually quite a few theories on how it originated— Never mind. It's a thing people say when you want to wish them good luck."

She sips her juice. "It's just odd to me. Why don't we say things like, hope you get laid off today, so people can, you know, keep their jobs?"

"You want that to catch on? We can try to make it a thing," I offer.

Hazel smirks.

"The point is, *I* said it," I continue. "And everything I touch lately turns to...not gold."

She stares at me. "Huh. And how would your theater-specific wording affect my nonactor brother in a different state?"

I rub my hand over my face. "I don't know. I think maybe we're now connected in this inexplicably bizarre way because of the fortunes."

"As much as we want to, we can't always explain why bad things happen," she says.

She's right. I'm uncomfortable, and I'm trying to find answers for why everything's gone the opposite of how they usually go in my life.

Hazel hands me her second slice. "You didn't break my brother's legs, Logan. Lately, there have been more fortuitous events than

I'm used to, but the rest of them? That's life," she says with a shrug. "That's how it goes."

"Not for me. Our past fortunes are irrelevant now. But your present and future ones were that you'll experience a loss, and that you'll have a painful event that will shake you," I recall. "Not only did everything I just told you happen, but we lost one of our main actors to a movie shooting in Hollywood. The new guy is taller than I am. We need to modify the height of a few doorways. We've been working around the clock."

"Losing an actor was your loss?" Hazel asks.

"Yeah, besides the destruction and chaos." I shake my head. "You know what, ignore me. I should be grateful that I have a smart, talented team who's willing to work through these problems. It's amazing I get to do what I do at all. This is my first time being a head carpenter. Of course there are going to be problems. What'd I expect?"

"It can still be frustrating," Hazel says, cataloging my reaction.

"I need to look at the bright side. I'm going to learn something from this. I'm probably delirious from the lack of sleep."

She makes a sympathetic face. "There's a really good chance that's true. Has anything gone right?"

I try to think of something, anything. "We put the fire out?"

"Everything you've said does sound chaotic."

"And my fortunes were that I'd come into abundance and that next month is when I should execute on any ideas or goals. Given that we're not in October, that one's still to be determined."

"How do I fit into this exactly?" Hazel asks.

"Technically, you were holding the lottery ticket when we won," I say. "That was my abundance fortune."

"That's a huge stretch. With my luck, we wouldn't win a contest where everyone's a winner." She eyes her plushies, looking skeptical as she says this.

Sounds like Hazel and I have both had challenges. I'm probably so off base with my fortune theory.

I try to focus on something else and land on the pizza. "Thanks for sharing with me. I may have to rethink my usual." As Hazel drags a fry through ketchup and lifts it to her mouth, her bracelet catches my eye. "Were you inspired by Doc and Marty?" I ask.

She reaches for her wrist. "This was my mom's. All the charms fell off except this bird one," she says, like, *See? Not good.* "I thought I had lost it forever. But then someone...found it."

"That's very—"

"Don't say it."

"Fortunate." I can't help but point this fact out.

"I'll admit that happening is uncommon for me," she says.

All this good luck and bad luck. We need answers. And if the bird on Hazel's bracelet isn't a sign, I don't know what is.

We need another fortune reading.

"What I do want you to tell me is"—Hazel waves the lottery ticket—"how big of a tip do we need to leave?"

Chapter 6

LOGAN

Wendy and her birds are nowhere to be found. Toffee really must've done a number on Doc and Marty.

We look everywhere, squeezing our way through the crowd. It seems like everyone in New York City showed up here tonight. In the middle of the street are costumed dancers and musicians. When there's a break in the rain, people trickle out from their hiding spots under store awnings, picking up where they left off at food and shop stalls.

"Today is the Moon Festival. It's a Chinese holiday that takes place every fall. There'll be lion dances and celebrations all night," Hazel explains. "Hey, have you ever had a mooncake?"

"A what?"

"I'll be right back," she says, disappearing behind a family in color-coordinated shirts.

As I wait, I continue to look for Wendy. My search is interrupted by my phone buzzing in my pocket.

"Mom, hi. What's up?" I ask, distracted.

"What's wrong?"

My knee-jerk response is "Nothing's wrong." I adjust the phone between my ear and shoulder, along with my tone. "I'm just in the middle of something."

"You're still coming up next month, right?" she asks. "I'm figuring out how many potatoes I need."

"Is Warren actually retiring this time, or is this another trial run?"

"He is, and it would mean a lot if you were there."

"I'm planning on it, but some work stuff has popped up."

"Issues?"

I set my jaw. "There are always bumps in the beginning. All good, I'm working through it!" My upbeat tone sounds forced. "It's..." Disorganized. Behind schedule. Messy. "A busy time."

I'm saying this more to myself, I realize, but Mom says, "Sounds like an opportunity in disguise. Be grateful for busy. That means you've got big things going on."

"It just might be hard to get away. Can I keep you posted?"

"Okay. Sure. Of course," she says, attempting to cover her disappointment. "Remember, Logan, life never gives you more than you can handle at once."

"Right. Yeah. I'm sure it'll be fine," I say. "I'm looking forward to seeing everyone."

"Keep your head up!" Mom says more peppily this time. "Good things happen for you. They always do."

We hang up and I take a second. This show needs to go well. It's my first big—and maybe only—shot. It's like Mom said: Good things happen for me. I need for that not to change.

Hazel's back with what must be a mooncake. "I got us a black sesame snow skin one," she says, handing me half of a small, rounded pastry. It's slightly cool to the touch, the translucent white exterior revealing black filling.

I bite into it. It tastes a little sweet and nutty, the snow skin smooth on my tongue. "Chewy."

"These are going for double what they cost a few years ago," she says. "Who knew mooncake inflation would hit so hard?"

"When we get our money, you'll be able to buy all the mooncakes you want without worry." I toss the rest of my half into my mouth.

Hazel looks at me uncertainly. "I don't know what that's like. To buy anything without worry."

"I know you literally just agreed to the money, but have you thought about how you want to accept it? Because we're splitting one ticket, we can't take it two different ways," I say. "I'm thinking lump sum. Yes, we'd get less—we'd hit a higher income tax bracket and owe a ton of taxes—but we'd get it all at once. That might be more useful, especially if you need it for hospital bills."

She shakes her head quickly. "We should take the annuity option." She pulls up a spreadsheet on her phone. "See? We'll get payments for the next thirty years until our amount is fully paid off. And we'd get graduated payments, so every year the annual amount increases."

"True, but with the lump sum, we can invest more of it right away."

"Annuity accounts for that."

I consider this. "Sure, but if we grow the lump sum amount at a better rate than what's estimated with the annuity, we can make more money in the future."

"You sound like Wendy," Hazel retorts, pushing her fingertip into the flower design of her mooncake half.

"And then we can go buy something totally unnecessary and lavish, like a yacht. It's cliché, but hey. How often do you win the lottery?" I ask, half seriously.

"You're hilarious," she says, her face unchanging. "After the win, I was curious, so I worked out what we could end up with." She scrolls down her phone, showing me rows of numbers. "The annuity gives us enough money every year to cover what we need without having to worry about..." She trails off. "Without having to worry."

It's less *what* Hazel's saying and more *how* she's saying it that gives me pause. I recall her short-lived enthusiasm after winning. How she finally accepted the money but is still seemingly tentative about it.

This then makes me think about how my father would warn my siblings and me that showing off money makes you more of a target. That we needed to be careful of being taken advantage of.

"On the other hand," I say slowly, "having more money upfront means having more money for people to want."

Hazel blinks up at me like she's relieved she didn't have to say the words herself. "Yes, exactly. And I appreciate you considering the hospital bills, but the annuity payment we'd get this year would more than cover them. Was there something you needed the lump sum for? I don't want to mess up your plans."

I don't need to think about it. I shake my head no. "There isn't. I've got what I need. Let's do the annuity."

Landing on this resolution was surprisingly painless. When my parents had different ideas on how to invest or spend money, it was never this conflict-free. My father would always get his way, and Mom would put on a smile and go with it. This, though, feels more like an understanding than a surrendering.

Hazel takes a small bite of her mooncake. "You want the rest? I honestly don't love these."

"Why did you get it then?" I ask before finishing off her half.

"Well, it's tradition. And because I've gifted it to you, that's me expressing best wishes," she says, smiling. "You know, for all the luck you apparently lost."

I smirk. "That's what we're here to find out. Come on."

We walk farther down the street and find a fortune teller not occupied with anyone. Signs around his booth tell me that this man specializes in tea leaf reading. My curiosity gets the best of me as I approach him.

"Logan, what are you doing?" Hazel reaches for my hand and pulls me toward her. "We are not getting our fortunes read again. And I'm definitely not drinking some random man's tea."

I look down at our hands and smile. "I'm sure it'll all be fine, but I just want to know if our fortunes got mixed up that day. Maybe we did get each other's cards. Or maybe Wendy read the cards wrong. I have to confirm I'm not imagining everything. Let's just see."

Hazel pulls her hand away, her eyebrows wrinkled in concern. "I can't sit through another reading where I'm told how bad my future looks. I already spend my life waiting for bad things to happen." Her arms are crossed firmly over her chest. "Even though it's all nonsense anyway."

"If it was nonsense, why were you doing it to begin with?"

"I shouldn't have been. Now it's written," she says slightly sarcastically. "I could've lived in ignorant bliss."

I dip my head. "You can tell me."

She bites her lip. "Their methods sound charming at first, but I know how fortune tellers really work. They take your money. Tell you a mixture of what they think you want to hear, sprinkling in something ominous for effect. You know why fortunes only last for three to four months? To keep you coming back."

"Or to help you in your immediate future," I offer.

"Why do people even want to know the future?" Hazel asks. "It's not like it's some mystery."

"You don't think the future... is a mystery?" I ask, confused.

"Ultimately, things don't work out. Even when they're good, everything bottoms out at some point," she says. There's a deep layer of sadness in her statement. "Wendy probably took one look at me and thought I was helpless."

As she says this, drummers and the lion dancers come twirling past.

"Hopeless?" I ask, cupping my hand behind my ear.

"That, too!" she shouts back.

We wait for the performers to move down the block. "What if there is truth to it, though? What then?" I ask.

"Honestly, I do worry about that," she says with a sigh. "Logically, in my brain, I know superstitions are a way of dealing with uncertainty. Unpredictability. A lack of control. But what if there's really something to it? Did you know the psychic market is over two billion dollars in the United States? People want answers. Maybe they're really getting them." She shrugs. "It's more likely people are profiting off our fears, though."

"You've really looked into this."

She twirls her umbrella back and forth. "Going to see Wendy was a lapse in judgment. I wanted answers, especially when everything felt so...unknown. But now I can never unhear what she said. What she said about what was on my cards, that's now officially lodged deep in my brain, so that's fun."

"Or on *my* cards," I say.

"Maybe the cards you got were supposed to be mine. Maybe they weren't. I only wanted to hear something good." She steps closer to me, lowering her voice. "The day I—we—had our fortunes read... I got laid off."

"Shit. That's a lot." No wonder she was having a bad day. I don't want to bring her even lower. She's stressed enough as it is. "But then you won the lottery!" I try as an attempt to lift her spirits.

"Yeah, well, I'm sorry for how I acted that day," she says.

"It's fine. Really. Bad days remind us to be grateful for the good ones. I do think we need to understand what's going on, though. If I get a good fortune here, then I can confirm I'm overreacting and let it go."

Hazel stands a little straighter at this.

"You don't even have to do it," I tell her. "We just need to know mine. I volunteer my future."

THE FORTUNE FLIP

"For both of you, I'll give a discount," the older man says behind me. His black hair is gelled into a comb-over, and he wears spectacles on the tip of his nose. "Fifteen dollars for two readings."

"It'll just be him," Hazel says as we take seats next to each other.

The man writes something down on a notepad. "Ten for one reading."

"You're not going to negotiate?" Hazel asks when I agree.

"We have lottery money," I whisper to her. "We can afford to pay full price."

"We technically don't have any of that money yet," she says. "Ohhh, right. You want a good fortune. I got you. Make sure to add a generous tip."

The man won't give me a good fortune just because I overpay him. At least, I don't think he'd do that.

I hand the man a twenty-dollar bill just in case and tell him to keep the change.

The fortune teller, who tells us his name is Bo, instructs me to choose which tea I want from the glass jars containing loose leaves. I select lavender mint tea, but when I go to scoop a teaspoon into my cup, I drop the spoon. Tea leaves scatter all over his table.

I try again, this time with success. Bo pours hot water from a kettle into a small, white, rounded cup with an equally tiny handle. He explains that I'll drink the tea once it steeps, leaving just a little bit of liquid left in the cup. I blow the steam away as Hazel watches eagerly from her seat.

My gaze drifts back toward the fair. Wendy doesn't appear to be here, and on a holiday, probably one of the busiest days for business.

"Do you know where that fortune teller with the birds went?" I ask Bo.

He shakes his head. "For a few days now, she's had restless birds. They refused to leave the cage," Bo replies. "I haven't seen her since."

Hazel gives me a pointed look.

Great. I've rattled Doc and Marty. I read somewhere that crows hold grudges for up to seventeen years. I hope sparrows aren't like that.

"Do you know when she'll be back?" I ask.

Bo shakes his head, his sparse, gelled hair staying firmly in place. "She didn't say. Good for my business, though!"

I busy myself with the tea. It's still hot and burns the tip of my tongue. I'm flustered enough that I swallow a few tea leaves.

"Is there a specific question you'd like answered for this reading?" Bo asks.

I cough into my sleeve. "What does my future look like?" I say, going with the same question we asked Wendy.

Bo nods. "Swirl your cup three times counterclockwise."

I do as Bo says and then turn my cup over onto a towel he's laid out in front of me.

With both hands, he taps my cup a few times before flipping it over. He positions the handle toward me.

"Now," he says, smiling, "let's see what your future holds."

I inhale in anticipation. This was good. Bo will clear everything up. It's just been an off week, and my luck will be back in no time. Bo pushes up his glasses and analyzes my tea leaves lining the sides and base of the cup.

Hazel scoots closer to me and presses her cheek up against my shoulder to get a good look. I angle my head down toward her and catch an undercurrent of strawberries and sugar. Her scent blends with the lavender mint tea, and every single sweet note intoxicates me just as it did when she kissed me outside the bodega.

When she looks up at me, our lips are inches apart. It takes every

THE FORTUNE FLIP

ounce of self-control not to kiss her again right here, right now. I've already scared away one fortune teller.

"Just trying to get a better angle," she clarifies, immediately righting herself.

I scoot over and tug her chair closer, so she has the better view.

Bo adjusts his glasses. "Okay, let's see here. Closest to the rim, do you see those two triangles?" he says, describing the shapes formed on the side of my teacup. "The tips are facing each other, like a tilted hourglass."

The loose leaves don't look like anything but a random scattering of tea. Calling that left shape a triangle feels like a stretch, but I go along with it. "Am I gaining more time?" I ask hopefully. I could really use it at work.

"No, your time is running out," Bo states.

"His time—like his life?" Hazel cuts in.

Bo chuckles. "Oh, sorry. I can see how that sounds, though that's not incorrect. We're all running out of time. This one generally relates to a countdown, a timeline. Something's coming up for you, and you're racing against the clock."

Hazel looks over at me, her eyebrows pinched together. She knows exactly what I'm racing toward... and all the obstacles that have blocked my path this week alone.

Bo hovers his pointer finger over the middle of my cup. "Do you see two lines with tea leaves across, like a ladder?" He leans in closer and focuses his attention like he's trying hard to analyze what he's seeing. "In a couple of weeks, you might be advancing in your job. Climbing higher. Or, climbing down. Something like that. The shape is in the leaves and the white of the cup. This could be positive."

"Could be?" I ask. "Which means it could also be negative?"

"I'd say 50/50," Bo confirms. "You will be going somewhere."

Perfect. A 50/50 fortune.

Bo wavers. "It's not very distinct. Better to avoid ladders for a while in case this isn't so metaphorical."

With my job, that's not going to be easy. I try not to think about the *climbing down* aspect, but of course, my mind floods with all the recent events at the theater. If we don't have the sets ready by the time previews start, I really could be climbing down from my first job as head carpenter.

I suppress this last thought and instead focus on the other 50 percent. I'm great at concentrating on the other 50 percent. The glass half full. If I can have the sets ready on schedule—no, *ahead* of schedule—that would only help my career. But not just me. Mrs. Walker, Richie, my crew, the cast, the creatives. This show means something to all of us.

"Let's go with positive, then," I say, forcing a smile.

"At the bottom of your cup, we have an airplane. You have travel coming up," Bo says with more confidence than his first two predictions. "Some kind of adventure."

An airplane. This feels like a good direction.

I attempt a joke. "I'm visiting my family soon. That is usually an adventure."

Bo frowns. "The shape is depicted by the leaves themselves. That's... not the best."

"You sure that's not a bird?" Hazel tries. "Though we haven't had much luck with those lately."

Worry creeps back in. "Right, like maybe the airplane wings are actually bird wings?" I try.

"Do either of you actually know what birds look like?" Bo asks.

"This is like a Rorschach tea test," Hazel mutters. "If we don't see it, does that mean it won't come true?"

"You will still have an adventure," Bo says, "but I'd avoid flying if I were you."

"Avoid ladders *and* planes? For how long?" I ask. "What else do I need to steer clear of?"

Bo collects the teacups, indicating that our session is up. "I'd give it a few months to be safe" is all he says.

Based on the half-hearted way he states this, I'm never flying again.

"That's it! I wish you a very happy life," Bo says, waving. "Thank you! Good night!"

And just like that, Hazel and I are back on the streets of Chinatown.

But this time, I have the bad fortunes.

I give Hazel a *what did I tell you* shrug. "See?"

"If that doesn't prove that it's all nonsense, I don't know what will," Hazel says, but her voice is shaky.

"What it does tell me is that I'm not reading too much into what happened this week. I feel...relieved." What I don't tell her I feel? Stressed and confused. Also slightly panicked.

Hazel looks confused. "You're relieved?"

No. I feel like I just overpaid for bad news.

"Well, I at least feel like I didn't make it all up," I say. There's some truth in that. "I also..." What's the word? Comforting isn't it, though for a few moments there it felt nice to believe that someone had the answers for our situation. "I appreciated the clear guidance. Wendy didn't give us that."

She lifts a brow at me. "Guidance feels generous. He loosely told you what to avoid and couldn't even give a firm timeline."

"If it saves me, I'll take it," I say. "My luck is just temporarily on hold until I can figure out how to get back on track. It's all going to be fine. I got this."

Hazel opens her mouth before closing it again. I can see her reworking her choice of words. "You think you can get your luck back on track?"

"I have to before previews start," I say.

"When's that?"

"At the end of next month. For the crew, previews are practically opening night. Lines and songs can still get cut between previews and the official opening night, but for us, the set is pretty much done. That's when we need to be ready."

"Okay," Hazel says, thinking. "There's still time. A lot can happen in a month."

"You're probably right, but this show's too important to me, and especially to Mrs. Walker," I say. "Her late husband wrote it, which is why she's worked really hard to get it made." Also, she changed my life. I need to make sure this show is the best it can be. I refuse to be the one who ruins it.

Hazel takes a step closer, the colors of the lanterns above us playing off her smooth skin. "Look, Logan. For what it's worth, I still think it's all made up," she says. "Not even the best fortune teller in the world can get predictions one hundred percent right."

A tired smile crosses my lips. "Maybe it's all meaningless, but in the off chance it's not, we can't have my bad fortunes compromising anything."

Hazel shakes her head. "Like what?"

I take the lottery ticket out of my wallet.

"Like this," I say, handing her the ticket. Given everything, it's best if she hangs on to it. "We need to get that money."

Chapter 7

HAZEL

Turns out, we're not the only winners.

We'll be splitting the thirty million with three other people. Then Logan and I will divide that amount in half, leaving each of us with $3,750,000. After federal and state taxes, our annual payout for this year will be just under forty-four thousand.

Unreal.

"I can't believe there were four winning tickets," Logan says with a disbelieving laugh. "You know how hard it is for one person to win?"

"It's still a lot of money," I say.

"Yeah, it is."

In the week since Logan and I had our second fortune reading, we each met with financial advisors, lawyers, and tax accountants. We filled out the right forms, checked all the boxes, and agreed to the press event and public announcement that New York requires, which is where we are this afternoon.

My phone vibrates with a text message from Emma. **Excited for you to start on Monday! Getting matching aprons. (Gloria insisted.)**

I imagine us all in tangerine-colored aprons, filling up candy jars. I wonder how much my employee discount will be.

"What are you smiling at?" Logan whispers to me when we have a moment to ourselves.

"The thought of candy half off. I accepted a temporary job until I can land a full-time role," I tell him. "I couldn't accept this money and not be working." I nod toward the stage. "I thought we just got a check, smiled for the cameras, and went on our way. But an interview? On TV? This was a bad idea. Very, very bad."

All the winners are gathered in a nondescript building in an unmemorable room with a wide backdrop printed with the New York Lottery logo against a white wall. Given that their brand is big money, the lottery doesn't hold fancy press events. I guess it's because we're the ones walking away with the checks—metaphorically, that is—and not them.

"Keep answers brief and don't make direct eye contact," Logan coaches. "They'll see through our eyeholes. And maybe stop playing with your jowls."

I lift my fingers from the soft jowls of the hyper-realistic silicone mask covering my entire head. We decided to go with Logan's idea to disguise ourselves, and his Broadway friends helped out. My name will be made public, but it could conceptually be any Hazel Yen. And if someone goes one step further to find the photo, I won't look like myself.

We picked from his friend's premade silicone mask stash. Our options came down to the masks of lagoon creatures or older people. As much as I'd love to be green and have scales for a day, we went with the obvious choice. I went from being a single twenty-nine-year-old to being a married eighty-year-old. A cover-up story Logan and I created together.

Easily removable masks also allowed us to show our real faces at check-in when we had to be verified against our IDs. They aren't accurately representative of what we'd look like—Logan's friend didn't have a mask of an aged, mixed-race Chinese American woman—so today I'm fully white and thankfully haven't been asked about my last name.

THE FORTUNE FLIP 73

Logan's sporting a crew neck sweater over a button-down, which covers the edges of his mask. His khaki pants are a tad too short for his long legs. Socks and loafers complete the look.

My own mask extends down over my neck and chest, the flap tucking under my white T-shirt and cream-colored cardigan. I knew Coastal Grandmother was the look I wanted from the second we decided to go as older versions of ourselves. Because we'll be holding checks and our arms and hands will be on display, we've aged those, too. I squeeze my fingers into a fist. I need to relax. We've been in this room for fifteen minutes, and no one's seemed suspicious of us so far. This will be fine.

"How's your arm doing?" Logan asks. "Healing okay?"

"Surprisingly well," I say. "I don't think the scratches will leave scars. Which is odd. With my skin, I can't even get rid of papercuts."

He shoots me knowing eyes. "It's the fortunes. You're lucky now."

My instinct is to deny this. To tell him he's wrong and that he needs to forget about the fortunes. That it'll be a self-fulfilling prophecy if he keeps thinking about them every single day.

But the truth is, I've been noticing differences.

There have been small things: more jobs than I anticipated there being in industries I'm actually interested in, the guy at the cupcake shop who always gives me the wrong flavor accidentally giving me three of the right cupcakes instead of two, and a movie I wanted to watch being free on the streaming site that's included with my cell phone plan.

There have also been big things: Jerry calling to tell me that the total cost of the surgery will be $5,000 less than he anticipated. That he's recovering well but still wants space.

While we're waiting for the event to begin, I check my emails. My heart speeds up when I see one from a recruiter.

> Hazel,
>
> Thank you for your interest in the Sr. Data Analyst role. I'd like to set up a phone interview to learn more about your background. If you're interested, we're also hiring for a manager role that I think you might be a great fit for. Including the <u>job description</u> for your review. Let me know when a good time to chat might be.
>
> Best regards,
> Milly Wilson | Talent Acquisition Partner

I gasp, the sound muffled under my mask.

This mask takes away all peripheral vision, but I feel Logan's arm move as he turns to me. "What is it?" he asks.

"I got an interview request," I say. I don't know if it's because we're dressed like an old married couple or what, but I hand the phone to Logan like this is standard behavior. "It's for a job that's way higher than the role I was in before."

He scrolls through the email. "This is great!" he says, handing my phone back. "Congrats. You're one step closer."

"Logan, I was qualified for half of the bullet points in the senior analyst job description." I don't share that I only applied because the application process just required uploading my résumé.

"I seriously doubt that if they're asking you for an interview," he says. "Looks like they're eyeing you for the manager role, too."

"That makes no sense," I say. "I don't have experience. It's probably a mistake."

Any minute now, a follow-up email from Milly will come in about how she meant to send that to a different candidate.

Logan fixes the buttons on his sleeves, adjusting his watch and red string bracelet. "This is the second fortune," he says. "The one about executing on your goals. You did that, and it's officially October."

This, again.

"Wasn't that not supposed to be driven by money?" I recall. "This goal was specifically driven by the need for money."

"Part of the fortune was that you have everything you need to make your dreams a reality," Logan says. "I think you'd make a great manager. This is a good thing, Hazel. You're allowed to enjoy it."

I don't know what about me makes him think that I'd be good at managing people. Before I can ask, a tall woman in a yellow dress and chunky jewelry taps on her microphone so we can get started.

We watch the first winner, Marlin from Queens, talk to the woman, who introduces herself as Gretchen. Marlin's wearing a Knicks jersey that appears to be signed, which makes me wonder if he's already received his money.

"I went lump sum," Marlin tells Gretchen. "I need the funds for Marlinworld."

"Marlinworld?" she asks.

"A water park," he says like it should be obvious. "There'll be an area with rides and slides, but you'll also find the most exotic sea life you've ever seen. I'm talkin' deep-sea stuff."

"Wow! You've got a whole plan," Gretchen says. "Which exotic marine life are you most excited about?"

We never do find out. Before he answers, two police officers burst through the doors. There are gasps and murmurs in the crowd of media.

Logan positions himself in front of me as the scene unfolds. Instinctively, I grab his arm.

"Marlin Mavers?" one officer asks.

"Shit," Marlin says, tossing his microphone and running toward the door across the room.

A third officer steps between the doorframe, blocking Marlin. In a flash, the guy's handcuffed and escorted out. The whole scene is captured on cameras and phones.

Guess there won't be a Marlinworld after all.

I expect the press conference to be rescheduled, but Gretchen has a *show must go on* attitude and doesn't miss a beat. Which means we're up second.

"You still good to do this?" Logan asks.

Once my heart rate settles, I feel oddly relieved. We're here. We're dressed up. I need the money. So yeah, I better be ready. And after that excitement, no one will even be thinking about Logan and me. This might not have to be a big show, after all.

Still, Logan leans in and whispers, "We got this."

It's the way he says it, low and steady, that makes me believe him.

As we approach the podium, Gretchen's assistant hands us a replica of our ticket. The numbers Logan picked are slightly blurry with how blown up they are. I stand to Logan's right, keeping him between me and Gretchen. The lights of all the cameras shine directly in our faces. I worry that the brightness will reveal our fake creases.

"And now we'd like to congratulate Logan Wells and Hazel Yen!" Gretchen announces, stretching the "n" in my name for a few seconds with enthusiasm. "Married all these years, and still different last names, huh? How many years has it been?" She flips the microphone over to Logan.

This is hell. I am living my actual nightmare.

Or...wait, this is good. Gretchen thinks we're really in our golden years. This boosts my confidence.

Apparently, Logan's thought it all out because when he talks, he sounds nothing like himself. Instead, he's an older...Australian man? "Fifty beautiful years," he replies. "Give or take."

And because we're not just supposed to look like a couple who's been married for five decades but need to act like one, too, I wrap my arm around Logan's waist. He follows my lead and drops a kiss right on my fake forehead.

Gretchen doesn't miss a beat and continues to announce our winnings. She calls out the bodega and when we purchased the ticket. "How long have you been playing the lottery?" she asks, spinning the microphone back.

Logan takes this one, too. "Ever since I can remember."

Gretchen laughs. "It's finally paid off! Anything special about these numbers?"

I feel Logan straighten ever so slightly next to me, like he's excited to share his rationale. "Well, actually—no," he says. There's a course correction in his tone.

"Oh, okay," Gretchen says, her smile and eyes wide. "With the lump sum, you've got a lotta cash to spend—"

"We actually went with the annuity," Logan corrects. "Because we have many beautiful years ahead of us."

"Oh yeah, of course you do," Gretchen rushes out. "I bet your children are thrilled for you, too!"

Yes. I'm sure our nonexistent children will enjoy inheriting our boatload of cash.

We continue giving Gretchen pathetic answers, yet she acts like they're amazing. She's really good at her job. I wonder what it feels like to be her, to be surrounded every day by people coming into new money. Is she envious? Genuinely excited? Or is she, at this point, totally indifferent?

"What are your plans for the money?" Gretchen tries.

"Investments," Logan says, staying on track and keeping his answers more succinct than I think he'd prefer. If I weren't here, no question he'd be making new friends with Gretchen and every reporter and photographer in here.

Gretchen presses us on this one. "Oh, come on! You gotta do something fun! You're not going to buy a yacht? A car? Go on a dream vacation?" She pushes the microphone into my face.

I respond with the first thing that comes to mind. "We'll go on our second honeymoon," I squeak out to satisfy her. I have no idea where that idea came from, but I regret the words as soon as they leave my crinkled lips. "I mean, we'll go out to eat." Apparently, the best fake voice I can put on is one much higher than my typically low, raspy voice. I sound like an unoiled hinge.

"That is so precious! Tell me more," Gretchen says, lighting up. I've given her too much fake information.

"It's a secret," I say, not wanting to risk using my voice too much. I instinctively cross my arms and then straighten them down to my sides. How would eighty-year-old me stand? I fold my hands together in front of me, settling on that.

Gretchen deflates. I know she would've liked more from us, but that's all we can give her. She wraps things up by asking if we're ready for our photo opp. Gretchen's assistant takes the oversize ticket from Logan.

While he adjusts his sleeves, I, out of habit, tuck my wig hair behind my silicone ear. We're handed a giant cardboard check that's just for show. We were told we'd get the money electronically in a few days, but I'll believe it when I see it.

After dozens of photos and awkward silence, Gretchen instructs us to stand off to the side and to keep the check held up. All the cameras refocus on the third winner.

"Nice job," Logan says once we're out of the spotlight. "And your impression of your future self? Wow, that was…"

I laugh a little. "What I would sound like inhaling helium? What it sounds like running over a rubber duck? And who knew you become Australian when you're put on the spot?"

"Learning new things every day," he says with a chuckle. "Another thing I've learned? I look pretty good with all these wrinkles." He shifts his hand positioning on the check. "If only it were easier to slip in and out of. It's nice to not feel like myself for a second."

With all the bad luck Logan's been having, I can understand that. Ever since we met, my life has been like one long, unusual, and disorienting press conference, and I've had more of the good than the bad.

"The real me is racing against the clock, potentially unemployed soon, and can't take air travel," he recalls. "Good stuff."

Hourglass. Ladder. Plane.

Gretchen taps her long, blue nails against the third winner's oversize winning ticket, the clacking drawing my eyes to the numbers.

How unreal that this group of people is here because of a few tickets that had the exact combinations of numbers. What does these winners' luck look like in their day-to-day? Did we win the lottery because Logan bought the ticket when he was lucky? Or did we win because it was in my possession?

No. It's random. Pure chance.

Given everything, though...

"Maybe you were right. Somehow our fortunes—our luck—flipped." I shiver. "Maybe we should try to get struck by lightning to switch them back," I joke.

Logan half laughs. "Maybe step on a live wire?"

"What if it was the cat? Toffee literally flipped the fortunes the first time. Then you brushed the ticket against him for good luck."

"Like the static electricity did something?" he asks. "That's impossible. Right?"

"I don't really know what's possible anymore," I say, taking in the scene in front of me. "*This* is impossible, and yet we're holding this comically large check."

Gretchen has moved on to the fourth and final winner, a woman named Tiff from Westchester wearing a baseball cap and sunglasses.

A wild thought flashes into my mind. What if... what if it was the kiss?

Heat floods my face, creating a mini steam room under my mask. I push the thought out of my head. Switching bodies, switching fortunes—that doesn't happen in real life.

Still, something odd is happening.

"Whether or not I have good luck, what if I don't want my bad luck back?" I pose. "Can I hang on to it for a little longer? Maybe until I secure a job?"

"I don't want to take anything away from you," Logan says. He turns to look at me, his piercing eyes meeting mine. He keeps them there for a few long seconds. The crinkles on his silicone exterior look just as lifelike as his real-life ones. The ones I look forward to seeing every time he smiles.

We're in the present, looking like the future. It's surreal, in a way, being here with Older Logan. We look as though we've spent decades together when I've only known this man for half a month. It's like we're role-playing a prediction, if that prediction were to say Logan and I ended up together.

For the length of Tiff from Westchester's interview, I let myself live in that version of reality. Logan ordering pizza and chocolate milkshakes, bandaging up my scrapes. Logan being patient, keeping promises. Logan coming up with ridiculous-but-smart ideas like disguising ourselves on TV just so I'm comfortable. Logan smiling every time I come into view, looking at me like he really sees me.

And these are just the memories from knowing him for two weeks. What would a lifetime look like?

I blink the vision away, but I'm left with a truth: I'm attracted to a man I hardly know.

"I don't want you to have bad luck, either," I say, realizing I've been quiet for several minutes. "I feel bad."

"Thanks, but I don't want your pity."

"You sure? Because if I got the fortunes you did, I'd want your pity."

He straightens, the check lifting higher on his side. "Setbacks are an opportunity. The same goes for bad fortunes. This is a challenge I can overcome," he says, and his upbeat tone almost makes me believe him, but I hear a bitter edge in his words. "I've done it before. I can do it again. This bad luck streak can't possibly last forever."

The fourth winner poses excitedly with her large check. She's the first person to actually look happy about her win. I would've thought the other winners would've been jumping up and down with millionaire joy.

Watching everyone claim their money, it seems like there might be something to what Logan was saying about how we're bonded in this highly unusual way. I feel weirdly emotional about these people I don't know and will never see again. We'll always have in common this press conference, this one Powerball that changed our lives. Once we step out of here, we're back to being strangers. Ones with "lottery winner" attached to our names and our stories, the ones we tell and the ones others tell about us.

Well, not me and Logan, since we're not telling anyone. We're the only ones who will know this tidbit about each other. We'll forever share this secret.

"I can't just take your luck and leave you to fend for yourself," I say, knowing everything that's at stake for him. I pat his shoulder. "When I was having a rough day, you helped me. Now you're going through a rough time."

It's not guilt that's driving this, though I do feel that. The man honored his word and split the winnings. He doesn't deserve this.

At the same time, we look at my hand on Logan's shoulder before our eyes find each other's. A rush of heat up my neck is apparently my auto-response to touching Logan.

"I'm going to help you," I blurt. I puff out my cheeks, my own words surprising me. I don't take it back, though. While I'm job hunting and working at the candy shop, I need a distraction. A bigger purpose. This will give me exactly that, while being able to return Logan's favor.

"And how exactly are you going to do that?" he asks.

Given that I just came up with the idea, I have no idea. "I'm good at fixing things. Have been for eighty years."

It's a joke, but sometimes it really does feel like it's been that long.

My attempt to make him laugh works. His low rumble is deeper underneath all that silicone molded with loose jowls, forehead wrinkles, and ingrained laugh lines. It's a sound at odds with his older exterior. A shock of pleasure cuts through the center of my core.

I can't fix Logan's sets or make his work go faster. And it's not like we can really flip anything back, obviously. But just like Logan slipped the lottery ticket into my bag, I need to do the same for him. Theoretically speaking. He wanted me to have some of his luck. He insisted on it.

That's it.

"You wanted your luck to rub off on me, but now I need to rub your luck back off on you," I say. My words come out faster than my thoughts. I shake my head, and my mask jiggles side to side. "Wait, no. No one's rubbing anything."

Logan's eyes sparkle with amusement.

I can practically feel the red filling in my face. "I've said rub too many times," I mutter. "The point is: I owe you. I got millions, even though you picked most of the numbers. I'm the same way as you about debts, but I can't pay you back one-to-one."

"You owe me nothing. If I hadn't met you, we wouldn't be here right now. And besides, you're all over this ticket," Logan says.

"What do you mean?"

"10. 13. 30. 31. 23. 6." He says it like a mantra. "Ten and thirteen are for your birthday, which you told the fortune teller. And if you were born in 1996, that makes you about to turn thirty in a couple of weeks. Thirty-one is how old I am. We met on the twenty-third."

So there was something special about these numbers. Thankfully, he didn't share his rationale on camera. The last thing we need is my birthday out there confirming that Older Hazel Yen is actually Young Hazel Yen.

"Why did you pick six?" he asks as he rubs his artificially sun-spotted forehead.

I turn away. "I don't want to say."

Logan laughs. "What? Why not? I just told you my reasoning."

"Because."

"Okay, well, now you have to tell me," he says.

More heat. More red. I'm going to overbake in this mask. "You... You have three crinkles next to each eye when you smile." I don't have to look at him to confirm this. I do anyways. He's wearing a goofy grin under his mask.

Logan doesn't say anything. He just moves his hand closer to mine under the check until our pinkies are grazing.

From the very beginning, he had been paying attention. Seeing me.

And I had been seeing him.

I've witnessed enough with Dad to know how to help Logan. Or at least to know where we can start. Whenever he goes to the casino, Dad does his rituals. Brings his lucky charms. Wears his lucky colors. Has his lucky numbers. He does what he thinks he has to in order to beat the odds and improve his chances.

More times than not, his efforts don't work.

But…sometimes they do.

I don't know where the luck will come from. We'll just have to hope there's enough of it to go around to get Logan to opening night.

This is going to be just like the fortunes, probably. Futile attempts in the name of control.

But we have to at least try.

We need to attract luck. Increase it, somehow. That's what I'm going to help Logan with.

And I'm not going to let his hesitation deter me. Because of his choice to buy the ticket, I can help my brother. I might even be able to clear my own debts. It's life-changing, this gift he's given me.

"My dear, darling husband," I say, linking my temporarily aged pinky with his. "You need to get lucky."

Chapter 8

LOGAN

Sunday morning begins with thanking a police horse named Pancakes.

Pancakes was the key to our first action item in Hazel's plan that she's calling Operation Lucky Charms.

As we made our way uptown on the subway, Hazel prepped me on our first order of business: securing a horseshoe for luck and protection.

That's what led us to Central Park to ask a mounted police officer if he had any extra horseshoes on him or at the station. Apparently, that's not how horseshoes work. I think this is about to be another Advil moment where Hazel doesn't find what she's looking for, lets it go, and moves on.

But she doesn't. She's persistent and asks if there's another police horse nearby. This prompts the officer to contact the mobile horseshoe unit, which was currently on its way to meet an officer across the park.

Which is how we end up sprinting to the east side to watch a blacksmith change out the shoes on Pancakes. It didn't take much convincing from Hazel to get them to agree to let us keep the horseshoe.

And now, Action Item #2 involves us crawling around on the grass looking for four-leaf clovers.

"They're Celtic charms. Finding one is very rare. There are like, ten thousand three-leaf clovers for every single four-leaf," Hazel explains, referencing the printout she's brought along. "Look for general shapes. Four-leaf clovers will look more like squares, not triangles. I'll be over there." She points to an area half a football field away. "If you find one, give it to me, okay? That's supposed to double your luck."

She heads to her own patch of grass, leaving me to mine.

Never have I ever had to seek out luck. It's always found me. But I'm open to trying, no matter how many questions I have about Hazel's plan.

Two hours later, once Central Park looks like one giant, blurry square without a four-leaf clover in sight, we take a break.

Hazel releases a quiet groan as she pushes her knuckles into her lower back. She pulls her printed-out plan from her bag. "There are only twenty-five days until opening night," she reminds me. "We should look for ladybugs while we're here. What do you think our chances of seeing a shooting star are?"

"Rare, but not impossible."

"Good, that's the spirit." She skims her list. "How do you feel about goldfish? You might need to adopt one. Getting a horse is probably out of the question." She pauses and looks up at me for confirmation.

After a couple of seconds, I realize she's serious and still waiting for an answer. "Mrs. Walker—my landlord—she probably wouldn't allow it," I say. "And we've already reached our one-horse limit for the building."

"Maybe you need to move to a prewar. Heard they have a two-horse limit," she teases. "Wait—Mrs. Walker, like Toffee's owner, Mrs. Walker?"

I nod. "The one and only."

"Okay, well, what about rabbits?" she asks. "I didn't have it in me to add a rabbit's foot to this list. But a real one with all its limbs, that might work."

"Mrs. Walker might be okay with it, but I don't think Toffee would be."

Hazel sighs. "Fine. You can't say I didn't try."

No. I can't. It's incredibly sweet how hard she's trying.

"In some cultures, cats can ward off evil spirits and protect humans," she says, tapping her thumb against her printout. "Maybe you need to keep Toffee with you at all times."

"He'd love that."

Hazel smiles. "It'd be terrible for the birds of New York City, but good for you." She points to her sheet. "Pennies. If we find any, don't walk on by. Pick that shit up! Only if you see heads, though. And if we find a rainbow, we should probably follow it." She looks up at the sky, seemingly weighing in her mind the chances of seeing a rainbow on this sunny and cool October day.

"I'll keep an eye out," I promise. "You think these charms are actually going to work?"

"This is just Phase One. We need to get the obvious out of the way."

There's no way she believes in this stuff, and yet she's going along with it. For me.

"You know the Charging Bull statue down on Wall Street?" she asks. "Rumor has it, rubbing its...you know...is supposed to be a good omen. Thoughts on that?"

Instead of going with "hard pass" like I want to, I say, "I'll rub a bronze bull's family jewels if I must."

"Let's circle back on that one. How do you feel about crystals and stones?"

"They have great energy," I tell her.

She smirks and checks her phone. "Come on. It's time for lunch. Keep your eyes peeled for wishing wells."

We make our way out of the park and cross over a couple of avenues to the nearest grocery store, where Hazel makes a beeline for the precooked food.

"Hope you're hungry," she says, lifting a steaming container of rotisserie chicken.

"I'll grab forks." I also snag a few napkins and a couple of sparkling waters.

We cross back to the park to eat, but because it's a beautiful fall day, it's packed, and all the benches are taken.

"We could do that," I say, pointing with my shoulder toward Central Park Lake.

"If there aren't benches, there won't be boats. It's first come, first serve," Hazel says. "And we have a lot left to do today."

"Let's just see," I say. "But you should probably be the one to ask, given...you know."

Hazel reluctantly agrees, going down to the dock to talk to the attendant. She waves me over.

"Those two are done," she says about a couple stepping out of one of the boats. "Good timing."

"I'd say. Have you ever been out on one of these before?" I ask.

"At thirty dollars an hour? Absolutely not. You can see all that"—she waves her hands toward the skyline—"from there." She points to land.

"It's a nicer view on the water," I say. "And I guess now we can take our time out here, huh?"

I row us out to the center of the lake, where a dozen other people are floating in their boats. The blue backdrop of sky illuminates the shimmering skyrises sprouting up from a quilt of orange-, yellow-, and red-leafed trees. All the colors swirl together in the reflection of the surface of the algae-green lake.

Hazel turns her body to look behind her. "Wow."

"You should see it from this angle." I grab the left oar to spin the boat around so that she has the better view. As I do, my phone buzzes three times in a row with yet another spam call, probably someone requesting donations or pretending to be tech support. With my other hand, I scroll through the voicemail transcript.

"Hey! Logan!" Hazel's voice breaks through my distraction. I only realize I've been spinning us in circles when I notice her clinging to the sides of the boat. "Everything okay?"

I hold the oar firmly against the water, straightening us out. "Oh, everything's great." I set my phone down. "You wanna hear about an amazing investment opportunity? I've got three for you to pick from."

Hazel glances at my phone. "Apparently, I have five sets of grandparents in trouble who need my social security number." She rolls her eyes. "I've always gotten spam calls but never this much. It's been two days. How did these people even get our numbers?"

"With our names out there, I'm sure a simple Google search did it."

"I do think the disguises worked," she says. "I haven't heard from anyone that I know. I guess I don't mind the texts and calls as long as they're from strangers. Makes me feel like I've got a robust network of friends."

I nod in response. "Did you get a chance to enjoy the view, or was it all a blur?"

"I'm only a little seasick," she jokes, refocusing on the skyline. "Being so far downtown, I always forget there's a literal lake in the middle of the city. I've forgotten how much I love Central Park."

"If it weren't for all those skyscrapers, I might even forget I was in the city."

"And those hot dog carts."

"That, too."

"Summer's my favorite time of year," Hazel says. "This, though. This is giving it a run for its money." She looks content. "Fall feels like being covered with a heated blanket on a cold morning."

I grin at that image, especially because I know that she runs cold. When she turns her face into the sun to catch some of its warming rays, I feel a different kind of warmth as I watch her eyes flutter closed, her thick lashes curled against her smiling cheeks.

Hazel feels like fall.

We're in a small rowboat in the middle of Central Park Lake because this woman is embracing my wild fortune flip theory and recognizing that something's off for both of us. Instead of running away from it, she's running toward it.

With me.

My heart catches in my chest at this. Ever since I first laid eyes on Hazel, I've been a goner. The kiss solidified that.

Between this and the sun and the rowing, I'm now starting to overheat. I pull my sweater off, setting it on the seat beside me.

Hazel's already turned back to me, her eyes snapping up from my arms to my eyes. She's visibly flustered as she clears her throat.

The air is charged again, and this time, I think she feels it, too.

Would it be too much if I reached for her hand? Pulled her closer to me and re-created what she initiated on the first day we met? I've never wanted anything more...

"Chicken," Hazel says.

I lower my eyes to meet hers. I'm not one to back down from a challenge—

Then she reaches into the bag with the rotisserie chicken and pops the lid off.

Oh. *That* chicken.

She balances the container on her knees.

"Do you know what you're going to do with the money?" Hazel asks.

Ever since we agreed to claim our share, I've given this some thought. I've learned before how money can have strings attached. This lottery money, though... this doesn't.

I twist off the caps of our sparkling waters. "I'll invest it. It's more money than I'd need in a lifetime, so I'll probably donate a good chunk, too," I share. "But not to anyone who says, 'I've got an opportunity that'll make your head spin!'"

"Or to anyone who promises to double your money in ninety days," Hazel says, making a goofy face.

I laugh. "No way."

"So no yacht or five-star hotel vacation?" she asks, poking her spork into the chicken skin.

I consider this. "Have you heard about those yearlong cruises? A guy I used to work with once told me that after his brother-in-law's cousin came into money, he bought tickets for him and his wife. He paid in full for a suite, but even with discounts, I think it was, like, $110,000 per ticket."

Hazel tilts her head. "Let me guess. It ruined their lives and their relationship."

"Apparently, but it wasn't the money that got them. It was the nearly three-hundred-day trip and being trapped on a boat together."

"Maybe that's the true test," she says.

I grip the side of the rowboat. "Are we being tested now?"

Hazel smiles softly. "Can you imagine three hundred days in this thing?"

With her? Happily.

"This might surprise you," Hazel says, "but I think I would love that."

"Yeah?"

"Being around all that water sounds amazing," she says, and I realize we're talking about very different things.

"This is doing it for you then?" I gesture toward the lake.

"Like you wouldn't believe." Her shoulders come up with the corners of her mouth, like her whole body's smiling. "Since moving to the city, I haven't been able to swim. I feel like a yearlong trip would have to allow time for that, right?"

"Maybe a lap or two."

"And the trip itself...I haven't been out of New York since college, and that was to visit my brother. We rarely took trips when I was a kid, and when we did, my dad took us to Atlantic City or Mashantucket."

I adjust my hat. "What's in Mashantucket?"

"One of the largest resort casinos in North America," Hazel says, her eyes dropping. "My travel budget is slim. Nonexistent, really. Between rent, bills, student loans, and"—she waves her spork around—"everything else, I wanted to save whatever was left, not spend it."

"Everything else?"

Hazel meets my eyes, but she's quiet. She seems to be deciding whether she wants to share something. "I want to keep my grandparents' lake house in the family," she finally says. "I pay for half of the mortgage to help my dad. My grandpa built the house himself."

"Seriously? That's a dream of mine, to do something like that."

Hazel's face lights up. "Really? You've got all the skills for it, I'm sure. What kind would you build?"

"Honestly, I think a lot of that depends on who I'm building it for—or with."

"Like your special someone?" She says it with forced nonchalance.

"Exactly," I say, holding back a smile. "But there's not— I don't have...there's no one special in my life. Other than Toffee, of course."

This doesn't feel truthful. I'm practically living in an oil painting right now with a beautiful woman who cares about me enough to help me increase my luck. This feels pretty special. *She* feels pretty damn special.

"Yeah, well, special someones are hard to find these days," Hazel says.

"Are you going to pay off the house with the winnings?"

Her chewing slows. "Oh," she says, swallowing. "I don't...the total mortgage is more than I would be able to cover with the annual payments. At least for right now." She sets her spork down. "Do you ever feel guilty about winning? Like it was too easy? Money isn't this easy to make." She watches another boat pass us before speaking again. "It feels like, I don't know, a dream or something. The money. The fortunes. This. All of it." She peers up at me through her lashes. "Meeting you."

"Your life can change in a second," I say. "Doesn't mean you change just as fast."

"Yes. That's exactly it."

We float into a ray of sunlight, and Hazel's eyes brighten as her dark hair takes on a reddish hue. She's as picturesque as the trees and skyline behind her. Winning the lottery might not feel real. This, though. This doesn't either.

I can't help but feel the spark of luck again. It's too good, being here with her.

"But I...yes," I say on an exhale. "I do know that feeling." Of guilt. Of pressure.

In fact, I know those feelings a little too well.

"Do you feel like you need to give the money to anyone? To

family?" Hazel asks, her eyebrows furrowed. She sits up straighter. "Sorry, oh my god. That's such an intrusive question."

"Hazel, we won the lottery together," I say. "We're bonded for life."

This gets a small smile out of her, and I think, maybe, relief?

"But to answer your question, no," I answer. "They don't need it."

Hazel twists her spork into the chicken breast. "Mine's the opposite. My dad is bad with money. Whenever money came in, it went right out. We'd go from having a nice dinner one night to eating frozen pizza seven nights in a row."

She doesn't elaborate, so I say, "That's a really big swing."

She nods. "I don't trust the lottery money. This game has been such a disaster for my family. And now it's part of my life forever."

"Or at least until the annuity runs out."

"Right, I'll have that annual reminder," she says with a half smile.

"It's just surreal being on the other side of it. I really can't gripe with money coming in like that every year, but I also can't just ignore how I've felt about gambling for basically my entire life." She lets out a huff of air. "I'll use the money for my brother's emergency. But otherwise, I want to pretend like the money doesn't exist."

"Some things in life we're allowed to do, or keep, just for ourselves," I say, this time more seriously. I mean it.

I see the moment my comment lands as Hazel's mouth twitches in surprise. Her eyes lift to meet mine. "Ahh!" She ducks and reaches for her shoulder.

"Wait!" I say, grabbing her hand. "That's…"

Her eyes widen. "No."

"Bird poop," I say, pressing my lips together. "Hold on."

I tip my sparkling water into a napkin.

"On me and not you?" she asks excitedly. "I knew it was a good thing you held on to the horseshoe."

THE FORTUNE FLIP

At the mention of it, I remember the weight of it in my coat pocket. "Birds pooping on you is supposed to be a good sign. You didn't need a fortune teller to confirm your luck. Life's doing it for you."

"Oh, right," Hazel mumbles. "What's with me and birds lately?"

"Can I get it for you?"

"Please." She leans forward, and I lift the droppings off her shoulder with a dry napkin, wiping the spot clean with the wet one. Every time we see each other, we're touching in little ways. It feels natural, like it's an inevitable part of our day.

"You're all good," I say, feeling the curve of her shoulder beneath her sweater.

"Thanks." And as though she's used to stuff like this constantly happening to her, she continues eating. At this point, we've made a good dent.

"There!" Hazel says, tapping something with her spork. "The wishbone." She digs it out of the chicken and sets it on a napkin next to her. "It needs to dry before we break it."

"You thought of everything."

"I take my responsibilities seriously," she says. "Especially because of all the good things happening for me. Another recruiter reached out."

"Hazel, I want the very best things for you."

"You hardly know me," she whispers.

"But I want to," I tell her. Because it's true. I do. I want to know everything about Hazel. I want to know which countries she'd look forward to most on a yearlong cruise. I want to know why she got a tattoo of Mickey Mouse. I want to know what her grandparents' house looks like and what season of the year she loves it most in so I can know what she loves.

Those all feel like more intimate questions somehow, so I start with a basic one.

"What made you want to become a data analyst?" I ask, remembering the role the recruiter mentioned in Hazel's email. When we drift too far into the shade, I grab the oars and row us around the lake, guiding us toward the Bow Bridge.

Hazel looks out over the water. "Data is chaos I can control," she says. "My dad was always analyzing stats and numbers for the games he watched. I didn't see them as numbers, though. I saw them as stories. If you can hear past the noise of all the data that comes in, you can understand what it's really saying. We use that chaos to interpret and forecast future trends."

I don't even try to hold back my grin.

"Why are you smiling like that?" she asks.

"You're like a data fortune teller."

Hazel challenges my statement by making a face.

"Maybe you going to a fortune teller makes a lot more sense," I reason. "You had data, you wanted a forecast."

Hazel laughs once through her nose, like she doesn't believe me. "Yeah, well, sometimes the data doesn't tell you that you're about to get laid off."

"Or that the cat you're walking is going to change your life."

There's a shift in the way Hazel looks at me. I don't know if it's the way the sun slants against her face or the glow of the vibrant trees behind her, but she seems more relaxed.

We float under the iconic Bow Bridge that spans the lake, passing rocks on the other side of it. Hazel points to one with five turtles lounging. "Look! They're part of today's operation. Turtles are supposed to protect you from evil and are good luck."

I pull the left oar harder against the water. "Great, grab one. Check it off the list!"

"I was kidding, but sure. Let's steal a turtle," she says. "The only downside is that I've heard that turtles being low maintenance is a marketing ploy. And they'll probably outlive you."

"Before I die, I'll make sure to drop it off here," I say. "On this very rock, where these turtles will still be sunbathing."

"Don't say that!" Hazel says. "Take it back. You're not going to die."

"Ooookay, I'm not going to die?" Hazel glares at me, and I say it again without a lift at the end of my sentence.

"Thank you. It's a Chinese superstition. We don't like to talk about…that." She waves her hands in front of her. "Not that I'm superstitious. But it's better to be safe."

"Not touching that one."

She looks down, remembering the wishbone. "You have one more chance."

I make a dramatic show of stretching out my neck, arms, and fingers in preparation.

"Put your thumb up closer to the top, okay?" Hazel instructs, holding the wishbone up to the sky to analyze it. "Take this side. It's bigger."

"Does the wish count if it's rigged in my favor?" I ask, reaching for the bigger side of the bone. As I do, a bird swoops down and plucks it out of Hazel's fingers.

"No!" she calls after it.

I stand to reach for the wishbone, but the bird is faster. It's got the wishbone in its beak, hovering in the air before it flies past my head. I lean back to avoid getting struck, the boat wobbling with my movements.

I wave my arms around to steady myself, but it's a useless attempt. I've leaned too far back.

And then everything goes dark green.

The lake isn't as cold as I thought it would be. Or I'm in shock.

When I emerge from the water, Hazel's hand is clasped over her mouth.

"Can you swim?" she shouts.

I rub my hand down my face as I tread water. "I'm rethinking the yearlong cruise!"

"I'm coming in." Hazel quickly sheds her coat and starts to unzip one of her boots.

As much as I'd like to see where this goes, she can't jump in after me. This lake is filthy.

I swim over to the side of the boat and wrap my arms over the edge. "Were you really going to save me?" I ask, grinning up at her.

Hazel zips her boot back up and lets out a mock-irritated sigh, but there's a playfulness in her eyes. "Just get back in here, will you?"

"Sure, but steer clear," I say. "There's a chance I'm waking up tomorrow with the ability to glow."

And that's when Hazel's whole face brightens. Her laugh feels like the exact moment when slats of wood that have taken hours to measure, cut, and chisel end up fitting perfectly. The sound of it is so satisfying, so rewarding.

I swish around in the water. "I think a fish just swam up my pant leg."

She laughs more. I let the sound of it wash over me before slowly climbing into the boat, taking extra care not to tip it. I ring out my shirt, ditch my hat, and push the wet strands of hair off my face.

Hazel watches my every move. "So," she says, amused, "rain check on the goldfish then?"

Chapter 9

HAZEL

The money is deposited on a Wednesday afternoon.

It's staggering, the amount. One second it wasn't there, the next it was.

I was certain we'd get a call after the press event about how there was some sort of mistake. A mix-up in the numbers or the winners. A processing error. No metaphorical *but* came.

Logan texts when he sees his own deposit, his message appearing above Jerry's latest update: Healing process doing its thing. Ever since Sunday, Logan and I have been texting. I updated him on how smooth my first day at Sweet Escape was, how I've already memorized the names of more than 75 percent of the inventory, and progress on the job hunt. Yesterday, I had a call with the recruiter who emailed. The salary for the senior data analyst role was more than I anticipated. If I go for the manager role, it's even more than that. Milly is moving me forward for both. Logan gave me play-by-plays from the theater. The set piece mix-up was worse than he thought and two of his stagehands quit.

Now Logan's insisting on celebrating our win. I only agree if we don't call it a celebration.

Later that night, I meet him on the corner of Varick Street and North Moore Street in Lower Manhattan. Logan's waiting for me, dressed in medium-wash denim—well-worn, as always—sneakers, and a blue sweater with a white shirt peeking out from underneath. It's just like the one he wore when he had his very own Mr. Darcy moment in the middle of Central Park Lake.

At the memory, heat collects under my thick gray wool sweater. I couldn't even be bothered to try averting my gaze after he pulled himself out of the water. The way the wet cotton hugged every inch of muscle on him. The way it revealed the beginnings of a tattoo sprawling up his shoulder. It was blurry through the fabric, though I could tell the design was of the roots of something. I wanted to reach out to touch him. Find out what those roots led to.

Logan smiles when he sees me. He does that a lot, I've noticed. Smile. But the ones he saves for me are different. They send my heart into overdrive. I hope that never stops—his smiling or the fluttering.

"Hey," I say softly.

"Hey yourself. We'll be here tonight." He points to the building across the street, which is only three stories tall, the top portion of it brick. On the street level, a giant, arched red door tips me off.

It's a firehouse. But why does it look so familiar?

I read the words above the door. Hook & Ladder 8. "This is from *Ghostbusters*."

Logan tips his head. "Come with me."

The red door opens, revealing a massive, shiny firetruck behind it. Inside, *Ghostbusters* signs, stickers, melted phones, and clocks cover the doorways and walls.

Logan waves to a group of firefighters across the firehouse. Everywhere he goes, he's like a social butterfly collecting friends. It amazes me how he does that. I didn't have a lot of friends growing up. I don't even have friends now. I lost touch with everyone from college. I wouldn't go to happy hours with coworkers because I needed to save money. More often than not, work consumed my weekends. I've hardly explored the city.

I follow Logan to the back stairs. They're a little uneven, and the railing's wobbly, but it's a historic old building. There's a type of charm in the imperfection of these places that I adore.

At the top of the second flight, I grab Logan's arm. "I'm not lucky enough to break the law, and you're definitely not in a position to push it more than you have. Are we allowed to be here?"

"It's okay," he says. "A buddy I used to work with is a fireman here."

"And he's just letting us hang out on the roof?"

"No, of course not." Logan pushes the door open with his back. "He's letting us *eat* on the roof." He smiles. "I made a sizable donation as a thank-you."

"Not even twenty-four hours into getting the money and you're already paying people off," I say dryly. "Money really does change a person."

Logan laughs as he leads me to a table set for two with paper plates and cups. In the center, a votive candle flickers.

"They're battery-powered," he says as he slides out my chair for me. "Though this would probably be the safest place to burn a candle."

The building's so low that there's not a great view of the city. But because it's on the corner, the entire sky stretches out in front of us. The horizon burns bright orange with streaks of red flickering underneath as the sun moves. It's a fire no one needs to put out.

Logan reveals a few paper bags filled with an assortment of white takeout boxes. He pops the lids open. "On the menu for this evening, we have egg rolls, white rice, lo mein, Kung Pao shrimp, sautéed string beans, dumplings, sesame chicken, egg drop soup, hot and sour soup, fried rice, beef and broccoli, and General Tso's chicken." He rubs his hand behind his neck. "I didn't know what you liked, so I got everything."

The man literally brought me a feast.

"Chinese takeout. Just like the movie," I recall.

"And for dessert we have…" He shakes a box of Twinkies, another reference from the movie. "Got the sense you have a sweet tooth."

Playing along, I add, "For hors d'oeuvres,"—I pull out a bag of candy and drape it over my arm—"an assortment of gummy numbers, for good luck."

Logan gives me a questioning look. "Eights and sevens?"

"Eight is auspicious in Chinese culture. The pronunciation of it sounds like how you say *to make fortune*," I explain. Dad never let me forget this. "And you mentioned having Welsh grandparents. Seven is supposed to be lucky."

He takes the bag from me and smiles at it. "You remembered that?"

I remember everything about you, I don't say. "This is the good stuff. It's from the shop," I say instead. "You got me candy, so here's some back."

He rubs his neck. "Thank you. I'm a little embarrassed I got you bodega cherry gummies."

"Candy is candy. I don't discriminate."

He plops the bag in the center of the table for us to share. Even when he's doing something mundane like popping the lids off takeout boxes, he wears a small, permanent smile. It's too cute.

Suddenly, I'm nervous. "You really didn't have to go through all this trouble. The last thing you need to do is spend money on me."

Logan nods toward the candy without missing a beat. "It's no trouble, and I could say the same to you."

"Sugar and renting out a firehouse are not the same things."

"Maybe not, but we both wanted to do something nice for each other." He glances up at me, his eyebrow arched. "You don't need to reciprocate this."

"Fine. I'll cancel my ask to the police precinct," I joke.

Logan laughs.

"Thanks for planning this," I add. "I've never been inside—or on—a firehouse before."

"I thought you'd like it because you mentioned the Ecto-1 at the pizza shop."

Did I? "How do you remember that?"

"I remember everything about you," he says, sounding entirely serious.

Oh.

His earnestness catches me off guard. My nerves can't catch a break. "What was it with the eighties and cars?" I ask, trying to distract myself from the fact that maybe what I'm feeling isn't actually nerves but...excitement? "I'm marathoning eighties movies, and wow, did they love their vehicles."

"You enjoyed the movie, though, right?" Logan asks, scooping a heaping mound of rice onto my plate.

"Enough for me to remember the car's name."

"Good. Otherwise, this really would've been a bust."

"Ha ha." I add a spoonful of General Tso's onto my rice. "I had never seen a ghost movie before. Do you find that weird?"

"I find nothing about you weird," Logan says, though he can't help but ask, "So you've never seen *Casper*?"

"My dad's superstitious. He wouldn't let us watch any movies with ghosts in them," I share. "Especially after my mom..." I swallow. "After my mom died."

Logan sets his chopsticks down. "Hazel—"

"It's okay. I'm fine. It was a really long time ago," I say, waving him off. "But when people face uncertainty, they lean into superstitions. That's my dad in a nutshell. He grew up hearing how ghosts could be harmful if provoked and didn't want anything to do with them."

Logan watches me for a second with concerned eyes before following my lead and moving on. "But you're not a believer in ghosts, superstitions, the paranormal?" he asks.

"I believe in that as much as I believe in fortune-telling," I say.

He nods, like he hears me but isn't entirely convinced by what I'm saying. "They drink Budweiser in the movie, but I don't drink, so I hope it's okay that I brought these," Logan says, setting onto the table a ginger beer and a root beer. "You can try both and take whichever you like best."

My heart softens at this. "Why are you always so nice to me?"

Logan sits back against his chair, which looks too small with him in it. "Do you think it's annoying? Me being this nice?" His question comes out serious.

I almost spit out the ginger beer I'm taste testing. "Annoying? Oh my god, no. I just...no one's ever done something this sweet for me before."

His jaw clenches at this. "You deserve nice things, Hazel," he says, expelling a frustrated breath. "My ex, she just always thought I was too nice. Which I don't get. I'm too nice, so that makes me a bad person?"

"You're the perfect amount of nice."

Logan's shoulders relax. "Sorry, I didn't mean to get all intense. She even said I smile too much, so it was probably doomed from the beginning," he says in a more lighthearted way. "What am I supposed to do? Not smile?"

"That would be a tragedy."

At this, he smiles. Because of course he does.

"Well, cheers to nice things," he says, holding up the root beer I didn't choose. "Like winning the lottery."

I slide my drink closer to me. "Cheers-ing is too celebratory. We're not supposed to be doing that."

"No, we're not supposed to be *calling* it that," he clarifies. "But fine. How about... cheers to other nice things. Like this."

"This?"

"Tonight. Being here, with you, after a whirlwind of a week." He's still holding up his root beer. "You're not gonna leave me hanging now, are you?"

Logan's bathed in golden light, the diffused rays highlighting his eye crinkles and a subtle dimple in his left cheek, just outside his smile lines, that I hadn't noticed before. He's looking at me like I'm the one who concocted this entire magical evening. Like I'm the one who won us a fortune.

Leave him hanging? How could I possibly?

I hold my drink up to his. "Okay. I'll cheers to that."

I want to relax into this night. Enjoy the view and Logan's company. But I can't help but feel on edge. Nothing ever goes this well.

The sunset becomes more vibrant as the minutes tick on. I grab my phone and take a quick picture. It reminds me of the sunsets on the lake.

Then Logan says, "From your grandparents' house," and I realize I've said this out loud.

I'm not used to talking about my grandparents' house with anyone as much as I have with Logan.

I nod.

"Tell me about it?" he asks.

I've never been asked this before. Where to even start. "It looks like a mix between a cabin and a cottage. It has gingerbread decorative trim," I start, recalling every detail so easily. I tell him about the wraparound porch. The dining room set in a bay. Windows everywhere so you can see the lake from each room.

When I'm done, Logan has a faraway look, like he could actually imagine it. He finishes off his egg roll. "My mom lives in Maine now, so I'm just used to the sunsets on the bay, but I think I get what you're saying. There's nothing like a sunset on the water."

"Is that where you grew up? Maine?" I ask between bites.

Logan moves a few noodles around on his plate. "No. I'm from Washington state. No one in my family lives there anymore, so I have no reason to go back."

"What brought you to the city then?"

"What I do now. I wanted to get away from home after...I just needed to get away," Logan says. He doesn't elaborate. "I got lucky and found carpentry. I loved it, and that brought me here."

I swallow a bite of broccoli. "What is it you love about carpentry?"

Logan stretches out against his seat. "A lot of people stick with things because they love them. Me? I hated it at first. It was the hardest thing I had ever done. I was not good at it. Like, really awful. Someone should've taken the saw away from me." He pushes a piece of shrimp around on his plate. "It wasn't something I was naturally good at, but I got a little better each day. Eventually, I was good at it without fully realizing how I got there. I think I fell in love with it because it challenged me."

"You had to work for it."

"I did," he says, punctuating this with a single nod. "Once I got the hang of it, I started to love the little things about it. The history in it. The smell of the wood. The feeling of a cut board before it's sanded and smoothed. The feeling afterward."

"So you could make something out of"—I point down to a tree lining the street—"that."

"Sure, what would you like?"

"Surprise me. But if you get caught chopping it down, I don't know you."

Logan grins. "I'll have to get my disguise back on before I do it."

"No way. There's photographic evidence that ties you to me in that thing," I say.

"Right, right," he says, rubbing his chin. "In fact, that version of me was your husband."

"Maybe that's better. Spousal immunity."

"Did we just begin our life of crime together?" Logan asks.

I gesture toward the rooftop. "We're up here on a bribe. I'd say that's a good start."

Logan laughs hard, his whole heart showing.

"That's really great, though. Sounds like carpentry brings you a lot of joy," I say. Despite recent events, it really seems to. Logan looks peaceful as he shares all this. It guts me that something he loves so much is challenging him all over again. "I'm sorry things aren't getting better at work."

I can't properly analyze his expression, but based on his long silence, I imagine he's working through something.

"Our set designer left," he updates as I bite a string bean in half. "She took a job Off Broadway. We have a new guy, but he wants to move some of the sets around. Which, of course, complicates how everything was meant to be arranged, and we need to make adjustments. So that's the latest."

The hourglass from his tea leaf reading comes to mind. *Something's coming up for you, and you're racing against the clock.*

"That's frustrating," I say.

The look of concern Logan wears is new to me. But as quickly as it comes, it vanishes. "The show will be better for it," he says. "New vision, new energy. And I do my best work under pressure."

It's a classic Logan move, I've noticed. Whenever anything bad, or even mildly annoying happens, he spins it. Makes the situation positive, but in a forced way. It's like he doesn't want to talk about—no, *feel*—the negative.

In perfect universal timing, the distant roar of a plane's engine draws our attention. Our eyes meet, both of us probably thinking the same thing.

Avoid planes.

"I figured out Phase Two," I say suddenly to fill the silence that follows as the plane flies farther into the distance.

Logan offers a weak smile. "More charms?"

"We're past the trinket stage. But remember to keep an eye out for the clover," I remind him. "If you find one, let me know, and I'll add it to my tracker."

He arches an eyebrow. "Your tracker?"

"I'm tracking all the unusual activities that happen in your life. And our efforts. You should probably let me know anything else that's happened. I've made a mental note to add the set design change-up."

"You're cataloging the bad things that happen to me?" Logan asks, somewhat amused.

"I've got data all the way back to the day we met," I explain. "I'll make sense of the numbers and give you a nice visual report. I have a particular data visualization style that I was kind of known for at work. Why are you looking at me like that?"

He smirks. "You're trying to control the chaos."

I set my chopsticks down. "I'm trying to track your luck," I correct. "Then we can do more of what works. I'm hoping we'll have enough to forecast when your bad fortune might go away."

He laughs to himself. "Sure. As much as I appreciate you tracking everything that goes wrong in my life, and as grateful as I am that you're even helping me at all, let's forget about it for now. We're celeb— No, sorry. We're *acknowledging* that the money came in."

"Do you commemorate everything?"

Logan takes a bite of his egg roll, swallowing as he nods. "I try. When something's good—big or small—I think it's worth celebrating. Or at least recognizing it."

"So tonight's an acknowledgment. Is tonight also supposed to be...a date?" I feel bold asking this, but I want to know how he views me. And part of me wants...something else. Something other than what my life looks like. I think subconsciously I've wanted that since we kissed.

A warm glow from the battery-powered candlelight illuminates his face as his eyes search mine. "I would never trick you into a date. I really did want us to have fun," he says.

"Oh. Yeah." I wave my hand. "No, of course—"

"But I would love nothing more than to take you on a date," he adds, his gaze filled with heat. It's directed right at me, and I feel the warmth of it all the way down to my toes.

I'm on the verge of melting into this moment when my mind pulls me back to reality.

"I..."

Logan leans forward in anticipation, resting his arms on the table. There's a beat of silence until the air shrieks with the whoop of a firetruck siren. He jolts, his knees knocking into the table. He manages to catch it, but we lose the last of the sesame chicken and rice.

We both kneel to clean up the mess with the extra napkins. "Are you going to add that to the tracker?" he asks, our faces inches apart.

I grin. Instead of answering his probably rhetorical question, to which the answer is a definitive *yes*, I surprise myself by saying, "I would love nothing more than for you to take me on a date."

Logan's smile brackets deepen, his blue-green eyes a shade darker.

"But we need to go slow," I quickly add as the siren fades down the avenue. "I used to be married. Which you already know because you saw the divorce papers."

And that's a classic me move. When things are going well, I have to self-sabotage. Not that there's anything wrong with being a bad dater or being divorced, but really? I had to bring that up now?

His head tilt turns into a slow nod.

We're still on the ground, huddled together under the table. "I'm not very good at dating," I admit.

Logan's probably being polite when he says, "Who is?"

"I still can't believe I even had to get divorced." I worry this topic is a mood killer. Even so, I lean into it. "I only knew him—my ex... husband, technically—for seventy-two hours. Our marriage lasted six months, which was mostly because we wanted a no-fault divorce."

Good ol' impulsivity. The exact kind of thing I try to not do. It reminds me too much of Dad.

"Seventy-two hours, huh?" Logan asks.

"It was around the time my dad had won big in Atlantic City," I share, fidgeting with one of the splintered chopsticks.

I don't know why any of this comes out. It must be because Logan opened up to me, and, I don't know, I feel like I owe him something in return. He's given me reason to trust him, so I do.

"He promised he'd put his winnings against the mortgage to help pay it down faster. Then he ended up losing everything in a last-minute bet on the playoffs. I just..." I throw my hands up weakly. "I was tired of being the responsible one. The one who doesn't get to be spontaneous. I wanted to feel free from it all. I married the first single guy I met at a belated New Year's party at the office. A party that we were required to attend." I groan. "That's humiliating."

"I don't think you're guilty here. It should be illegal for office parties to be required," Logan says softly.

It catches me so off guard that I can't help but laugh a little. "Funny. I should've said that in my exit interview."

Logan's quiet as he takes my hands in his. He probably doesn't know what to say. I don't know what I'd even say to everything I just dumped on him.

I start to backtrack. "I probably shouldn't have told you all that."

"No," he says, his expression and tone serious.

"Sorry, that was—"

He lifts my chin up gently. "No, Hazel, I'm glad you did. Seriously. I want to know you."

"I want to know you, too." And I do. I really, really do.

"And we've been through something big—something impossible—together. We know what each other's futures hold," Logan says with a little humor in his voice. He's trying to cheer me up. "That's got to count for something, right?"

I grab a handful of gummy numbers from the bag on the table. "Yeah, maybe like fifteen," I say, holding up a seven and an eight.

He playfully bites the eight out of my hand. "Now we're here. If that hadn't happened, and if I wasn't *such* a nice guy," he says with a playful roll of his eyes, "then we wouldn't be on this rooftop. Together." Logan gently holds my face between his hands. "Believe me when I say we all do things we wish we could take back. I sure as hell have. You're not the only one who's made a mistake."

"Thank you," I whisper. This man really doesn't have a mean bone in his body.

Logan pulls me into him, holding me until I'm ready to let go. He smells like sawdust and pine. There's an entire forest in his skin.

He reaches for the bag the takeout came in and removes two fortune cookies. "Here. These are always a nice little boost." He jumbles the two plastic-wrapped cookies together like a magician performing a sleight-of-hand trick.

I choose the cookie from his left hand. "After the tea leaf reading, I thought you'd be done with fortunes."

"No restaurant is going to give you a bad fortune," Logan says, tearing his open and snapping the cookie in half. "That wouldn't be smart for business."

His smile fades when he sees that his slip of paper is torn into three squares.

"It must've been baked into the folds?" I guess.

"Does this cancel out whatever's written here?"

"Maybe? Here, let me see." I puzzle the pieces together against my thigh, which I quickly learn is useless. There are only words printed on one of the squares.

—give up.

"The first part is cut off," I say, turning that piece over. "I'm sure it was supposed to say something encouraging that ends with 'never give up.'"

"Or it says, 'You should give up.'"

"No. *No.* Let's go back to that restaurant and report this. They can't be giving out cut-off fortunes! Or maybe there was a printer error. I'm sure they're all like that." I crack my cookie in half, pull out my fortune, and start reading. "Time teaches us everything we need to know. When to start, when to stop. When enough is enough. In twenty-four hours or a lifetime, many lessons can be learned." I take a breath. "There's no need to rush. Time is your friend."

Logan laughs as he shakes his head in disbelief. "All of that was on your fortune?"

"Probably a verbose intern wrote this. It was their first day, and they didn't know they had to keep their predictions to one line. That's Fortune Cookie Writing 101," I say, turning my slip over. "Either way, fortune cookie fortunes don't count."

He looks slightly relieved. "You don't think so?"

"No," I try to say confidently. "But just in case, maybe we should confirm it." Down below, the sounds of the city's noisy night scene echo off the buildings. I stand and help pull Logan up. "Come on. We're going back to that restaurant and getting you a new fortune cookie."

His eyes sparkle in the lights from the neighboring buildings. "If you insist." He sweeps our plates and empty takeout boxes into the bag, tossing his fortune in after it.

I follow him across the rooftop. My steps slow as we reach the door.

I hesitate. For some reason, this is the moment my mind decides to recall Logan's third tea leaf reading.

He pulls the door open. A gust from the stairwell blows my hair back.

The tea leaves indicated a ladder.

I'm sure Logan is around ladders at work, but he hasn't mentioned anything.

I scan the stairwell. There's not a ladder in sight. Because why would there be?

I squint in thought, breathing in sharply when it hits me.

The firehouse.

Hook & Ladder 8.

I reach for his arm. "Logan, wait!"

But it's too late.

He trips over the threshold and grabs for the railing to balance himself. It's too wobbly to sustain his weight and pops out of the wall.

Logan makes a grunting noise before tumbling down the stairs. The takeout boxes and his fortune go down with him.

Chapter 10

LOGAN

Turns out, it was a metaphorical ladder.

"Nine weeks? For a broken wrist?" Mrs. Walker asks on the other end of the line.

"It could've been twelve weeks or longer," I say.

Huh. Maybe my luck is turning around after all.

After my fall down the stairs, Hazel insisted on taking me to the hospital, refusing to hear my *I'm fine*s. Nothing about the sharp, burning sensation felt fine, but she didn't need this burden, especially with all that she has going on with her brother. She stayed with me the entire time at the hospital, asking the doctor questions and typing notes into her phone. A couple of hours later, I was sent home with a cast. Hazel picked the color: lucky red.

And now I'm home earlier than usual from work on a Friday. Not only did I break my wrist, but my entire body is sore. I should still be at the theater managing my crew, moving things along, but Richie promised to make life hell for me if I kept pushing through the pain.

"Tell the doctors you need it done faster," Mrs. Walker says in her no-nonsense British accent.

I make a face she can't see. "What can the doctors do? It's the body's timeline."

"Then will your body into obedience. At the beginning of any cold, I tell my body, *No! You do not have time for this.* And it works. I've had mild colds that only last two days since 2010."

Nothing about that sounds healthy, but I don't fight it. Celine Walker is a powerhouse in her personal and professional lives. A former actress headlining in shows, she's now transitioned into producing them, mostly on Broadway or the West End, and she doesn't have time for whining or excuses. Which, apparently, includes my wrist.

"I suppose I'm being a smidge dramatic. You're taking time to recover, I hope?" Mrs. Walker asks, her tone a warning. "The theater will still be there next week, you know."

If she had seen what's been happening, she wouldn't be saying that.

"There's still a lot to do, but I'm managing," I say, keeping it vague. I flick the waving arm of a lucky cat figurine that Hazel had delivered to me this morning.

Mrs. Walker groans. "Spare me the bullshit. Is everything okay over there?"

"Okay? It's better than that. It's fantastic. This show's going to be...great." I don't need to worry Mrs. Walker about her most personal show and biggest investment to date when she's halfway across the world. No one wants to be around negative people.

"Okay, well, good," she says. "Because I've decided that this is my last show."

I'm so glad this isn't a video call because then she'd see the look on my face.

"Your last show?" I ask, hoping she can't hear the panic vibrating through me. The final show she produces cannot be this one. Not when it's on the verge of crashing and burning. "But aren't there still so many stories you want to tell? You're just getting started!"

"Roman will never get to see it come to life, but I'll get to. I figured, why not go out on a high with the musical my husband spent half his life working on?"

"Half his life, wow," I say, tapping the lucky cat's arm so hard the whole thing falls over. "Great. Well, can't wait for you to see how things are progressing. You're going to be..." Disappointed. Upset. Alarmed. "Surprised."

"Pleasantly, I hope," she says.

"Yep! Totally." This comes out so emphatically that I kind of believe myself.

Mrs. Walker doesn't seem to be buying it. "Logan, you've always had a can-do attitude, but not everything you can do. Not everything you *should* do. Which reminds me, please don't make me Christmas biscotti again this year, I beg of you."

I huff out a laugh. Each holiday season, Mrs. Walker and her late husband made biscotti for their neighbors. Ever since I met her, I've been baking her a batch during the holidays since she no longer wants to do it without Roman.

Something I learned about Mrs. Walker is that she prefers her biscotti burned to a crisp. According to her, my perfectly golden ones were "expected." Mrs. Walker's a don't-follow-the-recipe kind of person.

"This year you're getting two boxes," I say as she laughs and goes *uh-huh*. Little does she know, I'll probably unintentionally burn every batch of biscotti I make, even if I set a timer for a shorter bake time. Maybe she'd actually eat them this year.

"Roman couldn't stand it. To him, golden was overbaked," Mrs. Walker says with a rare laugh in recollection.

"You were married for a long time. What's your secret?"

"Share all your pieces with each other," she says right away. "The beautiful, the ugly. The messy, the shiny. Don't live your life in hiding."

I vocalize my head nods with an *mmm* to acknowledge I've heard her.

"How's my Mr. Mistoffelees doing?" Mrs. Walker asks, her voice still soft. It loses its edge whenever we talk about her husband or her cat.

"I thought he was with you," I deadpan. Toffee meows from on top of my shoe where he's lounging.

"Hah. Those birds better not have traumatized him too much," she says. "You've seen Hitchcock's movie, right? Birds can be vile creatures."

I still worry those sparrows are going to find me one day.

"Oh, Logan, you added too much to rent this month," Mrs. Walker says, the sharpness in her voice back. It's not that she's unkind; she just doesn't put on unnecessary niceties.

"It'll take some time, but I'm going to pay you back for the discounted rate you've been giving me all these years," I explain. "And will, from this point forward, be paying what you could be renting this place for." It's a staggering amount—Tribeca isn't cheap—but it's fair.

She groans. "But then it's not a good deed on my end. You know I'm nothing without my good deeds. How are you affording this?"

"I won the lottery."

Mrs. Walker laughs at this for a long time. "Logan, I'm serious. I know what carpenters make," she says once she catches her breath.

"I'm serious, too."

Now that the money's cleared, I update her on my situation. I've already spoken to a financial advisor, but she offers to put me in touch with hers. She also insists I, at the very least, cut off $1,000 in the rent for cat sitting.

We end the call agreeing on a happy medium of $500.

As I'm leashing up Toffee, I hear a knock at my door.

Hazel's on the other side, holding a large bag and two to-go cups.

I attempt to take them from her, awkwardly placing my cast under the bottom of the bag to steady it, but she pulls back before I get a good grip.

"You're"—I look at my watch—"three hours early. I'm about to take Toffee on a walk."

"In your texts, you said you were home," she says, setting everything down on the counter. "I just got off from the shop. I thought I'd come by to see if I could help with anything?" She hands me one of the cups. "I'm a cinnamon latte girl. I got you the same. I hope that's okay."

"You didn't have to get me anything."

"I couldn't show up here with just a beverage for me," she says. "I know it's a little late to be drinking coffee but the craving hit."

I take a sip from the cup. It's delicious. "I think I'm a cinnamon latte boy."

Hazel smirks as she takes the end of Toffee's leash from me. "I can do that. You need rest." She guides me back to the living room.

I grab my hat from the entry table. "I need fresh air, and my body needs blood flow, movement, something vertical."

She shoots me a look that says, *Fine, you win*. "No more than ten minutes, tops."

As soon as we enter Rockefeller Park, it's clear the walk is going to take more than ten minutes. Toffee insists on smelling every blade of grass and soaking up each ray of the lowering sun.

"Let him have it. He only has a couple of months left," I say.

Hazel drops to her knees and gives Toffee a side hug. "I'm sorry I was ever mad at you."

I play my words back. "Oh no. Like, he only has a couple of months left before temperatures drop too low for his toe beans to touch pavement, and he's taking full advantage."

She releases Toffee from her grip. "I'm still kind of mad at you," she whispers to him. She accepts my outstretched hand to help her up, her eyes lingering on me. "You're always wearing that hat."

"Thanks for noticing."

"What's the story?"

I lift my hat to run my hand through my hair. "I've worn it during some tough times. Ever since then, I guess it's kind of become a habit."

She nods slowly. "Your lucky hat. I'll note it in the tracker."

We continue our stroll through the park, taking small steps to keep up with Toffee's pace. "Hey, uh, did you also get the interview request?" I ask. "For AARP?"

"Like the magazine for retired people?"

"Yeah. They want to put us on their cover."

Hazel's eyes widen. "The disguises were good, but they couldn't possibly have been put-you-on-a-cover good."

"If there were a Tony Award category for Best Makeup, my friend would win," I say.

"And maybe we'd get a nomination for Best Actor and Best Actress," she says. "We must've been a pretty convincing married couple."

I can't explain why my first thought is *being married to her wasn't hard*.

A pigeon lands in front of us, and Hazel grips Toffee's leash tighter. "How do you even know this?" she asks. "You're not actually listening to all your voicemails, are you?"

We wait for a biker to pass before crossing over to the water's edge.

"I can't help it," I admit. "You're not a little bit curious?"

She scoffs. "I know what they're all saying: *We want something from you.*"

"Not all. Some people want to *give* us the chance to help them."

Hazel makes a face. "While we're on the topic of helping, I saw that you got a goldfish. That's information I need to know, Logan."

"Yeah, but...wait, you were in my apartment for ten seconds. How did you see that?"

"I'm visiting your apartment alone. I was assessing it for danger."

My mouth quirks at this. "But you'll go on a roof with me alone?"

She half smiles. "There were three fire escapes. Besides the suspiciously large, practically human-size fish tank, your place looked safe enough. For now. I'll get a better look later."

I couldn't bear the thought of trapping the goldfish in a small bowl, so I got the biggest tank I could carry. Then I went back to get the fish a friend.

"I'm surprised you listened," she says.

"Not only did I listen, I got two."

She looks pleased. "I'm not used to anyone following my advice."

"Well, apparently their gold color is lucky, and their movements create good energy," I say, repeating back to her what she told me after I fell into the lake.

"I love when my research is put to good use."

"You want to name them?"

Her face brightens. "Really? I've never had a pet." She looks out at the Hudson River, the choppy waves reflecting the glow of orange above the horizon. "What about Goldie and Kurt?"

"It's perfect. I take it you made it to the amnesia portion of your movie marathon."

"I watched *Overboard* this past summer," she confirms as Toffee jumps up onto a bench and sniffs the air. "Isn't Toffee supposed to be Mrs. Walker's cat?"

"Officially, he is. Toffee stays with me when Mrs. Walker's out of town. She's helped me out a lot over the years, so when she travels, I return the favor."

"Well, your apartment's really nice."

"Come on, I'll give you the full tour," I say. "You can even look in the closets and my medicine cabinet."

"I'm for sure doing that," she says with humor in her voice.

Back at my apartment, Hazel removes her shoes at the door and takes her time looking around while I wipe Toffee's paws.

"I feel okay spending the next few hours here," she says.

I make a show of wiping my brow. "What's happening in the next few hours?"

She pulls another bag of gummy numbers out of her purse. "For you."

I laugh at this ongoing joke. "I hope you're getting a good employee discount."

"Dangerously good. Gloria, my pseudo-coworker, somehow got ordering privileges. She's obsessed with trying to find candy Emma has never heard of. It's like, her whole personality right now." Hazel laughs a little like she's remembering something funny. "So she got these matcha KitKats, which of course Emma had heard of. Anyway, I brought some for you to try."

She drops a handful of individually wrapped KitKats on the counter.

"Sounds like you're enjoying it," I notice.

Hazel looks surprised by my comment. "Oh. Yeah. I guess I am. The customers have been pleasant, too," she says. "No matter what kind of day you're having, you can't go into a candy store and be mad, you know?"

I snap half a green KitKat between my teeth. "It's a law."

She removes a cookbook from her bag. "Ready for Phase Two?" she asks, holding up two fingers. "I call it *Lucky Foods*."

"Hey, I know them!" I turn the cookbook around to face me. On it, Chrysanthemum Hua Williams and her aunties smile from behind a kitchen counter. "I stayed at their inn once."

Hazel glances over at me. "Really? Looks like they heal heartbreak."

I nod but don't want to bring down Hazel with the details. That years after the accident, I wasn't physically broken, but I still felt it. That my mom had heard from a friend of a friend's cousin about this small inn on Whidbey Island and had to practically beg me to go. That by the end of my week there, I was changed for the better.

"Yeah, I was going through a rough few years. Feels like a lifetime ago." I turn the cookbook over, skimming the words on the back. "I didn't realize this had come out already."

"It was on the New in Cookbooks table," Hazel says as she unloads the bags of groceries she brought. She stops me when I try to help. "Their food's supposed to be very healing."

"It's also delicious." I organize what she unpacks so I have something to do. "I was so thankful for their help that I made them a bunch of heart-shaped chairs," I recall with a laugh.

That place meant a lot to me. Knowing that other people were going through something similar, having the safe space to be able to voice the heartache. I've forgotten what that's like. I've forgotten how to do that.

"Those sound pretty. Did you make that, too?" She nods to the far wall. A trunk of a tree is rooted in place, its branches stretching up along the wall. At various points, custom shelves sprout out from the branches, holding up all my thriller and nonfiction reads.

"I made everything in here," I admit. "But before you're impressed, know that I created a lot of my furniture when I was just starting to learn. I can't open half of the drawers that hold my clothes, and I wouldn't recommend sitting on that chair."

Hazel smirks. "Your clothes are trapped, so you're left to wear that." She points to my orange and yellow swirled long-sleeve shirt.

I feel a smile start. "I know they look goofy, but Mrs. Walker made these for me, thank you very much, and she'd be appalled to hear you say that, even though she'd agree. She went through a tie-dye phase." I shrug. "Honestly? They're some of the most comfortable shirts I own."

"That's actually sweet." She runs her hand down my arm, rubbing the cotton between her fingers. "Somehow, you pull them off. And that's a big compliment," she says with a chuckle before growing serious again and giving my hand a squeeze. "For you to go to this inn…you must've really been hurting."

I consider what to say that might help alleviate her concern. "I needed to get away."

It sounds dramatic, but at the time, it felt true. Urgent. Necessary.

For a second, I forget that my left hand is out of commission, and I ram it into the bag while trying to reach for a can of pears.

"Go rest while I make food," Hazel says. Then she points at my casted arm. "Hope an infection sets in and you never heal."

I laugh, remembering the night at the pizzeria and our break-a-leg conversation. "Okay, maybe we shouldn't make that a thing."

She nods in agreement. "Probably for the best."

I resist her commands by stepping closer. "I'm not making you cook for me while I lounge." Walking Toffee, being here, unloading groceries…it all feels so natural with Hazel. We've slipped into an easy rhythm together. I make a point to remove a bag of rice with my hurt arm. "See? I'm fine! If anything, it's my ego that took a hit. There's no graceful way to fall down a flight of stairs while ending up covered in lo mein."

"And that flip you did at the end, wow." She draws a loop through the air with the taro she's holding. She turns serious. "This is a lot, especially with everything going on at work for you. And now you have to miss work. It's so shitty."

I'm unsure how to respond. She's not downplaying my fall or comparing it to something worse. There's no mention of luck or good timing. She's just calling it as it is.

And shitty is exactly what it is.

She peers over her shoulder at me. "Are you doing okay otherwise? If there's anything else I can do to help, please tell me."

Share all your pieces.

My arm hurts. I'm stressed. Everything's falling apart, and I don't know what to do.

"I could've broken my back" is what I end up saying. "At least I'll still be able to be at the theater and help where I can."

Hazel stops what she's doing, holding a package of goji berries midair. Instead of pushing back, she just nods. "I'm making almond tofu with fruit, pork, and taro stew, and eight-treasure sticky rice. They're lucky foods, which is the point. In some European countries, almonds have been a good luck symbol. We'll eat those with oranges, which in Chinese culture represent good fortune."

"I bought you a Band-Aid. You're making me a three-course meal. This hardly feels like a fair exchange."

"It isn't," Hazel says with a grin. She moves to the sink and washes her hands. "But it's happening. You did also keep your word about splitting the money. I sent the money to my brother."

What a relief. "I'm so glad to hear that."

"I did also pay off the rest of my student loans."

"Congrats! That's great."

"Yeah, I never thought I'd see the day." She sucks in a long breath through her nose, shaking her shoulders on the exhale. "I've never spent that much money all at once before." She looks over at me. "Hey! Why are you not on the couch?"

"Tell you what," I say, standing firmly in place. "While you make that, I'll make dessert."

"No. You'll just get in my way."

I place my hand over my heart. "I'll stay so far out of your way. All-the-way-over-on-this-side-of-the-counter out of your way."

She props her hand on her hip. "You think that flirty voice you're using is going to work? On me?" She takes a confident step forward.

Hazel's strong. She has her walls bonded together with mortar. She's also soft. She's given me glimpses of her pieces, which show me that her walls may be strong, but they're not very high.

And if I need to be a chisel to break those walls down, or if I need to climb over them to meet her on the other side, I will.

"I do think so," I say, dipping my head. "Or maybe I just hope so. I found a new recipe for a dessert I think you'll like."

"Unlucky, but still pressing your luck," she says, a smile playing on her lips. She takes a long breath in. "Just because I'm not picky with candy doesn't mean I'm not picky with desserts."

I take a step. *The* step. The one that closes the distance between our bodies. The one that leaves no question what I want.

"I won't let you down," I say, looking directly into her eyes. The tips of her fingers graze my uncasted forearm as she leans slightly into me.

I miscalculate how far I need to bend to reach Hazel. Our mouths miss each other entirely, my lips landing on the tip of her nose instead.

A surprised laugh spills out of her. "That was...really special."

"Promise I'm not normally that clumsy of a kisser," I say, feeling my cheeks flush.

Hazel angles her chin up, giving me an easy target. "Prove it."

So I do. And this time, it's a bullseye.

She wraps her hands around my waist right as the sound of something hitting the floor startles us.

Toffee's sitting on the edge of the counter with his paw midair, looking down at the pumpkin seeds he's just successfully bopped to the ground. We freeze for a second, regarding each other. Waiting for the other to make a move.

There's a fifty-fifty chance Toffee will have ruined yet another moment.

Hazel still has her arms around me, though, so I like my chances. Her eyes sweep from Toffee over to me. She takes one hand off me, and now I'm sure this is the end of whatever it was we just started.

But then she swipes the box of Lucky Charms cereal straight off the counter. It lands on the floor with a soft *thud*.

Without breaking eye contact, I mimic her movements, toppling the bottle of peanuts sideways.

Hazel taps a bag of jujubes that flips midair to the floor.

I knock the walnuts on top of those.

Toffee gives us an annoyed meow before jumping down.

"Who knew Toffee was such a sore loser," I say.

"We just defeated a cat at his own game." Then, without another word, Hazel sweeps the other ingredients to the side, clearing the counter next to us. I lift her up onto it with one arm.

I position myself between her thighs as she slides her hands over my triceps, resting them on my shoulders. I inch forward slowly, and this time, she drops a quick, soft kiss on the tip of *my* nose. She bites her lip as she smiles, bending forward the rest of the way to catch my bottom lip between hers. Gone are the clumsy near-misses. Unlike our first rushed, spur-of-the-moment kiss, this one is slow and purposeful.

I keep my hands steady on Hazel's waist as she hooks her calves behind my thighs and pulls me closer, wrapping her arms more tightly around me. We release twin sighs—hers breathier while mine's released from somewhere deep. Somewhere needy.

"Didn't even have to make the food," I whisper against her lips, "and the ingredients are already doing their job."

Hazel searches my face as she traces her thumb across my cheek. She pulls her hand back and drops a whisper-soft kiss in its place. "They're useless on the floor," she finally says. Then she pats my chest and hops down. "We should start cooking."

A low grunt escapes my throat. I don't want to stop kissing her. Then I recall what she said at the firehouse about wanting to go slow. "I'll get the oven going."

"I meant it when I said I was going to help you get lu—" She clamps her mouth shut before finishing her sentence. "Get some luck."

My eyes don't leave hers as the air crackles around us, just like it did that first day. Like there's a static fuzz that makes time stand still when we're around each other. That's what spending time with her feels like: moments frozen in time. Like nothing bad can touch them. Like nothing bad can touch us.

We spend the next few hours cooking side by side, me only getting in Hazel's way twice on accident and once on purpose.

She skips the eight-treasure rice because it turns out that the rice needed to soak, but my M&M-covered chocolate pizza makes up for it. Hazel likes it so much she eats three slices.

As the evening slips into night, I share more of my pieces with Hazel. The messy, the shiny. The clumsy, the smooth.

And in return, she shares more of hers with me.

Chapter 11

HAZEL

When it came to working in a candy shop, I thought the hardest part would be avoiding snacking on the inventory all day long.

I didn't think it would be constantly trying to avoid distractions. And by distractions, I mean Gloria.

"Why peach?" Gloria asks as she scoops out sour peach lips from one of the jars on the round table in the middle of the shop into a small glass bowl. "Peach rings, peach lips, peach rounds, peach skulls. Did every candy maker congregate and agree that peach was *the* flavor? Was it the cheapest flavor option?"

"Maybe because they taste the most natural?" I say toward my laptop, where the past year's sales and customer data from the point-of-sale system are downloading.

She pops an entire pair of lips into her mouth. "Do dey, dough?" she mumbles. I think she means *Do they, though?*

Emma comes in from the shop's back room with a box of sour watermelon skulls. "Gloria, restock this, will you please?" she asks.

Gloria plays with one of her silver hoop earrings. "I don't get a paycheck from you."

"Okay. Do you plan on paying for that?" Emma asks, nodding toward Gloria's bowl, which is her third refill of the day.

Gloria hides it behind her back. "Friend special?" When Emma arches a sharp brow at her, she surrenders. "Oh, fine! Did you like the way I organized the bats yesterday? I brought some bodega pumpkins to scatter around the jars."

With three weeks until Halloween, Sweet Escape has been packed. In addition to contributing pumpkins, Gloria's taken it upon herself to add faux cobwebs to the front door and windows.

Where I mostly spend time is at the register, which is situated along the opposite wall with other products that people tend to impulse buy on the way out: candles, mugs, and hats.

"Maybe you should start paying her," I suggest to Emma.

She laughs. "I've tried. She won't accept a penny. I think she just likes having something to do during the day, having somewhere to go."

"It wouldn't be the same without her," I say. It feels true. "Oh, I have something for you." I grab a box next to my bag behind the counter and hand it to Emma.

She lifts the lid and peers in. "You got me cupcakes?"

"It was Sweet Escape's two-year anniversary yesterday, right? They're dirt cupcakes."

From where she's standing, Gloria lets out a loud *aww*. "I'll grab the worms!" she calls out.

"This is so thoughtful," Emma says, wrapping her arm around me in a hug. "Thank you."

Gloria joins us at the checkout counter and sets a few gummy worms on top of each dirt cupcake.

"What's with this?" Emma asks when she notices a plump bag of gummy numbers tied neatly with an orange ribbon.

"I paid for it," I say.

"No, I'm just curious why you do it," Emma says before biting into her cupcake.

"Oh. It's just this thing I do for…"

Gloria waves me on with her half-eaten cupcake. "For…?"

"For myself," I say before taking a bite, the dark chocolate crumble perfectly sweet and rich.

"Lies!" Gloria shouts. "Who are you doing this for? I've seen you devour candy by the bagful, but even this would be excessive."

She and Emma huddle closer to me like we're gossiping at Sunday brunch and not work.

"It's for a friend," I say.

"Oh. I had a friend like that once," Gloria says with a knowing smile. "We gave each other buttons. Come to think of it, where are those buttons?"

"This is the fifth bag of"—Emma analyzes the contents of the bag—"numbers since you started working here," she says. "Does your friend eat it all, or what?"

"I don't know what he does with it," I say. Him eating it isn't really the point.

"Why numbers?" Gloria asks.

Obviously, I can't tell them about the lottery. Money changes dynamics. It changes relationships. "Why buttons?" I ask her.

Gloria's lips curl up. "To replace the ones we lost when we were ripping each other's clothes—"

"What's your friend's name?" Emma cuts in.

That's an easier question to answer. Still, I hesitate. "Logan."

"I met a man named Logan once in the seventies. He was quite the looker. Is your Logan a looker?"

Logan is not *my* Logan. Or...maybe he is? I don't know what he is.

"He's a looker," I say with finality. I don't want to go down this path. Gloria and Emma are getting way too invested in my personal life. I move the trackpad on my laptop so that the download doesn't get interrupted.

Emma shifts the conversation, as though she can sense my unease. "So you get Logan candy numbers. That's fun."

Gloria nudges me with her elbow. "And cute. Look at you two having inside jokes."

"It's not an inside joke if you two know about it," I point out.

Emma holds her hand up. "Look, I get it. You don't have to tell us about what you're doing with Logan. New feelings can be fragile. You don't want to jinx it."

"What? No," I say. "I'm not superstitious about me and Logan."

I don't think I'm the only one who notices that I don't address the *feelings* part of Emma's comment.

"Look at the three of us, talking about feelings like we're in middle school." Gloria sighs. "In middle school, I had a crush on Jim MacCreary. Now he was a looker."

"You can talk about feelings as adults, Gloria," Emma says.

Gloria flaps her hand at us. "Not in my generation, you can't."

"Anyway," Emma says, turning to me, "it's been nice having you here, Hazel. You're job hunting, right? How's that going?"

Good. Work is a safe topic. Work I can talk about. I update them on my upcoming round of interviews and how I'm being considered for manager. They listen eagerly. They act excited for me. They're encouraging. They're so friendly, and I…I just smile and nod in return. I'm not used to having people to talk to. Lately, between these two and Logan, I've had it in spades.

Our huddle is over when a customer comes in and asks for suggestions on what to buy for her Halloween party–slash–baby shower.

I check my phone. Two missed text messages. One's from Logan that just says FYI. The second is from Bank Frances.

That's literally how I added her name to my contacts. Bank Frances works at Dad's local bank in upstate New York. She helped us with the mortgage. She told me to reach out if I ever had questions, which was nice of her to do but also probably something she regrets. Honestly, I think Bank Frances took pity on me for being in this position in the first place.

For putting up with me—and Dad—Bank Frances gets boxes of chocolates during the holidays and cards on her birthday. Nearly a decade in, I've never missed one. This year, she's getting the largest box they've got.

> **Bank Frances (4:31 PM):** Hey Zull, hope the Big Apple's still cheating you well. Listen, we've got a bitch of a situation here. It's short hair on your account that there are perfumist payments. Give me a call when tucan, k?

Bank Frances must be using her phone's speech-to-text feature again. I tell Emma I'm taking a quick break and go to the stock room to make the call, needing typo-free, speech-to-ear answers.

"Hazel! You got my text?" Bank Frances says after a third ring.

"Hi," I say. "You're back from leave already? How's your mom doing?"

"It was three long months, but she's doing better now. Thanks for asking. Listen, Hazel."

Uh-oh.

"I got back this week and am still playing catch-up. They had Bobby cover for me, but unfortunately for all of us, he's new. Mary Margaret was also out for the past month on vacation and, long story short, the monthly mortgage amounts still haven't been paid," Bank Frances says, her tone steady as it always is. "I'm still trying to figure out the details, but I thought you should know right away."

I log in to my banking app. "I'm looking at the transfers right now." I scroll down to the past few months, identifying each of my $600 payments. "They've all gone through successfully."

"Ah." Bank Frances clicks her tongue in realization. "That's the issue. You're still short."

"Oh, well, yeah. My dad pays the other half," I remind her.

"After six hundred gets paid, there's still..." Bank Frances hums as she types. "Eight thousand left."

"Eight *thousand*?" I choke out. I visualize the numbers she's mentioned, trying to make sense of them. That makes the new mortgage amount $8,600. And *that* makes my new monthly half... $4,300. "Maybe it's a processing error? Our full monthly mortgage amount is twelve hundred dollars." Not over seven times that amount. The confidence in my voice has vanished.

Bank Frances is quiet for a moment. "Look, Hazel. Another letter's gonna go out—"

"Another letter?" I ask, my voice wobbling. "I didn't get any letters."

"Because you don't co-own the house, Bobby couldn't include you in the communications."

Which, sure, that technically makes sense. I don't have the same kind of relationship with Bobby like I do with Bank Frances.

"Looks like the amount increased in..." *Tap, tap, tap.* "May."

The new amount is going to be impossible to afford. For me and Dad. This doesn't make any sense.

"It's a good thing I caught this when I did," Bank Frances says. "There's still time to make it right."

The air deflates out of my lungs like a popped balloon. "Make what right?"

"The house going into foreclosure, sweetie. I'm emailing you a copy of the latest pre-foreclosure notice."

"I'll call you right back," I mumble, distracted.

Increase in May. $8,600. Foreclosure.

It takes three tries to finally get through to Dad's cell phone.

"Give me a break, ref! That's a hold" are the first words I hear. "Hello?"

"Dad!" I shout-whisper into the phone. I'd really prefer that my coworkers and customers don't hear this.

"Hazel! You watching the game?" Dad asks.

I slide a box filled with ribbon aside with my foot, moving as far from the door as I can. "No, we need to talk—"

"Who do you think will win?" he asks.

I pull one of the precut orange ribbons out. "I haven't been keeping up. Can you turn the volume down for a second?"

"You're missing a great game. I have a good feeling about it. This morning, I found a pair of sunglasses I thought I'd lost. The last time something like this happened, I won big," Dad says excitedly.

I can practically see him in the living room now, on the La-Z-Boy he won in a sweepstakes. To the left of the TV would be the sliding doors with a porch overlooking the lake. I read every issue of *Sweet Valley High* in that living room. It's also where I beat Grandma, Grandpa, and Jerry at every game of Monopoly. I was always the banker.

Doesn't feel like much has changed.

"Bank Frances called," I say, cutting to the chase. "She told me about the pre-foreclosure notices. Please tell me there's been some misunder—"

"Jesus," Dad says quickly. The sound of muffled cheers from the crowd on TV becomes quieter on the other end. "I was going to tell you about those, okay? I had some other things to take care of first."

Not a misunderstanding then.

On my phone, I pull up the email Bank Frances sent with the latest foreclosure letter. It's time-stamped from two months ago. The words become a blur. I make out just enough to start piecing things together.

"We have until the end of this month to pay the missing amounts before they open a foreclosure case," I say, reading the letter.

"Your monthly amount was supposed to stay the same," Dad mumbles.

"My amount was supposed to stay the same," I repeat as I process his words. "But your amount...increased? You were just, what, going to pay eight thousand dollars on your own?" *In what alternate universe?* I stop myself from asking.

"You didn't need to concern yourself with this. I needed the cash, and Bill needed his car paid off," Dad says, as though this absolves him.

Slowly, it clicks into place. Dad remortgaged the house, keeping my monthly payments the same so I wouldn't know. And somehow, he expected to be able to pay more when, really, he couldn't pay any of it. Which explains all the missing payments.

My heartbeat throbs in my ears. "Did you take out more cash on the house...to pay off Uncle Bill's car payments?" I manage to ask in a steady tone.

"I had some other things to pay off."

"What kind of things?"

"Things," Dad says firmly. I hear between the lines: *none of your business*. "I just need some more time. Luck wasn't on my side. I need you to believe me, Hazel, I was gonna figure it out."

Too late for that.

"Why didn't you tell me about the letters? About the refinancing?" I know this is pointless. With Dad, there are always excuses.

"You weren't supposed to be impacted," he says.

"I'm impacted when you miss payments." I don't want to feel like a nag. I don't want to have to state what should be obvious. "There's over twenty-four thousand dollars to make up for. If we don't pay it, they're going to open a foreclosure case. Do you know what that means, Dad? We could lose the house." This comes out in a level tone. I'm trying to get through to him without a hint of emotion, so I don't frighten him off or upset him.

The full weight of the potential consequences lands squarely on my chest. I sit down in Emma's desk chair, crossing one arm over myself. I just paid off Jerry's hospital bills and my student loans. I have enough in my savings to pay down one month at the new amount, which would leave me with only one month left for my rent. And that doesn't include the fact I still need to eat and would like to have running water.

But after next month, I'll be wiped out.

My mind whirls into overdrive. I really need to focus on getting that manager job. The higher salary still wouldn't cover the new monthly mortgage payments, but it'd be something. Then, when next year's lottery payment comes in, I'll be able to cover more.

"We can probably get them to give us more time," Dad says with the confidence of someone who hasn't earned it.

"There's no more time. There's a process," I say, standing to pace. I'm trembling a little. Cold, probably. "I'm trying to help you here."

"Let's not pretend you're not trying to help yourself, too," Dad snaps. "Maybe I should just die, and then you can have the house. Would that make you happy?"

My stomach churns. "Of course it wouldn't. And you're not going to die. I just—"

"I know, I know, I shouldn't have done it, okay, HazeyDazey?" Dad says, pulling out all the stops, childhood nicknames included. "You think I want to lose this house? I live here. Your mother's father built it. It's all I've got left of her. This house means something to me, too." There's enough annoyance in his tone that makes me back down.

I grit my teeth. Finalizing the divorce has distracted me, and I let this fall to the wayside. Have I really not checked in with Dad in the past few months like I normally do? How could I have let this happen?

"We can still fix this." I say it calmly, or risk losing him completely. Sounding like we're in this together has always been more productive than it being him versus me.

Dad lets out a loaded sigh. "I have a plan, okay? I'm taking care of it."

"A plan," I say flatly. "And what's that?"

"I'm in Atlantic City."

"You're in Atlantic City." I walk to the very back corner of the stock room. The part where the light doesn't fully reach. "Like, right now?"

"Just 'til Wednesday." Dad's tone switches back to upbeat. "I showed up at brunch right as they brought out a new hunk of roast beef. My luck changes today. I can feel it!"

An hour ago, I might've said, *Same*. But this? What's happening right now isn't lucky. It's very, very bad. So much so that I'm starting to think Logan's and my luck flipped back.

Great. Now I'm officially in too deep thinking that Logan's theory is real.

"I'm going to win back enough to cover at least a portion of the payments," Dad says when I'm quiet.

He's probably using what he took out in the refinancing to fund his trip. This is like the time he took the money my grandparents left us in their will, which only covered one college tuition, and tried to double the money. He lost every penny.

Have I learned nothing from the past? Of course this was going to happen again.

I bite the inside of my cheeks. Hold back everything I don't know how to say. He sounds happy.

"I've put too much into it. I can't stop now. I'm due for a win," Dad adds. "And don't worry, I've got a strategy. Jim's with me, too."

Jim. His pocket-size golden toad he carries with him for luck. He's had it for so long that Jerry named his van, Frogger, after it.

I don't mention how trinkets won't save him. Or how his odds are the same every time he gambles. Putting in more money doesn't mean better chances. He never hears me when I say this. Special strategies, good feelings, hope, and wishes will not result in wins.

"A strategy," I mutter. "Are you working?"

"Not at this exact moment, no," Dad jokes. My silence must speak volumes because he adds, "I'm in between jobs right now. I've got a lead."

I rub my temple with one hand. "Okay, well, right now we need to sort this out with Frances. This is serious—"

"Can you talk to her?" he says. "Last time we talked, she threw me off my game. I'm in a good place right now. There's something in the air, too."

I don't want to leave Bank Frances hanging, especially when she might be our only hope. And I don't want either of us to be the reason why Dad's high comes crashing down. That's the last thing he needs in Atlantic City.

I pick at the fraying ends of the ribbon. "Sure. I'll take care of it."

"That's my girl. What would I do without you?" he asks.

Question of my life.

"Game's almost over. When I'm rolling in dough, you're the first person I'm calling, okay?" he says. "Promise."

I nod at the corner I've tucked myself into. "Yeah, sure. Bye."

The call disconnects. I don't want to move. Don't want to think. I just want to stay here in the half darkness. Let everything fall apart. Even when I try to keep it together, it still breaks. What's the point in trying when it always comes down to this? I can hardly keep my head above water as it is. It's even harder when Dad keeps dragging me down.

I stand there for who knows how long, my eyes going blurry as I stare at a toppling pile of boxes filled with ribbon and candy. To the right of that is Emma's filing cabinet. Corners of bank statements and contracts poke out of the drawers that won't close. The side is dented, the black metal etched with long white scratch lines. The key lock is missing, making the entire point of having it useless. This part of the store is a disaster compared to the orange creamsicle just past the door.

My phone buzzes in my hand, startling me. There's a pile of shredded ribbon on the ground.

> **Logan (5:01 PM):** Toffee is so hangry right now omg
> **Logan (5:02 PM):** And he escaped down the hall and made it to the second floor somehow??
> **Logan (5:02 PM):** Then he started using my cast as a scratching post when I carried him back up
> **Logan (5:03 PM):** This cat, I swear
> **Logan (5:04 PM):** That was an unhinged number of texts in a row, I apologize

As quickly as a puff of air escapes my nose, I inhale another just as fast. It reminds me I can still breathe. I haven't sunk yet.

> **Logan (5:07 PM):** I'm thinking of ideas for how to increase my luck, too. I don't want you to think it's all on you. I really appreciate you and your help.
> **Logan (5:08 PM):** That's what I meant to text in the first place ☺

Chapter 12

HAZEL

Logan's still at the theater by the time I get off work and make my way uptown. I had to scroll back through old texts to find which theater he works at. There are so many of them on Broadway.

He's sewing a rip in a curtain when I get there. I watch him for a few minutes from the back of the theater as he finishes up. He's focused as he tries to thread a needle with his casted arm. Finally, he gets it, pulling the thread in and out of the fabric. Repairing what was broken.

He looks up at me as I step into the light. From all the way over here, I can see his smile. The one for me.

I walk down the aisle toward him, dazed. Drawn in.

"Standby line closed at three," he says, his voice managing to reach me. "But you can enter the Broadway lottery for a later show."

"No more lotteries," I hear myself say. I step up onto the stage.

Logan puts his needle and thread away in a little box. "Right. I win once and think I'm invincible. You found me at a good time. Everyone's on dinner break—"

I finish his sentence with my mouth on his. The force of my body pins him up against the wall behind the curtain. It's all tongue, quick breaths, hands everywhere. I run my hands down his chest, feeling the topography of his muscles under my fingertips. Every touch is charged; static electricity from the buildup between us.

I slip two fingers into the waistband of his jeans and tug him toward me. The low grunt he makes sets off what feels like the world's longest sparkler running from my chest all the way down to my toes. Our lips glide against each other in hurried want, our tongues going back and forth in a chaotic but satisfying rhythm. They're greedy, our movements, as though we haven't already won enough.

I don't have to think. Don't have to feel anything but what's happening right now.

It's exactly what I need.

"Bathroom," I whisper against his neck. "Take me there."

Logan freezes, his hands sliding down my arms. "You want to have...bathroom sex?"

I pull him back to me, kissing his lips, his cheeks. "Don't stop."

"Hazel, hold on," he says with a forced laugh. "Are you okay?"

"I will be once you kiss me," I say, annoyed.

He adjusts his hat as he dips his head. "What's going on?"

I glance away. He'll know something's wrong if he takes one look at my eyes. "I just want to feel better," I say weakly.

"We can't do this here. Not like this," he says gently. He looks over at the door, where probably an entire crew is eating their dinners.

"You're rejecting me?" I ask, blinking. "Oh my god." I take a few steps back. "I shouldn't have come here."

"Hazel, talk to me," he says, reaching for my hand. "Tell me what's wrong."

I yank it away. "I don't want to talk! I just...I needed you, and you can't even be here for me." There's a bite to my voice. It's sharp and ugly and filled with the pain that I'm in. I don't want it inside of me anymore.

My stomach feels like it's folding in on itself as I recount the last couple of minutes. My face is on fire. This is beyond humiliating. It's soul-crushing. How could I have done that? Logan means more to me than acting on some desperate desire.

The back of my eyes sting. I press my knuckles against them before I start to cry. "I should go," I say, barely getting the words out.

"Hazel, wait," Logan says, following me a few steps. "Please don't leave."

For some reason, I listen, pausing halfway down the stairs in front of the stage. I wait for a scolding. I almost want it. I want Logan to shout back. To be mad at me for doing this. For trying to come on to him here of all places.

But he doesn't. Logan stands right where he is. He doesn't look at me any differently than he always has. He doesn't seem to be disgusted or mad. I don't get the smile reserved just for me, but I do get a look of consideration I've never seen him give anyone else.

Then he steps closer, meeting me on the middle step. He cups my cheeks in his hands, the cast rough against my skin. When he looks into my eyes and says, "I'm here," the tight knot of anger inside me loosens, just a bit.

I'm a mess. I'm out of control.

And he doesn't *not* want me.

I wonder if he can sense all the pain I feel. Can he see me for who I really am?

Logan holds my gaze for a second longer. "Come with me," he says.

"Don't you have work?" I say, gentler this time, as he leads me outside through the back door.

"I'll let my team know I'm taking my dinner break now."

We walk a few blocks, the silence hanging between us. I let him guide me wherever we're going. He'll probably drop me off at the subway station where I can take myself home. Shower. Eat. Sleep off whatever he thinks is happening here.

It's only when we're in an elevator that I snap out of my daze. He's not sending me home. He's taking me somewhere.

The elevator doors open. We're on some sort of observation deck. Logan gives a knowing nod to a guard keeping watch.

"You're someone who knows everybody, aren't you?" I ask.

Logan smirks. "Once I meet that guy," he says, tilting his chin toward a person painted a deep turquoise and dressed like the Statue of Liberty taking selfies with the city backdrop, "then yes. I'll officially know everybody."

Despite my bad mood, a soft laugh slips out.

"You ever been to Top of the Rock before?" Logan asks. He's still holding my hand.

I shake my head.

"We're above Rockefeller Center," he explains as he leads me to a corner where we can see the entire city laid out before us. It looks like a miniature town, gathered up in the palms of someone's hands. The skyscrapers are gray and orange against a smear of purple and yellow sky. From this angle, the Empire State Building is smack dab in the middle of the city, the Upper New York Bay just beyond it.

It's dusk. The transition hours. It's a time of day that's always made me sad. At the lake house, it's when I had to turn back into a human after being a fish all day long.

Now I realize that there's something beautiful to it. Most of the day is behind you, but there's still a whole night ahead of you. It's like the ending and the beginning of something at once.

"This is where I come to think sometimes," Logan says. "During breaks, after work. Sometimes before. I know it's touristy, but the view gets me every time. It's a city of stone and glass, but it was once mostly wood and brick. It reminds me how much something can change, and how beautiful it can stay."

"Except for that really tall skyscraper in midtown," I mumble.

Logan half laughs. "True. That one ruined the skyline."

I gulp in a lungful of air seventy stories above the ground. It takes the edge off my anxiety. The churning in my stomach that's been there since my conversation with Dad slows.

"I like that you can see the water," I observe, taking in the glow from the structures downtown.

"Sometimes when people ask where I live, I tell them I live on an island," Logan says. "Partly to mess with them, but also, I'm curious what the first place is that pops into their minds. I get a lot of Hawaii, Nantucket, or San Juan Islands."

"Huh. You struck me as a Martha's Vineyard man," I say playfully.

Logan doesn't sound like he's joking when he says, "My mom does spend her summers there." He slides his hands into his pockets. "Mostly, I'm fascinated by how differently we all think. What's an island to one person varies from someone else's definition of one. What's lucky to me may not be lucky to you. We all have our own mental models. None of us is wrong."

I sit with this as I soak in the view. "Sometimes I forget I live here," I finally say when the overwhelming beauty of the city becomes too much. It's a loaded statement, if I've ever said one. "Like in the city." I shake my head. "I haven't had a chance to enjoy it." I swallow down the tightness in my throat.

"Your slim budget?" Logan asks, remembering.

I nod. "That extends to the city, too." The twinkling artificial lights brighten as the sky's glow fades. "Growing up, I felt trapped. I wanted to come here because it felt like freedom. And it seemed fun. I didn't get to have a lot of that, either." A cold breeze sweeps across my cheeks. It feels cleansing in a way. I almost feel brand-new. "Here, I could be anyone I wanted to be." Whoever that is. I think about all the versions of me I imagined myself being when I moved here for my first—and only—job. Independent. Explorative. In control.

"It's the best place for reinvention," Logan says.

That's what I had hoped, but life doesn't go that way.

"It's nice being away from it all for a second. Peaceful," I say.

And now, given everything, I might need to leave. How can I still justify living in one of the most expensive cities in the world?

He gives me a small smile. "What happened today?"

I think I might start crying again if I look at Logan, so I stare at an orange, cone-shaped roof to the left of the Empire State Building. "My dad refinanced the lake house. We might lose it."

Even though I've had some distance from the afternoon, the floor feels like it's falling out from underneath me for a second time today. Paired with how high up we are, my legs stiffen more, and I cling to Logan. It's disorienting, being practically on top of the world but feeling so low.

Logan holds me steady as he releases a tense breath. "No. That can't happen."

"We only have until the end of the month to cover the missed payments."

"Okay, so you still have the house," he says. "That's good at least. There's still time."

"I don't have the money to cover all of it." I don't even want to think about what would've happened if we didn't win the lottery. At least now, I can still help a little.

"Do you need more money? You can have mine," Logan offers without a second thought.

Now I can't help but look up at him. My jaw has dropped. He's just casually offering me his annual lottery winnings? "I don't borrow from those I care about, and you've given me enough. But that's generous of you," I say. "I shouldn't have paid off all my student loans. I just wanted to do something for myself, you know?"

Paying off my debts felt too good to be true. How did I not hear the alarm bells ringing?

"It's not like you bought a boat," he says. "You paid off your education."

I nod distractedly. "Maybe I can take out a personal loan. Though I'll need a job for that. Maybe we should've taken that lump sum."

"It's nice that you want to help, but won't there just be more problems?"

Undoubtedly.

"I need to figure something out." Maybe this time I can convince Dad to transfer the house into my name so that this doesn't happen again. "Dad and Jerry need me."

They probably always will. I've had so many conversations with Dad about gambling and getting help. I know my pleas alone won't change anything. They won't cure his addiction.

My voice is tense when I say, "I have no idea what to do."

Logan positions me in front of him as he wraps his arms around me. I nestle in, leaning back against his chest. We stand there for a few minutes, my body rising and falling in sync with his every breath.

"I'm so sorry about earlier," I say, turning to face him. I try not to feel again how desperate I was. How I try to eject myself from a shitty situation only to find myself in a different problem. "I shouldn't have done that. I wanted to feel something good."

Of all the bad things that happened today, how does what I did to Logan feel like the worst of all of them?

Logan raises one eyebrow. "And I was that something good?"

"You're something more than good," I say. "You didn't deserve that."

He kisses the tip of my nose. On purpose. The simple, tender act of it locks something into place. I like this man. A lot. I never again want to do anything like I did earlier tonight to jeopardize a future with him.

Another breeze blows over the observation deck, this time so forceful that my jacket puffs out. Like if it were one degree stronger, I could lift off. With the city so small beneath me, it appears less chaotic. More controllable. I can see all of it at once. The bigger picture. It's a fleeting moment, but what it feels like is a wake-up call.

If I'm always reaching for temporary fixes, I can never make long-lasting ones. I'm keeping myself in a feedback loop. It's a loop where I'll never be truly happy.

Before anything solidifies deeper in my brain, it blows away on a much lighter breeze. No liftoff today.

"When we do this," Logan says, his voice low and unhurried, "I want it to be mind-blowing, not mind-numbing."

My mind only hears *when*. After all that, Logan still wants to be with me.

"And not in a highly trafficked bathroom," I contribute.

"You have no idea what you were asking," Logan says. "By this time in the day, that bathroom is a disaster."

Despite everything feeling uncontrollable, I do the one thing I can control. I smile. And then I kiss him. "Mind-blowing, not mind-numbing," I repeat like a promise.

I scan the horizon. Dad's only in the next state over, though Atlantic City might as well be a world away. It's like we're existing on totally different planets. He's probably in his lucky red shirt, using whatever auspicious number he saw multiples of today. He's definitely got his lucky penny in his pocket and Mom's wedding band on a chain around his neck.

Then it hits me. Maybe I've been acting too much like Dad. Logan and I need to try something different. What we've been doing isn't going to work.

I glance back up at Logan. The soft, purple light of dusk makes his sharp angles softer. I commit to memory the planes of his face as he looks out at the city. Our city.

At least for now.

"Thank you," I say, my breath falling in rhythm with his heartbeat.

He gives my shoulder a light squeeze. "You're not alone in this."

Chapter 13

LOGAN

"What if our luck didn't actually flip, but we both got bad fortunes?" Hazel asks first thing on Monday morning when we meet at our spot in the now-gone Good Fortune Fair. "Logan?"

I snap out of my daze. "Sorry, I was distracted by—" I point at her shirt, which looks more like something I'd wear. "Are you... Do you realize you're wearing a very colorful, very floral Hawaiian shirt?"

Hazel smooths out the front of her tropical pink and yellow short-sleeve button-down. "We do live on an island, haven't you heard?" she teases. "I know. I look like someone who presses her luck."

"Hey, if you got it, press it," I say. "This style suits you. I like it."

"Yeah. I forgot I liked these shirts, too." She refocuses and hands me a bag of gummy numbers. In return, I hand her one of the two cinnamon lattes that I picked up on the way here. "You don't have to give me something just because I bring you something," she comments.

"But it's our thing," I say.

Hazel smiles at this and says, "You're right. It is." Then she takes a long sip.

I take one, too. At this point, I'm so caffeinated from the all-nighters I've pulled trying to sort out the set pieces. We finally figured it out at 2:00 a.m. After this morning and a nap, I'll go back to the theater and keep working.

"But seriously," she says. "We need to try something different. Charms and symbolic food, they're nothing but false hope."

"The money tree you sent me grew another leaf, so that feels promising. I'm usually only good with plants once they're dead." As soon as the words leave my mouth, I remember what happened this morning. "But the arm of the lucky cat fell off, so maybe let's not read into the charms."

Hazel gives me a look like, *see what I mean?* "What we're doing, it isn't working."

"There's still more we can try," I tell her between sips. "What does your tracker say?"

"The data's inconclusive."

We take the subway to Brooklyn, drinking our lattes in silence, walking the rest of the way to Empire Fulton Ferry Lawn in Brooklyn Bridge Park.

"What do you do with the candy I bring you?" she asks.

I drain the rest of my coffee and toss it in a nearby garbage can. "I eat too much of it, and then I give the rest to my crew. They think it's a countdown to opening night."

"That's kind of funny," she says without a trace of amusement. I can't tell if she means it.

"I'm not complaining, but why candy?" I ask. "Is it because they're numbers?"

"Candy symbolizes the sweetness of life in Chinese culture," she says.

I pull the ribbon off the bag. "You just assuaged any lingering doubts I had for eating sweets every day," I say, popping a gummy eight into my mouth. "Hey, so your birthday..." I slow my pace to match hers. "It's tomorrow."

Hazel's so focused on her drink that she nearly runs into a jogger. "Is it? Oh."

I wrap my arm around her shoulders and guide her into the park. "Thirty was a great age. You excited? New decade!"

"I haven't felt my age in years," Hazel says.

"Do you have any plans for it?"

"Interview prep. I'll eat noodles."

I swivel toward her, my arm dropping away. "That's it?"

"I hate birthdays," she mumbles.

This raises more questions in my mind, but I spot a man in his fifties with a thick mustache and a head full of gray curls. "Pretty sure that's him," I say.

"Him who?"

"I think we needed to try something more tangible, so I enlisted the help of an expert."

"An expert? In what? Luck?" she asks.

I subtly gesture toward the man. "Exactly. I've hired a luck consultant. He's got this multistep plan for how to increase it."

It kind of sounded like a scam when I found him online, but I don't tell Hazel that. I've been racking my brain to come up with ideas to contribute, and I couldn't bring myself to suggest turtle theft, though I did reconsider it. I don't want her to feel like this is all on her, especially when she's doing this for me.

"A luck consultant?" she asks skeptically before considering it. "It couldn't be worse than trinkets." She holds her cup up to her lips and says discreetly, "Maybe we should have a safe word, just in case this goes south?"

"Good idea," I agree. "How about...Shirley MacLaine?"

She just nods, not questioning it, and we quickly agree on our exit strategy.

The luck consultant waves as he approaches. "The way you're

looking at me makes me think you're Logan. I'm Max Strout, but I prefer Maxwell." We do introductions before Maxwell guides the conversation to the real reason why we're gathered here this morning. "In your intake form, you said you wanted to increase your luck. We'll talk about methods on how to do just that. I teach psychology and conduct research on this very subject and have worked with dozens of couples like yourselves."

Neither of us corrects him on this last point. It's probably easier to just go with it than try to explain whatever it is we are to each other. Fortune thieves? Luck swappers? Or, in more standard terms, maybe we're even friends?

We sit on an oversize blanket Maxwell has laid out on the grass. Hazel and I face the Brooklyn Bridge, the skyline of the Battery sitting just behind it.

Maxwell opens his briefcase filled with painting supplies and divvies up tubes of paint, brushes, palettes, and canvases. "So, tell me, Hazel and Logan, do you consider yourself to be lucky or unlucky?" he asks.

Hazel frowns. "Like right now? Or in general?"

Maxwell considers her. "Is there a difference?"

She casts me an unreadable glance. "I'm usually unlucky."

Maxwell nods before turning to me, adjusting the collar of his navy turtleneck, which he's paired with brown corduroy overalls.

"Normally, I'm lucky," I answer. Noticeably absent is the usual confidence I feel when I say this.

Maxwell finishes unloading the suitcase. "Today I implore you to open your minds. We're here to talk freely. I've found with clients that a change of scenery can help with this, hence the park." He hands us each a paintbrush. "As we talk, you two will be painting something of your choosing."

"Is that required?" Hazel asks. I can practically hear her thinking, *What does this have to do with luck?*

THE FORTUNE FLIP

"You're not gonna like what I have to say," Maxwell says.

"Great," she mumbles.

"You're gonna love it," he says.

Hazel looks confused while Maxwell carries on. He directs our attention to everything he's brought. "What we do and share today is up to you. I won't force you to do anything. Now," he says, "why is it you consider yourself unlucky and lucky? Hazel, let's hear from you first."

I scan the horizon for something to paint as Hazel takes a paintbrush between her fingers, spinning it as a distraction, like she's weighing how much to share.

"Well, my family has never been very lucky," she says.

"Never? Are there any moments you can recall?" Maxwell asks. "In work or life? Have you ever won anything?"

Hazel swipes her paintless brush against her palm. "The only thing I've ever won is a spot on a two-week-long jury duty."

Maxwell nods. "What about your family? Or in relationships?" He smiles. "Or, I suppose, prior to your relationship now. Maybe your luck has changed."

Hazel's eyes lock with mine for a few long seconds before she quickly shakes her head. "Maybe. I don't know. But we're not here for me."

Maxwell shifts his entire body toward me. "Logan, why do you consider yourself lucky?"

His use of present tense throws me off. "Well, good things always happened for me." I reach for the easy examples first, along with a tube of yellow paint to keep my hands moving. "I've won a lot of giveaways and contests. I've met people purely by chance at times in my life when I unknowingly needed them most. I beat out thirteen other people for my job. My entire family has been fortunate enough to be comfortable in life." I squeeze a blob of paint onto my palette. "Am I supposed to do this while I talk?" I ask Maxwell.

"I don't need you to paint," Maxwell says.

"Oh, okay." I'm not sure if I should continue.

"I want you to paint," he finishes.

Hazel and I catch each other's eyes, and I can see in them that she's amused.

"Right," I say, adding more colors onto my palette. I let my hands take over with the mixing and painting as I talk. The strokes pour out of me as I dab light pink onto the canvas.

"Should we paint the bridge or..." Hazel asks, glancing around. "The skyline?"

"There's no right or wrong answer," Maxwell says. "If you see anything you like, paint that!" He holds a hand against the side of his mouth, like he's letting her in on a secret. "The carousel and the ferries are fan favorites."

Hazel grabs the tube of red paint. "Those seem harder than the bridge. What are you painting?" she asks me.

"All I have is a circle," I say. "I'm seeing where it goes."

"I'm so bad at art," Hazel states like it's an objective truth.

"You get to keep what you make," Maxwell offers. "And you don't even have to show us at the end if you don't want."

Hazel dips her brush into paint and attempts the activity. I think, more than anything, she just wants to keep busy. With the tip of her brush, she stabs at her canvas.

"Logan, I want to dig a little deeper into the people you've met in your life. You say it was by chance," Maxwell says, picking up the conversation. "You happened to be in the right place at the right time, is that it?"

I nod. "I was. Each time. I met Mrs. Walker at an inn I stayed at." Hazel looks up when I mention this. "She's the reason why I'm in New York. I was looking to get out of my hometown, and she's a Broadway producer. She knew of people looking for stagehands and carpenters, and I fit that bill. She connected me with the right people, let me rent out one of the apartments she owns for a price I could afford." I keep my eyes trained on my painting as I talk. "Meeting her changed my life. So did meeting Mr. Patterson."

"Who's Mr. Patterson?" Maxwell asks.

My audience has directed their full, undivided attention on me. All at once, this feels like a makeshift escape room we must paint ourselves out of. The brisk morning air turns hot, the trickle of sunlight streaming through the trees suddenly a spotlight.

"Oh. Uh..." I trail off.

I wonder if I've ventured too far. Under normal circumstances, I wouldn't think twice about opening up like this. I've always loved connecting with people, talking to them, learning about them. And I don't mind people knowing me in return. But now... everything's different.

"You don't have to tell us," Hazel says, throwing me a lifeline. An out. If I wanted to Phone-a-Friend, she'd be the one to pick up, and all I'd have to say is *Shirley MacLaine*.

Hypothetically, that's when one of us would feign a stomachache, like we discussed. I'd tell Maxwell that we need to cut the session short and thank him for his help.

But I don't say our safe word. I surprisingly don't feel uncomfortable or like we're being taken advantage of.

"I was in an accident when I was younger. For underage drinking and driving," I confess, keeping my voice steady and my hand even steadier as it sweeps more paint onto the canvas. With part of my focus on painting, sharing this story feels more approachable. Like it's part of something else and not the only thing that matters.

Because at one point, it was all that mattered to me. I've grown a lot since I was twenty, though, and I'm proud of who I've become. I'm proud of who I'm *not* anymore.

Hazel pauses what she's doing, just for a second. I catch her reluctance to keep going once I've dropped a statement like that. She slowly keeps moving, but I can sense she does so for my benefit, to not make me feel like I'm under a microscope.

"It was just another Friday night when I thought I was above it all. Above the law," I say. "I borrowed my dad's car when he explicitly told me not to, just to show him that I was above listening to him, too. I raided my parents' bar, started drinking, didn't stop, and got behind the wheel." I dip my brush into brown paint and spread it across the canvas. "I crashed the car. Drove right through my neighbor's fence and through his daughter's playhouse. Thankfully, it was at night, and she wasn't inside playing. It could've been... it could've been more of a nightmare than it already was." As I relay this, I realize I've turned toward Hazel like I'm telling this story just to her. Like this piece of me is just for her.

"Were you okay?" is the first thing Hazel asks.

"Physically, yes," I say. "I was fined, and my license was suspended. My neighbor, Mr. Patterson, didn't press charges, but it was only on the condition that I rebuild the fence and playhouse. I went over every day when I didn't have classes. It's how I learned carpentry. The entire trajectory of my life changed. Was saved, really." I run my hand over my shoulder. "Of all the yards I could've driven into, it belonged to someone who was not only forgiving but who actively helped me out of a bad situation. He taught me the foundations of woodwork."

"That must've been really scary," she says, leaning over to grab my hand.

It was terrifying. It was the worst experience I've lived through, still to this day. Even worse was that I felt completely alone throughout it all. Anytime I wanted to talk about it, Mom would just remind me how much worse it could've been, and my ex-girlfriend didn't want to constantly hear about it.

So I convinced myself that everything was good. That I was good. After all, I did survive it in the literal sense.

But there's a reason I'm behind the stage and not on it. My act wasn't convincing enough, and my relationship with my ex was never quite the same. When I couldn't move on from the accident, she moved on from me.

For years, I stayed in town improving my carpentry skills, forcing down any negative emotions when they came up. The heartache—related to my ex or the accident, I couldn't tell anymore—lingered. That's when it was time to do something about it. I went to the inn, and then, after that, to New York.

Somehow, it feels better that Hazel knows this about me. I want her to know the whole person she's graciously decided to help, but I also don't want to bring her down more than I already have. So I squeeze her hand back and say, "The accident made me stronger. Scary is what happened to this canvas while I was talking."

Hazel's gaze lingers on me for an extra beat. "Right. Of course." She watches as I adjust my hat, her eyes lingering on my head. "Your lucky hat. It was the one you were wearing the night of the accident."

It's not a question, but I nod anyway.

"And the accident, the aftermath...that's what you believe was the right place, right time?" Maxwell asks, reminding me that he's here, too.

"I don't believe it. I know it," I say, my eyes drifting back to my canvas. It's now that I realize I'm painting a portrait of Hazel. I don't have anything close to the skill level it would take to capture her beauty, but it's abstract enough to be presentable.

"I can see how that feels lucky. No one got seriously hurt; you were introduced to a new career path. Maybe people even reminded you how much worse it could've been." Maxwell runs his fingers down his mustache. "With Mrs. Walker, how did she know you were a carpenter?"

"I told her. That's when I learned she worked in the theater."

Maxwell nods thoughtfully. "And when that opportunity was presented, you said yes?"

"I stayed in my hometown way too long after the accident. I would've said yes to anything at that point," I say. "The opportunity... it just presented itself. They always have."

"It was an opportunity you acted on," Maxwell says. "You were in the right state of mind to say yes to begin with. With your accident, too, you didn't have to say yes to Mr. Patterson. In fact, several of my clients don't say yes when opportunities like that come up. I take it you're not a soft worker." He pokes the air with his pointer finger. "You're a hard one. Would you agree with that?"

I don't pretend that I'm not a hard worker. I have been ever since Mr. Patterson gave me that second chance.

"You were exposed to people. You made yourself easy to get to know. You shared your life with people. Your interests," Maxwell continues. "You were open to opportunities. You said 'yes.'" He holds his hands out, palms up. "That's luck *you* made."

Luck that... I made?

"I was born lucky," I correct.

"I don't have good news for you," Maxwell tells me. "I have really good news for you: There's no such thing. We can make our own luck. In fact, anyone can. And if you can harness this mindset, you'll find yourself getting a little luckier."

As he says this, a dark blue dragonfly circles us, landing on my canvas.

Hazel gasps and sets her hand gently on my cast, giving my fingers a squeeze. "Dragonflies represent good fortune," she whispers.

The irony isn't lost on me that we're here to get practical and grounded advice, yet are still reading into the symbols around us.

Maxwell gives us a few more minutes to finish up our paintings and invites us to share what we've been working on. I don't expect Hazel to let us see her art, but she does. Slowly, she turns her canvas around. I'm staring back at a person's very colorful, very abstract face.

"It's Logan," she reveals. "Well, it was supposed to be."

While I was over here painting a portrait of her, she was doing the same of me.

If you see anything you like, paint that.

"Hazel, I don't like it," Maxwell says. He claps his hands together. "I love it!"

I have an oversize square head with big eyes and spiky yellow hair. She's given me pink lips and dressed me in a spiral-tie-dyed, long-sleeve shirt.

"The resemblance is uncanny. It's very cubist," I say of her piece. "Are you one of those annoying people who say they're bad at something but are secretly really good?"

"I can't explain this," she says, tucking a windblown strand of hair behind her ear.

"Maybe it was the lucky combination of good morning light, quality supplies, and your muse?" Maxwell poses. *Muse, really?* "Or once you moved beyond 'no,' were you in the right mindset? You started off negative, saying you'd be bad at this, but you still did it. And look what happened!"

"Well, no. This is a fluke," Hazel pushes back. "Art is not my strong suit. Seriously. You should see my stars. They look like a toddler drew them."

"Maybe." Maxwell tilts his head. "Maybe not."

Hazel goes quiet as she processes this, so his message must have the desired effect.

Maxwell pats his chest, removing his phone from his overalls' front pocket. "Excuse me for a moment. If this call is what I think it is, I need to take it."

"In case I wasn't clear, I love it," I tell Hazel when Maxwell steps away to answer his phone. "Would it be okay if I kept it?"

"You want this?" She glides her pointer finger along the top of the canvas. "I've seen your apartment. This would not fit."

"I think it's exactly what my place is missing."

"Uh-huh," she says. "Let me see yours."

"Unlike what you claim, I'm not actually all that terrible at drawing." I cringe and turn my canvas around. "But this...I'm really sorry."

The corners of Hazel's mouth curl when she realizes she was my inspiration.

"You look scary," I say. "I mean, not *you* you. But this version of you? It might haunt me." Saying it's a disaster would be an understatement. I got so caught up trying to capture the exact shade of her eyes the entire time that the rest of her ended up as straight lines.

"I love what you did with my hair," she says, delighted at how I went overboard with brown paint. Her hair looks more like a hat that's been puffed up by static electricity.

I take another look at my portrait of her and bust out laughing. "You know, I actually thought this was decent at first? Then I saw yours of me and damn."

I didn't anticipate any of this making her blush, but maybe it's because I've embarrassed her?

Hazel rocks from one side to the other. "My eyes are following me."

"We should probably never speak of this again," I say, running my hand across the back of my neck. "At the very least, it needs to be burned and then divided up across garbage cans so it can't somehow come back together."

Hazel takes my canvas, smiling down at my poor attempt. "Can I be honest? There's something about it I resonate with. I'm the mature, responsible one," she explains. Her expression turns contemplative. "And this stick figure version of me… Well, it feels like I don't have to be totally put together. All this can get is better."

I nod in confirmation. "It literally couldn't get worse."

She brushes her thumb along the side of the canvas. "I'd like to have it."

"Then it's all yours," I say. "But I won't be held responsible for nightmares that may occur."

A laugh bubbles out of Hazel's throat. I wish I were better at art, for no other selfish reason than to paint this moment of her sitting on a picnic blanket under the Brooklyn Bridge as we attempt to chase a little luck. I want to capture all of her, every single detail, in every vibrant shade this canvas can hold.

But it's more than that, I think. I don't want just portrait-level with Hazel. I really do want to know everything about her, and the only way I can do that is for us to spend more time together. If that means I have to continue being unlucky to do so, then so be it.

Maxwell rushes back to us. "Thanks for waiting. There was a last-minute cancellation at a restaurant I keep putting myself on the waitlist for. It's finally paid off!" He rubs his hands together. "Now, where were we? Mindset is just the beginning."

Chapter 14

HAZEL

Unknown Number (6:46 AM): Happy birthday!!!!!!!!!!!!!!!!!!!!!!!!!!!!!

First, the spammers get my number, now they have my birthday? When will it end?

Unknown Number (6:47 AM): For the record, that's 30 exclamation points. One for each year of your life, which deserves to be shouted about.
Unknown Number (6:49 AM): (I fully recognize how excessive and annoying you'll probably think that is. I'm not sorry!)
Hazel (6:55 AM): Logan?
Unknown Number (6:56 AM): Oh, sorry, yes. It's me. It was fun feeling popular for a second but then the calls just got annoying.

I add Logan's new number to my contacts.

Logan (6:57 AM): I was sad to lose my 206 number, though.
Hazel (6:59 AM): Some people say you're not an official New Yorker until you have a 917 area code.

THE FORTUNE FLIP

Hazel (7:00 AM): BTW, that was more exclamation points than one should have to see this early in the morning.
Hazel (7:02 AM): But thank you.
Logan (7:04 AM): No rules on birthdays. I know you don't celebrate, but maybe you'd be open to acknowledging it?
Logan (7:07 AM): If you are, please select from the following answers:
A: It needs to be low key
B: It needs to be low effort
C: It needs to be low cost
D: It needs to cost a lot
E: I'm open to a surprise, just this once
F: I'm not open to anything, but thanks

I'm not in a festive mood—let alone an acknowledging one—yet I'm smiling as I scan the list. I have my box of De Cecco spaghetti, my résumé, and a list of potential questions the hiring manager might ask me in my interview in a few days. I've decided to go for the manager role, since I've basically been managing people my whole life. But hey, this job pays more.

I'm about to send option F. I stop myself before I do.

Every year I've spent my birthday with pasta and a movie. Those were plans I could count on.

You want something else, a voice in the back of my head supplies.

It's the same unhelpful voice that drove me into my ex's arms that night we met. The night filled with impulsive decisions that led to a short-lived marriage with someone I hardly knew.

But Logan is not my ex.

And this year, my same old plans don't give me butterflies.

I've prepped so much that I have my interview answers

memorized. I can spend a couple hours acknowledging that I'm one year older.

I have no idea what Logan has in store. But just the thought of doing anything with him is enough to make me excited in a way that doesn't instill fear. It inspires hope.

I delete F and retype my answer.

Logan sent a cryptic text in the late afternoon with a time and place: the Battery, 8 p.m. By the time I arrive at the corner he specified, he's already there waiting. Located at the very bottom of Manhattan, the Battery is surrounded by water and, therefore, wind. A gust whips off the Hudson River, sending my hair flying as I wave hello.

"Surprise!" he says, opening the door to a glass, shell-shaped structure.

Inside is a sea-themed carousel with thirty or so glass fish figures with seats. The ceiling and walls are bathed in cobalt and teal, the swirly patterns giving me the feeling of being in a handblown glass paperweight. He's brought me to the human equivalent of a fish tank. This must be how Goldie and Kurt feel.

"Where is everyone?" I ask, looking around. Every square inch of the floor is covered in balloons. On the other side of the glass, people walk with purpose in their hunched-over post-work-drinks commute.

"It's just us," Logan says. "And Sam, who will operate the ride, but he'll be outside until I text him that we're ready for a spin." He spreads his arms. "Welcome to the SeaGlass Carousel!"

"I said I was okay with a surprise. I should've also said low cost," I say, hesitation bubbling inside me. First, the firehouse. Now this. I step away from him. "Why did you do all this?" I'm not even trying to hide the emotion coming through in my voice. I try to swallow it down, which just makes my throat tighter.

"I didn't think you'd want to spend your birthday with strangers and screaming children," Logan explains. "I wanted to do something nice."

"Are you doing this because I'm helping you? Because you don't have to." I shake my head. "This must've cost you a fortune."

"Good thing I kind of have one?" he says. "This is what I want to spend my money on. You." He tilts his head. "I've also been eyeing a nice, custom Japanese chisel set, but still. Mostly you."

I'm still lingering near the door. If I step in, I commit to this... present? Gift? Those words don't quite capture what this is. Extravagance? Overindulgence?

I don't know what my face is doing, but Logan must sense my reluctance. He steps closer and says, "Birthdays are supposed to be big."

I cross my arms. "That's not how my birthdays have been."

"Maybe that needs to change."

"Let me pay for half."

"Half of what?"

"Half of this," I say, waving toward a giant, glowing fiberglass fish.

"Seriously? No," he says. "This is part of your gift."

Part of? I don't want to be this way or ruin tonight. But I also don't want Logan spending all his money on me. I tell him this.

The excitement in Logan's face dulls. I hate to be the one who caused it.

"I understand," he says, "and I'm sorry if this is excessive. I didn't mean to make you uncomfortable."

"This just... it isn't why I'm spending time with you. I don't need fancy things."

"I mean, I'm glad you're not into me for my money," he says, shifting to his other foot, "but I don't know, it's the first time I've had excess money in a while. I mostly prefer to spend my money on other people and experiences, not stuff."

It is his money. He can do what he wants with it. Even if that means spending it on me.

"And if it wasn't your birthday, I'd be some random, lonely guy renting out a carousel for himself," he adds.

I imagine it and a very small laugh escapes. "No, you wouldn't."

Logan's eyes brighten. "No, I wouldn't. Because this is for you. It's all for you. And that smile right there is exactly why I'd rent a hundred more carousels a hundred more times." He shuffles closer to me, balloons bouncing off his legs. "But I do hear you, and I'm going to cool it on the big gestures."

Now I'm full-on smiling at him. I don't know how he does that. How he turns my mood around and works through what it is I feel. He gently pushes back, but ultimately, he listens.

"Thank you," I say, deciding to go with whatever it is he's planned. The money's spent. There's no use wasting a perfectly good carousel.

Logan grins and opens his arms for a hug. "Happy birthday, Hazel."

I can't get into his arms fast enough. I squeeze him back as I continue to take it all in. Against the curved far wall is a table with candy boxes shaped like a cake next to three chocolate pizzas covered in M&Ms.

Logan notices me looking. "Since I burned dessert the last time we cooked, this time I made several but set them at different bake times, just in case."

I open my mouth in surprise. All that comes out is a puff of air. I'm actually speechless.

Logan takes my hand and guides me through the river of balloons to the setup. There's spaghetti in glass containers, premade tomato sauce in a Mason jar, and a block of Parmesan.

"You mentioned something about noodles, so I went in that

direction," Logan says, shaking the jar and twisting off the lid. Steam rises from the top. "And it's red for, you know, good luck." He lifts his arm, showing off the cast I picked out that night he fell.

He looks a little nervous, like in a way where there's some percentage of doubt in him that thinks I might not like this. Like in a way where he wants this night to be special for me.

As he stirs, the veins in his forearms swell. Tonight's shirt is dark green and blue. It's like he's worn his fanciest tie-dye for me. The fabric hugs his chest and back in all the right places.

It makes me want to do the same. I come up beside him and wrap my arms around his waist, my cheeks squished against his chest. "Longevity noodles symbolize a long life," I say. "It was something my dad taught me when I was a kid."

It's only now, in my first day of being thirty years old, that I realize how superstitious that tradition is.

"In that case, you get more," Logan says, transferring noodles from his container into mine.

I never got stuff like this for my birthday. These big gestures, it's exactly what Dad made promises about. The ones that never came true. I needed Dad in the small ways. To make us dinner, to keep the heat on. Flashy gifts don't mean much when the important things are forgotten.

But Logan didn't just do flashy. He also cooked.

The way he's looking at me heats all of me up, my adrenaline, and anticipation, and desire a slow simmer bubbling just below the surface.

I don't want to feel this. It's too happy. Happy things like this don't last.

I glance around, looking for something, anything, that will make this experience less shiny. But it's not cold in here, it's not noisy, and the carousel is so artfully done I can't help but be mesmerized by the scene. In fact, the underwater sounds are set so low that it's peaceful. As is the shimmering light flickering across the space to make it feel like we're underwater. And there's Logan wearing his usual—navy hat included. Strands of hair stick out from behind his ears, windblown from standing outside.

It's a perfect visual. One that I can't believe is happening in my real life.

I wait and wait some more for the crushing low to hit after feeling so high.

The sensation never comes. Instead, I feel warm inside. And then a tear has the nerve to roll out of my eye and down my face.

Logan brushes his thumb against my cheek to wipe the tear away. Being with him, it feels right. All I want to feel is this.

"Hey," he says in a soothing tone, "what's wrong?"

My throat is dry as I swallow. "Every single thing about this, about you...it's too good. Too nice."

Logan frowns. "And that's bad?"

"No," I say, remembering that his ex had made him feel bad about that exact thing. "*No.*" I say it twice, so he knows I mean it. "I'm just not used to it."

"Does it have something to do with why you hate birthdays?" Logan asks.

I look over at the noodles all tangled together in the containers and cross my arms. "Why are we celebrated for being born anyway? I didn't do anything. I just came out."

Logan gives me a look that tells me he's not buying it. In past relationships, if I was dating someone and my birthday happened to come around, no one's ever questioned my requests for no presents, no celebrations.

Then Logan came along...

I sit in a blue angelfish that's double my height and lit from below. Logan picks the butterfly fish closest to me.

"Truthfully, it's the day after birthdays I hate," I share. "Birthdays themselves were like a giant PAUSE button. They were days my dad had something else to focus on other than gambling."

I immediately wish I could take back the words. I've always kept this part of my life hidden from everyone. Then I realize Logan already knows so much. Too much, probably.

But he doesn't budge an inch. He waits patiently as I spill my guts inside the fish's.

"Birthdays were generally fine days," I continue. "Not amazing, but good enough. Better than the others. There'd be cake sometimes. I'd even get a present on years when my dad had a recent winning streak, but usually he'd just promise something extravagant. My brother and I didn't fight." I release a humorless laugh. Just a soft puff of air, really. "But the day after? Everything that had been held back came rushing forward like the previous day had never happened. It just made me wish birthdays never came around."

"That's a mind trip," Logan says, nodding in a way that makes me think he can relate.

"They were. I haven't heard from my dad today." It tells me as much as I need to know about how Atlantic City went. This is always how it is when the games don't go his way: His mood plummets, plans get canceled, and I have to tiptoe around him trying to figure out how to fix it. I did, however, receive an animated card from Jerry in lieu of a daily check-in. It featured dolphins wearing party hats singing *Happ-eee-eee-eeee Birthday*.

Logan makes a face. "Seriously?"

"Not that I want to talk to him," I mumble without thinking. "I feel bad for feeling—and saying—that."

Part of me expects Logan to reply with something positive or for him to point out the silver linings, the way he has the entire time I've known him. But what he says next surprises me.

"Parents tend to be people we want to love and connect with, even when they disappoint us."

I nod. "Birthdays were especially hard after my mom died. They were her favorite," I say, feeling safe in the privacy of the fish. The sea glass–colored fish soothe me, sparking a distant memory. It was my birthday at the aquarium. The last party Mom organized for me. The last birthday party I ever had. "She once made me a mermaid cake. Twisted streamers to look like seaweed. She set up bowls with gummy sharks and Swedish Fish."

The rest of the details are fuzzy, but the memory itself is the color of deep-sea blue. From the massive tanks we were surrounded by, probably. Still, to this day, the color calms me.

I had forgotten until tonight how much Mom loved celebrating birthdays. Any major event, really. I don't remember much about her, but I do recall her being a celebrator. Just like Logan.

"I think she would've loved this night you planned," I say. Another tear springs out of the corner of my eye.

"Hey, it's okay," Logan says, jumping out of his fish, squeezing beside me in mine. The seat's so small I end up on his lap, my arm draped around his shoulders. "Use my shirt."

It reminds me of when we met. As he gently dabs my cheeks dry with his sleeve, I say, "These are happy tears, I think. I've never talked about this with anyone before." It's uncomfortable to share about my family. It exposes the underbelly of the vulnerable and messy sides of me. But this moment has also made me realize something else. For a long time, I haven't trusted others. And maybe even myself. "I like talking to you, though. This was the best present you could've gotten me."

Logan takes my hand in his. "Well, I did get you a physical present, too."

We step out of the fish so Logan can grab a bag he's hidden under the table. I push past the blue tissue paper and remove eight small boxes, piling them in my arms. I use the carousel seat as a makeshift table, opening the first box. It's a gold charm of a wrapped-up flower bouquet.

"They look like bodega flowers," Logan says. "You didn't want them, but that day we met, I wanted so badly to buy you flowers."

I open the next box, which is a gold cat charm.

"Toffee. So you always remember him," he says.

"I'll give the bird charm some distance from him," I joke.

The rest of the boxes hold more charms: a four-leaf clover ("because we couldn't find any"), a turtle ("so we don't go to jail for stealing one"), a ladybug ("they're even harder to find than clovers"), a lightning bolt (ha-ha), and a horseshoe ("in case Pancakes doesn't need his shoes repaired next time we see him").

The last box is a charm of Mickey Mouse.

"I was inspired by your tattoo," Logan says, pleased.

For a split second, I'm confused. Then it clicks. A delighted laugh bursts out of me.

Logan lets out a velvety, low one that stops when he realizes we're not laughing at the same thing. "Wait, what's so funny?" he asks.

I pull my sweater sleeve up and point to my tattoo. "You thought this was Mickey Mouse?"

"Isn't it?"

"This was the tattoo I got BAFG. Before Alleged Good Fortune," I say. "For something so permanent, I really should've had a plan. A visual, at the very least. My brother was supposed to visit but bailed last minute. So I took the money I saved up for us to go to a few restaurants and museums and got a tattoo instead. Midway through, the guy started telling me how excited he was for his upcoming family trip to Disneyworld. Clearly, this"—I gesture to my arm—"is what he had on his mind. So instead of a water molecule with covalent bond lines connecting the oxygen atom with each hydrogen atom, I got a Mickey Mouse head."

"You're telling me that's a water molecule," Logan says, biting down on his fist.

"It's my way of bringing water to me when I can't get to it," I say. "I haven't been able to afford swimming here. But yeah, when life gets hard, add water."

"You really could've saved me at Central Park Lake then?"

"I was a competitive swimmer in college. So, if it came down to it, yes. You really would've needed to have been flailing, though."

"Noted. Next time, more flailing," he says.

"This is just a little taste of what my luck looks—looked?—like," I tell him as he adds the charms to my bracelet. "Tattoo artists going rogue. And I've never been to Disneyland or World so I can't even tie it to any kind of memory." I look down at the Mickey Mouse charm. "Actually, that's not true anymore."

Logan's smile is so big it sets in motion a fresh ripple effect across his cheeks. Like a stone skipping across a still pond. Before I know it, I've flung my arms around his shoulders, tipping up on my toes to meet him. "Thank you for these. Thank you for this night. I love y—them," I say, a flush of heat rushing my face. "I love them."

I cover up my embarrassment over that near emotional miss by kissing him. As though that's really any better.

Thankfully, Logan doesn't seem to notice my flub. Or he did and he's just nice enough to let me kiss my way out of it.

Logan's blue eyes are the same shade as my happy childhood birthday memory. "Thank you for letting me spend today with you," he says.

And then we're both done talking.

I smile against his mouth at the thrill of being this close to him. And not just physically. To kiss Logan, to let my feelings run wild for him, these aren't spontaneous responses. These are conscious decisions.

Logan lifts me up against the side of the giant fish.

"Your arm," I mumble against his neck.

He doesn't seem concerned. "You might be surprised by what I can do with one hand."

I tighten my legs around his waist. As he drops kisses down my throat, I run my hands through his hair, knocking his hat off. I grip the strands gently, pulling him closer to me. I can't get Logan close enough. Still, I try.

The pressure of his body against mine sends millions of little zaps of electricity up and down my skin. I burrow my face into his neck, inhaling the faint scent of wood shavings and basil. I'm there for a few seconds before needing his mouth on mine again.

I nip greedily at his bottom lip as I feel my way under his shirt. If I'm honest, I've never particularly cared much for muscles on a man. His are incredible, yes. But they're nothing compared to his eyes. Those I care very much for. And Logan's are so warm and expressive. Maybe subconsciously, that's what got me that very first day.

It's those same eyes that do me in now. The crinkles around them from the smile that forms whenever he sees me. It's the way he looks at me—now, any other time—that has always told me what I need to know. I have seen from the very beginning that Logan is a good guy. Decent. Honest. *Mine*, my brain adds last minute.

"Hey," Logan says below me. "Where'd you go?"

"Into your eyes," I whisper.

He grins and sets me down, propping his arm up against the fish. I turn toward his uncasted forearm and give it three kisses. He bends down to cut me off, taking my bottom lip into his mouth. As he kisses me, all my thoughts and worries about the past and future melt away. I'm only focused on this present moment. With him.

It's a rare kind of quiet I only experience when his mouth is on mine. To test the theory, I kiss him again. The noise of my overcrowded, loud brain dulls to a peaceful, low hum.

Since day one, we haven't known normal things about each other. Who meets a random stranger and learns what their future holds? I finally get what Logan was saying about how we're connected in this inexplicably bizarre way. Because of the fortunes. Because I did something out of character.

Something Maxwell said stops me. *Lucky people try new things.*

And I guess I did.

For the first time since all of this started—and since everything awful that has happened in the past few days—I feel lucky in this moment. Lucky to know Logan. Lucky to be here with him tonight. Lucky to remember happy moments from my childhood. The ones that got pushed down under the crushing weight of all my responsibilities.

I want Logan to feel what I do.

Past Logan's shoulder, I spot a pack of long, glittery candles. Nothing about me screams glitter. Yet I love them. And somehow, he knew that.

"Make my wish," I blurt out.

He balks. "You're off luck duty tonight. And I'm not stealing your birthday wish."

We can talk like this, I find. Picking up pieces of conversation that we left off. Communicating without having to say too much.

Look at you two having inside jokes, Gloria had said. I've never had inside jokes with anyone.

THE FORTUNE FLIP

"It's not stealing if I give it to you. In fact, I wish you would take it," I say. "Seriously. Blow out my candle."

Logan kisses my palm as he wraps his hand tighter around me. "Is that what the kids are calling it these days?"

"My birthday candle," I say, nudging him. "You should blow it out and make a wish."

"Are you seriously trying to fix my luck right now?" Logan says, arching an eyebrow. "Because I'm feeling pretty damn lucky." He trails his hands down to the waistband of my jeans, tugging at the loop until I'm pressed up against him.

I bite down a smile. It's like he's just read my mind.

Little fireworks explode along my skin. As we kiss, the intensity grows. I want this. I want him. So, so much.

Too much. I've overheated, my emotions reaching a dangerously high temperature.

It's too good. You're too good. It won't last.

I try to break the feedback loop. But this night is as close to perfect as it gets, and the only way to go from here is down. Things between Logan and me have spun too far out of control. There's an overflow of happiness. Instead of rising with the waves, suddenly I'm drowning in them.

But before I do, Logan pulls back.

"I want this. I want you," he says, our chests rising and falling in perfect sync. "But you matter too much to me to rush this. We met fast, and we won fast, but I want to be with you nice and slow."

I press my lips together as I nod quickly. I don't want us to flame out before we've had a chance to light up. "Yes. Please."

Logan touches his forehead against mine. "Great. Also, we're surrounded by glass. I build the sets. I'm not the one putting on the show."

He diffuses any lingering tension with this joke. I'm grateful for the warm release of laughter.

He grabs the charm boxes and pats the seat. "Get comfy."

Logan texts Sam, who comes back in and powers up the ride. For three and a half minutes, we slowly rotate, rising and falling in a waterless current. Balloons bounce off the fish and each other, floating around us, like bubbles in a bath.

It's the best birthday acknowledgment I've ever had.

Chapter 15

HAZEL

My first two days of being thirty are a blur.

Emma, Gloria, and I have been working around the clock preparing for a last-minute pop-up collaboration with New York City's hottest ice cream shop, Worldly Scoops, and a travel company, The Cheshire, that owns luxury hotels around the world. Fittingly, the theme is Going Places.

When the small business providing chocolate, caramel, and butterscotch sauces dropped out earlier this week, Worldly Scoops immediately reached out to Emma. They wouldn't have sauces to drizzle over ice cream, but they could have candy.

Worldly Scoops spent months securing the permits for the two-day pop-up at Grand Central Terminal, an iconic train station and landmark on the east side of Manhattan. It's bustling with people who have come far and wide to shop, eat, and admire its awe-inspiring architecture and jade-hued celestial ceiling with gold-leaf constellations.

We'll be in one of The Cheshire's luxury train cars that's been rolled into the expansive main terminal. The Cheshire's latest rail-travel venture launches this month across England, Wales, and Scotland, so they want to give a peek at what to expect with their redesigned train cars. Apparently, a famous movie director with a well-known visual style worked with them on the revamping.

"Doesn't everything about this go against that old saying about never getting into vans with strangers offering candy?" Gloria says as she sets out scoops next to the jars on the bar where we've set up shop at one end of the train car. Next to us, the Worldly Scoops founders, Cole and Jonathan, are arranging their tubs of ice cream.

Emma stashes an empty box under the bar. "What about any of this"—she motions around the interior of the car that has splashes of bright colors and a mix of textures and patterns—"reminds you of a van?"

Gloria looks out a window draped with the same high-quality cornflower blue fabric that the dining chairs are upholstered with. Through the glass, I notice that people have already started to line up, waiting for us to open. "The wheels?" she says.

Emma and I share an amused look. "Ooh, I'm nervous," Emma says, shaking out her shoulders. "You know how many influencers and reporters will be here? Like, dozens. If this hits, it could be a game changer for us."

"Interior design and travel magazine photographers will be here, too," Gloria says, waving to the customers in line. "It's going to be fabulous, darling. We caught a lucky break to get this level of exposure."

Emma nods. "I can't believe we pulled it together in time."

Honestly, me neither. Emma almost passed on it. There wasn't enough time to order new batches of candy for the pop-up, so we took our supply from the shop. While Emma took care of event logistics and coordinated schedules for her two other employees to cover for us at the shop while we're here, Gloria managed the marketing and updated the website and social media. I was in charge of acquiring more jars and bags for customers, though I did have another idea that I went ahead and ran with.

"Emma, got a sec?" I hold up a small box.

Emma shakes a bag of French nougats into one of the jars. "Of course, what's up?"

I remove the lid and take a postcard-size paper out. I found a print shop near Washington Square Park that was able to get this printing done in under twenty-four hours. "I wanted to show you these passports I had made. Well, passcards," I say, hearing my voice reflect my internal excitement about them. "Every customer gets one. For each candy and ice cream flavor they try, they get a stamp in one of the boxes. And for the ones they don't try, they can come back to our shops and keep filling out their passcard."

"What happens when every box has been stamped?" Gloria asks, peeking over my shoulder.

"I was thinking they'd get ten percent off their next purchase," I say, only now realizing that in the rush of getting everything together, I forgot to ask Emma for the green light on this detail.

"Hazel..." Emma shakes her head.

"I'm really sorry I didn't run it by you first," I rush out. "I wanted to be helpful since you were so busy. I already took care of talking to Cole and Jonathan. They're onboard with it."

"Oh my god, no, I'm not mad," Emma says with wide eyes. "I love it. It's so creative."

"It's also backed by numbers," I share. "Based on the zip codes of our store customers, eighty-nine percent of Midtown residents are the ones buying candy like the mixed fruit Turkish delight and Aero peppermint bars. We brought some of our top sellers, but I also snuck in some of the candy many people in this area tend to love." I pull a box from a large tote and grab one of the individually wrapped bubbly chocolate bars. "I figured, since they're always coming to us, I wanted to show that we're paying attention when we come to them."

Emma lets out an amused sound. "I didn't realize we were such a destination."

"Several times a month, actually," I say. "Which told me that, if people are willing to go all that way for international candy, there's a strong chance they'd be willing to hop around to Worldly Scoops' stores, too. Hopefully, this passcard will inspire them to keep coming back to try new candy. And they'll get rewarded for it."

"Wow, you went above and beyond what you needed to do," Emma says. "This passcard, looking through the data...that must've taken you a lot of time."

"Honestly, I find this kind of thing fun."

Dissecting purchasing patterns of customers and thinking through how to attain optimal inventory levels have already been more interesting to me than the type of data I worked with in health care. And Sweet Escape's data is something I can personally act on instead of just building reports to hand off to someone else.

"That makes"—Gloria points at Emma, then herself, and then me—"one of us," she says. "Where have you been all of Emma's shop life?"

"Oh, I've been there, just consuming most of her inventory," I half joke.

Emma laughs. "That's true. You've been right here with us from the beginning." She gives me a side hug. "I'm so thankful for you."

I breathe out a slow exhale of relief. "Please, I'm the thankful one," I say. For the job, yes, but also for their kindness they've consistently shown me.

"No, seriously," Emma says, "I've had enough wading through legalese in my life that trying to decipher reports is just...Well, it's not why I went into the candy business. This is great. Thank you, Hazel." She lifts one of the passcards and admires it. "When you've got more ideas, I'm all ears."

I don't try to contain my happiness. At my last job, my manager acted like encouragement and being open to new ideas were above his pay grade. We did things his way, and he did things the way they had always been done.

"Okay, yes, thank you," I say, grinning so widely that my cheeks start to ache.

I get to work breaking up the Aero bars into smaller pieces. Once the candy jars are ready to go, I set the passcards in a neat pile on the far end of the bar closest to Worldly Scoops, where customers will start off. The first few people start trickling in, ordering ice cream flavors like ricotta with crushed pistachio, oolong tea with ribbons of mango jam, and baklava with layers of crisp phyllo dough and a trio of nuts. Jonathan had explained during setup that these flavors were inspired by their travels to Sicily, Taiwan, and Greece.

As Cole presses a mini spoon-shaped stamp onto one of the passcard boxes, a pang of longing thrums through me. It suddenly hits me, standing here in this luxury train with all its possibilities of where it can travel, that I want to be the passenger. The desire only solidifies being next to tubs of worldly flavors I've never experienced in person and serving candy that Emma's picked out on her own adventures. I want to taste mangos in Taiwan and pistachios in Sicily for myself. I want to see the Greek Islands with my own eyes.

This urge is unfamiliar but strong. I rub my knuckles across my chest, the ache only slightly lessening.

The next stop on the customers' journey is to our candy buffet, where they can top their ice cream with gummies and chocolates. I pull myself out of my thoughts and answer questions about where we source our candy and if the banana marshmallow candy really tastes like banana. (It doesn't *not* taste like banana.)

The booths and dining chairs fill up fast. Everyone has their phones out, snapping their sweet treats from various angles. Some have small clip-on ring lights on their phones for a more flattering image. I assume those are the influencers Emma was talking about.

A brunette with tight curls steps up to our section of the bar, holding bright purple ice cream. "Which of these would go best with ube, do you think?" she asks.

I reach for the coconut-coated licorice candy. "I'd recommend—"

"You're here! Hi!" Emma singsongs beside me. "Hazel, this is Chelsea Rogers. She's a writer at *Out of Office*." I must look like I'm drawing a blank because Emma adds, "It's one of the most popular online travel magazines in the country. And Chels, this is Hazel Yen. She's our newest hire and data queen. I'll introduce you to Gloria in a second."

Chelsea does a double take. "Hazel Yen?" She looks at me for a few long seconds. "Sorry, I thought you were someone else for a second."

Someone else like Older Hazel Yen by chance?

"Oh, no worries," I say, busying myself by wiping sugar off the counter.

"Who'd you think she was?" Emma unhelpfully asks.

Chelsea taps her polished finger against her bowl before addressing me again. "Did you know you share a name with someone who just won the lottery?"

I freeze in place as my eyes dart up to her. Is that a look of recognition? The moment passes before I can be sure. Gloria zips over to us, so I assume she's overheard this tidbit.

"Oh, really? Wow," I squeak out. So it's when I'm uncomfortable that my voice becomes shrill. Cool.

"A lottery winner with Hazel's name?" Gloria asks. "What are the odds?"

Oh, just about 100 percent.

Chelsea gives me another once-over. "It was a husband and wife. She was much older than you, though. And white." She sidesteps to keep the line moving. I don't bother trying to tell her that I'm also white. "I'm surprised you haven't seen the press conference photos. They've become the 'it' couple of the moment because of how elusive they've been."

Great. Ignoring every text and call has only made us more mysterious. And therefore, intriguing.

"Elusive, but also cute," Chelsea self-corrects. "There are a bunch of lottery winners, but their stories aren't as adorable as this couple's. After decades of marriage, they still had this, like, really intense chemistry. You need to look up the photos."

I swallow. "For sure, will do." There's a very real possibility that my cheeks are as bright as the red ropes in the jar in front of us.

"If the first thing that comes up is the arrest of Marlin Mavers, keep scrolling. You'll find them," Chelsea reassures me, though it's not at all encouraging. I don't need photos of any of it. I witnessed—and experienced—the whole thing firsthand.

"An arrest?" Gloria asks. "Sounds exciting."

That's one word for what it was.

"The press conference was partially a setup for the police to catch the guy," Chelsea elaborates. "Marlin had a warrant out for his arrest on theft and possession of stolen property charges. Something to do with sports jerseys and exotic fish? But then get this. He was bailed out by, you guessed it, his lottery winnings."

Now, that part is news to me. Maybe Marlinworld will live to see the light of day, after all.

"Are you serious? He seemed—" I stop myself. "*That* seems...like a lot. But I don't really keep up with that kind of thing." I punctuate this with a shrug that I hope implies I'd like to move on from the conversation.

"A guy named Marlin stealing exotic fish?" Gloria asks with a smirk. "Sounds made up. Good for that couple, though. Talk about a sweet retirement plan."

"My editor has been trying to reach them for a feature," Chelsea shares, dropping a tong-full of candied ginger over her ice cream. "She wants to fly them out to a location of their choice for their second honeymoon."

I knew that slipup about our nonexistent honeymoon would come back to bite me. Why couldn't I just stick to food?

Gloria snorts. "Why is it that rich people get all the free stuff? You see celebrities getting sent clothes, bags, and skincare all the time. Like, why? They're the ones who can afford it!"

"Why would they be flown out if they had just won the lottery?" I ask. I can't help myself. I need this to make sense.

"It would be in exchange for an interview and a few photoshoots during the trip. People need good news right now. This would be such a feel-good feature," Chelsea says. "I heard that the *Today* show has been trying to book them, too."

I take in air to speak, conscious of what my voice might come out like. I need to *not* sound like high-pitched Hazel Yen from the press conference.

"The *Today* show, really?" I ask, overcorrecting too low. I clear my throat. "Interesting." There we go. I take in a long, slow breath to calm myself. I'm nearly through this. "Well, is there anything else I can get you?"

Chelsea isn't ready to end our little chat, though. "We'll keep trying. No one's featured them yet, so it'd be a huge get and a love story for the ages." She shuffles forward past more candy jars and toward the register. "They'd be put up in five-star hotels, and it's all expenses paid. I don't know why Hazel and Logan wouldn't want to do it."

I might have gasped out loud when she said Logan's name. I can't be sure since I've gone totally numb. I do know I'm overheating and likely sweating through my shirt, which just might be what ends up giving me away.

"Logan?" Gloria asks, her head snapping back toward us. "Well, that's just freaky!"

"What a strange coincidence," Emma chimes back in after helping ring up a customer. Has she been listening this entire time, too?

I force out a laugh. "Yeah. So, so...strange!"

These are all the words I'm good for right now. If Chelsea doesn't realize it's me, it'll be Emma and Gloria.

Chelsea looks between the three of us, confused. When she opens her mouth to say something, Emma asks, "Will that be it for you?"

The line's getting longer behind Chelsea, who just now realizes this. "Oh yeah. That's it!" She pays for her ice cream and candy with the tap of her phone. "Emma, so good seeing you. I'll be sure to tag Sweet Escape in my post. Nice to meet you, Hazel and Gloria!"

Emma rounds the bar to give Chelsea a hug as Gloria turns to me. "Hazel and Logan. Life really works in mysterious ways, huh?" she asks.

"I—I guess," I start, not sure what I'm about to tell her. A bond has just started to form between the three of us. I don't want our friendship—is it too soon to call it that?—to include lies. "Gloria, there's something—"

"You look a little sweaty," Gloria interjects. "Take a few minutes. I'll cover for you." She squints both eyes closed. Was that a wink, or am I now paranoid about blinking?

I nod and turn around, needing a second. That was close. Logan and I really need to be careful where we're seen together.

I walk up to the window, highly alert. Past the glass, tourists point their phones up toward the ceiling as commuters fast-walk to catch their trains. As they cross paths, I follow their invisible footprints and let myself wonder about where they might be going. Uptown, downtown? To Long Island? The airport?

I fumble for my phone in my apron pocket.

> **Hazel (10:31 AM):** If I could get us two tickets, all expenses paid, to a place of our choice, where would you go?

Of course I'm not serious, but I am curious. Logan responds right away.

> **Logan (10:32 AM):** The foliage in Japan is supposed to be amazing this time of year. I do find the French Riviera stunning in the fall. Rome, too. I can take you to my favorite gelato place.

Has he actually been to these places? I can't tell over text if he's serious or not.

> **Hazel (10:32 AM):** I'm tossing Sweden into the mix for how good their candy is.
> **Logan (10:33 AM):** Yeah, great. I'm not picky with my free trips.
> **Logan (10:33 AM):** What's the catch?

I smile and write back, Oh, nothing big. We'd just have to be in our lottery disguises the entire time.

> **Logan (10:33 AM):** Doable. I'll just quickly learn a decades worth of makeup design, BRB.

> **Logan (10:33 AM):** Is there still time to change my answer to Iceland? Lots of layers, clothes. And gloves! Wouldn't have to worry about aging the hands.
> **Hazel (10:33 AM):** Iceland it is.
> **Logan (10:34 AM):** So you finally checked your messages? Was a scammer convincing enough about a free trip?

I roll my eyes to myself. I haven't listened to a single voicemail since the calls started pouring in. All the unknown-numbered texts get immediately deleted.

> **Hazel (10:34 AM):** It was a travel magazine.
> **Logan (10:34 AM):** Ah. The "love story for the ages" people?

I had forgotten Logan was actually checking his messages.

> **Hazel (10:35 AM):** And the *Today* show.
> **Logan (10:34 AM):** I'm kinda jealous of Future Us. Think we should give the disguises another go?

A buzz of energy surges through me. It's like I'm having a sugar rush, even though I haven't had any candy yet today.

I think if we push our luck one too many times, we're bound to be found out, I text, practicality winning.

The typing bubble bounces and stops a few times.

You're probably right. Shouldn't chance it, he finally writes back.

I send a thumbs-up and tell him I need to get back to work. The rest of the afternoon is pretty much my dream work scenario. We serve candy, talk about candy, and eat candy. Passcards get stamped. Customers tag us on social media. I observe them up close and personal to better understand their behaviors. To listen closely to the kinds of questions they're asking.

Every hour, more ideas sprout from the corners of my brain. We can pair up with a chip company for a play on salty and sweet. Or we could do a joint event with a popcorn brand at outdoor film screenings in the park. We can offer gingerbread houses to decorate at Christmastime.

Between rushes, I sample flavors of Worldly Scoops' ice cream and imagine myself in those faraway places. Being surrounded by sweets that are more well-traveled than I am makes me hungry for something I've never had.

It's freeing, this type of dreaming. It makes me curious again. I feel that same sense of adventure I had when I first moved to the city. As mango jam lights up my taste buds, I imagine myself in Japan, France, Italy, Sweden, and Iceland.

In every destination, Logan's right there with me.

Chapter 16

LOGAN

Dress rehearsal starts next week, and we're nowhere near having the stage ready. The mechanical pieces still aren't rolling on and off their marks properly. My notepad with the set designer's feedback has gone missing. And now the HR controller is insisting that the new automated payroll system be in Excel with a safety measure and countermeasure process that has only led to payroll mistakes. I'm convinced HR gets off on messing with us on purpose.

Earlier, Richie sent me a meme of a dog sitting in a chair in a room that's on fire with the words This is fine. It captured what this entire show has felt like.

I slam my laptop shut, letting my mind take me back to Hazel's birthday. It felt like we were in our own little world. Reality felt so far away. That's how it's always felt with Hazel, but maybe that's because most of what we've experienced together has been surreal.

"You got a visitor," Richie says behind me.

I run my hand down my face. "If it's Frank's team again, tell them we need our sidewalk today—"

"Okay, okay. You can have the sidewalk," Hazel's voice says behind me.

I spin around, tucking my pencil behind my ear. Despite

everything that's gone wrong already today, I can't stop the ridiculous grin that forms every time I see her.

"Sorry about that," I say. "We set up a temporary woodshop on the sidewalk when it gets too crowded in here. Sometimes it's a battle with the other theater crews."

"Geez," Richie cuts in. "Can I get a smile like that every now and then? Hey, Joe had an idea for how we could get the sparklers to go off without catching fire." He explains something involving way too much fireproofing spray.

After having started one fire already, I'm weary. "I don't know if that'll work."

Richie looks surprised. "You got a different idea?"

"No." It's a shit answer, but it's all I've got. I don't know what else to do or try. Nothing seems to work. I fix one problem, and another pops up.

"Okayyy, well, take some time to think on it. I'm sure you've got a couple ideas somewhere in there," Richie says, tapping on his own head. He waves bye to Hazel. To everyone else backstage, he tells them to take thirty, and the place clears out. Over his shoulder, he shouts to me, "Don't forget, you owe me fifty bucks!"

"Fantasy Soccer. I lost," I update a confused Hazel.

"So that's your best friend, huh?" Hazel says, watching Richie go.

I huff a laugh. "Is that what he said?"

"Among other things." She holds up a bag with takeout boxes inside, along with a bundle of candy. "This is for you."

Inside the container are a few slices of pizza and waffle fries. "You came all the way uptown to bring me lunch?"

"You mean dinner?" she asks.

"Is it that late?"

A flash of concern crosses Hazel's features. "You need to eat something," she says, nodding to the food. "I wanted to thank you for the other night. And for the cake you had sent to Sweet Escape on Wednesday. Everyone was confused by the *Happy Day After Your Birthday* written in icing. Didn't stop them from eating it, though. Gloria took the new order of champagne bottle gummies and lined the entire sides of the cake in them. Emma was so mad." She laughs. "But it's more like this fake-mad act. We can't really ever be mad at Gloria."

I smile. It really seems like Hazel's enjoying her time at the candy store.

"I'm glad you all liked it, but I didn't do it so you would return the favor," I say. "That's not how this works."

"How what works?"

"This." I move my finger back and forth. "Us."

"Us," Hazel repeats, like she's trying out how it sounds coming from her own mouth. "How exactly does 'us' work then?"

"We don't need to repay each other," I clarify. "I can do nice things for you, and that can be that. This isn't transactional."

"Well, then. Likewise," she says, crossing her arms.

I pull her into a hug. "We'll work on it. Also, hi."

She unfolds her arms and wraps them around me, burying her face in my chest. She lingers longer than usual, refusing to break the hug first.

"The milkshake machine is still down," she informs me.

"Figures," I say on a sigh. "How'd your interview go?"

"I'm being moved forward to team interviews," she says flatly, releasing me.

"That's great news! Congrats."

"Thanks," she mumbles. She doesn't say anything else about it.

"What about the pop-up? How was that?"

She brightens. "So great. Both days were pretty much nonstop," she says. "Now that the event's behind us, I want to see how I can help with inventory management. I've got ideas for processes that might help with allocation, replenishment, fulfillment...Sweet Escape got a lot of coverage. Speaking of, we need to be more cautious about being seen together."

"Wasn't that the point of the disguises? People don't know what we look like."

"But they know our names. So no more introductions. We can make up new names if we need to."

I can't tell if she's being serious, so I play along. "I can go by Gan, and you can be Zel."

Hazel's mouth curls into a smile. "We just need to be careful." She fills me in on Marlin and her near-miss with the magazine writer, which explains what prompted her texts. "Anyway, the event was a nice distraction from...everything."

"I'm sure. Are you still thinking about—"

"Taking out a personal loan? Probably? I don't know," she says, looking around like she's ready for a topic change. "So this looks like it's coming together."

"Don't let appearances fool you." I clench my jaw.

I walk her back to my office and set the takeout container on my desk. I offer her a slice of pizza, but she doesn't want one.

I'm quieter than usual. We both are.

"You okay?" she asks. "I know you've got a lot to do. I can come by another time."

"I always have time for you," I rush out. "Unless you're tired and need to go? You had work and an interview."

Hazel leans against my desk. "I've still got a little left in the tank. So, tell me. What's up?"

I wait a few long seconds before finally admitting, "I'm just trying to remain calm, I guess."

I leave tomorrow for Maine, and I already know I'll be putting Richie in a tough spot.

"Did something else happen?"

"It's all fine," I say. It comes out forced.

She nods slowly. "Well, that right there"—she points at the spot between my eyebrows—"tells me otherwise."

I drag my hand over my face. "Better?"

She smooths out the lines on my skin. "Now it is. What are you working on?"

I grunt. "We have this new Excel payroll system, and I need to fill out the hours today, but the system's messed up."

"Oh, I can help you," she offers.

"You know payroll processes?"

"I know Excel."

I show her the problem on my laptop. She sits in my chair and starts typing.

"I do most of my data work in Excel," she says a few minutes later. "It's not ideal, but..." She turns my laptop to face me. "You should be able to plug in your crew's hours in that cell."

I exhale in relief. "Thank you. You're a wizard."

"Actually, I'd be a witch—"

As she says this, there's a loud crashing noise out on the stage. It's the faux antler chandelier from the dining room set.

Hazel jumps up and runs over to assess the damage. I'm close behind.

"Is this how bad it is still?" she asks.

"It would've been worse if someone had been under it." If Richie had waited for me to let everyone go for the day, someone could've gotten seriously hurt.

She kneels and pokes the dull tip of a faux antler. "Should we try to save any of this?"

"It's mostly wood. I'll work with props to get a new one made." I add the task to my growing to-do list. "That wasn't my best work anyways."

I grab a broom and a garbage bag and start sweeping as Hazel collects the larger pieces. "This is stressful. And dangerous," she says, shaking her head.

"It's going to be okay," I say on instinct. I shrug like I'm trying to prove how relaxed I am, but it ends up looking like I'm trying to touch my shoulders to the tip of my ears.

"Actually, nothing about this seems okay. Like at all," she says.

"This experience is going to make me stronger."

Hazel shakes her head. "Don't fortune cookie me. I don't want to hear pithy, positive statements."

"Depends on whose fortune it is. If it's yours, there's nothing pithy about it. If it's mine, I'd cut myself off midsentence."

"Talk to me," she says gently. She takes the broom from me and lays it on the stage.

I release a breath and shake my head curtly. "I don't want to complain. Maxwell said lucky people see the positive in bad things that happen. That's what I'm doing. Hell, it's what I do!"

"He also said lucky people don't linger on those bad things."

"I'm fine—"

"So don't linger." Hazel takes my face between her hands. "But can you at least acknowledge? You don't have to pretend you're okay."

"Honesty is one of my favorite traits about you, Hazel. I like that you don't sugarcoat things, but it's not as easy for me as it is for you to just say how I really feel." I mirror her usual crossed-arm stance. "I don't want to bring you down, and I don't want to feel bad." There's a finality in my tone, but Hazel pushes past it.

"Down? That's where I've been. Come hang out," she says, sliding her hands across my chest, breaking my arms apart, and grabbing my hands. "If you did, what would you feel bad about?"

My core is tight as I say, "This is all just part of the process."

"What would you feel bad about?" she repeats.

Hazel's not giving up on this. She's not giving up on me. I take in a full breath. If Hazel can acknowledge her birthday for me, I can do this for her.

"I feel bad about every single thing that's gone wrong on this show," I finally admit. "And people quitting out of nowhere. That's been rough. Having two weeks until opening night and not having my shit together." I hold up my cast. "Falling down the damn stairs. That hurt like hell."

She winces. "Yeah."

"I feel bad that your brother's in the hospital, probably because I told someone to break a leg. And when I fed Goldie and Kurt this morning, the entire bottle top popped off and all their Vitamin C–enriched flakes fell into the water. Into their home. I feel bad about that."

My heart pounds against my rib cage, but at this point, I can't tell if it's the stress or adrenaline or Hazel doing this to me. I'm being negative, and Hazel's not running away. She's in this with me. I've never had anything like it before.

Now I'm pissed off, thinking about Hazel's situation with her dad and the house. She doesn't deserve to be treated the way she has. "It's not fucking okay," I say, gritting my teeth.

Hazel looks up at me, blinking. "What isn't?"

"How it all falls to you. You can't carry everyone's burdens. It's. Not. Okay." Deep inside my chest, I feel frustration. It's grating at my insides. I think it has been for a long time.

In response to that, Hazel gives me a smile that doesn't reach her eyes.

"I even feel bad that I hyped up a milkshake you never got to try," I continue. "I feel bad that our night at the firehouse got cut short and that you had to spend hours in the hospital."

"I needed to make sure you were okay," Hazel says, her voice softer. She gives my unbroken hand a light shake, my arm moving with the gesture. It makes me realize how rigidly I'm standing and how every muscle in my body is tight.

I take in a long breath and hold back the air, the discomfort, the shame. I haven't been this worked up about anything in a very long time.

"For the past few weeks, there's been nothing but problem after problem. Because of me. I hate that feeling," I say, sitting on the edge of the stage.

"Or because of me," Hazel says, looking down. She sits beside me. "Remember that's my luck you have."

"No. Now it's mine. You didn't do this. I don't want you to feel any blame." Admitting that I'm not okay still hasn't scared Hazel off. It emboldens me. "When my parents got divorced, my mom changed. She became so...positive. After my dad's affair, I think she wanted to put on a good face for me and my sisters. She wanted to pretend everything was fine, but I heard her crying in her room every night after he left. In the morning, you would never know it."

I pause, waiting to see if this is too much for Hazel. She's alert, though, and waiting to see what I'll say next, so I continue.

"After the accident, I wanted to talk to people about it. My ex-girlfriend, my mom, hell, even my dad. Any time I tried, I would just be told how lucky I was or scolded for how negative I was being about something that turned out okay. I couldn't help but think that if I had just gone into someone else's yard at a different time of day...what could've happened?"

"It sounds like you needed to process it," Hazel says.

"Maybe so, but everyone in my life only wanted to see the positive in things. Which, I get it. Who wants to feel bad?" I ask. "At some point, I just kind of accepted it, I guess. That became my role. My siblings and I all fell into line to help our mom. For a while, it felt like it worked. I was so out of control as a teenager. My parents were clearly unhappy, and alcohol numbed me. My actions felt like something I could control...until I couldn't." I frown. "So then I started controlling my thoughts."

"Yeah," Hazel says. "Sounds like you suppressed negative emotions and put a positive spin on everything."

"I didn't want to inconvenience anyone with my stress or shame. Still don't," I admit. "I'm the lucky one, and I'm so grateful for what my life has become. I survived, I got opportunities, I like my work. Things could've turned out very differently for me."

"Just because you're lucky and grateful doesn't mean you're not allowed to feel bad," she says. "I don't say this because I want you to feel low. But even if you positive platitude your negative feelings away, they'll still be there. Your issues will still be there. Recognizing when things aren't okay—when you're not okay—is just as important as spotting the good." She frowns a little as she says this, her eyebrows briefly pinching together.

It doesn't take long to recall all the problems that need fixing at work and on my own body. I still have weeks to go in this damn cast.

"Yeah. I'm starting to realize that," I admit. From the beginning, Hazel has been here, seeing me fail, make mistakes, be my least smooth self. It all could've easily driven her away by now, but it hasn't. I wrap my arm around her. "There's more I feel bad about."

"Okay. What else?" Hazel asks, resting her chin on my shoulder as she looks up at me. Gazing into her brown eyes brings me a sense of calm, but my next words are still filled with something strong.

"I feel bad that it's taken me this long to tell you how wonderful you are," I tell her. "You're smart, and you have such good ideas, and I really like hanging out with you. Also, have I told you you're beautiful? I feel like I probably haven't said that enough." I squeeze the bill of my hat as Hazel lets out a quiet laugh.

"The way you see me..." she says softly. "I've never really seen myself that way."

"I wish you would. It's one hell of a view."

She nudges me as her cheeks pinken. Something about the honesty of her reaction makes me want to open up even more.

"Mostly, though," I continue. "I feel bad that the other night I tiptoed around telling you exactly how I feel about you."

She bites down on her smile. "And how is it you feel about me?"

"I feel really fucking good about you, Zel."

She side-hugs me harder. "I feel really fucking good about you, too, Gan."

"I feel really fucking sad about that chandelier," Richie's voice says, startling us both. "You know how long it took me to hang that? What happened in here?"

Hazel and I jump up to meet him.

"Chaos. It's all chaos," I say, grabbing the broom and sweeping up the last bits of debris.

"I swear this theater is haunted!" Richie says, grabbing the garbage bag from me. "Logan, you look like hell. Take that break. I've got you covered. If I see you in here this weekend, I'm reporting you to HR."

"I want to report HR to HR," I say to him.

Richie lifts his hand above his head as he's walking away, like *I don't want to hear it*. "I don't want to see you 'til Monday!"

With that parting comment, Hazel looks at me with curiosity. "You're taking a break?"

"It's not a break."

"Where are you going?" she asks.

With everything going on, I must've forgotten to tell Hazel about Maine. "I told my mom I'd visit. I'm driving up early Saturday and coming back Sunday, so it's a quick turnaround. I typically work shows during the holidays, so I won't be able to visit for the rest of the year." And since I'm on a roll, I add, "I do also feel bad that dress rehearsal starts next week and I'm leaving for the weekend at literally the worst time."

"And you're driving because of what Bo said, aren't you? To avoid planes?"

"Exactly. The drive will eat up most of the time I could've spent there, but better to be safe."

She nods. "If there's no way you can get out of it, then let's go. I want to make sure you're okay."

I raise an eyebrow at her. "Let's?"

"I don't like the idea of you driving alone in a car for that long, given...you know," she says. "I'm off from the shop this weekend."

She's right. With the way things are going for me, I'll probably get two flat tires.

"It could be good for us to get out of town," Hazel adds. "The press conference coverage won't be as intense in Maine as it is here." She rubs my shoulder. "And I know what it's like to not want to go home. Maybe it'll be more...pleasant...if you have someone there with you to get through it."

I can feel that damn smile again.

"It would mean a lot to have you there. I would really like that," I say. "But you don't need to do that for me. I can't ask that of you."

"You're not asking. I am," she says with more certainty. She looks me straight in the eyes when she says this next part. "Logan, you're not alone in this. You're not alone in any of it. Not anymore."

I didn't know I needed to hear that.

"Okay?" she says.

Half of me falls in love with Hazel right then and there, but I keep that part to myself and just say, "Okay."

Chapter 17

HAZEL

Logan and I meet at the crack of dawn on Saturday morning at the rental car place to begin our journey north.

It's only when I'm buckling up that it fully hits me that I invited myself—on a whim, of course—to Maine. To meet Logan's family. It seems I'll never learn.

I half expected Toffee to be waiting in the car, but apparently Logan gets a break from cat-sitting duties when Mrs. Walker's back in town. I'm half disappointed by this.

Logan sets a pouch in my lap. I 100 percent didn't expect to be gifted a road trip kit from Logan. Inside is Advil (for my headaches), more Hello Kitty Band-Aids (just in case), water, a USB car charger, a granola bar (to stave off hanger), and, of course, cherry gummies.

We manage to beat the traffic going out of the city, spending the first hour in a peaceful quiet. We slowly wake up with the help of our cinnamon lattes and bagel sandwiches. Thankfully, my nose acclimates to the rental's overly strong Fall Spice air freshener as soon as we reach the highway.

I have the heat blasting on my side while Logan has his temperature set in the high sixties. He drives with his hands firmly placed on ten and two, his concentration on the road ahead.

In exchange for the early wake-up call, we're rewarded with a sunrise that bathes every inch of sky, tree, and road in gold.

I learn that Logan isn't a big talker when he drives—he's too focused—but he does like listening to classic rock.

Somehow, an hour zooms by. Logan seems to relax a little more. Now, he holds the wheel steady with his casted hand, his fingers wrapped around the base. Three hours in, he surprises me by grabbing my hand, holding it all the way up until he pulls into a gas station somewhere in Massachusetts and turns off the car.

There's a bright red neon sign shaped like a hand—palm lines included—just past the gas station's building. "Palmistry and Tarot Reading," it says, taunting me. Logan gets out of the car to fill up, clocking the sign only once the pump has been inserted into the tank.

He catches my eye. "No," he says immediately.

"I'm the one who says that," I say, climbing out of the car to stretch off the last few hours. "You're the one who says 'yes,' remember?" I peer over at the sign again. Of all the gas stations we could've stopped at, it had to be this one.

"Logan, I think we need to check it out." I tilt my head to the side to work out a kink in my neck. I'm too sore to consider the consequences.

"We're not going to a gas station fortune teller," he says.

"That building isn't *in* the gas station. Let's just see?" I say, using what's practically his own catchphrase to entice him.

He shakes his head. "There are basic life rules to live by. You don't eat gas station sushi, sandwiches, or salad. Same rules apply to gas station fortune tellers."

"It'll be like a temp check. To see if our efforts are doing anything," I reason. "More data will help."

Logan pushes the gas pump nozzle back into its holder. He

glances at me. I must look convincing—or desperate—enough, because he finally nods in agreement.

Turns out, the palmist's building is attached to the gas station. But in my defense, it has its own front door. The words "Fiona's Fortunes" are printed on it in swoopy lettering.

It's surprisingly modern on the inside. Behind a simple white podium, another neon sign spells out "#HighFive" and an @ sign with the business name and a few numbers.

This has less of the vibes of a tourist trap and more of someone who might read our palms and film it for social media.

"Hiiii!" A young woman, who looks to be in her early twenties, pops out from behind a pink curtain. "Sorry, I was wrapping a Live."

By that, she must mean an Instagram Live, which only sounds familiar because Jerry had to once explain the difference between that and a Reel to me for one of the brand deals he had "in the works."

"Welcome! I'm Fiona Lee, and this is my place!" she says, smiling brightly at us. "Well, my dad owns the gas station next door."

"I'm... Zel, and this is Gan."

Beside me, Logan laughs into his fist.

"You two are so cute. Can I get a high five?" she crosses over to me, her hand held up above her head. I awkwardly return the gesture. She turns to give one to Logan when she sees his cast and fist bumps him instead. She waves us both farther into the space. "Come! Let's get those palms read. I promise, readings are quick because you're at a gas station. Clearly, you're on your way somewhere."

A part of me is worried Fiona learned her knowledge of palmistry from social media and that this will be a huge waste of time and money. It might even throw us off course with everything we've tried. But I don't want to judge Fiona by her neon signs and intense energy. She deserves a chance. And if it's all nonsense, we'll wipe our hands of it.

I'm laughing to myself about my pun when Logan takes me by the elbow and whispers, "Remind me why we're doing this again?"

"We're collecting data," I whisper back. Admittedly, I'm also kind of curious to know what about our lives is already written on our bodies. I keep this one to myself.

Fiona guides us to a back room where there are pillow puffs and a low, wooden, antique table. Fairy lights drape across the ceiling with posters of hands covered in intricate lines layered over the walls. In the corner are stacks upon stacks of boxes of candy bars.

"My dad uses this place for storage," Fiona says with an eye roll. "But I get the place for free, so I can't complain. Please sit where you like."

Logan and I sit on puffs next to each other. His knees knock mine as he crosses them, his long limbs pretzeling over each other on the ground. Fiona sets her phone on a charger behind her and sits across the table from us.

"Because the palm lines vary on each hand, I prefer to read both, but I see that won't be possible for you," Fiona says to Logan. "Are you both right-handed?"

We nod.

"Let's focus on your dominant hands, then," Fiona decides as she pumps sanitizer into her hands before offering it to us. "Readings are forty dollars each. I'm fast, but I'm good at what I do. That's what you're paying for. I've been doing this full-time for years. I have 1.2 million followers on my socials, and I was taught everything I know by my auntie, who's a fortune teller in Taiwan. Does that help?"

Fiona's got good intuition, I'll give her that. Or my skepticism isn't as subtle as I think.

I give it a second for regret to sink in. Surprisingly, I find that I trust Fiona, and not because she has over a million followers. I glance at Logan, who shrugs.

I nod to Fiona, and we begin.

Fiona reaches for my right hand and stretches it out. I stare at my palm that I've never paid much attention to, tracing the way the lines carve their own path in my skin.

Fiona runs a long, pink manicured nail over my palm. There are diamonds pressed onto her nails in the shape of arched lines. Like palm lines.

"Your hand lines reveal your personality and character traits. I focus on the five big ones: Life, Wisdom, Love, Marriage, and Fate," she says, her bubbly voice surprisingly reassuring. "Ooh, clear palm lines. You've had good luck recently."

Logan gives me a knowing look.

"You have a solid Life line," Fiona says, pulling my attention back to her. "It's long and deep. You have a strong life energy."

"Are you able to tell how long I'll live?" I ask curiously.

Or...wait. Do I even want to know that?

"Common misconception," she replies. "That's not what the line's about." She runs her nail horizontally across my palm, tracing another specific line. "Your Wisdom line overlaps a lot with your Life line. You're careful, but you worry too much."

Now I'm sweating.

On the next line, Fiona's nail crosses from just below my middle finger to the edge of my hand, moving downward. It's a particularly sensitive and more ticklish spot. "Your Love line is shorter. You're a little irrational, a little narrow-minded."

I take this in but don't respond.

"The way it curves down like this and has these splits, though"—Fiona pokes at my skin where the line breaks off—"means you're willing to sacrifice everything for it."

"For what? Love?" I want to laugh. "No, I don't think so."

Fiona hums. "You say that so confidently, but your palms don't lie." She taps the outside of my palm. "Your Marriage lines. Long means you're picky."

Not picky enough, given my track record with marriage.

"And your Fate line, which is also your Career or Money line," Fiona says, leaning in closer. She traces twice vertically from my wrist to the center of my palm. "You have two!"

"Does that mean she has two different destinies?" Logan asks. He's been quiet this entire time, watching very closely.

"It means you have big changes ahead," Fiona says. "In your life or work. Maybe both. They're straight, though, so you have a lucky future ahead. Your life looks stable."

Stable. I've never considered my life to be stable before. Not as a kid. Not as a young adult. Not even as a lottery-winning adult.

Something about this experience is weirdly comforting. It's like, in this world filled with uncertainty, there are at least a few knowns right here in the palm of my hand.

Fiona instructs me to press my fingers together side by side. She holds my hand up to the light. "You hardly have any gaps between your fingers. You don't let money slip through easily," she says.

A very thin crack of yellow from the overhead light peeks through below my knuckles. That sounds about right, too.

Logan grips my thigh softly and gives me an uneasy smile. Probably because he knows he's next.

Fiona turns my hand over in hers and gives it a little tap. "Thank you for sharing your lines with me." She gestures to Logan. "You're up!"

He doesn't take her hands. Instead, he apologizes, stands, and leaves. My mouth drops open as he disappears behind the curtain.

"Don't worry," Fiona assures me. "That happens a lot."

I stand to follow him, hesitating at the door. "Fiona, from what you saw..." I say, turning back around, "do you think I—things—will turn out okay?"

She gives me an encouraging smile. "Only you can decide that."

Feels at odds with her whole business of interpreting-lines-literally-etched-into-my-skin, but okay.

I thank Fiona for her time. She points out the QR code for payment. Even though Logan didn't get a reading, I decide to pay for both sessions. Plus, a big tip. Past me couldn't imagine spending this much money on something like this.

Before I go, Fiona stops me at the front door. "Zel! Remember, your palm lines don't solely decide your future," she says, her tone laced with a different, more thoughtful tone. This isn't the peppy Fiona who I've spent the last ten minutes with. "I captured you now in this moment, but over time, your palm lines evolve. Just as you, too, evolve. I've shared my interpretation and my insights, but we all have the power to change our lives. To change our fortunes."

"How?"

"Stop doing the things that aren't working for you," she says simply, her easy-breezy attitude back. Then she waves goodbye, leaving me alone out front with that fortune-cookie advice.

Chapter 18

HAZEL

Logan's parked outside waiting for me in the car. Once I'm buckled up, he starts driving. As soon as we're back on the highway and moving in the right direction, apologies spill out of him.

I stop him mid-sentence. "Logan, I'm the one who's sorry. I should've never put you in that position. You told me no, and I didn't listen."

He shakes his head. "No, you were right. I'm the one who normally says yes. I just didn't want to hear anything bad." He's white-knuckling the steering wheel. "I freaked out."

This is Logan, the guy who joins strangers' fortune readings on a whim. The guy who sets up impromptu dates on firehouse rooftops. The guy who, up until this very moment, has never turned down a new experience. That Logan was overconfident and unafraid to push his limit. Now he worries how a palm reader will interpret his hands.

Maxwell talked about mindset and trying new things and seeing the positive. All things, I've come to realize, that Logan has already done for a lot of his life. Lately, though, he's been retreating.

"Also, I'm pretty sure this hand has my better lines," he says, lifting his casted arm.

I feel a smile form.

Logan taps against the wheel with his cast. "Damn, okay. Thought that one was pretty good."

"That was funny," I say.

He looks confused. "Was it? I couldn't tell."

"I smiled."

Logan finds the right moment to steal a longer look at me. "I must not have caught it. Sometimes I have a hard time knowing what you're feeling."

I rock back against the seat. "You do? I thought I looked amused, I guess?"

"It's my bad. I just didn't see it is all," he says, setting his jaw.

I twist to face him, even though he's focused on the road. "Do you feel like it's hard..." I swallow, bracing myself. "To connect with me?"

Logan reaches for my hand. "I've never connected with anyone so quickly the way I have with you."

I'm relieved. But I can tell there's more he wants to say.

"I didn't realize I wasn't reacting," I admit. "Is this what it's been like since we met?"

"You were pretty annoyed when we met," he says with a half smile. "That much was clear."

I cross my arms over my stomach. "Yeah, I guess that wasn't hard to tell."

"I'm used to connecting with people through emotions," he says. "Which we established a couple days ago is probably not great if it's only through one particular emotion, but...yeah, I like getting feedback. A frown if I've said something you don't like. A laugh if my joke is funny. Otherwise, I guess I feel alone in an experience."

I had no idea I came off like that. It's like having a mirror held up, and instead of a reflection I'd expect to see, I'm faced with a different version of myself. Strangely, this one feels closer to the truth of who I am than any I've seen before.

"I feel that, too," I say quietly. "Lonely."

As bizarre as it sounds, his noticing my lack of reactions makes me feel...seen.

"I was so young when my mom died. It was quick and sudden. But it was earth-shattering," I say, my voice shakier than I intend it to be. I clear my throat.

"Even an earthquake that only lasts a few seconds can be damaging," Logan says.

I nod. "That's how it felt. Life as we knew it changed overnight. It became such an emotional roller coaster with my dad." I look out the window at the blurring landscape. "He'd gamble, make bets, lose so much money one day but then win the next. I got exhausted from feeling the highs and the lows." My voice levels out. "So, at six, I had to grow up and take care of everything and everyone. To do that, I had to turn off my reactions and emotions."

Logan grabs my hand and brings my just-read palm to his lips, gently dropping a kiss on what I remember being my Love line. It's his way of encouraging me to continue.

"If something hard is happening, I try to level out," I tell him. "I reach for the nearest thing that can make me happy, so I don't have to sit in the lows."

Quick marriages. Tattoos. Bathroom sex.

"Or I'd rather feel nothing," I say. "But I'm numbing the good stuff, too. When nice feelings pop up, I don't let myself stay there because I know that happiness won't last. Staying in the zero-feelings zone is easiest."

"Is it, though?"

I blink. "No. Well, maybe it was once. And now it's what I'm used to. God, I'm such a hypocrite. At the theater, I told you that you're allowed to feel bad. Who am I to say that when I don't allow myself to feel the bad or the good?"

"You were trying to help me," Logan reasons. "It's easier to see what others need than what we need ourselves."

"I've kept everything in for so long," I say. After a long pause, I add, "Too long."

"We've both been keeping too much in," Logan says. "Maybe we can sit in our lows together."

"What about the highs?"

Logan shakes his head. "Nah. We don't want to be *too* happy."

I shake my head, playing along.

"I've been living in muted shades," I say. "But it's like ever since meeting you—"

Ever since meeting Logan, everything's been a bit brighter. More vibrant.

Oh. *Oh.*

He's still looking at the road, focused on our safety. Which is good. I need the moment to collect myself.

"Ever since meeting me...?" Logan asks. His hand slips from mine to my leg, right above my knee.

"Ever since meeting you..." I say slowly. "I guess I've...I've felt a wider spectrum of emotions. It's like meeting you has cracked me open, just a little." It's a lie. He's cracked me wide open.

I'm shallow breathing now, my chest rising and falling faster at this admission. It's scary, being vulnerable.

Logan gives me a small grin. "Toffee did most of that."

I laugh. Out loud this time. I catch Logan stealing a glance as I do, like he wants to capture my pleased reactions.

I trail my finger down my forearm where the two long scratches have faded. My fingers land on my charm bracelet. I find the cat and rub my thumb over its nose and ears.

"What kinds of emotions do you have?" he asks.

My fingers drop from the charm. "What?"

"Tell me what you're feeling, good or bad. Let's start with the good."

I see what he's doing. He's creating his own version of what I did to him at the theater.

I look around at the car's dashboard and cupholders, as though I'll find my response there. Out the window, there's nothing but highway and trees and signs. In the distance, gray clouds loom. We're driving straight toward them.

I spot the Wendy's logo on an exit sign. "I feel good about Frostys."

"I like those, too," Logan says. "What else?"

I note the eighty degrees I've set the heat to on the passenger side. In my defense, I'm always cold. "I feel good about the temperature."

"You feel good about the temperature? Like outside or in the car?" Logan clarifies. He's taking this more seriously than I am.

"In here. It's comfortable."

"Well, your limbs are always cold so that makes sense," he says, waiting. "Is that it?"

Of course that's not it. Lately, there's been so much to feel good about. Mostly because of him.

"I don't want to say it out loud," I finally say.

"Why? What will happen if you do?"

I wait a few beats before saying, "It might go away." I shift against the leather seat. "Speaking the good into existence feels risky. When my dad won bets or when certain teams won, he'd talk about his luck and how good he had it. How on top of the world he was. But the high never lasted, and that only led to disappointment. Even when we first met, you were so confident about how you always won games and how things worked out for you. And then they didn't. It feels like jinxing."

"I knew you were a little superstitious." He squeezes my leg. "You know, Hazel, when something good happens for you, you're allowed to enjoy it. You're even allowed to say when something makes you happy. Doing so won't take that truth away. I'm not going to say something cliché like you have to know the bad to know the good. I want to, but I won't."

"You literally just said it."

Logan laughs. "The reality is happy feelings won't last forever. But what does?"

"So with that logic...if the good doesn't last forever, then that means the negative feelings won't either, doesn't it?" I ask pointedly.

He narrows his eyes at me, understanding right away what I'm getting at. "Fair enough. That's...yeah."

I check the car's temperature, which has stayed at eighty this entire conversation. Even after I mentioned it.

"I feel good about the interviews I've done," I say without being prompted, answering his earlier question for real. Though I do still have team interviews. "We'll see what ends up happening. I still might not get the job."

Clearly, I can't help myself.

"Regardless of what happens, though, you're happy with how you handled it?" Logan asks.

"Actually, yeah. I am." I prepared. I had solid answers. I gave my very best.

Admitting this is like shedding an invisible weight. A sense of comfort courses through me, and I feel compelled to say more. I reach for whatever comes to mind first.

"I feel good that I was able to help my brother. I even feel good about that painting I made of you." This next one's easy. "I feel good about celebrating my birthday."

"You mean acknowledging?" Logan asks.

"That night was a celebration if I've ever seen one."

I get a ripple-smile for that comment.

"I feel good about being here with you. Even though we're on our way to Maine. To meet your family," I say.

Logan laughs. "Stranger things have happened in the past month."

That is so true.

Turns out, I feel good about a lot of things. And nothing can take away what I've just spoken out loud. Contentment bubbles up through my center. Every time I'm with Logan, this is how I feel. I almost dare to imagine a future where every day could be like this.

I'm probably getting ahead of myself, but I've burst open the dam of positive feelings, and now they're all rushing toward me. I expect them to topple me sideways with their velocity. Send me tumbling into the deep end. After a few long, agonizing seconds, that's not what happens.

Instead, the deluge of emotions lifts me up. I get to ride this wave. And it's not excruciating.

It's exhilarating.

So I continue to linger in this moment. Push it a little further. "What if I said I could see a future with you in it?" I ask.

Yeah. I've definitely gotten ahead of myself. Logan and I have known each other only a short while. It's too soon to be saying stuff like that. I jumped to our future, and we're still just trying to get through the present. And now we're stuck in a car together for another four hours.

But Logan's beaming from the driver's seat, his grin big and goofy and just so, so happy. He looks at me like I've hung the daytime moon. The one that requires an extra second to find it, like it's a special sighting that needs to be earned. The one we see when we least expect it.

"I predict that we'd be happy, even though sometimes we'd be sad, too," he says. "But we'd have each other. And together, I think we could get through anything."

When he says this, it feels true. Even in four and a half weeks, we've gone through so much. But I haven't bolted. And Logan has only been a steady presence.

I feel the smile grow on my lips. I hope I'm reflecting how he's looking at me. I want him to feel what he makes me feel.

I spoke my happiness out loud, and it was returned. When I glance out toward the gray clouds, they're still there. We have a ways to go before we reach them, though.

Until we do, I'm going to enjoy the sunshine.

Logan flicks on the turn signal and takes the next exit.

We're now straying from the directions on his phone. "Are we out of gas already?" I ask.

"My girl feels good about Frostys," he says. "So that's exactly what we're going to get."

Chapter 19

LOGAN

The second half of the drive is scenic. We pass houses that look like boats, inflatable lobsters on top of restaurants, and in one person's yard, a moss-covered stone well so picturesque that Hazel insisted I pull over so we could make a wish in it.

We get to Mom's in the late afternoon without getting a flat tire, running out of gas, or getting into any accidents, though I do somehow manage to run over a few pots of mums lining the driveway.

Hazel and I walk around the house and up to the deck, where all the noise is coming from.

I point out everyone I know to Hazel: my mom, my stepfather, my older sister and her boyfriend, my younger sister, my oldest stepbrother and his husband, my other stepbrother and his girlfriend. Everyone else must be friends and coworkers. They're all paired off in conversation, warming themselves next to space heaters and the fire pit.

We meet Mom at the outdoor dining table that's covered in bowls filled with chives, sour cream, cheddar cheese, diced bacon, and butter balls. My stepfather, Warren, sets a giant silver tub of foil-wrapped potatoes onto the end of the table, completing the baked potato bar. When he sees us, he doesn't bother taking off his oven mitts before wrapping Hazel and me into a group hug.

Originally from Canada, Warren was transferred to a hospital in our town in Washington. That's where he and Mom met as nurses after my parents had divorced. After a couple years of dating, they got married. Warren's kids were also in their teens and twenties, so we were all off doing our own thing. We mostly get to know each other at holidays and gatherings.

"Thanks for coming," Warren says to us. "You really didn't have to go to the trouble."

"Wouldn't miss it," I say. "This one's for real?"

"You can only retire so many times, I suppose," he says, clasping his mitt-covered hands together. Warren has retired about four times at this point. He never sets an end date, which means he keeps showing up to work.

"Have you had your last day yet?" I ask Warren.

"Last Friday. I had to make sure my patients were in a good spot," he says, eyeing my mom. "Your mother is happy."

"It's going to be great!" Mom says, overhearing our conversation and meeting us at the head of the table. "We'll have more time for traveling. We can seriously think about that boat you've always wanted."

Warren nods. "It'll be great," he echoes.

Mom has tongs in one hand, an empty plate in the other. It takes her a second to notice my arm. "Oh my god, Logan!"

"This? It's nothing," I say, giving her a hug. "Just a scratch. Mom, meet Haze—"

"It's clearly not. What happened?" Mom asks. She's wild-eyed, her tone coated in concern.

"I fell down a few stairs." I shrug.

She gives my shoulder a shake. "Oh, honey, this could've been so much worse. You could've broken your whole arm."

"Yeah," I mumble. "Phew."

THE FORTUNE FLIP

Mom glances over to Hazel. "Honey, it's so wonderful to meet you!" she says, sweeping her into a hug.

"Your house is...wow. It's beautiful," a wide-eyed Hazel tells Mom. "I love the scallop siding. Was that part of the original house?"

Mom looks delighted, her worry no longer present. "Thank you for noticing," she says. "Logan did that. A house on the coastline needs pizzazz."

"It looks like a mermaid's house," Hazel says, staring up at the 2,800-square-foot house painted a sea foam green behind us. "I mean that as a compliment."

Mom beams. "I take it as one!"

Hazel looks like she's lost in a daydream. "I'd love to do something similar with my grandparents' house. I'm taking notes."

Mom's house is perched on the rocky coastline overlooking Penobscot Bay. It's an unobstructed view with endless blue water in the distance, trees flanking the house on both sides. At this time of year, the leaves are painted every shade in the warm color palette. Set against the bright bay and sparsely clouded sky, it's practically a fall paradise.

Mom points to the round windows built into the dining room nook and on the second floor. "Logan added those, as well as the cabinetry in the kitchen. Oh! And that entire setup," she says, directing Hazel's attention to the long dining table and benches I built. "Obviously, the backs of the benches needed to look like shells."

"*Obviously*," my oldest sister, Eva, says as she and her boyfriend, Roy, join our trio. She jerks her thumb toward me. "If it can be built, this one'll do it."

"You start your own carpentry business yet, or what?" Roy asks me.

"Logan just made head carpenter on Broadway," Mom says proudly as she emphasizes her last word. "He's very busy."

"Head carpenter already?" Tina, my stepbrother Joe's girlfriend, asks. "Did I miss this announcement?"

"I didn't make one," I tell her.

Roy makes a show of blowing out a big breath of air. "You're living the dream," he says. "I don't know how you do it on a carpenter's salary. I wish I could live in the city."

"We talking about Logan?" Joe asks, a half-eaten whoopie pie in hand. "I need some of your luck, man. I'm up for a promotion at work."

I shift uncomfortably at this, but no one seems to notice. Except Hazel. She puts her hand on my lower back and rubs it in small, slow circles.

At this point, everyone's gathered around, so I introduce them to Hazel.

"I didn't know you had a girlfriend, Logan!" Jane, my younger sister, says, oblivious to the fact I haven't actually labeled her as such.

Hazel doesn't correct Jane. Neither do I. We talked about our future but not what we officially are to each other. It's not something we anticipated having to address, which, looking back now, was a big oversight. What else was my family going to think about me bringing someone home?

But this isn't just someone.

"Guess Logan's not big on sharing much these days," Eva says.

Mom sets the tongs and plate down and picks up a ceramic jar. "Has everyone entered the raffle? Warren, make sure your colleagues have put their names in, will you please?"

Warren sets off as my siblings groan. There's always some sort of annual competition, but today's sounds less involved than usual.

"Why even go through the effort? Logan's gonna win, like always," my other stepbrother, Nick, teases.

Bruce, Nick's husband, nudges him and shoots me an apologetic look.

"Think positive, Nick," Mom says. "Maybe then you'll win this year."

"Remember that one year we had to whittle?" Jane asks Nick. "That competition was rigged."

Eva laughs. "Lucky Logan never misses."

If only they knew. Though if I lose this competition, there will be questions. In years prior, I've won pumpkin carving, soufflé baking, lobster roll cook-off, and, as mentioned, whittling.

If this were any other time, if I weren't so shaky in my luck, I'd laugh at this comment. I'd joke that Nick's just jealous. That I can't help that I'm naturally good at these random skills.

Today, though, my siblings' comments nag at me. *Easily?* Besides the whittling, which took me years to learn how to do well, those competitions weren't easy. Nor did they come naturally to me. But while everyone else either gave up halfway through or half-assed it, I took it seriously.

Maxwell's words replay in my mind. *Once you moved beyond 'no,' were you in the right mindset?*

Has it been luck, then, like everyone's always told me? Like I've always thought?

This is too much to process right now, especially with a group of people irritated at my winning streak. But for the first time, a surge of self-compassion trickles through me.

My shoulders drop as I relax a little. Maybe I'll lose and break my streak this year.

Maybe that's okay.

I push down my annoyance and focus on Hazel. My family's always seen me in a certain lucky light, while Hazel's always doubted that part of me. For the first time, it strikes me how freeing it is to not be viewed like that by her.

"There will be more than one winner," Mom says. "Just look at all those prizes!"

On another table, closer to the house, there's an assortment of items: bottles of wine, a basket of cookies shaped and iced to look like fish and fly rods, a few gift cards, and golf ball boxes tied with ribbon.

"Whatever the biggest prize is, Logan will get it. I'd put money on it," Jane says. Nick takes her up on her offer.

I don't bother trying to convince Jane otherwise.

Those of us who haven't entered write our names down and drop the slips into the jar. Then we eat.

"I'm obsessed with this baked potato bar," Hazel says flatly, and mostly to herself. I wouldn't have been able to tell she was into it if she hadn't said so. Then she looks up at me, and there's the tell: a slight crinkle in her eyes, a glimmer of excitement. "The red onion is a great touch."

Hazel may have learned to dampen her expectations for good things and to keep her reactions under wraps, but they're still there when you really pay attention. With time, I want to learn all her tells.

"Let's go! The butter's melting," Jane sarcastically says behind me, nudging my back.

I take my time putting a potato on my plate, just to mess with her. The weather's in the fifties. The butter's not melting anytime soon. I cut down the middle of the potato, a curl of steam escaping. I scoot forward toward Hazel before Jane makes comments about the bacon.

Ahead of me, Hazel's eyebrows are furrowed slightly as she considers how much sour cream she wants. The tip of her tongue pokes out the side of her mouth as she thinks. It's the cutest damn thing I've ever seen.

"I can feel you watching me," she whispers, landing on two scoops of sour cream.

"I could watch you do this all day."

A smile plays on her lips as she blinks at me through her long eyelashes.

"Logan, what the hell?" Jane says over my shoulder. "Seriously?"

"Oh my god, Jane. We're getting chives, and then we're done," I tell her. What's her problem today?

Jane pushes her phone into my face. "I'm not talking about chives, Logan. I'm talking about you winning the lottery."

Beside me, Hazel drops the spoon into the bowl of shredded cheese.

My siblings look confused. Behind us in line, Mom laughs. "The lottery? Logan would never. Jane, you're a riot today." She claps her hands together. "Come on, get moving. We've got twenty nurses and doctors behind us who know how to use a scalpel and aren't afraid to use it."

"I'm being serious. My friend just messaged me this photo," Jane says, following us over to the prize table. "Logan and...Hazel? You both won?" She shakes her head. "I don't get it. Why do you both look old?"

My siblings have all heard Jane and surround us, quickly loading up their plates. Warren's coworkers look pleased as they scoot closer to the food.

"Logan won the lottery? Wow, I'm so surprised," Nick says sarcastically, his mouth full of potato.

Eva twirls her fork in the air. "Lucky Logan strikes again!" she says.

Jane hands me her phone. "Explain."

"Do you think it was the reporter?" Hazel whispers to me.

We both stare at the screen and try to process what we're seeing. Glaring back at us is a social media post with the photo of me and Hazel at the press conference. We look eighty years old. Sure, our names are on the giant check, but we knew that would happen. It was a risk that my family and their friends might recognize the names if the news spread widely enough.

And up until now, it hadn't.

"Okay, it's a photo," I say. "What about it?"

"Did you go through all of them?" Jane asks. "It's a carousel."

"Is it supposed to move? What does that mean?"

Jane makes a motion with her thumb. "Slide through the photos."

My family huddles up behind us, trying to catch a glimpse. The press conference photo was just the first photo of many. The second photo is a snapshot of security camera footage. There I am in black and white at the counter with Hazel on the day we met, when I bought her bandages and candy. When I bought the lottery ticket.

It's old us and young us. I'm still not seeing the connection. The silicone masks weren't even close to our likeness.

Hazel reaches over and swipes across the screen to the third photo. It's a zoomed in image of my arm and the stuff on the counter with a timestamp in the corner.

"Logan. Your bracelet," she says, pointing to the screen.

My stomach plummets like it's an elevator and my body is a drop tower.

My hand shakes a little as I slide to the next picture. Hazel and I are back in our disguises, but the photo is zoomed in on my arm.

And what's poking out from underneath my sleeve? My red bracelet.

The last image is of a man standing in front of a bodega with his arms spread wide. He's grinning like *he's* just won the lottery.

THE FORTUNE FLIP

"Why does that guy look so familiar?" Hazel asks.

I tap the name above the photo, and it takes me to a page with a lot more pictures in a grid. Interior shots of a bodega, new items on sale, and, more recently, a promo of the growing Powerball number. Then I recognize something that brings me back to how all the dots are connected: an *Indiana Jones* shirt.

It's the social media page of the bodega clerk.

I skim the caption: Thanks, Logan and Hazel, for stopping by the shop.

He goes on to say more celebratory-toned words about how the Powerball ticket was sold at his bodega, along with a list of store hours.

Hazel grips my arm and shakes it. "Plane. The plane!"

Right there, on the bodega clerk's shirt, is the vintage airplane bursting through the clouds.

"This guy really knows how to tell a story," Nick says. "That was a journey."

Someone's finger pulls down on the screen, and the page refreshes. "His follower count jumped by a hundred in the time it took us to look through those photos," Bruce says.

"It doesn't seem malicious," Warren says, who joined the huddle at some point. "The guy's excited. You know how much business this will bring? They might even have lines out the door. He has a lucky store now."

Lucky. I wish that word never existed.

"How did he even find out?" Hazel asks.

"Doesn't the bodega get money when they sell the winning ticket? When the payout hit, he probably wanted to find out who it came from," Jane guesses.

Warren nods slowly. "If that's his shop, that would make a huge difference for him."

Roy gives us a thumbs-up. "Good for you guys for shopping local."

I already know how this will land with Hazel. "This is an invasion of privacy," I say, handing Jane her phone.

Jane takes one look at my face and then does what we all do when things get hard. "Why are you upset?" she asks. "You won the lottery! I mean, it's a lot of money, but it's not as much as what you would've gotten from Dad—"

"Jane, stop," I say, not wanting to hear the rest of that sentence.

"Your faces are blurry in that footage," Eva says, probably trying to be helpful.

It's like we fall into roles when we're all back together, saying the words from a script in the name of comfort. I find myself trying to spin this into something that will hurt a little bit less.

"This is really bad," Hazel says, forcefully mushing her toppings into her potato.

"Your names were already out there," Jane says flippantly, swiping back to the first photo. "Like, literally. Logan Wells. Hazel Yen. Why'd you even bother with disguises?"

"None of you knew until now," Hazel says. She's still distractedly mushing, her potato and toppings now a thick paste. "Obviously, we didn't want to be outed if we were in disguises. Now our real faces are attached to this."

"I don't think anyone's gonna care too much about this," Mom chimes in.

Hazel abandons her plate on the table, breaking free from the group and moving to the bench on the edge of the deck.

I make a move to follow her, but Jane cuts in front of me. "I don't get it, Logan," she says, not even trying to disguise her irritation. "You won't accept your inheritance, but you'll take lottery money? If your luck ran out and you needed help, you could've come to us."

I glare at her. "You don't know what you're talking about."

"I know that you almost risked our inheritances because you didn't want yours," Jane nearly shouts. I can't remember the last time I've seen her get this worked up. "We can't all be as lucky as you, Logan. Our lives don't just fall into place like yours does."

Jane's gone a step too far, and she knows it. Eva knows it. Mom knows it.

"When you see me, all you can think of is luck," I shoot back. "You assume everything's so easy, like it's just happening to me, but maybe you need to take a better look."

"Okay, everyone take a deep breath," Mom says, trying to diffuse the situation. "Everything happens for a reason. Just think of what you can learn from this."

"Yeah, like don't ever rob a bank," Joe says as he crushes his second whoopie pie. Tina nudges him in the side.

Mom holds up her hands like she has the answers. "If we can just stay positive, this will get better. Freaking out isn't going to do anything. Let's just—"

"Actually, Mom, this really sucks," I snap.

Everyone goes quiet.

I have the floor. I might as well take it. "Hazel and I are allowed to feel mad about this. Freaking out might not fix this, but happy thoughts sure as shit won't either," I say. I'm frustrated, and I sound it. I haven't taken this tone with Mom in decades.

If Mom's stunned by my outburst, she doesn't show it. "Stop worrying. This is hardly news. It'll blow over in a few days. You'll get through this," she says evenly.

She's not hearing me. No one is.

That's not true. Not no one. Hazel hears me.

And the worst part about all of this is what Hazel must be going through. She's got her legs tucked up into her chest, her chin resting on her knees. She's staring out at the sparkling bay. In a place that feels so free and open and wide, she's made herself small.

The happiness that lit up Hazel's face earlier is long gone. I'd do anything to put it back there.

I walk over to her and reach for her hand. "Shirley MacLaine," I say.

She looks up at me, a little dazed, but doesn't hesitate to place her colder-than-usual hand in mine.

And then we get the hell out of there.

Chapter 20

HAZEL

We coast down the highway in silence. I keep checking my phone, waiting for a call or text message from Dad about the news.

Or Jerry. He's the one who's chronically online.

There's a chance they'll never know. But the waiting to find out is the worst part.

I stare at the ocean through the windshield. It helps dull some of what I'm feeling. I imagine jumping into it and swimming away from all my problems. A muscle in my arm twitches, longing for the burn of a butterfly stroke.

"What's with your safe word?" I finally ask Logan, curious about the name that actually did help us escape one of my problems.

Logan loosens his grip on the steering wheel. "Shirley MacLaine got lucky when she was in *The Pajama Game* on Broadway. Her life changed when she filled in for Carol Haney, the star of the musical, after she sprained her ankle," he explains. "MacLaine hadn't rehearsed but pulled off the show. And who was in the audience? A Hollywood producer who was impressed enough with her performance to offer her a contract. She was in the right place at the right time."

"So we say her name to get out of being in the wrong place at the wrong time," I say.

"Exactly."

Logan turns onto a road that leads to a narrow bridge. After a few more turns, we're pulling into a gravel parking lot that's just steps from the harbor. There are picnic tables scattered over the grass and pavement and Adirondack chairs facing the water. A coastline is dotted with rocks in the distance. A small red shack perches on the water's edge with a sign that reads "Luna's Lobster Shack." Below that is a smaller sign with "Last day of the season" and its hours printed on it. We made it right before it closes down for the winter.

"I'm not even gonna say it," I say.

Logan lets out a humorless huff. "You said when life's a shitshow, add water. So that's what we're doing. We need to talk, but we're not doing that on an empty stomach. The situation calls for the best lobster rolls, and these are it."

We take our place in line. It goes fast, and we each order a lobster roll with chips and a blueberry soda. Logan points out an empty picnic table in an ideal spot on the deck, but as soon as he heads toward it, a family cuts in.

We keep looking, but the place is packed and the hunt for open chairs is competitive. Logan heads back to the shack when his name is called for our order. Just as I begin my solo search, two Adirondack chairs on a secluded patch of grass become available.

"These are the hardest seats to get!" Logan says, returning with the seafood-filled tray. He places it on a table connecting the two chairs.

I pour melted butter over thick chunks of cooked lobster as Logan rips open his bag of chips. The toasted bun gives way between my teeth as the fresh lobster, butter, and mayonnaise burst across my taste buds. The salty butter and the sweet lobster are a perfectly balanced and thoroughly satisfying combination.

Once our rumbling stomachs are satiated, Logan angry-wipes his mouth with a napkin. He turns to me. "Hazel, I'm so, so sorry," he says. "I've had to say that a lot lately, and I'm sorry for that, too."

I set my lobster roll into the food boat. "Logan—"

"Wait, I'd like to say this," he says, looking more stressed than anyone should be next to this breathtaking view. "Our identities being revealed, that's on me." He pats his chest. "This is my fault. At least we get lobster out of it?" He frowns. "Wait, let me try that again. This sucks."

His attempt at vulnerability kind of works. My face relaxes slightly, but everything still feels too heavy to fully commit to a grin. "It was an honest mistake," I say.

It's a knee-jerk reaction. Hearing it out loud in this context startles me. It's a phrase I use with Dad and Jerry when they apologize for blowing their savings and then ask me for money. When they break promises and try to make excuses. With them, I try to justify their actions. But I say those words without meaning it, without trusting that they are actually sorry. What else am I supposed to do? They're family.

With Logan, though, when I say "it was an honest mistake," I realize I actually mean it. In our entire time of knowing each other, he's never once given me any reason not to trust him. He's kept every promise to me. He's remembered the smallest commitments. He's owned his mistakes. He's owning it now. Logan is reliable in all the big and small ways.

"It was an accident, but it doesn't make this okay," he says. "If I could take it all back, I would."

I try to resist the immediate distrust that spins up inside of me.

If I could take it all back, I would. They're words I heard constantly when I grew up. Yet, while I'm sure Dad wished he could redo his actions, could go back in time to get the money he spent back, he never did anything about it. In the future, history would repeat itself. Maybe his words weren't lies, but they certainly weren't the truth.

I swallow my bitter skepticism and replace the taste with another bite of lobster roll. I finish chewing and then ask, "Would you really? Take it all back?"

The look on Logan's face shows me how much this is eating at him. Behind his eyes, I see an entire debate playing out. I envision a positive platitude popping up in his mind and him whacking it down. Pop up. Whack down. Repeat.

He takes off his hat and runs his hand back and forth through his hair. The strands stick up in every direction. "I don't know. But I do know that…I feel bad," he starts. "I feel bad that I messed this up for you. I wish I could blame the fortune, but this…this wasn't about luck. It was stupidity. My own. I failed to think about the details. The masks, wigs, costumes…the accent! It was all pointless because I wasn't careful enough."

"We can escape the city, but we can't escape the Internet," I say.

I glance down at Logan's wrist. And right there, poking out from under his long-sleeve shirt is the tail of his red bracelet. Our true identities were revealed because of…string? The whole thing is absurd. The anxiety bouncing around inside of me mutates into amusement.

Suddenly, I bust out laughing at the sheer ridiculousness of it all. "Seriously, don't beat yourself up about it," I say, catching my breath. "It's harder to remember things when you're eighty."

Logan starts laughing, too. We go on like this for a minute or two, leaning back in our chairs with food boats rocking in our laps. The laughter feels like a release. Like the sunshine and lobster rolls and water are doing their jobs.

I'm laughing in the middle of my worst-case scenario. No. *We're* laughing in the middle of our worst-case scenario. I'm not alone in this.

Instead of feeling numb, I'm tingly and light. I steal a look at Logan, and my heart skips a beat. I hold my hand against my chest, willing it back to a steady rhythm. It speeds up.

I think I love Logan.

Oh god. This is a horrible time to think this.

Which probably means I really do. Love him.

I gasp as though a corset is being pulled around my middle. The tightness in my ribs squeezes harder.

And then Logan looks over at me with his just-for-me smile, and the corset is ripped off. Air fills my lungs, and my heart swells to three times its size.

I'm buoyant again. Just with a new realization. A couple of extra laughs popcorn out of me.

"There are fewer seagulls than you'd expect out here," I say.

Logan huffs a laugh. "What?"

"Seagulls," I repeat. There are a few birds in the distance flying lazy circles over the boats. "You'd think more of them would be hanging around trying to steal bites."

"Maybe they're more into French fries than chips," he says, popping a salt and vinegar chip into his mouth.

I roll my head against the seat to look at him. "You really didn't want your family to know either, did you?"

It takes a few seconds for Logan to nod in agreement. "My dad's side of the family is well off," he explains, smoothing the chip bag out between his fingers. "The Maine house was our summer home. My dad set aside money for my sisters and me for our inheritances, but after his affair, I didn't want anything from him. In the divorce, my mom got money and the house. They broke up, he left, and my relationship with him hasn't been the same."

Logan squints out at the horizon. "It wasn't just that, though. After my accident, my dad tried to pay off our neighbor, and not in a sorry-for-the-trouble kind of way. He wanted to pay him off, as if he was doing me this big favor by saving me. What that really would've meant, though, was that I'd have to follow through on what was expected of me, which was to work in the family business. He reminded me of the inheritance I stood to lose if I didn't do what he wanted. All I wanted was to do right by my neighbor. If there was going to be a debt to pay off, I would've rather it have been to him, not my dad. Anything he paid for came with a price."

"You would've owed him."

"I didn't want to be anyone's puppet," he says, resting his elbows on his thighs. "I decided to cut myself off. My dad didn't like that and used my sisters' inheritances as a bargaining chip. It was a whole thing. It got figured out, but it only validated my decision. I transferred to a community college to stay local. I wanted to be there for my ex-girlfriend, and I said I was going to rebuild what I broke, which is exactly what I did. I kept my word, and no one can take that from me."

Unlike money, he doesn't say.

He says this like it was the only choice he had to be truly free. Like it's plain and simple. But I know it couldn't have been easy.

"It's difficult to justify turning down a lot of money without looking like an asshole," he says. "And then here I go winning millions."

I draw figure-eights into the condensation on my bottle. "You made choices for your own reasons. Some things in life we're allowed to do just for ourselves, right?"

Logan half smiles at my use of his words. "Yeah."

My head spins with all this new information. The way Logan lived, his parents' approach to money, his fiscal responsibility, the built-in security. His siblings didn't even ask for money when they found out he won. They didn't even think it was a lot. I try not to remember the years I had to steal cash from Dad to mail to the utility companies. "The way we grew up could not have been more different. Too different, do you think?"

"Money can be a sensitive and complicated topic no matter how you grew up," he says. "If anything, I think that's something we can both relate to."

"I didn't want to go around announcing that I had lottery

money," I say, processing everything. "So I get why you wouldn't go around telling people that you come from money. Or that you turned it down."

Suddenly, our night in the pizzeria becomes clear. Logan really would have walked away from the money. He's done it before.

"You took the money for me," I manage to get out. The thought sends a sharp pain shooting right through my center. I scoot closer to the edge of my seat so I can grab his hand.

Logan rocks forward, tilting his head to meet my eyes. "It wasn't a hardship to accept it," he says, his jaw flexing as he works through something in his head, "I just don't want money to lay the path for me so easily, I guess. I like the life I'm creating for myself. I learned how to support myself my way. That means something to me."

"I can understand that." I think of all the times Dad believed the lottery was his answer to everything.

"We beat the odds, though," Logan says, squinting at the view. "Sometimes there are things in life you can't turn down. I'm realizing that the lottery winnings aren't free of strings, but accepting that money was not the same as accepting my dad's."

That, I get, too. But for me, those strings feel a lot more like guilt.

Logan pulls his hat over his windblown hair. "I'm grateful to have had luck on my side," he pushes on. "I just...I had no doubt that I was going to figure it out and be okay. That knowledge was comforting, for both me and my mom, when I moved away. Also, I was born a white man in America. I know that helps me."

I nod, thinking about how my dad's life might've been different if he were a white man instead of a Chinese one.

"You know you're allowed to have made the decision you did and still have struggles, right?" I ask.

Logan doesn't answer this, which gives me time to think.

I follow up with, "Expectations."

"What about them?"

"It's like Maxwell said, you didn't question good things happening to you," I rush out. "You expected them to happen. Because of that, you still went after what you wanted. Doing so got you closer to your goals."

"I don't know about all that."

"If you always expected to lose, you probably wouldn't have taken action the way you did. Every time you try, you're giving yourself one more chance to succeed."

It's nothing Logan hasn't heard before. But now that I'm learning more about him, Maxwell's rationale seems more plausible for why Logan considers himself lucky.

"You think what he was saying could be real?" Logan asks.

"No, I don't," I say. "I *really* think what he was saying could be real."

He laughs at this. "I think we might've picked up a little too much from Maxwell."

"I know you were always told you were lucky," I say. "But being told you're something doesn't make it true. You made everything that's happened in your life come true."

This logic is great for Logan, but not so much for my situation. Because if it is, then logically, wouldn't it be the opposite for me? If all I heard growing up was how unlucky we were, did that make me fearful to try new things? To say yes? To expect that anything exceptionally good could happen for me? Have I only been paying attention to the bad?

I take a sip of my drink, washing these thoughts down for another time. A time when we aren't dealing with a crisis.

Logan leans back against his chair and lets out the kind of sigh that accompanies newfound realization. "Huh."

I'm glad to have gotten through to him. I gesture toward the waves. "And that's why we add water."

A light breeze sweeps over us. Logan breathes it in.

Ahead of us, the fishing boats sway from side to side on the surface of the water like they're stuck in place. The sound of the waves lapping over each other becomes louder when I turn my attention to them.

After a few quiet moments, Logan says, "You're right. There aren't that many seagulls here."

"More food for us, I guess." I finish the last of my roll.

"I can't believe the damn plane was a warning about the clerk. You think we can fly back to New York?"

"It's not worth the risk," I say. "And who knows? Maybe we'll find a face-reader fortune teller on the way back."

"At a rest stop, probably," he quips, taking a long chug of his blueberry soda.

I laugh. "My năi nai once told me I had very lucky cheeks."

He chuckles. "They are very cute cheeks."

"Who knew you were the wealthy New York girl going to the fancy Catskills resort, and I was the dance instructor?" I ask. "All this time I could've been calling you Baby."

He smirks at my *Dirty Dancing* reference. "I'm Rose, and you're Jack."

"I'm Noah, and you're Allie."

Then, despite the heaviness of our situation and the fallout that inevitably awaits, a ripple-smile flashes across Logan's cheeks.

And that smile on his face does more for me than all the water in the world combined.

Chapter 21

LOGAN

We avoid reality for as long as we can and get back to Mom's house shortly after 10:00 p.m., narrowly avoiding the storm that's just started.

"Mom, hi," I say quietly as we enter through the back door. She's reading in the living room with a cup of tea.

She sets her book down and removes her glasses. "You're back. Would you like tea? I can get—"

"All set, thanks." I sit in the armchair next to the couch while Hazel heads upstairs to the guest room. "Is Warren officially retired now?" I ask, trying to keep the conversation light.

"We're closer than before," Mom says.

"Sounds like this has been a hard transition for him."

She grabs her cup, the scent of her chamomile tea drifting over to me. "He'll be fine. These things take time getting used to is all," she says. "So... the lottery? You really played?"

I settle back against the cushion. "On a whim."

"Isn't that something?" Mom wonders. "Are you and Hazel okay now?"

I rest my elbows on my thighs as I lean forward in thought. "More sites are picking up that social post. You know how many people win every week? A lot. They just don't go to the lengths we did to try to hide our identities. That's what everyone's entertained by." I shake my head. "It was my idea, too."

"Sounds like you were trying to help," Mom says.

"I really was."

Mom tucks one leg underneath her, adjusting to face me. "At least the security footage was flattering."

That's one way to look at it.

"I'm sorry for snapping," I say as a crack of thunder booms overhead.

She sighs and pats my cast. "It was a nice time while we had it. Logan, I know you've had your challenges, but you come out stronger for them. Always remember that."

This is the point in the conversation where I'd nod and agree or stay silent and not push back.

But I can't do that anymore. "Do I, though?" I ask.

"What do you mean? Of course you do," Mom says with a light laugh. "You have a good job, you live in New York City, you've got your health. You won the lottery for goodness' sake! Just look at everything you've been through and have overcome."

The room is dimly lit with just the small lamp on the table next to the couch. Still, I can see that Mom's trying hard to put on a good face.

"Overcome or ignored?" I ask.

"Ignored?"

"Hard conversations, hard feelings. You don't think we've just conveniently not dealt with those?" I ask.

"Where is this coming from?" Mom asks, her voice tight.

"I know when I transferred schools and went into carpentry and moved to the city, you were worried, especially after what had happened," I say, processing this as it comes out, "But I didn't want you to be concerned, so I pretended everything was okay—I pretended *I* was okay—all the time."

"I'm your mother. Am I not allowed to worry?" she asks. "You cut yourself off and changed your life after going through something huge."

It was something we all had to go through, and every one of us kept things positive. There was never any honesty, any realness, even to this day. I know I'm not innocent in this.

"You were the one I probably didn't need to worry about as much, though," Mom adds. "You've been my lucky boy since birth."

"See? That right there," I say, holding my hands out, "is not helpful."

"Well, you have been!" Mom says with a shrug, her tea nearly sloshing over the sides of her mug. "Quite literally, too. Of all my children's births, yours was the shortest and the least painful. How lucky is that? You practically walked out."

"Nope! Too much," I say, covering my ears.

Mom swats my hands down. "So you've had luck in your life. Why are you acting like it's a bad thing? All your success, the accident. You know how much worse that could've been? You could've died." She shakes her head. "So no, your luck isn't a bad thing. I, for one, am grateful for it."

"I'm grateful I was okay, too, Mom," I say. "But that was a really hard time."

"It made us stronger," Mom says.

"I needed you." My voice is a low whisper, but my words are clear. I only have to say it once. "I felt so alone."

A small gasp comes out of Mom's mouth. "And we got through it." She closes her eyes. "Help me understand. Would you rather be unlucky? Would you rather not have good things happening to you?"

"Maybe I'd rather it be neither," I say, scanning over the shelves of books and the vases of flowers. I can sense my focus is drifting, probably so I can avoid confronting this truth. "And everything isn't just happening to me." I feel hesitation as this comes out.

Because if everything isn't happening to me, how do I explain everything in the past month that has felt like that? If I'm claiming to not have been a recipient of good luck, then maybe I haven't been a victim of bad luck, either.

"I've never rubbed my luck in any of your faces, but it's kind of feeling like you all think I have. When you attribute my hard work to luck, it devalues what I've worked for," I add, gaining confidence. "It erases who I am, in a way. There are opportunities I made for myself over the years, hard decisions I had to make."

"Ah," she says, murmuring to herself. "So this is where it's coming from. You're stressed."

I rub my hand along my neck. "Yes, I am, but that's not why I'm saying this."

"How can you be stressed when there's so much to be grateful for?" Mom asks.

"I'm stressed *and* I'm grateful," I say. "I can't help but have emotions. Neither can you, and that's okay. But never processing those emotions? We're not doing ourselves any favors when we do that."

Mom grabs her cup and holds it firmly between her hands. It's unlikely I'll break through to her in a single conversation, but at least I've said my peace.

"I'm not sure what you want me to say here," she says.

"This isn't a test. I just wanted to tell you that."

"Okay."

"And one more thing. I didn't try to win the lottery." I feel the need to clarify. "I wasn't looking for an easy out."

Mom looks confused. "Isn't anyone playing the lottery *trying* to win?"

"It was about a girl."

She smiles. "Earlier on the deck. You and Hazel...you shook us, I think. Don't be too mad at Jane. She's also stressed."

This gets my attention. "Is she okay?"

"She...well, she doesn't want to be part of your father's company anymore," Mom reveals. "I think maybe she sees you doing what you want, and she's jealous. Your sisters, they've never had your luck—" She holds her hand up. "They've never felt like they could make decisions in the way you have."

While I was so adamant about figuring everything out on my own, my sisters followed the path our dad laid out for them.

I hear Maxwell's voice in my head. *Mindset. Expectations. Listen to your gut. Be open to new experiences.*

"Jane doesn't need luck," I tell Mom. "Neither does Eva. They can make their own." I start to stand but drop back down in the chair to say this last part. "Please tell Warren I'm sorry, too. Maybe go easy on him. It sounds like he might be struggling with saying goodbye to a career he loves."

"Warren loves his work, yes, but he's the one who's talked about retiring," Mom says. "It's time."

"Doesn't mean it's not still hard." I stand and squeeze Mom's shoulder. "See you in the morning."

"Goodnight. Oh, and Logan?" Mom whispers. I turn from the archway entry. "Sorry to be the bearer of bad news, but Hazel won the raffle. I hope she likes golf."

I laugh dryly. "Well, isn't that just my luck?"

She smirks and flips back to where she left off in her book as I head upstairs to the guest room that Mom's made up.

I quietly open the door as the room lights up from a shard of lightning.

Hazel turns over to face me. "Is that my doing? Or are you Zeus now?" she asks, pointing to the window. "I can't keep the fortunes straight."

"I honestly don't know anymore."

I reach for a pillow to make up my bed on the floor.

"You're not sleeping in the bed?" she asks.

"I...didn't want to assume," I say, clutching the pillow.

Hazel pulls back the comforter, welcoming me in. She's wearing one of my tie-dye shirts that falls just above her upper thighs.

"You make them look so good," she says, biting down a smile. "Does it look goofy on me?"

"It looks better on you," I say, taking off my jeans and flannel button-down. Her eyes darken a shade when I remove my T-shirt. "Please, take them all."

"One's plenty for now," she says.

I slide in next to her. She meets me in the middle, the sheets cool. Hazel's hands and feet are colder.

I gasp when her toes graze my shin. "Fuuuuuu—how long have you been in here?"

"I'm looking into compression socks," she says, rubbing her hands together. "I fear my toes are frozen to the point of no return."

I slap my thighs. "Come on. Get them on here."

Hazel doesn't wait for me to say it twice. She tucks her feet under my legs and wraps her hands around my stomach.

She releases a contented sigh. "I'm regaining some feeling."

I shiver. "G-good."

She laughs and burrows her face into my neck, and the tip of her nose is cold, too. I make a mental note to buy her a truckload of hand and toe warmers for when I'm not around to keep her warm myself.

A deluge of rain beats against the windows and roof, unsynced and chaotic. I feel safe in here with Hazel. Cozy, even. I've never had anyone to weather the storm with.

"It's an oak tree," Hazel says. "Without leaves?"

She must be looking at my tattoo.

"It's the stage where the tree has lost everything except for what's necessary for it to survive. For it to get through the impending winter," I explain. "In time, though, those leaves come back stronger." I pause for a moment. "This is the tree that stopped me from crashing into my neighbor's house, right after barreling through the fence and playhouse."

She reaches out to touch the dangling root of the oak, stopping before her fingers make contact with my skin. She finds my eyes, like she's asking for permission. I nod.

Slowly, she drags her finger from the roots at my triceps up to a tree trunk and its barren branches sprawled over my shoulder.

"Trees have hard years," Hazel says quietly. "They survive droughts, windstorms, flooding. They weather storms. They're resilient." She takes her time, sliding her finger over to my biceps. I wonder if our contact sets everything within her on fire, too. "They earn every inch."

She stops at my shoulder, the pads of her fingers finding a raised groove.

"Scar from the glass," I explain, filling in the blanks.

"It must've been really hard going through that," she says. "I wish I could've been there for you."

"Me, too."

Hazel turns onto her side so we're chest to chest, intertwining her legs with mine like the roots on my arm. She leans over to kiss the scar, trailing her kisses down the tree. As she does, I drop a kiss on her temple.

"Did you know some trees can predict the weather?" she says.

"I think that's a myth."

"A belief," she says. "Some people think you can look at a tree's leaves and know a storm is coming. The leaves will curl or flip over. But it's because of the wind. Or humidity."

"Isn't the prediction kind of true if the leaves are doing that, and then it does rain or storm?"

"I guess it depends on what you want to believe," she says, sliding her arm under her pillow to prop her head up more. "The leaves can make a prediction about the weather. But there's nothing else about how strong that storm will be. Or how long it'll last. Or how much damage it'll do."

"That doesn't sound very useful."

She considers this. "Maybe, as long as you're not hiding out in fear of the storm, the heads-up can be helpful."

"So that you can get ahead of it?" I ask.

"If it helps you to take action, yes. And if there isn't a storm, then you're ready for the next one."

I adjust my head on the pillow so I can see her better. "Well, whatever's coming, we can face it. Together."

A streak of moonlight slips past the curtains, providing just enough light for me to see Hazel's face and the glimmer in her eyes that tells me she agrees.

She leans back, holding up my right hand in the blue light, tracing her fingertip across my palm. It's a more sensitive sensation than I'd anticipated. She follows each line, winding up, down, around.

"I have bigger gaps between my knuckles," I analyze. "Doesn't that mean money's slipping through my fingers?"

"Only when it's my birthday," Hazel teases.

"Oh yeah?" I squeeze my fingers tighter together, the light vanishing. "What does my palm say?"

She traces her pinky across the center of my palm. "This one's very long. I believe it's the Handsome line." She surveys my face. "Yep, accurate."

I gently fist my hand around hers, trapping her pinky. She lets out a laugh and then quickly says, "Okay, okay. All I remember is that this is the Love line." Her voice drops to a whisper as she runs her thumb along the line closest to my fingers. "And yours looks clear and unbroken. As for the rest of them..." Hazel slowly presses a kiss against each line, "that's the best I can tell you."

I kiss her knuckles in return. "If that's what my future holds, I'll take it."

Hazel clasps both her hands around mine and presses them to her chest. We're able to make direct eye contact lying down like this. If I leaned forward a few inches, I'd be kissing her. It's the predicament I've found myself in lately. When I'm not kissing Hazel, it's all I want to do. When I'm kissing Hazel, it's all I want to keep doing.

This is what I'm thinking about when Hazel presses her lips against mine. In reaction, I brush my fingers along her jawline and down her neck, feeling her pulse beat steadily against my thumb.

We're tangled up in a queen-size bed, trading quiet kisses back and forth. Our very first kiss was hurried, the second curious and indulgent. But these... these kisses feel like a promise. These are the ones that don't have to lead anywhere because we have all the time in the world for more. They are the end destination.

"This moment. It makes me happy," she says when she pulls away. "You make me happy. I want to feel it. I want this to last."

So that's what we do. We stretch out this moment for as long as we can. We talk until our voices are hoarse from whispering, and when we're not talking, we're kissing.

Hazel snuggles into my shoulder, and I hold her in my arms in the blue light of the moon as the wind chimes clang outside in the storm. It's sometime after the rain falls to a steady thrum that her breathing finally slows, and she falls asleep smiling.

Chapter 22

HAZEL

The next morning, I'm up before the sun. The guest bedroom's window overlooks the bay, giving me a front-row seat to streaks of peach and gold trickling over the horizon, the colors lazily stretching across the sky. I'm aware of every passing second, grounded firmly in this moment, in this room, in this bed. The sun looks like it's climbing up out of the water before it takes a rest, bobbing on the surface like a beach ball. It's a once-a-day occurrence, but catching the sunrise now, here, over the water...it somehow feels like a stroke of luck. Within a few minutes, the rays poke through the curtain, stirring Logan awake.

He rolls onto his side, bumping into me. His eyes slowly blink open.

"Hi," I say, brushing his hair off his forehead.

"Hey," Logan says, his throat husky. It's his sleepy voice. My heart squeezes at this. I want to know all his voices. "How long have you been awake?"

"Long enough to hear you mumble my name."

"We were on a lobster boat," he says, running his hand down his face. "But it was an actual giant lobster that was carrying us over the water, like a boat, and then you fell overboard. Well, more like overclaw because that's the part we were on."

"Did you come in after me?"

Logan shakes his head decisively. "Nope, you didn't want me to. You swam alongside us." He gives me a soft smile.

I want to curl up in those curved lines that form on his cheeks. I settle for kissing them instead. "Normally I don't love listening to people's dreams," I admit. "Yours I like, though." I roll onto my side to face him. "I was thinking...I want to get ahead of the news with my family."

"You're reading the tree leaves," Logan says.

"Yeah. I don't want to wait around living in fear. And I haven't been to the lake house in a while. It would be nice to see it."

And Dad's not responding to any of my calls or messages. We only have a couple of weeks left. We need a plan.

Logan rubs his eyes. "I can understand that."

"Would you mind dropping me off at the rental car place? I'll be heading out a little early."

He sits up. "Your dad's in upstate New York, right? We'll go together."

"We were hardly here. I don't want to take you away from your family."

"We'll have breakfast with everyone and then leave after that."

"It's really not a—"

"I'm coming with you," Logan says, kissing my knuckles. "We weather storms together."

"Well, isn't this my lucky day?" Dad says when he swings the door open and finds us on the other side.

Great. He's cheerful. A good mood should help.

"Surprise," I say with a little wave of my hands. "Hope it's okay we're dropping by unannounced."

Without any unexpected stops this time, the drive didn't take as long as it did yesterday. Getting back to the city tonight should be another three hours.

"It's your home, too," Dad says.

Home. Something about this place doesn't look like the home it once felt like. The exterior paint is peeling. Shingles from the roof are missing. The second step up to the front door has sunken in on itself. Houses require a lot of maintenance. Especially lake houses. There's erosion, water damage, dock maintenance, repairs, various insurance, and higher property taxes. I wonder if Dad ever looks at the spreadsheet that I created for him with the annual checklist of tasks to take care of. I make a mental note to resend—

"Rick Yen." Dad's voice cuts through my thoughts.

"Logan Wells," Logan says, shaking Dad's hand.

"Come on in," Dad says, ushering us through the door. "Game's on, and I'm making a burger. Let me throw some extra patties in the pan."

When this house was my grandparents', they didn't own a TV. Grandpa's favorite yellow chair faced out toward the lake, which he called "nature's television." That chair has now been replaced by a dark-gray reclining sofa.

"Where'd grandpa's chair go?" I ask.

Dad sets his grill glove on the kitchen counter that we're all gathered around. "Eh, it was practically falling apart."

What I hear: *I needed the money.*

"It was well loved," I say.

"I won that sofa," Dad says with a proud grin. "There's nothing like loafing around on something you got for free!"

"What about the La-Z-Boy you won?" I ask.

"That thing was getting old. It was time for something new," he says.

"I once won a Cuisinart bread maker for winning a crossword puzzle contest," Logan says, probably at the mention of the word "loaf."

Dad's eyes light up. "You brought a winner into the house," he says, clapping Logan on the back. "Can you stay for this game? I've got money on the Giants making three touchdowns in the first half."

"We actually don't have much time," I interject. My eyes dart over to the living room wall where a rustic hutch used to hold all of Grandma and Mom's antique finds. Those are gone, too. "We need to get back to the city tonight. This isn't a pop by for fun. I need to talk to you." To Logan, I say, "I got this."

Logan nods and squeezes my hand before slipping out the back door that leads down to the dock. From here, I can tell there are two missing boards on it. Next to it, though, is a shiny red boat.

"Another win?" I ask, dragging my eyes back to Dad.

"You want tomatoes?" Dad asks, ignoring my question.

"I'll do it," I say, grabbing a cutting board to slice tomatoes and onions. "So, Dad—"

"Let me guess," he interjects. "You're here to talk about the plan."

"Yes. Yeah. That's part of it," I say, thinking through what I have rehearsed. A last-minute thought interjects. Maybe while I'm here, I can convince Dad to transfer the house into my name, so this doesn't happen again. "We still have a little time. We do need to act fast, though."

"We?" Dad says, raising his eyebrows. He adds two more patties to a platter.

"The house is under your name, so yes, we. I did the math. We owe—"

"What am I missing here?" Dad asks. "You're still saying 'we.'"

I resist the urge to audibly sigh. "If you let me finish, I'll tell you."

"Hazel, I don't have the money right now for the payments."

"But you put money on the game..." I say, pointing toward the TV with my knife.

"Well, yeah," Dad says with a shrug. "If I win, then I'll have money, but that isn't the point. Even then, I still won't have enough to cover it all." He looks at me expectantly. "You do, though. I'm a little confused on why you're dragging this out." Dad peers over my head at the TV. "We're up one touchdown, and I need to see how the rest plays out."

"Dragging out..." And then it clicks. We've really been on different wavelengths this entire time. For our entire lives, really. "Oh. You know."

Dad's practically shaking with excitement. "My daughter wins the lottery and waits weeks to tell her old man. Don't you know what a big deal this is for us?"

I slice down on the tomato a little too hard.

"I always knew one day our luck would turn," he continues. "You were always on me about those tickets and yet look at you now." He chuckles. "The irony! That was a hefty chunk of change, too."

"What have you seen?" I ask.

"There were all those photos, Hazel. The disguises were very funny."

"So you already knew who Logan was when we got here."

"Well, he looks a little different now," Dad jokes. "Thought it was all part of your big reveal." He frowns. "What's wrong? Has the money not come in yet? It should've—"

"It's not that," I say. "I just...I haven't decided what to do with it yet."

Dad cranes his neck toward me, his forehead crunching in confusion. He laughs through a smile. "Well, I wouldn't mind an early Christmas gift," he says, as if I were welcoming suggestions. "Raising you kids wasn't cheap. Man, I had no idea until Jerry sent me that link—"

"Wait, Jerry told you? Jerry knows?"

"I guess he saw it on social media?"

I blink. "You're talking to him?"

"Uh, yeah? Why wouldn't I be?"

"What do you talk about?" I ask.

"What's with the interrogation? I'm not allowed to talk to my own son?" Dad asks, grabbing American cheese slices from the fridge. "Hey, can you stay until next week? Jerry's coming by, and it'd be nice for us to celebrate together."

This freezes me in place.

"Jerry's coming?" I say, vaguely. I have no idea what he's told Dad. He hasn't updated me in days. He did say he'd tell him about his situation when the time was right. That could've been... anytime he felt the time was right.

Maybe he and Danielle will roll up in their van, and his broken legs will be a surprise to garner sympathy. He shouldn't be putting weight on his legs yet, but maybe they found a way to make him comfortable in their drive across the country.

"Next week," Dad says again, slower this time. "I have a good feeling for when he gets here. My luck always turns when Jerry comes to visit. I've got my eye on a couple of games."

"And you're going to take care of him?" I ask. "How long will he be here?"

Dad grabs ketchup from the fridge. "Just for a few days before he's off to New Hampshire. Or was it Vermont? Wherever you can see the leaves change colors. Young people have so much energy. I envy everyone in their twenties."

"He's thirty-two," I say.

Dad squirts a spiral onto the bottom of each bun. "Is he? I thought you were thirty-two."

"I'm younger."

"You've always seemed older."

No kidding.

"Ah, shit. You just had a birthday, didn't you?" he asks. "I'm working on getting you something nice. I just need some more time."

"I don't care about that. Don't get me anything."

Dad balks. "Of course I'm gonna get you something."

"Seriously, don't. The best present you can get me is to talk through a plan. I worked out a couple of ideas—"

"What ideas? You're loaded now. Pay off the missing amounts. You can afford to pay the increased payments now, too!"

"You think I should pay off the entire amount?"

"You do want the house, don't you?"

"Well, yeah. One day. But we had an agreement—"

"An agreement before you went and won the lottery!" Dad says.

"There's also a lot here that needs work. Last time you said you were going to fix the screen door. The rip in it is bigger now."

Dad waves me off. "Eh, nothing's getting in through there."

The dock needs work, and the windows need the deepest cleaning the company offers. Everything in here looks worn down. Unloved.

Across the kitchen, Grandma's baking corner is filled with boxes of blenders, shoes, and baseball cards. It used to hold glass jars of flour and sugar. That was the perk of Grandpa building a custom home. They could add special details like a kitchen space designated just for Grandma's hobbies.

"Mom's candy jar. Where is it?" I ask, scanning the counters.

"What?" Dad asks. "I don't— What'd it look like?"

I stack my hands vertically, a foot of space between them. "It was pink. It looked like a strawberry. It had all the sour strawberry drops she used to eat." I'm up out of my seat, opening cabinets and drawers. Looking behind piles. "You know the one. It was antique." I scan the walls where my grandparents' art used to hang. "You didn't sell it, did you?"

"I can't keep track of everything in here," Dad says as he adds mayonnaise to the other buns. "This place was getting cluttered. If I see it, I'll let you know, okay?"

I look in one last place where I might've stashed it before I left for college. The hallway closet with all the Fenton glass vases Mom and Grandma found at their estate sale hops. The closet's completely empty.

I round the corner back to the kitchen as Dad says, "Here's what we do: We get the house paid off, get it all fixed up, and we increase the value"—he snaps—"just like that. It'll be great, Hazel. Then one day, when I'm too old to walk upstairs, it'll be yours." His tone is upbeat and confident. If I weren't on edge, it might even be convincing. "Or maybe we put in an elevator."

Dad doesn't have the money in hand, and he's already spending it. I haven't agreed to pay anything off. Or to give any of the money to him.

The thought goes as fast as it comes. Am I horrible for thinking it? It feels like a betrayal, in a sense. I know all the reasons why Dad and Jerry getting even a modest amount of this money would be a bad idea, but how can something this incredible happen to me and I not share it with them?

"What if I hadn't won the lottery?" I ask.

"But you did," he says, his eyes dimming. "We can't lose this house. So if you want it, you're going to need to use that money. It's like you said. We still have time to fix this. How often do you get second chances in life?"

My jaw aches. I've been grinding my teeth so hard that it's locked.

"You can't just go and refinance the house and expect me to pay for it," I say. "That's not how—"

"Jesus, Hazel. I learned my lesson. Don't make me feel bad about this."

I swallow. "I want to know why you did it. Why did you refinance knowing it'd put us both in a harder spot?"

He knows I've been putting money toward the mortgage every month for the past decade. I don't travel, I restrict how many times I go out to eat and do things, and I limit what I buy. I help out Jerry so he doesn't have to. I went into a career that made good money so I could contribute.

All this time, I've lived such a responsible life just for him and Jerry to have an irresponsible one.

"I needed the money, okay?" he says, turning to wash his hands at the sink. He doesn't say anything more. Shutting down, like usual, when a topic he doesn't want to talk about comes up.

"When you gamble, you gamble with my life," I push.

Dad spins around. "Great. Now you're making this about you. You win the lottery, and you still have something to bitch about. Why can't you just be happy for once?"

My throat constricts. "Happy?" I manage. "You think I should be happy?"

"Why wouldn't you be? I've been working my whole life to win something like you did, and you get it on a fluke. It's hypocritical, is what this is."

"I have rent, bills, loans," I say. "I can't afford this refinancing."

"It was a mistake!" he shouts.

I squeeze my eyes shut. "Your mistakes affect everyone around you. What about my goals? My dreams? My desires? I've been the sea legs of this family. Steady so when you and Jerry rock the boat, we're not tipping over and drowning."

"You want your dreams to come true? Join the club," Dad says. "I'd like for just one thing to go right."

"When you wrecked the car, I got a job after school to help pay for it. All so you could get to a job you only worked at for six months before quitting because you thought it was throwing your numbers off. When the water got shut off, I did extra chores at the neighbors and would walk to town to pay it off in person."

"You become a millionaire, and suddenly you're ungrateful for your whole life. Well, sorry you had it so bad," Dad says. "It wasn't easy for me after losing your mother."

"I lost her, too!"

The toaster springs, the burger buns popping up.

"I'm probably going to take a job I don't even know I want so I can make more money to help," I say. "I do what's right, even when it's hard."

"You always do what's right," Dad says. "You're so responsible. Are you looking for a thank-you? Because sure, thanks. Thanks for all you do."

"I don't care about thank-yous. I just want help!"

Dad lets out a gusty sigh. "You're clearly emotional. Let's talk when you've calmed down."

An intensity swirls inside my chest and then...clicks off. Detaches. Goes numb. It's a particular feeling where I'm eerily calm. I can barely feel my heart beating.

"I want to know why you needed the money," I say, my voice monotone. I feel like a zombie as I move from one end of the kitchen to the other to toss the ends of the onions and tomatoes into the trash.

"Why does it matter so much to you?"

"I want to know what's more important than your daughter."

"Oh, come on with that crap," Dad says.

I detour to the other side of the counter, marching up to him. "No. What's more important than me?" I repeat, choking out the words. "Tell me."

Dad takes a step back.

"Tell me," I say more forcefully.

He heads toward the couch, waving his hand dismissively. "Jerry needed help."

My voice dies in my throat. There are a few seconds of dead air until I find it again. "What did you say?"

"You heard me. Jerry needed help," Dad repeats, rubbing his forehead. "I can't catch a break."

I see dark spots in my periphery. "You needed money...for Jerry?"

"What was I supposed to do? He sprained his ankles. Hospital bills aren't cheap," Dad says, laughing bitterly under his breath. "And you don't think I do anything."

"He didn't sprain his ankles, Dad. He broke his legs."

Or wait.

"He didn't, did he?" I ask.

This is going to be expensive. Those were Jerry's exact words. Forty-five-thousand-dollars expensive.

I huff out a sound of disbelief. I knew it. I fucking knew it.

"*I* gave Jerry the money for his legs," I say quietly.

Dad just stares at the TV and says nothing.

After a long minute, I speak again. "You took out way more than what Jerry would've needed."

More silence follows. Dad gets up from the couch and moves to the corner of the living room. I follow his gaze out the window. He's looking out at the dock where Logan's on all fours investigating the missing planks.

"Sometimes when we're in a hole so deep, the only thing we know how to do is to keep digging," Dad says. The smell of burning meat snaps him out of whatever he's thinking about. He rushes to the stove and slides the pan off the heat.

Slowly, the pieces click into place.

Lucky people listen to their intuition, Maxwell had said.

When it comes to Dad and Jerry, I should've trusted my gut.

I don't know how to process any of this.

So I don't.

The game goes to halftime, and the Giants make only one touchdown.

I don't want to know how much Dad just lost. I don't want to know if this will require him to take out another personal loan or borrow from more family members.

I don't want to know anything anymore.

Chapter 23

LOGAN

"We need to de-haunt the theater," Hazel declares as she walks down the center aisle.

We got back to the city late last night, but she was up early texting me to meet her at the theater this afternoon. It's everyone's day off, so we have the place to ourselves.

Over the weekend, the star drop refused to lower, which means the actors would have to sing against a plain navy background that does not at all evoke romance. Also, the canoe used during the moonlit float scene isn't rolling out to center stage. Not that they could even get into the canoe from the dock, like planned, since one of the dock legs collapsed.

With the show opening next Thursday, we're almost out of time. At this point, we won't have a functioning set if there are any more issues.

"So now we're ghostbusting?" I ask.

"We can't control much. But we can control our environment. I've hired a feng shui expert," Hazel informs me. "I've heard stories where they've helped eliminate negative spirits in homes and castles. If they can do that there, they can do it here. Her name's An-Ming, and she's going to get a feel for the energy of the theater." At my skeptical expression, she adds, "I know, this feels a tad superstitious, but a lot of people consider feng shui to have positive psychological impacts. We may not have been able to protect our identities, but we can still save your show."

Ten minutes later, we're letting An-Ming through the front doors. She's a petite older woman with her black hair tied back in a low bun. She breezes past me, focusing on the lobby. After assessing the space, she takes a note in her phone.

We introduce ourselves to her with our real names. If An-Ming knows who we are, she doesn't show it. The heightened attention did entice a few scammers to set up social media profiles impersonating us, and I now know the names of more accountants in the city than I'd ever know what to do with. We don't have to hide now, though. The amused articles and quizzes about what to dress up as if you win the lottery will blow over in a week or so to make room for the drama about some celebrity couple breaking up.

An-Ming refuses to hear what's been happening here or have us guide her around. Apparently, it's necessary that she feels the energy of the theater without any preconceived notions.

I follow An-Ming's gaze over to the concession stand. "What's feng shui supposed to do?" I whisper to Hazel.

"It's a Chinese practice of balancing the qi patterns in our natural environment," she explains as An-Ming examines the space, typing as she walks. "There are items and arrangements that bring good luck and good flow. I thought this place could benefit from some harmony." Hazel shrugs. "And I reached out to her last week and prepaid, so we might as well try."

Hazel and I meet An-Ming next to aisle F.

"Mind if I take a look backstage?" she asks.

"Okay. Sure. We'll just be around," I say.

"She's supposed to be one of the best consultants in the city,"

Hazel reassures me. "I did extensive research before spending a dime."

"What happened here?" An-Ming asks. She's pointing to the corner of the dock resting on the stage. The shattered leg lies next to it.

"The Spirits of Broadway?" I offer unhelpfully.

The lights from the dining room chandeliers flicker on and off after I say this. Hazel steps closer to me as a chill shoots down my spine.

An-Ming squints toward the ceiling. "Interesting." She makes a note. "And do you actually have the ability to make changes here?"

"I'm responsible for the theater and set here, so yeah," I say, though I maybe shouldn't have agreed so willingly. I have no clue what she's going to propose.

She seems satisfied with my answer and continues her work.

Hazel walks to the edge of the stage, turning around to face the fictional world I'm desperately trying to help bring to life. "Do you like what you do?" she asks me.

That's a loaded question.

I stand next to her. "Like generally or with this show?"

"As head carpenter," she clarifies. "You have a crew. You do payroll. You're a manager now. Do you build anything anymore?"

"Oh." I consider her questions. "Sometimes, but not as much as I'd like. I traded my workbench for a desk. When I got into this, I just loved working with my hands and getting out of my head. Making something from nothing. I love creating worlds." I wave toward the sets behind us. "I do miss the actual hands-on part of it."

"Is this what you've been working toward?" she asks.

"Wow. Honestly, I didn't really know what I was headed toward. Once I got into it, I worked hard. It all fell into place from there."

She nods to herself. "Do you regret taking the job?"

I breathe in. Another tough one.

If she had asked me this a month ago—or even just two weeks ago—my first instinct would've been to immediately say no. To express how great challenges are and that I'm better off for them. I haven't been better off for them, though. It's like I'm paralyzed with fear and don't want to ruin anything else. It's made me useless around the theater. I can't even give my crew decent answers for simple questions.

"I regret not having a better handle on things," I admit, toeing blocking tape with my shoe. Most days, I've wondered if it was too much too soon. The way things are going, this is going to be my first and last show as head carpenter. Maybe it should be. I can hand off my work to someone who knows what they're doing—who can't curse this place with their bad luck. I make a mental note to figure out how to make that happen.

"What about managing people? Do you like that?" Hazel asks.

"I do, actually," I say. "I love talking to people, getting to know them. Problem-solving together. Helping them work through their shit. There's more politics with my new job, though. That part's been trickier to navigate."

Hazel nudges me. "You want to keep everyone happy?"

"Something like that," I say with a shrug of one shoulder. "Have you heard back about the job yet?"

"Team interviews were this morning. So any day now," she says flatly, crossing her arms low over her stomach. It's a gesture I've noticed she does when she seems to be working through something.

"How are you doing?" I ask, lowering my voice a bit. "Do you want to talk?"

On the drive back, she filled me in on what had happened with her dad and brother, but she was mostly quiet. After everything Hazel has done for them—that she continues to do for them—and this is how they treat her. They don't deserve her.

"That's how it always is. How he always is," she says with a shake of her head. "I'd pay off his debts, always wipe their slates clean. In these moments, I always thought I was helping. But maybe I haven't actually been. I've taken away any potential consequences. I always caved, and there'd be no lessons learned."

"So you've been here before."

"I don't even think real consequences would make a difference at this point. The addiction's too strong. They need to get real help."

I can tell she's trying to keep her voice steady, trying to numb any bad feelings. Battling the emotions that pop up, keeping them all in a neutral state, it's got to be exhausting.

"Have you ever talked to them about that?" I ask.

"So many times," Hazel says. "Those conversations were worse, and you know how the last one went. They just become better at hiding their problems. Became scrappier at figuring out how to borrow money. Got more creative with excuses..." Her voice trails off as she works through it. "But what about the house?"

I angle myself toward her. "You either help your dad and enable him to keep the house that you love, or you don't help and lose the house that you love. What a shitty situation."

"At least I don't have to worry about them finding out about the lottery anymore," Hazel says in an attempt to spin the situation.

"Now you sound like me."

Hazel releases a tight breath mixed with a chuckle. "Anyway, I want to focus on this. On helping you."

An-Ming's busy capturing dimensions with her tape measure.

"Come with me," I say to Hazel, taking her by the hand.

I lead her around to the resort's dance hall set that we shockingly haven't had any issues with. It has exposed ceiling beams and large windows overlooking a lake that's been repainted on a backdrop. We climb the staircase built along the rear of the set that leads to the roof of the dance hall, where the lead actors sneak up to look out over the lake together just before intermission.

"Another roof?" Hazel asks. "You sure you want to risk it with your last good wrist?"

"For this view?" I say teasingly, gesturing to the rows and rows of empty seats. "Definitely."

We sit on the slanted roof in the hidden seats built for the actors' safety. Hazel looks up at the tiered levels, her head tilting all the way back as she studies the intricate detailing of the theater's decorative molding and the paintings on the walls above us.

"It's so nice in here," she says. "You know, I've never seen a show? Until I met you, I had never actually been inside a theater."

"Really?" I hook my elbows around my knees and turn toward her.

"One time we were supposed to. For my tenth birthday. My dad bought tickets to *Wicked*. He was going to take me and my brother." Hazel runs her hand along one of the wood shingles. "It was going to be this big weekend trip to the city. I saved up every last penny from chores I did at my neighbors'. You know the only thing I wanted as a souvenir was a MetroCard." She laughs softly. "Like, what? I was nine."

I smile. "Freedom."

"Exactly," she says, regarding me. "For me, New York City just existed in movies. We only lived three hours away, but it might as well have been thirty. My dad set money aside for the trip. We were going to go to Central Park, get Frrrozen Hot Chocolate at Serendipity 3, go see the Empire State Building. You know, New York-y things."

I nod, watching as the last trace of her smile fades away completely.

"Then my dad bet the money on a game," she says after a few moments. "And that was that."

I shake my head.

Hazel swallows thickly. "I learned never to get my hopes up for things again. You don't get disappointed that way. I've lost everything I've ever loved." She blinks up at me. "I know this is too much. I'm too much. Logan, if at any point you want to walk away, you can. I promise I would understand."

I wrap my arm around her and stay right where I am, showing her I'm not moving from this spot. "Never once have you been too much for me, Hazel," I tell her, the words coming easily. "Don't think you're getting rid of me that easily."

"Good, because I don't want to lose you, too," she says.

I've lost everything I've ever loved. My brain trips. Did she imply that she loves me?

Because I also feel it.

"Bad things happen, but that doesn't mean that's how it'll always be," I say, the instinct to cheer her up kicking in.

"Right." She shakes her head like she's snapping out of the memory. "All that to say, it's pretty cool to be in a theater now."

"I'd love for you to come to opening night," I offer.

A small smile grows on Hazel's lips. "I'll be there. Is it a play or a musical?"

"Musical. *Windfall*'s about an estranged family that inherits a lakeside resort that used to be the go-to destination in its heyday. Now it's falling apart, and they have to decide whether to work together to sell the place or bring it back to life," I explain.

Hazel straightens a little. "Wait. The show is called *Windfall*?"

"To the family, this was like winning the jack...pot..." I trail off. How had I not made that connection before?

"Is it life imitating art or the other way around?"

"We'll never know."

Hazel kicks her leg out and leans back on her palms. "We used to watch the sunset like this at my grandparents' house. My grandpa built a special sunset-watching spot on the roof deck."

"The perks of building your own home."

"I had always wanted to make that my sunrise-watching spot," she says wistfully. "But this isn't too bad, either."

Hazel really is in an impossible situation. All her life, she's fixed things for her family because she's never had anyone to fix things for her.

"It's not your responsibility to anticipate everything that can go wrong," I say. "Or for your bullshit detector to be one hundred percent accurate."

"It's usually pretty accurate," she says.

I so desperately want to do more to help. To say something positive to try to make her pain go away completely.

But just like Hazel doesn't have to fix her family's problems, I don't need to fix this.

"I'm here for you," I say. "I'll be right here *with* you. I promise. I'm not going anywhere."

I hold my breath, feeling my heart beating in my ears. I think maybe I've failed or let her down. I could've found more useful words to make her feel better. Was not doing so the wrong approach? What I said probably wasn't helpful. Maybe I did need to show her the silver lining.

Hazel looks up at me with an expression I haven't yet seen from her. I can't decipher it or tell if I've messed this up for good.

But then she moves closer to me. She wraps her arm around my waist, smushing her cheek against my chest and pulling me in for a hug.

"Thank you," she says emotionally. She half groans, half grumbles into my shirt. "My detector tells me you're not bullshitting me."

I rest my cheek on her head. "Not even a little."

"It's all just stuck"—I feel her move her hand over her chest, the pressure of her knuckles against my stomach—"here. I don't know what to do with it or how to get it out."

I hold her a little tighter. "Then we need to get you unstuck. I may have an idea."

"There's a lot of wood in here," a voice says below us. We startle, but neither of us falls off the roof, which feels like a minor miracle. An-Ming has been so quiet I nearly forgot about her.

We meet her down at the bottom of the lodge's stairs. "Can we add some metal weights under that bed?" she asks. "That will help with productivity and moving this project along. Is opening night on an auspicious day, do you know?"

"I...don't," I say.

"Okay. Is that something you have control over?"

"Unfortunately not."

An-Ming tilts her head. "The positioning of the stage is not ideal," she adds. "But I suppose there's nothing to be done about that, either." She waves toward backstage. "It's too cluttered back there. Tidy spaces allow energy to flow through better."

"I'll organize it," I say.

"Oh, and fire!" she says.

"Pretty sure you can't say that in a theater," Hazel deadpans.

"Actually, it's Macb—" I snap my mouth shut. "Never mind."

An-Ming looks back at her phone. "The fire element is severely lacking. We need to bump up the visibility and passion in the space. Can you get more lamps back there? Too many dark corners." She scrolls more. "Also, you have no water. Is that something you can work on?"

"Like water bottles?" I ask. "We have some in the—"

An-Ming gives a firm shake of her head. "Not water bottles. Flowing and moving water," she clarifies. "A small fountain or water feature?"

In a theater? "That's not..." I trail off. "Oh! I do have a tank for my goldfish."

She perks up at this and types into her phone. "Goldfish? Even better." Hazel and I exchange glances, pleased with ourselves, as though we've passed some sort of test.

I have no idea where I'll put something like that, and there's no way the theater's letting me bring in fish. But at this point, getting in trouble for sneaking in marine life is the least of my worries.

Chapter 24

HAZEL

"You want me to do *what* with this pipe?" I ask Logan, who's standing ten steps away from me. He's wearing a face shield, goggles, a helmet, gloves, closed-toed shoes, and a long-sleeve navy and purple tie-dye shirt and pants. He looks ridiculous. Which means I also look ridiculous, because I'm basically in the exact same outfit.

"Swing it at that." He points to what looks like a castle balcony. "Give it everything you got."

When Logan asked if he could see me after work on a Thursday night, I didn't anticipate we'd be going out to a New Jersey storage building filled with... old Broadway sets?

This place is the size of a six- or seven-car garage. There's an open area, where we are, that's surrounded by sets and props. Some are exposed while others are covered in drop cloths. It's eclectic, but handwritten signs hanging above various areas of the unit create a sense of organization.

Under one of the cloths, the corner of a grandfather clock—or a coffin—pokes out.

"This feels like the start of a murder mystery," I say. "And not a cozy one."

Logan laughs. "This is the start of something, but not that."

"It's the start of my criminal record, isn't it?" I look around skeptically. "Is this private property?"

"Yeah. But we can be here."

"Who did you pay off this time?"

"Myself," Logan says. "To make extra money, I run a storage and transfer business. Mrs. Walker and some other producers store their old sets here. Some haven't paid me in years, and they don't care about those sets anymore, so..." He gestures again. "Have at it."

I hold the pipe up in the air and let it drop down on the balcony. If this were a murder mystery, I would not be very good at it.

"I left a mark," I say, analyzing my damage on the railing.

Logan runs his glove over it. "I can hardly feel it. Try again."

I bring my arm down with a little more force this time. The pipe nearly bounces back and hits me in the face. I do manage to take a little chunk of wood out.

I adjust my face shield. "Oops. I can fix that. A little wood glue, no problem."

"That's not the point of this."

"What is the point of this?"

"To break it."

"But it's too pretty!"

And it is. Even after years in storage. The balcony's curved front has an ornate vine-like pattern, the design underneath even more detailed. This balcony was made for a queen, for sure.

Logan doesn't fight this and instead moves the balcony out of the way. He's careful with his casted arm, but the vein in his right arm bulges as he grips the railing and pushes off with his legs to gain momentum. I should offer to help, but I'm too distracted watching him. He pulls an eight-foot faded yellow crescent moon from the shadows.

"I am not hitting that," I say. "Look at the moon's face! Those little cheeks!"

"You're breaking something in here, Hazel. It's either this or the next thing I bring out."

I wave the pipe. "Next. Mr. Moon doesn't deserve this."

Logan pushes Mr. Moon back into the shadows. Watching him disappear into storage, never to see the light of day, makes me a little sad.

"Whatever you're feeling right now, use it," Logan says. "On this." He slides out a four-foot chimney painted to look like brick. "It's from the *Mary Poppins* musical."

"You don't think Mary will want it back?"

"Given that it's been over a decade since they've used it, no," Logan says. "All of these sets have been here for years. They can sit in here for longer or they can be put toward something good."

"How is me smashing this up something good?" I ask.

"Because it'll be a release." Logan comes over to me and flips his face shield up. I do the same so there's one less barrier between us. "The other day, you said you didn't know what to do with your feelings. You've talked about how you numb yourself." He taps on the chimney. "Put your feelings here. Onto this. You're always giving so much of yourself to others, but who's giving anything to you? You deserve good things, too. You deserve love and support and help. All the time. Not just on special occasions."

"This sounds like a great exercise for you to try," I say, trying to hand him the pipe. "Express what you've been suppressing." He doesn't take it.

"Next time. This isn't about me," he says, running his hands down my arms. "We can talk about it more after, but right now, we're not here to talk. We're here for you to *feel*."

He doesn't need to spell it out any more than this. I know what he's getting at.

"You've been fixing all your life," Logan says. "Now it's time to break something."

I nod and flip my face shield down, and he steps back and does the same with his. He leans against a vintage car, waiting.

We're clearly not leaving until I demolish something, so the chimney will have to do. I decide to make this quick. The faster I smash this chimney up, the faster we get back to Manhattan. Logan promised me pizza afterward.

I raise the pipe over my head with both arms and swing it down hard and fast. I gasp as the lip of the chimney crumbles.

Drips of adrenaline trickle through my bloodstream. That felt... satisfying.

That one's going to be a little harder to fix, though.

Not the point, I remind myself.

I look over at Logan, who's beaming. "Amazing!" he cheers.

Fueled by his encouragement, I knock one of the two pipes right off the top.

After this strike, adrenaline is joined by dopamine. It rushes through me in tingly waves. They crash down on the feelings I've packed away neatly inside, chipping away at each one.

Dad is the first to come to mind. His manipulation. His lies. His selfish charm.

I go quiet and try to name what I feel.

I feel frustrated. I feel mad. I feel small.

I whack the second pipe off, and it flies into a sunset-painted backdrop.

Thoughts of my brother and his lies float to the surface.

I feel annoyed. I feel used. I feel betrayed.

THE FORTUNE FLIP

I take another swing, this time from the side. The pipe crashes into the chimney's walls. It collapses.

I think about losing Mom.

Whack!

Losing Grandma and Grandpa.

Thwack!

Losing myself.

I wallop the other side of the set where the paint has started to crack from the force.

Losing the lake house.

Thump!

Losing my sense of home.

Whack!

From behind a chandelier, the tip of the Empire State Building peeks out. It's a painted backdrop of the New York City skyline. This city is my home. It's where I moved to have freedom. To be my own person. It's taken me a while to get there, but now it's time. Time to start building not just a life, but *my* life.

I tighten my grip on the pipe.

The rest comes in bursts: my divorce. My job loss. Being alone. Feeling alone.

My nose tingles, and what's left of the chimney blurs. I blink through it, still swinging.

My heart is racing, my lungs burning from taking in too much air too fast. I've never felt more grounded in my body. I'm fully present for this.

The pipe is light in my hands. Almost as light as the cardboard check.

I feel surprised. I feel relieved.

Something breaks open inside me.

Just like this chimney.

I send the pipe straight into the center, polishing off the remaining bricks.

My chest warms as the stinging fades.

I think of Emma and Gloria, who I've kept at a distance. They haven't distanced me in return.

I feel included. I feel accepted.

I strike the base, breaking what's left of its foundation. The set is now in pieces all over the concrete floor. It's no longer a structure, just chimney confetti made by my own hands.

What was once whole is now shattered. It's a mess.

It's still beautiful.

I'm still beautiful.

I kneel into the remnants of the set, scooping up pieces of red and white flakes into my hands. I squeeze them into a soft fist before opening my hand again. The flakes fall through my fingers like water.

I glance over my shoulder at Logan. "I can definitely still fix this," I say softly.

A smile spreads across his face before he breaks into laughter.

I fling the pipe into the mess. I strip off my face shield, helmet, goggles, and gloves. He does the same.

I'm not alone anymore.

Then I close the distance between us and jump into his arms. My lips crash against his, his mouth parting to let me in. Our kisses taste tear-salted, but these are happy ones.

I pull back and lock eyes with him. The day's last rays of sun shine behind Logan's head, turning his sandy hair gold. I smile at the sight. This moment...it's exactly what being with Logan feels like—emerging from the darkness and stepping into the light.

"I love you," we say at the same time. My version comes out urgent. Desperate. Like I need him to know right this very second.

His version is steady and sure. Like he's had time to sit with this idea for some time.

"I love you," I say again, simply for the fact that it feels so fucking good to say.

This is *the* feeling. The ultimate one.

I laugh through my tears, this jumble of emotions bubbling up inside me and fizzing out over the rim.

Logan smiles, his cheeks wet with my tears. It's a perfect metaphor, I think, for what we've been to each other: safe spaces to figure out our emotions. He doesn't wipe them off.

"Hazel," he says. "I've loved you since the moment we pretended to be old together."

I blink the tears out. "Not when I hatched the plan to help you increase your luck?"

"I don't need you to fix anything for me. Not then, not now, not ever. I just need you to be with me."

I know how he means this. That's all I need, too.

But right now, I also need him in another way.

"Off," I instruct, surprised by my own directness.

Logan does as I say. As he pulls the shirt over his head, I'm reminded of how strong he is. How solid.

I lift my arms. Without further instruction, Logan tugs off my long-sleeve shirt. He does the same with my tank underneath. I push him back against the vintage car. He tucks one finger into the waistband of my pants and pulls me to him so he can undo my button. He's kissing me as he does this, and I mirror every single thing he does. Unbutton, unzip.

I shimmy out of my pants as he kicks his off. His eyes take in every inch of me while I do the same to him.

He reaches around to the door handle, pulling it open. I slide into the backseat, moving myself backward. Logan crawls in over me, resting his elbows on either side of my head, pressing our hearts together.

I part his lips with my tongue and kiss him like he's the best thing.

Because he is. He's the very best thing.

Logan drops a trail of kisses from my forehead to my nose to my lips to my chin. He makes his way down my neck and collarbones, his breath hot against my chest.

"Holy shit, we won the lottery," I whisper, the full impact of our win just now hitting me.

He grunts. "Yeah."

I grip his hair as he draws a line down my stomach with his tongue. I try to pull him back to me to give him kisses. To express everything that's pouring out of me. He shakes his head.

"No more giving. No more fixing. Now you get to take," he says as we shed the last of our clothing.

So I do.

For the rest of the evening, I manage to take while still giving just enough back. I can't help it. What we do, it's the opposite of mind-numbing. Mind-blowing isn't quite what I'd call it, either. How we finally get to explore this tension and how gentle yet commanding he is, how he unravels me from my very core... it's mind-melting.

Logan says he loves me. I say it in return.

I feel elated. I feel safe. I feel loved.

And without needing a fortune teller's confirmation, I know I'm going to feel this way again and again and again in the future.

Chapter 25

LOGAN

On day one of dress rehearsals, one week out from opening night, Richie figures out the star drop problem. A new issue pops up: A full moon backdrop was never painted. That's how it's been for the past few days. We take one step forward and two steps back. We rebuild the dock's legs, but the new corner snags on the curtain. The canoe now glides out to center stage, but it's wobbly on its track, making the actors, who are now rehearsing in full hair and makeup, nervous.

What's making me nervous is that Mrs. Walker is here for today's rehearsal. Her presence brings an entirely new energy to the space. And that's on top of the questionable energy An-Ming called out.

Since An-Ming provided her recommendations for bringing more balance into the theater, I organized everything from top to bottom over the weekend. I did manage to get clearance for a few plants, but it was a *no* to the fish tank.

During one of our breaks, I head out to the woodshop we've set up on the sidewalk outside the theater. I clear my head with fresh air and a personal project that takes me out of the world of *Windfall*. It feels good working with my chop saw and building something again with my hands, even for just thirty minutes. Maybe I should've never stopped being a carpenter.

"Logan! Are you avoiding me?" Mrs. Walker asks over the buzz of my saw.

She's bundled up in an oversize wool jacket, her shoulder-length, highlighted blond hair styled in its usual way.

I cut the power and remove my goggles. "Impossible. You know where I live."

Mrs. Walker smirks. "It's true. I'm unavoidable." She checks the time on her gold watch. "Got time for a break? I need to get my joints moving."

"Of course," I say, holding out my arm for her to link hers through for stability.

"It's nice to see my creations getting some wear," she says, motioning toward my tie-dye shirt.

"They're perfectly good clothes," I say. "I've worn them for almost every show I've worked on." I always thought they were lucky, but now I don't know what they are.

Mrs. Walker subtly lifts her cheetah-printed silk scarf. "I've got one, too. Don't tell anyone. I just didn't peg you as the superstitious type."

We slowly walk toward Times Square, which is slightly less busy than it was twenty minutes ago. The matinee shows have started. "Why's that?" I ask.

"You've always struck me as a make-your-own-luck kind of guy," Mrs. Walker says, peering up at me through her bangs. "How are things? I've heard it's been a rough start."

Mrs. Walker has poured her money into this show. She's fought for it to get to Broadway. I don't want her to be more stressed or to think that we—I—can't handle it. Especially not after what she's done for me.

I can respond positively. *Challenges make us better*, I almost say.

Nothing we can't handle has been a comfortable go-to.

I'm grateful to even have this job. Another subtle way I've basically gaslit myself in the name of gratitude.

But that would be dishonest for what Mrs. Walker's really trying to ask.

I can redirect. Readjust. Or at least try. Clearly, this is a mindset that's going to take a while to retrain.

"It has been rough, yes. Very rough, actually," I admit. I practically have to bite down on my tongue from tacking on anything else that counteracts this statement. "Have you ever wanted to not produce?"

"You're asking if I ever wanted to quit?" Mrs. Walker asks as I nod. "Most days. I've thought about starting over. Going back into acting. Hell, I've even considered retiring. Long before now."

"Why didn't you?" I ask, keeping hold of Mrs. Walker by her arm.

"Working in the theater, it's demanding. What every single person does within those walls is hard work. But we're on Broadway! This is the dream." Her head swivels over to me. "Don't tell me you're thinking of quitting."

I glance up at the billboards featuring shows old and new. "I just… I thought I'd be more prepared," I say. "More ready. I don't know if I can do this. I don't know if this is going to make my rent go up, but… so many things have gone wrong because of me. I wanted to do right by you and Roman. I couldn't even do that after everything you've done for me."

Saying this to my boss and my landlord is probably not the way to handle this. I'm in charge. I should be portraying the picture of confidence, but that's just not where I am.

Mrs. Walker's mouth is a hard underscore before she releases a long sigh. "Ah well. Love does that to a person."

I do a double-take, looking over as her words take a second to sink in. Then I'm not so confused.

"Is it that obvious?" I ask.

She chuckles. "Is Times Square bright at night?" she poses. "I've never heard you utter a negative word in the entire time I've known you, so clearly someone's affected you in a good way."

"You think my negativity is good?"

"I think the fact you're being honest about how hard work has been is good," she clarifies.

I'm back to being confused. It must come across in my silence as I try to figure it out.

Mrs. Walker clasps my arm. "It's easy when a job is your entire life. It's all you have to think about, all you have to focus on." She looks up at me. "But when your life is your job *and* someone else, well, it's different. Love... it's the greatest thing in the world. It's also distracting."

"I promise you this show is important to me. I wouldn't do anything to jeopardize it."

We're in the thick of Times Square now, shuffling past people—tourists, mostly—in our lap around the block. Most people I meet think of this area as chaos. These five blocks contain the best theater productions in the world, plus shopping, restaurants, and the brightest lights in all of Manhattan. Chaos? It's more like an energy source.

"Of course you wouldn't," Mrs. Walker says as we pass a human-size Minnie Mouse. I immediately think of Hazel and her tattoo. "This work saved your life. I know how important it is to you. And now you've found someone who makes you want to put work second. And I don't mean it doesn't matter to you, but not everything can come first. When your priorities shift like this, growth happens. Growth is uncomfortable."

Can that be true? Do I really care more about Hazel than I care about my work? I couldn't even pinpoint the moment that happened. Ever since meeting her, she just gradually, naturally, became more important. She became my priority.

"When a show moves from Off Broadway to Broadway,"

Mrs. Walker continues, "there's a lot of discomfort that comes with it. It's hard to see something great change, but it must. You need more money, production becomes more complicated, the sets get bigger. The show isn't better or worse, but it is different. You have to learn to accept that."

"And I'm...Broadway now?" I ask, trying to keep up.

"Your life has more in it. You're on Broadway and in love," she says dreamily. "It doesn't get better than that!"

"So I need to learn to be uncomfortable with being bad at my job because I'm in love."

"As your employer, I'm probably required to tell you not to be bad at your job, but yeah. You have to make room for the other stuff, too." Mrs. Walker jabs her finger in the air toward a theater we pass by. "These shows come and go. Once-in-a-lifetime love doesn't." She taps my arm. "I care more about you than this job."

"Really?"

"I can't believe I even need to say it. I also care more about my husband in the ground than this job," she says, clearing her throat at the mention of her husband. "I met Roman when I was in *Cats*. Something changed inside me," she says. "I thought my world was going to come crashing down on me. Not unlike the *Windfall* set."

"Ha, ha," I mumble as we make a turn around the corner and away from the crowds. "Is that what happened to your world? Did it crash down?"

"The opposite. Love built me up," Mrs. Walker says. "My life expanded when I met him. Suddenly, my whole world wasn't just that one role I played onstage every night. It was so much more."

I nod, taking in every piece she shares with me.

"As for doing right by me and Roman, you already have, Logan," she says earnestly. "Don't you see? You were there for me after he died just as much as I was there for you. It was your excitement about getting to New York, about getting to Broadway, that reinvigorated"—she waves her hand in front of us—"all this for me. And okay, fine, the biscotti helped, too."

At this, a boulder lifts off my shoulders. All this time, she had offered me such tangible help—an apartment, a job—that I didn't think I was giving enough back. Maybe I was.

Mrs. Walker smiles toward the clouds. "As for Roman, he'd be thrilled something he wrote was being mentioned in the same breath as Broadway. Doing this as my last show...it's one hell of a way to go out."

"You've always known how to make an entrance and an exit."

She bumps me with her elbow. "Keep up the flattery, and I'll knock another ten percent off your rent," she says through a chuckle. We pause for a couple of latecomers sprinting toward a theater. "Sometimes we get too into the weeds with how we think things need to go that we forget to appreciate that they're even happening at all." She turns to face me. "There will be mistakes, Logan. They won't be the end of the world."

The words hit their mark. Mistakes won't be the end of the world because they won't be my entire world.

Once, this job was everything to me. Now it's not even close to being everything.

"It's your first show as head carpenter, and maybe even your first time in love. Go easy on yourself. Life will give you enough splinters," she says. "So will work. Take, for instance, what prompted me needing a bit of fresh air. We have no moon backdrop. In every mock-up I signed off on, there was a moon in the background of key scenes. And what do we have now, just days away from the show opening?"

"No moon."

"No moon," she emphasizes. "I'd go out there and do it myself, but do you know how hard it is to paint a perfect circle? What ideas have you got?"

THE FORTUNE FLIP

"Not sure that I have any," I say.

"Oh, sure you do."

I shrug. "I don't think I can be much help here. I'm doing more harm than good, honestly."

Mrs. Walker pulls back and shoots me a disbelieving face. "Do you remember for *Chicago* how we were missing a letter in the sign onstage? The one with the light bulbs?" she asks.

"Yeah. No one could find the *I*."

"And what the hell's a *Chcago*? You took down one of the dressing room mirrors and did something"—she boxes the air with her hands—"with it to transform it into a usable letter."

"I lucked out on that one," I say with a huff. "You know not all dressing rooms have those types of mirrors, right?"

"Luck? No. You made that happen. I think you also enjoy challenges, too," Mrs. Walker says. "I see a lot of myself in you. You take limes and turn them into key lime pie."

"Is this your way of making *me* go out there and paint an oblong moon?"

"You're very talented," she says. "But not paint-a-perfect-circle talented. I'm going to figure it out. It'll be a nice creative break from all the contracts I've been reading."

As we walk back into the theater, there's a loud thump as the wobbly canoe topples over.

"We're not going to be ready for previews," Mrs. Walker says definitively.

"There isn't a way to get more time?" I try. "Two weeks? Maybe four?"

She laughs. "That's why it's called previews. By the time critics come for the real opening night, we'll be ready."

Will we, though?

"Or as ready as we'll ever be," she corrects. "We rehearse and prepare to make our future easier. Yet, things still go wrong. They also go right. You know how the superstition goes: Bad dress rehearsals mean that opening night will be a success."

"Have you found that to be true over the years?" I ask.

"Yes and no," Mrs. Walker says, tilting her head in consideration. "Opening nights are never flawless, but never has one crashed and burned so spectacularly that we couldn't recover from it. There are mistakes that happen onstage and backstage. You know how many people notice? Very few."

She lets go of my arm, patting my shoulder in thanks. "When I was in *Cats*, I would prowl and leap across the stage. Now I can hardly get out of bed." She shrugs. "It means I've lived an active life, right? I'm glad to still be here."

"Yeah," I agree, finding comfort in this familiar, positive territory. "But it also kind of sucks."

Mrs. Walker laughs. "That it does, Logan. That it does."

The cast and crew file in for an afternoon of more rehearsals.

I turn to face her and, before we have to get back to work, say, "Can I ask you something? When you gave me a chance all those years ago, why did you do it?"

Mrs. Walker looks surprised. "Why do you think I did it?"

"I was in the right place at the right time," I say, fidgeting with my hat out of habit. "I got lucky meeting you when I did. You gave me my first break in this industry."

She huffs through her nose. "Luck will only get you so far." She peers at me. "You don't remember all the emails you sent me?"

"I think I recall sending a thank-you email, yes—"

"There was that, yeah," Mrs. Walker says. "But you also followed up with me every month with theater news you thought I'd be interested in and shows you expressed a desire to be a part of."

"So you helped me so I would stop annoying you, basically," I joke.

"Certainly that, but also it was your persistence that got you your first break," she says. "You not only knew what you wanted but you voiced it. It was like you knew something was going to happen at some point. It was a matter of when, not if."

"I don't remember it that way," I confess.

I don't remember it taking months for me to finally get to New York with a job. I don't remember the multiple follow-ups.

The process of getting here felt relatively quick, but maybe that's my mind smoothing over the bumps. I only remember telling Mrs. Walker what I was passionate about, but that's how I've always been.

"Very rarely do things just happen for people, Logan. We have more control than we think," she says. "You know what I loved about being an actress in the theater? Each night, everyone gets a chance to do it all over again. Not just the cast. Every single person, on and off the stage. Every show is a new opportunity. So, you, Mr. Wells, need to get back out there and try something you haven't yet. Your persistence is somewhere in there. Dig deep for it, because I want that moon. And as they say, the show must go on!"

Windfall was once an idea, and now it's a world with a set and lines and a cast and music and a whole team of people working invisibly behind the scenes. And isn't that really what luck is? Invisible, often unacknowledged work that we put in to make things happen for ourselves? Day after day after day.

Sometimes progress happens in big strokes. It also happens in small bursts, over and over again. When something's not working, we acknowledge it and try something else.

After my accident, I tried something else. I went in a different direction.

From the moment I said no to who I was, to my father, and to the money, I got closer to who I am today. Because I said *no*, I could say *yes*. Yes to opportunities, yes to this new job.

Yes to the lottery.

Yes to Hazel.

Every show isn't just a new opportunity.

Every day is.

Up until recently, I've said a hell of a lot of *yesses*. It's possible I really have been making a hell of a lot of my own luck, too.

It's time for me to own that, and whatever comes with it. Good or bad.

I see the stage and all the set pieces as a new problem to solve. I stand in the wings. I go backstage. I move down to the seats where the audience will sit and analyze it from that perspective. A seed of an idea forms.

I find Richie. "Instead of a canoe, what if we did a rowboat?" I pitch. "It'll give us the width we need, and we can add wheels underneath each corner. That way we can roll it forward from backstage, which gives us more room to work with, and the leads can sit side by side instead of facing each other."

Richie considers this. "Fucking finally. Where's that brain of yours been? That's great. It'll be safer for them, too."

"Oh, and I may have a solution for the moon," I tell him.

Before our second rehearsal of the day, I huddle up with everyone who's had a hand in getting this show to where it is now. The rest of the afternoon will be dedicated to figuring out what's not working, to making progress, to making opening night the best it can be with what we have.

We take it from the top and try again.

Chapter 26

HAZEL

"Halloween hasn't even happened yet, and you have Christmas candy out?" Gloria asks, hugging a jar of gingerbread people gummies. "Of all the people to play that game, Emma, I didn't think it'd be you."

Emma snorts as she sets a box on the counter. "The making-money game? Because I'm very much here to play that. That's literally how this store keeps its lights on. Here's the rest of the white-chocolate snowballs, Hazel."

"Snowballs? This is all too soon, darling, but hey, inventory management is above my pay grade." Gloria slices the box open and scoops a few of the chocolates into her bowl. We each try one. "Okay, those are delightful! I take it back. Give me all the holiday candy!"

"The chocolate turkeys are over there if you want something more relevant." Emma nods to the corner where she's also stocked maple candies. "And I can't take credit. It was Hazel's idea."

Chocolate melts on my tongue as I wipe down the checkout screen. "Having the holiday candy out doesn't put off the customers," I say. "When you put out St. Patrick's Day inventory at Valentine's Day, there was a huge bump in heart candy and chocolate sales."

"I accidentally ordered them too early," Emma says, grimacing. "Figured we might as well try to move it."

"Oh yeah, I remember that," Gloria says. "I thought you were confused about which month it was."

"What it does is put the more immediate holiday front and center and make people want to enjoy it more," I explain. "Trends across the industry also indicate that people are trying to stretch out the collective holidays for as long as possible. Have you heard of Summerween?"

"Summerwhatnow?" Gloria asks.

"A lot of people now celebrate Halloween in the summer," I explain. "We should definitely order more of those"—I point to the jar of candy bones—"in July."

"You've really been paying attention when ringing up customers," Emma says.

I spin my laptop around. "Actually, it's all in the data."

Emma focuses on my screen. "Is that...did you make a presentation?"

"It's still rough. I analyzed the point-of-sale data and created a few reports." I go to the next slide. "I hope that's okay. I have some ideas."

"Go on," Emma says, removing a notepad from the counter's shelf. She and Gloria lean in.

I bring up the next slide. "Have you ever considered a loyalty program?" I ask. "You have a lot of repeat customers. They come by every two weeks, usually between five and seven. A punch card or rewards app is a great way to give back to those customers. Maybe when they get all ten stamped, they get a free mixed bag of candy. It'd be a good way to promote new-to-them inventory."

Emma writes this down.

On the next slide, I have my graphs and numbers neatly arranged so it's easy to understand the story I'm trying to tell. "In the week before big holidays—Lunar New Year, Valentine's Day, Fourth of

July, New Year's—you have customers buying hundreds of dollars' worth of candy."

"People love to drop by to stock up on candy for their parties," Emma says.

"Have you considered putting together themed candy boxes or charcuterie boards for parties?" I ask.

"Candy charcuterie?" Gloria asks, intrigued.

I nod. "I think they'd be cute."

Gloria snickers. "Candy char-*cute*-erie."

I smile as Emma writes that down, too.

"If you did it, that'd make it easier for customers," I go on. "You could also take custom orders. And because your store has candy from all over the world, you could put together special boxes. Like a Tray of Togetherness for Lunar New Year with lucky sweets, chocolate coins, dried fruits, nuts."

"Yes! My family always has those. How did I not think of that?" Emma says.

"All the numbers from this"—Gloria places her hand on the laptop in its stand—"told you that?" she says, pointing to my screen.

"The numbers have stories to tell if you listen," I say.

"Well, isn't that romantic?" Gloria says. "But how do you know if they're saying something bad or good?"

"It's less about them being bad or good and more that I figure out how to interpret them," I say.

"How do these interpretations turn out?" Emma asks.

"Yeah," Gloria says. "Once you figure something out with the numbers, did you make your company millions of dollars?"

"There were times I saved them millions of dollars, yes. My forecasts weren't always accurate, though. Sometimes I'd have misleading results when I didn't have enough data to paint a full picture. Or there would be extreme data points that skewed my readings..." I trail off.

I play back my words. Readings. Forecasts. Interpretations.

You're like a data fortune teller, Logan had said.

I decipher data just like the fortune tellers have decoded our cards, tea leaves, palms. We both take numbers and fortunes and find the stories in them.

Sometimes, though, the stories had plot twists. Past data isn't a perfect predictor of the future. Though it sometimes does, history doesn't always repeat itself.

Which means I also know that just like with data, there is no insight without interpretation. Action still needs to be taken. Choices must be made. The steps Logan and I took were based on how we deciphered our fortunes.

Logan bought the lottery ticket. We drove, not flew. I said yes to an unexpected manager interview.

Gloria shrugs. "Close enough."

"This is amazing, but it's above and beyond," Emma says. "Don't feel like you have to do extra work. Seriously. You're valuable as you are, and this job is yours for as long as you need."

"How's the job search been going?" Gloria asks, leaning against the counter.

"It's been going well. Weirdly well," I say, realizing I haven't thought to update them.

"Weird?" Gloria asks. "What's weird?"

"The interviews?" Emma asks.

"I mean in general," I say, touched by their concern. "Things don't go so smoothly for me. Or better than expected. I was offered a manager role."

The news came in this morning. Gloria and Emma are the first I've told in person.

"That's incredible!" Emma says as Gloria shouts, "Whoopee!" and swings her arms into the air. I must be making a face because her arms flop down by her side. "Darling, does this not make you happy?"

"No. I mean, yes? It's great," I say. Because it is. It's a lot more money, which is exactly what I need. I'm moving up. Getting a more impressive title. I could pay for the house. Isn't that what I've worked for? Isn't that the dream?

But I've had a lot of dreams, haven't I? I've dreamed of a normal life. Of a father who I didn't have to worry about stealing from me instead of giving me birthday money. Of an older brother who protected me instead of hurting me. Of a lake house with a happy family inside instead of people who care more about themselves than each other.

Not all dreams come true.

"It's *really* great," I say too emphatically.

"What's your hesitation?" Emma asks. "Do you not want this job?"

Take the job, save the house.

Don't take the job, lose the house.

"I don't..." I stiffen. "No."

"You don't know?" Gloria asks.

"No. Yes," I say, backtracking. "No. I don't know."

I've never had a chance to get to know what I want. I've always been too busy doing what I needed to do.

What's the data telling me? I could put together an entire spreadsheet with all the times Dad and Jerry have dug themselves into a hole and lied to me about it, and with the ways I've sacrificed myself to help them out of it.

"What's your gut telling you?" Emma asks.

My gut?

I'm silent for too long, and they both lose interest and get back to work. Emma busies herself with a Post-it while Gloria fills up her candy bowl.

But then Emma walks over to the front door, tapes the Post-it onto the glass, and flips the "Open" sign around. Gloria waves me over to join her at the sitting area in the front of the store. "Come. Sit." They're not getting back to work. They're temporarily closing the store. For me.

Emma speaks first. "Hazel, Gloria and I have gotten the sense that it's hard for you to open up—"

"Trust people," Gloria says around a mouthful of candy, offering me the bowl. "You've always been suspicious. Of others. *You* aren't suspicious. Well, you kind of are with how secretive you—"

"Thanks, Glo. You know what, I got this," Emma says, patting her knee. She turns to me. "Hazel, we would never want to pressure you into telling us anything or doing anything you're uncomfortable with, but we want you to know that you can always talk to us. We might just be your coworkers—"

"I thought we agreed on candy crew," Gloria interjects.

Emma gives Gloria a look. "We might just be your candy crew, but we'd also like to be your friends."

Friends. I don't even know how to have friends. Or how to be a friend.

Gloria nods quickly. "Thanks to candy, we were all brought together. That's got to mean something. You don't have to talk to us now if you don't want, but we're here whenever you do."

"I—I..."

Emma and Gloria each take one of my hands in theirs. I draw in a tight breath. They've made me feel nothing but accepted.

"My mom died when I was really young," I say, starting slowly. "And from that point forward, I think I always viewed myself as needing to replace her in my family. To be the person who cared for everybody. Who fixed all their problems. Who put them above herself, at all costs."

"Oh, Hazel," Gloria whispers.

"I'm starting to realize that a lot of decisions I've made in my life maybe gave people—my family—the ability not to have to worry about their decisions. And maybe that scares me because if I'm not needed, then who am I?"

It's overwhelming to say this out loud. I don't try to numb it away. Instead, I let myself feel the weight of these words.

"Darling, you've got a lifetime to figure that out," Gloria says gently. "But also, what you've said, it isn't fully true. You are needed... by you. You've spent all these years looking out for others, but now it's time for you to look out for yourself."

"What are your hopes?" Emma asks. "What are your dreams?"

I look between Emma and Gloria. It's not that there haven't been people to trust. It's that I haven't let myself notice them. Before I glance away, in one of the reflections of the glass candy jar, I catch an oblong, blurry reflection of myself.

I haven't let myself trust me, either.

"I...I don't know. I was the one who had to think about everything," I say. "At some point, I started acting as impulsively as what I had witnessed growing up. Too-high highs made me scared for the drop. Too-low lows had me reaching for something that could bring me out of it. I'm impulsive, and I'm afraid I'll hurt people I don't want to hurt."

I recall my thoughtlessness with Logan at the theater, right before he took me to Top of the Rock. My heart rate accelerates. Wasn't our whole relationship built on recklessness? Me going to the fortune teller that led to a chaotic reading? My impromptu plans to fix Logan's luck without much success? I've brought him into my ups and downs.

"Maybe you've made impulsive decisions," Gloria says, her voice more serious than I've ever heard it. "And maybe those decisions have led to less-than-ideal situations. But I'd bet this entire candy store that some of those quick choices you've made have led to something good."

"Hey! Speaking of being rash," Emma says. "You can't be using this place as collateral."

Gloria waves her off. "On the day I first came into your store, Emma, I was supposed to meet someone for a date at a restaurant around the corner."

Emma looks confused before something clicks. "That's why you were dressed up. I'd never seen someone with so much fur on before. You looked like a bear."

"It was faux, darling," Gloria reassures us.

"You..." Emma blinks in surprise. "You hung out with me all night. You had a date?"

Gloria shrugs. "It was your opening week. You were panicking about how you were offered partner, and instead of accepting it, you quit your high-paying, stable, fancy lawyer job on the spot to open this." She looks around at all the worldly trinkets lining the walls. "We make thoughtless decisions all the time, whether we realize it or not. Sometimes impulsivity can lead to the very best things."

"You ghosted your date for me?" Emma grabs Gloria's hand, her eyes glistening. "Thank you."

Gloria taps her hand. "This is why I deserve more than a fifteen-percent discount on candy."

I huff a laugh at this as my thoughts wander to my hasty tattoo, which intrigued Logan enough to buy me a charm because of it. In my mind's eye, I see Logan and me dressed up as the older versions of ourselves. An act that ultimately led to our true identities being revealed, which led to the truth coming out to my dad. A truth that I hadn't been fully ready to face but needed to.

I think again of the fortune reading. If I had never made that impulsive decision, I never would've met Logan. The thought sends pinpricks down my body.

Sometimes impulsivity can lead to the very best things.

Take the job, save the house.

Don't take the job, lose the house.

Everything I've wanted before, it's not what I want anymore.

And that's okay. I can give myself permission. I can dream new dreams.

"I love what I do," I say, staring at the bowl of gingerbread gummies. "I want to keep working in data. But I don't want to be a manager. I've managed people my whole life. I don't want to do that anymore." I pinch my eyebrows together. "It feels wrong to say that."

"Because it's deeply ingrained in us to constantly strive and achieve more," Emma says as Gloria nods beside her. "I felt this when I left my job."

"Yes," I say, a little breathless. It's such a relief to know I'm not the only one who's felt this way. "We're supposed to climb the ladder, make more money. Do more, be more. Otherwise, you're getting in the way. You're a rock in a river while everyone rushes around you."

"Isn't it tiring living your life based on what other people think you should do?" Emma asks.

Gloria points a dark-purple-manicured finger at me. "What does Hazel Yen want?"

The lake house pushes its way front and center. Then my grandparents. And Mom. To lose the house Grandpa built, the house that Mom loved, would feel like I was disappointing them.

If we lose the house, it feels like losing them.

I run my fingers along my bracelet, feeling each of the charms. Mom's just as much in this bracelet as she is in that house. She's in me, just as much as she's in anything.

I make my way around to the bird.

"You know, phoenixes symbolize rebirth," Gloria says, watching me. "After destruction and hardship, they emerge stronger. They rise from the ashes and start over."

"This isn't a phoenix," I say, confused. "It's a dove."

Gloria squints at the charm. "That's a phoenix if I've ever seen one."

"Because it works better for your metaphor?" Emma asks.

"Precisely. Eagles are symbolic, too, if you'd be willing to meet me there," she offers.

Emma smiles. "Well, doves represent freedom and peace."

A laugh bubbles out of my throat. Phoenix. Eagle. Dove. All I hear is: more birds.

"When you quit your job to open this place," I ask Emma, "were you scared?"

"Shitless," Emma says without missing a beat. "But I had spent years working for others. It was time to do something for me." She looks around her shop appreciatively. "If there's anything I learned, it's that the future is not written. When I passed the bar, my fifteen-year plan did not look...this orange."

"A psychic once told me I was going to be married three times," Gloria says. "I've only had two marriages, but hey, there's still time."

We have so many people telling us what our futures should look like. Get a good job. Then get a better one. Get married. Have kids. Buy a house. Live in the suburbs.

But what if I don't want all of that? What if I want to change that vision? Make my own version?

What if I want a shoebox of an apartment with a boyishly handsome man with way too many tie-dye shirts?

What if I want to choose myself for once? What then? It's like Gloria said, there's still time.

And it's time—and my actions—that will tell what happens in my life. Not a bunch of fortune tellers. I want to have a say in what my life looks like. Present and future.

"I want to be here for the candy charcuterie," I blurt out. "I want to help with the register, and clean the shelves and tables, and fill up jars with candy. And when I have time in between that, I'd like to analyze your data."

Emma looks surprised. "You want to work here? With us?"

Gloria beams at her use of *us*.

"I do," I say. I feel so sure about it, too, I find. "I don't want to be a cog in a machine. I want to add real value. Our days make up a life. And I don't want to save a billion-dollar company millions of dollars."

"You want to save my candy store thousands?" Emma asks.

"I really, really do," I say with a little laugh. "Being here, helping customers, spending time with you two, that's made me happy these past few weeks. This place makes every customer who comes in here happy, too. I want to be part of something like that."

"I'd love to hire you full-time, but I can't afford to match what you'd be making as a manager, let alone a data analyst," Emma says, looking apologetic.

I smile. "I think I'll be able to make it work." These words, this decision. They're for me. That's something I need to get used to.

"You can make it work, huh?" Gloria asks, flashing me a wink. It reminds me of the day at Grand Central when she—and Emma, now that I think about it—didn't dig deeper into the lottery name coincidence. I just figured we were all busy and that they weren't interested in that kind of thing, but... had it been more than that?

The question is on the tip of my tongue when Gloria says, "Her analysis could be useful as you try to expand."

"You want to expand?" I ask.

Emma's nod turns into a head circle. "It's a far-fetched dream."

"At my last job, I did analysis on demographic information and consumer behavior in various areas to help my company figure out where to open new locations," I tell her. "I can help you. No. We can help each other."

Emma smiles. "I would love that. Okay, you're hired... again! But hear me when I say this: You had the job before you said all that."

I sit back. "Just like that?"

"Just like that," Emma confirms.

Leaving a six-figure job to work as a cashier–slash–data analyst at a candy shop for five figures? I don't think anyone could've seen that coming. I'm thrilled.

"Speaking of, we need to talk about my pay raise," Gloria says. "I want more money."

"You don't work here, Glo. I don't pay you anything," Emma says.

Gloria huffs. "Exactly. So you see my problem."

"Maybe I could take on the ideas I pitched about the candy boards and rewards program," I say. "And leave inventory and stocking to Glo?"

Gloria smiles at my use of her nickname. "Look at you promoting yourself and you haven't even been here a full month," she says with humor in her voice. "That's what I like to see. And darling, if any of this has to do with Logan—which I'm sure it does because even though you haven't mentioned him by name, seven decades on this earth has made my sense about these things very sharp—so here's what I'll say: Trust yourself."

I listen to my intuition on this one. It tells me Logan's the one.

It also tells me that Emma and Glo are good people.

I smile. Maxwell's lessons don't apply just to Logan. I can apply them to my life, too. Being in the right mindset, saying yes to new opportunities, trusting my gut. Maybe I really can make my own luck.

I continue with another one of his lessons: opening up more to my friends.

I start with the birds.

Chapter 27

HAZEL

Logan's making breakfast for dinner when I swing by his place after my shift at Sweet Escape. He's left the door open so I don't have to knock. So it feels like I'm not a guest.

I slip into his apartment, leaving my shoes in the foyer. He's taken the time to lay out quite the spread on the counter: eggs three ways on a platter. Homemade sausage patties on a plate. A pitcher of juice. A bowl of sliced bananas, apples, and blueberries. Place mats laid out with forks and knives.

My delight turns to surprise when I look at Logan and he's hatless. He glances over his shoulder at me as he runs his hand back and forth through his hair like he's not sure what to do with it. It sticks up in several places, like late afternoon bedhead.

"So that's what the top of your head looks like," I tease. "It's very appealing. You should show it off more often."

"I think it's time to give that thing a break," he says, greeting me with a hug and kiss before handing me a ceramic cup. "Half orange, half grapefruit."

"You remembered." I chug half of the bittersweet blend.

"How could I forget? Waffle batter's resting. I'll make them when we're ready to eat. Should be quick. You want whipped cream on top or on the side?" he asks, hand-whipping heavy cream in a bowl. It's tucked between his cast and a towel, snuggling it in place. Nothing will slow this man down, not even a broken wrist.

"Side, please," I say, admiring the food.

The sight of it all and Logan in his checkered apron cooking for me while Matchbox Twenty plays in the background only deepens my feelings for him. It solidifies the decision I've worked through in the past few days.

I can envision future nights like this. Making a home. Building a life together.

It's what I want. Now it's time to make that happen.

I walk over to his side of the kitchen. "I have something for you," he says, right as I say, "I need to make a call."

"A call?" he asks.

"Yes. And I was hoping you could be here with me during it." I'm more nervous saying it out loud than I had practiced in my head.

I could've made this call alone. It's a part of my life I've hidden from everyone I've ever been with. But the thing is, I don't want to do this on my own anymore.

I don't want to hide what the realities of my life look like from Logan. I've wondered why this is. Why is this relationship different? The best answer I could think of was that, before we knew anything basic about each other, we knew each other's futures. What an odd thing that is.

"Anything you need," he says right away, without knowing the context. He pauses his whisking. "Is someone from the press reaching out about the lottery again?"

"No, it's nothing like that." I set my phone on the counter. "I need to call my dad. I thought about going to the house, doing this face-to-face. But last weekend was so awful, and I know how the dynamic works." I shake a list I had tucked away in my back pocket. "And I have notes."

Because I'm nervous. Because I hate that I even have to do this.

Logan sets the bowl of half-whipped cream next to the waffle maker and turns off the music. "We'll do this however you want," he says, still in the dark about the details. He places his palm against my neck and strokes my cheek with his thumb. "You're not alone in this."

I turn my head to kiss his inner wrist before pulling back. "Wait, did you say you had something for me?"

Logan wipes his hands off on his apron. "I do," he says, walking to the closet in the hallway. He pulls out an object with a sheet draped over it.

He walks whatever it is over to the counter and sets it down in front of me.

"What is it?"

Logan smiles. "I could tell you, or you could just open it."

I pull off the sheet, revealing my grandparents' lake house that's the size of a dollhouse. He... he must've built this for me.

I open my mouth and then close it. That happens a few more times. "I..." Tucked inside the house is an envelope. I slide out two tickets for *Wicked*.

"Was it too soon?" he asks. "I didn't want to be all secretive, but I understand if this is too much."

"Too much?" I manage to squeak out. "It's... it's incredible."

Better, actually. Because this house, it's mine.

He's captured the mash-up of my grandparents' cottage and cabin. The gingerbread trim is in the same spots as the real thing. The wraparound porch has the exact angles. The bay-windowed dining room that juts out toward the lake is right there. He's even included the dock.

The only difference with this version is that he included scallop siding. Like a mermaid's house.

"You didn't even see the lake house until last week," I say, confused.

"You described it to me at the firehouse."

"That's when you started this?" That was before I knew about the pre-foreclosure. He was going to make this no matter what.

"I figured, even if you did one day own it, why wait until then when you could have a mini version of it now?" Logan says.

It's possible I've just fallen in love with Logan all over again.

"I have the house *and* the city," I say, more to myself. This gift unleashes a scratchy throat. A rush of tears.

I let them fall. Logan pulls me to him as my tears soak into his green and orange tie-dye shirt, little wet spots spreading on his chest.

"Your clothes are just my tissues and napkins at this point," I laugh out.

"I can't think of a better use for them," Logan says, gently running his thumbs over my cheeks. "Did you want to eat first or make the call?"

I clear the tickles from my throat. "Call, definitely. I don't want this hanging over my head for any longer than it has to."

I set my phone next to the miniature lake house and dial Dad. It takes three tries to finally get him to pick up his phone.

"Jerry and I just got pizza. Game's about to start," Dad says as soon as he answers. "Can this wait?"

"I need to talk to you now," I say, swallowing. Before I lose my nerve. "Both of you, actually."

"Fine, but hurry. This is the fourth game of a parlay I have going, and I gotta pay attention." The volume on the TV on the other end of the line lowers. "And before you get all huffy, the cashier forgot to charge me for my soda. I told you, my luck's back."

"O-kay," I mumble. "Sure."

"Putting you on speaker," he says. "Have you finally come to your senses?"

I inhale deeply and then let out the breath in one long whoosh. "I have."

And then I tell them my plan. The one I went back and forth between so much that my head spun. The one I lost several nights of sleep over. The one I know won't go over well, but that I think will be best for everyone.

"I'm not going to pay off the missed payments for the lake house," I start.

The metaphorical Hello Kitty Band-Aid has been ripped off.

"You're not— Then what's this grand plan of yours?" Dad asks, his tone still light.

My next intake of air is shaky. Logan senses it and squeezes my hand. I glance down at my handwritten notes, waiting for oxygen to do its job. "We're going to let the house go into foreclosure," I say on a calmer, steadier exhale.

"Wh-What do you mean, go into foreclosure?" Dad asks, coughing out what must be his free soda. "It's where I live. You're not— you're not kicking me out, are you?" He laughs a little like the idea is preposterous.

"The house is too expensive to maintain. We won't be able to fix it up, either."

Dad grunts. "I almost fell on those stairs the other day, though. You're not thinking clearly. This is a mistake. You could pay for it all and then some if you wanted. You won millions!"

"I actually couldn't." I don't go into specifics. "And that's not how I want to spend the money. This isn't my problem to fix."

Just like Dad can't control the outcome of the games he bets on, I can't control him.

But this? This I can control.

"When your grandfather built the house, he didn't think about the future," Dad says. "He didn't think about how hard it would be to find people who have the skills to fix real craftsmanship. Homes are built fast and cheap now, but that's why this home is so special. It meant a lot to your mom, and it means a lot to me."

It takes everything in me not to bark out a laugh. If the house meant something to him, it wouldn't look the way it does.

"And it means something to Jerry. Right, Jerry?" Dad adds.

For the first time the entire call, Jerry mumbles a "yeah."

"This house is part of the family. You can hand it down to your kids one day. Don't you want that?" Dad asks. "I can't believe you want to let it go, just like that."

It's not just like anything.

Dad continues talking, trying to convince me. I let him get it all out. I know this is a lot. I've just gotten started.

"All your summer memories you say you loved so much," Dad says.

"I hope it'll go to a family who loves it just as much," I say, having accepted that my dreams existed because of the circumstances. "I want nothing more than for it to go to people who can make happy memories in it, just as Grandma and Grandpa wanted. I think they'd like that."

"Do you really wanna do this, Hazel?" Jerry asks.

"This is your home," Dad says, borderline pleading.

"Actually, I have a home," I say, sliding closer to Logan. "And it's not the lake house. Not anymore."

"Well, I own the house, and I don't agree to that," Dad says.

"Then you can pay off one hundred percent of the mortgage," I say. "It is your house, and it's in your name. The responsibility falls on you."

"You know the Powerball only got as big as it did because of people like me, right? Your whole life you've always hated gambling, and now you do it? Hypocritical is what that is. You know you wouldn't have that money if it weren't for me, right?" Under Dad's flippancy, I hear desperation. "Think of this as a return or a thank-you."

"No." I push more air behind this word so it doesn't come out sounding hesitant.

Dad lets out a stream of curses. "My daughter wins the fucking lottery, and I get kicked out. How did I get so unlucky?"

I don't bother attempting an answer to his rhetorical question. But because I know he's hurting—we're all hurting—I offer, "I'll pay for grief counseling and therapy, if you want it. I've looked into a therapist for myself. I think it could help us process—"

"Rehab? Therapy? Jesus, Hazel. Oh, I meant to tell you that I'm gonna sign myself out," he tries. He's really reaching now. "The casino won't let me back in after that."

I hold strong. "I hope you do, but that doesn't change any of this."

Dad's voice takes an accusatory turn. "What's gotten into you? You're being reckless."

No. Reckless would be giving Dad and Jerry more money.

"This way you can live somewhere more manageable. You didn't have a choice in inheriting the house," I say, trying to come from a place of compassion. "You can have a choice now."

"Nothing about this feels like a choice," Dad says. "If you really want to help, you'll give us some of that money. You used to want to spend thousands on fixing up this piece of shit house, and now you won't even help your living, breathing family." He scoffs bitterly.

He's not listening.

"It's all I can do right now. And Jerry, I know about your legs."

Now it's Jerry's turn to curse. He says something to Dad that I can't hear. "Hazel, I seriously did hurt them," he says. "I swear, I did."

"I know you did. But they weren't broken. They also didn't cost nearly as much as you claimed they did," I say. "You lied to me. And you tried to use me. That's not okay."

It's not okay to be treated like this.

"Your brother was hurt, Hazel," Dad says. "Have some heart."

"Where did you even get those photos, Jerry?" I ask. "Google?"

He's quiet, which gives me my answer.

I focus on Logan's bookshelf tree, the rows of colorful spines. I remind myself that it's okay to be upset. That if I want to cry, I can. I'm allowed to feel my way through this call. I didn't come into this thinking it'd be easy.

"You won't be getting any more money from me," I tell him, my core twisting into more knots.

"You're cutting me off?" Jerry asks.

"I'm not your parent. Or your bank. Or your fiduciary," I say, any last remaining wobbles in my voice steadying into something more forceful. I've played fair with them my whole life. I've been living too much in the past, helping Dad and Jerry. Playing the role I always have. "You can get a job, and you can make your own money."

Jerry whines. "It's hard to find remote work."

I shake my head at my phone. "Then maybe it's time to find somewhere to live that's more permanent. You could—" I stop myself. "You'll have to figure that out."

"Is this because of the legs thing?" Jerry asks. "Look, I'm sorry. I had a lot of credit card debt, okay? I think you'd agree that I couldn't sell the van. That's how I make my living. Please don't punish Dad for what I did."

"Punish?" I repeat. "What I do with that money isn't about any of you. I get to make my own choices."

Before, I never had the option to choose. Or maybe I had the option all along, but I didn't feel like I did.

"So you're just going to abandon us?" Dad asks.

For a few long seconds, time loses its shape. I recognize this as the moment when I'd go numb. Try to detach. Not have to feel how horrible this is. But I do feel how horrible this is. And for the first time ever, I say something about it.

"If anyone on this call has been abandoned, it's me," I say, my voice firm. "I've spent my entire life paying for it and then some. I won't be used or bullied or manipulated anymore."

I glance at Logan, who's glaring at my phone. He looks furious, his jaw set and eyes dark. Like if he could take my phone and throw it out the window, he would do it in a heartbeat.

"Your mother would be so disappointed," Dad spits out.

Logan's eyes catch mine, and they soften around the edges. He shakes his head. "She wouldn't be. Not even a little," he whispers, pulling me into his arms. For the first time ever, I feel like I can handle the anger inside of me. The lows are suddenly bearable with his simple loving gesture.

Feeling my way through this gives me a new realization. Mom wouldn't want this for me. For any of us. And I don't think Mom would be disappointed in me. I think she'd be disappointed in Dad and Jerry. But I don't have to fight cruelty with cruelty. I can still have compassion and be firm in my decisions.

"I'm not calling to negotiate," I say. "These are my offers. You can take them or not. Up to you."

It's a tricky thing, being needed. It's validating, in its own weird way. It feels like being in control. If there's anything this experience has taught me, though, it's that I want to be needed for who I am. Not because of what I can give people.

"Didn't realize I raised such an ungrateful brat who puts her family last—"

I end the call, not waiting to hear the rest of what Dad has to say.

I blink at the wallpaper on my phone. It's a photo of the sunset from the firehouse. A daily reminder of the life I'm making for myself. A daily reminder of home.

"Oh my god, did I really use the word 'fiduciary'?" I ask, stunned.

"Sounded like it just rolled off your tongue," Logan says, running his hand down his face.

"I'm proud of myself," I manage to say.

"Sweetheart, there aren't enough words for me to express how proud of you I am, too," Logan says. His term of endearment nearly cracks me in half in my already fragile state. He looks like he's just won a contest after a long dry spell of luck. As though my wins are his.

This must be what it feels like to be in it with someone all the way. Because this entire time, I've been fighting for his wins, too.

I don't know what will happen with my family any more than I know what my future holds. But I do know that right now I've trusted myself to make the best decision with the information I have. That's all I can do.

Closure, I'm learning, isn't a sure thing. Messy parts of life don't get wrapped up in pretty bows. I'm going to have to live with the discomfort of situations not resolving quickly. Or maybe at all. Maybe not everything is meant to be fixed.

"If you really did get my fortunes, this must be what Wendy was saying about having everything you need to make your dreams a reality," Logan says. "Not that this was a dream, but everything you just did was already inside of you."

I had viewed everything happening with my family as bad luck. But flip or no flip, maybe being forced to face this, to stand up for myself, was good all along. I lose something, but I gain something, too.

I nod. "Maybe so."

I run the tips of my fingers along the little dock, remembering the last time I sat on it with Grandma and Grandpa. We were looking back at the house, the sun making a showy descent.

"That right there, that's my whole life," Grandpa had said to me. "One day you'll be that lucky, too."

I turn his words over in my head. Scaled down to the size of half a coffee table, I see the house and Grandpa's comment in an entirely new light. Air deflates from my lungs as it all suddenly becomes so vibrantly clear.

He was never talking about the house. He wasn't even looking at it. Only I was.

With Grandpa in my periphery, I had been admiring the way the sun's golden rays reflected off the house's teal paint.

And Grandpa had been looking at Grandma.

A small sound escapes my throat. I wanted this house because I was holding on to a dream. A dream that would never become a reality.

But there are other dreams—better ones—that I never dared to envision for myself. And right here, right now, they're already starting to come true.

"Thank you for this. For all of it. I love it. I love you," I tell Logan. They're not powerful enough words for what I feel. They'll have to do for now.

It's when he kisses my forehead and tells me that he loves me back that I lose it. I'm half sobbing, half laughing into my hands. I'm not even crying because I'm sad. I'm crying because, finally, I feel free.

Time to rise from the ashes.

"How do waffles sound?" Logan asks.

Phoenixes do need to eat.

"Like a dream," I say.

And it does. I want the big stuff, sure. A home, a grand love story. But the big stuff only becomes big because of the little stuff:

breakfast for dinner, rowboats, disguises, bags of candy, and cinnamon lattes.

I want more of that. With Logan. Every day. I don't know how I get more fortunate than that.

Logan jumps up, bending over to kiss the top of my head. "I'll get those going and reheat the eggs and sausages."

For the rest of the night, we eat breakfast and watch *Ghost*. I let worries about the future slip away, along with any happy visions about what a life would look like with Logan.

I'm living it now, presently.

And right now, this is the moment that matters most.

Chapter 28

HAZEL

I'm not religious, but the moment the scent of chlorine greets me at the entrance of the YMCA is a nearly spiritual experience. I make my way across the tiled floor, the flipping of my sandals matching the beating of my heart. I adjust my swimsuit strap as I approach the pool's edge, water splashing up over my toes.

I stare down the turquoise lane. My muscles twitch in eager anticipation underneath prickling skin, already preparing itself for the cool water.

I let my eyes fall closed for just a few seconds. I catalog the symphony of noises around me: splashes from the swimmer in the next lane over, voices traveling across the surface of the pool, a high-pitched whistle from the lifeguard settling in for duty.

The water, in all its sparkling glory, moves with the other swimmers' movements. It mirrors everything above it, including the overhead lights, the triangle flags, and the lifeguard's tall chair.

And me.

I blink, trying to focus on my rippling reflection. For the length of a breath, the water stills, and I can see myself clearly.

"There you are," I whisper.

I feel a smile take over my face as I jump in. The water's cold. Shocking. Glorious. I let myself sink down, my body tingling as small air bubbles roll off my skin and rise to the surface. I push off the black strip lining the bottom, blasting up toward the light.

When I pierce the surface, my arms shoot out in front of me, pulling the water back. I breaststroke down the lane. My muscles and lungs burn. For the next thirty minutes, it's just me and the water.

And it's right there in the Chinatown YMCA pool that I come back to myself. That I learn how to breathe again.

Chapter 29

LOGAN

The first night of the show is a mess.

The rowboat wheels get jammed, the blocking on the lodge's lobby set is off, and two actors forget their lines. One even drops a plate of fake fruit, plastic apples and pears rolling into the audience. The fan we use to blow the scent of campfire out into the audience decides its last day of work was yesterday.

The audience has no idea any of it isn't supposed to happen.

Good things happen, too, though. The dock's legs stay put, and the sparklers work when they should. Nothing catches on fire.

Mr. Moon makes his appearance just before intermission. As the show's leads sing from the rooftop, he's lowered from the rafters. Moon problem, solved.

From the wings, I peek out to the audience and immediately spot a laughing Hazel, who's hard to miss in her floral Hawaiian shirt. She had no idea about Mr. Moon's cameo. She points him out to Emma and Gloria, her two friends she brought with her. Probably she's telling them how I almost made her smash him to pieces.

The second half of the show isn't any better, but by the time the curtain closes, there's a buzzy energy going around in the front of house and backstage.

"Well, that was...not great," I'm the first to say once the show has ended. It wasn't even close.

"Yes, but our show is officially live," Mrs. Walker says. "Roman would've loved every second of it."

Richie pats my back. "You're still here, Mr. Big Bucks? I would've quit yesterday."

News ended up spreading across the city—and the theater. Truthfully, I consider myself lucky that this information didn't change the way my coworkers treat me.

"Then who'd beat you next year in Fantasy Soccer?" I ask.

"After how badly you lost this year?" Richie scoffs. "Yeah, right."

"We'll see."

Each team's got a laundry list of what to improve, fix, and talk to the actors about, but we did it. We made it to opening night. Tomorrow, we get a chance to try again. We'll just keep tweaking, and the next show will be a little bit better than tonight was. Same with the night after that.

Hazel meets us backstage, and I introduce her to Mrs. Walker.

"Apologies for my cat," Mrs. Walker says. "I heard about the trouble he's caused."

I don't know if she realizes she does it, but Hazel runs her fingers down the arm Toffee scratched. "No trouble at all," Hazel says with a genuine smile. "Your cat might be one of the best things to happen to me." Her eyes flick over to me. "I owe him."

Mrs. Walker raises an eyebrow. "Careful. He just might take you up on that."

Once we clean up and reset for the next day's show, Hazel, Richie, Emma, Gloria, and a bunch of the cast and crew head out for a postshow dinner. Mrs. Walker declines our invite, claiming that it's well past her bedtime and that Toffee won't appreciate being left alone for so long.

After shows, we'd sometimes celebrate at Curtain Call Pizzeria, which is where we're headed now. Or at least that's where I thought we were going. The street to the diner is blocked off. Construction, maybe?

Hazel grabs my hand and pulls me forward. "Come on," she says.

"Looks like it's closed."

She ignores the cones and signs. "Let's just see."

I follow her, and the group follows me. She leads me toward the pizzeria, which isn't under construction. Neither is the road in front of it. Right in the center of the street is a giant inflatable pool filled with plastic pit balls and oversize New York–themed stuffed toys. A medium-size crane is positioned along the fringe of the pool.

"Is that a four-foot soft pretzel?" I ask.

"I was hoping you could win it for me this time," Hazel says, her face lit up.

"Wait," I mumble. Hazel's bouncing on her toes, not fazed at all. "Did you do this?"

"All your hard work deserved to be celebrated."

"Should we really be celebrating a man in the front row being bopped in the head with a plastic apple?" I ask.

Delighted laughter spills out of her. "At the very least, it deserves to be acknowledged." She wraps her arms around my waist. "Congrats on your first show as head carpenter! I'm officially a big fan of musicals."

I can't get over what I'm seeing. "You. You spent money on"—I gesture to the human-size toy crane machine she's essentially re-created in the streets of New York—"that? But these are specifically the types of things you don't spend money on."

"Sometimes exceptions need to be made," she says. "Especially when the crane machine in the pizzeria is too unpredictable."

"This had to be expensive," I say. "I thought we were cooling it on the big gestures."

"*You* were," she clarifies. "I was due for one. And crane rentals are surprisingly not too bad. It was the shutting down of this block that wasn't cheap, but Gloria knew a guy."

I run my hand through my hair. "You saw what happened the last time I tried to play this game."

She nods in recollection. "When the games are rigged, you have to make your own game." That's wise, but I'm still on the fence. Hazel must still be able to sense this because she adds, "You literally can't lose this one."

"I don't know—"

"We're not here to talk. We're here to have fun," she says, guiding me to the crane operator. "Now get in there!"

The group huddles around as I'm strapped up in a harness and lifted over the pool of toys and pit balls. I point where I want to go, the crane operator controlling my movements. I laugh every time the crane pushes and pulls me. I feel like a big kid dangling in the air like this.

I point down once I'm over the plush Hazel wants. I loop my cast through one of the loops. As the crane pulls me up, I make too much of a show about it, and the pretzel slips off my arm.

"Come on now!" I shout. Down below, Hazel bursts out laughing.

Just before the crane operator can move me back to the start, I kick my leg out and flip the pretzel up in the air, catching it between my calves. To cover my bases, I wrap my legs and arms around the toy.

"I'm not taking any more chances!" I call out.

Hazel cheers me on from the edge of the pool. I ask the crane operator to bring me to her. I drop the soft pretzel in her arms from above, lowering just enough so I can kiss her midair.

"You won!" Hazel says, hugging the plush toy.

It's hard to ignore the fact that I'm strapped into a harness over an arcade game come to life. Yet all I care about right now is Hazel. She doesn't just say everything will be better. She makes it better. I take in her delighted expression, bright eyes, and wide-cheeked smile, and more than anything I've ever known before, I know this: Love was my real windfall.

"I really did," I say, hovering in front of her, my calves sinking into the pit balls. "Thank you for this. For everything."

Hazel sneaks in one last kiss. "You worked so hard to get to tonight. It was time for some fun."

A line has already formed with Gloria at the front of it. I'm taken back to the start for everyone else to have a turn.

While that's happening, Suze brings out trays of milkshakes, pizza, and waffle fries for everyone who's waiting. It's after 11:00 p.m., but we've got the glow of Times Square pouring in on one side and the lights from restaurant and store signs filling in the other. Our evening is soundtracked by the noises of the city: taxis honking, crowds of people brushing past each other, chatter from nearby bars, and the songs of Miles Davis played by a saxophonist on the street corner.

A month and a half ago, I would've chalked up a night like this to me being lucky. If I'm honest, that feeling is still there, just a little. To exist at the same time as Hazel, to live in the same city as her. There's a little bit of luck there.

The rest of this, though? It feels earned.

While the cast and crew mingle and celebrate tonight, I get a moment alone with Hazel. We sit next to each other in one of the seats outside the pizzeria, facing the ball pit.

"I saw your win. I'm adding a tally," Suze says, meeting us at our table.

"I'll add it to the tracker," Hazel says playfully. "The positive column will finally get a tally."

Suze hands us chocolate milkshakes. "Finally got the machine fixed. Sorry that took so long."

"It's right on time," I say as Hazel and I clink glasses.

"I'm loving this look on you," I tell Hazel after a long sip of my milkshake.

"We're a sight for sore eyes, huh?" she says through a laugh as she runs her hands down her turquoise and yellow top. "It was my mom's. She had a whole box of them, and I had forgotten." She smiles, and I can tell this discovery made her very happy. "I figured if I was surprising you with this, I might as well go all in."

Could I have predicted that it'd be Hazel giving me a run for my money for most colorful clothing? Never. Guess the future has surprises up its sleeve, too.

"This must've taken you weeks to plan," I say.

"I only came up with it a few days ago," she admits. "I didn't have much time to think it through."

"A spur-of-the-moment human crane machine. Impressive."

Hazel gives me a knowing look. "Sometimes impulsivity can lead to the very best things."

"Like you," I say.

"You took my line." She takes her first sip of milkshake, her eyes widening when she does. "Okay, you were right. That's the best in the city."

I laugh. "So glad you're in the know now. You want to know something else?" I ask. "I normally don't walk Toffee when there's even the slightest chance of rain, but I stayed later at work that day and felt guilty that he didn't get his daily fresh air. I took him out without looking at the forecast." I gesture between us. "So two impulsive decisions led to this."

Hazel grins. "A lot more than two impulsive decisions led to this." She takes another sip. "Being open to the unknown, my world has been better for it. I don't know... Maybe doing things on a whim is just as important as the things you plan out. The things you can control. Life feels a little more serendipitous in a way."

"Like in a lucky kind of way?"

"I meant it more, like, fortuitous," she says, cutting herself off with a shake of the head. "No. Wait. Like in an unexpected kind of way."

"Unexpected, huh? Are you also changing your tune on fortune tellers?"

"Never once has fortune-telling given me hope. You know what has?"

"The fact that people actually do win the lottery? Because sometimes it seems a little too unbelievable," I say, stirring my milkshake with the straw.

"Especially when the jackpot gets really high," Hazel agrees. "Like, no way there are people winning that thing. Well, there are, but yeah, that's not what I was going to say." She grabs my arm. "It was you who gave me hope. I owe you for that."

"You really don't."

Hazel looks uncertain. "Maybe fortune-telling isn't all nonsense. And fine, maybe the future really is a mystery," she says with a teasing eye roll. "I wanted someone to tell me everything would be okay. That my future would be okay. That *I'd* be okay. If I knew what was to come, I thought I might be able to control it or fix it."

"If there's anything we've learned from trying to flip my fortune, it's that not much can be controlled."

We watch as Richie attempts to do spins over the ball pit, making everyone laugh.

"Fiona from the gas station said we have the power to change our lives," Hazel says, going quiet for a moment. "And our fortunes."

"So maybe it's a self-fulfilling prophecy then," I say.

"Right. We can hear what someone predicts our future to be, but ultimately, it comes down to how we interpret the reading," she says.

"Completely."

"We were given insights into the current state of our lives. But we also got to think about different paths forward because of it. We had the power to make choices. To make change," she says, thinking for a moment. "And let's say I did know what those fortune readings really meant. I wouldn't have been able to stop my brother from lying. Or prevent my dad from letting the house fall apart and go into pre-foreclosure." She shakes her head. "Maybe we shouldn't know everything. Though I would like to know that Wendy and her birds are okay."

"You'd think she'd have seen Toffee coming, you know what I mean?" I joke.

A smile stretches across Hazel's face. "I didn't want to say it, but..."

"Next year," I say, "we'll go find her again. Make sure she and Doc and Marty are all right. Though I still feel like one day they'll come back to haunt us."

"Or protect us," she says, running her thumb over her bracelet's bird charm. A crowd has formed outside the barricades, trying to figure out what's going on as the lead actor of the show dangles from the crane and heads straight for a stuffed coffee cup.

"I'd much rather make a life than be a passive recipient of one, even if it means being unlucky."

"Even if that means you break your winning crane machine streak?" Hazel asks.

"Especially if that's what it means," I confirm. "I'm not going to say it's because losing makes the wins sweeter, but…"

Hazel laughs, playfully rolling her eyes. "You literally just said it. What are you going to say next? That acknowledging the negative feelings makes the positive feelings better, too?"

"I wouldn't dare be so cliché." I grab her hand and bring it to my lap. "Maybe I do need to say it, though, because you're the first person who has ever made me feel that for real. You're the first person who's wanted to know my thoughts, the good and the bad. I don't have to put on a constantly happy face with you. I can be myself. All of me."

"Your optimism, your energy…they're some of my favorite things about you," she says. "But your sad, angry, negative thoughts and feelings? I love those just as much. It shows me that you trust me. And that means everything."

I push the whipped cream down into the melting chocolate ice cream. "We're living proof that you can change your luck and your future. I'm still not flying for a good six months, though."

"I'd make it a year," Hazel says. "You know, there were times I did actually feel a little lucky. Meeting you. Knowing you. Loving you. You showed me what it feels like to trust. You've shown me a happiness that can last."

"I'll show you for as long as you let me," I promise.

Her eyes sparkle. "I believe you."

I would live in this moment with Hazel forever if I could, with our milkshakes, and pizza, and fries. With our friends, and the music of the city, and the accomplished feeling of having one show under our belts.

There are still hard times ahead, because of course there are. But when I'm up against my next challenge, I can face it with honesty and truth. I can face it with everything I am, and not just parts of me. I no longer have to hide.

After everything we've been through, I know Hazel and I can weather tough things on our own. What feels like a minor miracle is that we don't have to. We have each other.

And I intend on loving Hazel through it all, even when it's uncomfortable.

Seconds later, the sky releases a steady, soft drizzle over us, the rain only visible in the dark when the light of the streetlamps catches the droplets at just the right angle. I expect everyone to run for cover, for the night to be cut short.

No one even flinches. They abandon the crane and jump into the inflatable pool, having splash fights with the stuffed toys and balls. The saxophonist doesn't stop. Life goes on, even when it's uncomfortable.

Then something funny happens inside me. I don't feel the need to say something positive to try to save this beautiful night Hazel's organized.

Not that she'd even need it anyway. Hazel has her head tilted up to the night sky, letting the rain wash over her forehead, her eyelids, her lips. She's smiling from rain-soaked cheek to cheek. This moment is still perfect.

I stand and pull her up gently by the hand. "Dance with me."

Hazel follows my lead, standing to meet me in the middle of the street. She presses up against me, resting her palm in mine. We sway side to side, finding a rhythm of our own.

"There wasn't rain in the forecast," she says with a laugh.

"Who knows? Maybe we'll even get snow," I say, half joking.

"I'm not ruling anything out at this point."

Me neither. More impossible things have happened.

A zigzag of lightning flashes across the sky, and now we really should get moving. Instead, Hazel squeezes my hand and says, "We better be careful. It's easier to get struck by lightning than to win the lottery, you know."

I laugh through my nose. "With the way things have been going for us," I murmur, ducking my head to get a good look at her, "I'd say we have a better chance of winning the lottery again."

Hazel half groans, half laughs as she wraps her hand around the back of my neck and pulls me down to kiss her. Booms of thunder surround us, but this feels like the opposite of destruction, chaos, and pain.

It feels like we've hit the jackpot for a second time.

Epilogue

HAZEL

Eleven months later

Turns out, Wendy and her birds aren't okay.

They're more than okay. Thriving even.

We find them at the Good Fortune Fair. The setup is the same as last year, with food booths, and strung lights, and a festive atmosphere. It's like no time has passed.

By the looks of it, Wendy had caught wind of our news. There's a printout of our photo with the big check. The writing next to it: *Predicted the jackpot winners having abundance.*

At least it's the disguised version of me. Wendy's also taken the time to color over our names with marker.

What is there to do but laugh? Everyone's got to make a living.

Wendy's busy. The line to see her snakes down the block. Just before we move on, she looks up and catches my eye. There's a glint. Something knowing. I give her a small wave, and she looks away before I can tell for sure.

"Bo's here, too," Logan says.

He's focused on his work, reading tea leaves for two young women. I'm relieved that they're smiling at whatever it is he's saying.

We continue strolling, our stomachs filled with mooncakes and crispy lotus root chips. Logan wanders off to a stall while I browse colorful lanterns for sale. When he returns, he's picked up orange and yellow chrysanthemums from one of the flower booths down the block.

Whenever we aren't cat sitting Toffee, who insists on eating petals like it's his sole purpose in life, Logan brings me bodega flowers. He said he's trying to make up for all the times he never got to. I still don't spend money on that kind of thing, but I've come to love this gesture. And that it makes him happy. Which makes me happy.

I take the bouquet from him, giving him a kiss in return.

He nods toward the lanterns I've been browsing. "You want to get some for the apartment?" Logan asks.

Home.

The one we now share in the East Village. A neighborhood—and a place—of our very own.

"They're lucky, right?" he asks.

I lift one. "They are."

We end up buying two. Not that we need the luck. These days, we're making our own.

Logan never quit or got fired as head carpenter from *Windfall*. It took them a few weeks after opening night to work out the kinks, but from the start, it received rave reviews from critics and fans and is still the hottest ticket in town. The show was even nominated for Best Musical at the Tony Awards, a first-ever nomination for Mrs. Walker as a producer. She walked the red carpet with Toffee in tow. It was a dangerous night for birds everywhere. Logan and I celebrated at the firehouse with Chinese food and extra fortune cookies. Just in case.

The show was extended, giving Logan some time to settle in until the next show moves into the theater. There's chatter that *Windfall* will hit the road on a traveling tour this spring. Logan's considering the head carpenter role to lead the traveling crew. I'd tag along for a bit and do some more traveling.

For the holidays, we took a spontaneous—and all-expenses paid—trip to Spain. Our magazine feature comes out next week. Yes, we got there by plane. Logan's still here. It's surreal that we got to see the Basilica de la Sagrada Família with our own eyes. There are dozens more countries on our list to visit in the coming years. But for now, we're content with the predictability of a routine.

Logan no longer runs his storage and transfer business. Instead, he's made room for more of what he loves: building, working with his hands, and turning wood into beautiful furniture—with drawers that open. He's been saving up his lottery money to open a woodworking shop for teenagers and young adults who have struggled with substance abuse. It's a place for a second chance. A place to restart.

I spend my days at Sweet Escape, working alongside Emma and Gloria, who's been on the payroll for months managing inventory while Emma's focused on growth and expansion. I do a little bit of everything at the shop, with most of my time going toward analyzing data. Making forecasts. Predicting trends. The usual data fortune-telling stuff.

I had told Emma and Gloria about my lottery win that day in the shop. They never again mentioned it out of respect for my privacy. It only came back up when I expressed interest in being an investor in Emma's second location after this year's increased annuity amount was deposited. We're working as quickly as we can to open a second Sweet Escape in the Meatpacking District in time for the holidays.

The house went into foreclosure. The highest bidder was a family with three kids in elementary school who love to swim. It's just my luck.

Even luckier, the family doesn't want to tear the house down. Instead, they wasted no time starting repairs and renovations to bring the house back to the version it used to be. I like to imagine the five of them making key lime blondies on Grandma's baking bar and sharing them with neighbors when they go out on their boat at sunset.

My relationship with Dad and Jerry was tense for the first few months after our phone call. I wouldn't say it's great, even now, but the ice between us is slowly thawing.

Dad begrudgingly moved into an apartment nearby. I gave him the number to my financial advisor, hoping he'd reach out to make good choices with the little money he got from the house sale, but I don't know if he ever did call. He still won't go to rehab or therapy. I talk to him mostly on his birthday and holidays. It's hard, but I try not to concern myself with the minutiae of his day-to-day.

Jerry's sprains healed up nicely. He and Danielle went their separate ways shortly before Thanksgiving. He's now in New Hampshire, focusing on his photography and working his way out of financial debt. He sold his van and is slowly working to pay me back for the fake surgery down payment he tricked me into. Plus interest. It hasn't been, like he guaranteed, the easiest money I ever made, but it has been the most gratifying.

Will I ever fully trust Dad and Jerry? Maybe, but I have a lot of my own work to do on that front, too. And that's between my therapist and me.

"Hazel. Hazel!" Logan calls out, drawing my attention from a booth serving Peking duck wraps. "Look!"

He's hunched over on the sidewalk. I run, concerned. When he looks up at me, his bracketed smile tells me everything's okay. Great, in fact. Because there, between the cracks of the sidewalk, is a bright green four-leaf clover the size of my thumbnail.

"You pick it," he says. "Then give it to me. It's supposed to double your luck."

"I'm not taking your luck."

"Well, I'm not taking yours."

"We can't just leave it there!" I say, ignoring the stares we're getting from passersby. "Or...maybe we can."

"We searched for hours. My eyes will never be the same. I was seeing squares in my dreams for weeks!" Logan runs his hand through his hair. "And now you want to leave it?"

"For someone else," I say. "They might need the luck more than we do."

Logan stands and takes my hands in his. He got his cast off just before last Christmas and hasn't broken any more bones since.

"Okay. I like that." He drops a kiss against my temple. "And I already get to love you. That makes me the luckiest."

I wrap my arm around his waist as we wind our way through the fair, checking out the other stalls.

Logan comes to an abrupt stop. "What would you say to checking out that place?" He points to a stall with the words "kau chim" written on its sign.

"I say no way."

I've been trying not to overthink anything that isn't within my control. That's just another way of trying to predict the future. And I have no idea what's going to happen.

For now, I'm learning how to trust life as it comes. I'm continuing to learn how to trust myself.

Logan nudges me. "One more for old times' sake?"

"Absolutely not."

"We might go home empty-handed, or we could win big," he says, thinking this will tempt me.

I'm skeptical, but also kind of intrigued. "We already did win big, in more ways than one." I glance back over at the sign.

Haven't we pushed our luck enough? Everything's been going so well. Yes, metaphorical shoes have dropped, but Logan and I have been there to catch them. Together. We've made our own fortune. It's what we've been doing since the beginning.

"You want to do a temp check? After all this time?" I ask.

"Let's just see," Logan says. "I owe you dim sum after."

I take a deep breath in as we head toward the fortune teller. She has availability now, inviting us to sit down in the two chairs across from her. A red tube sits on the table between us, patterned cloth spread over the surface.

"Have either of you done Chinese fortune sticks before?" she asks after introducing herself as Mel.

We shake our heads no. And while it's true, it doesn't feel accurate. We haven't done this kind of fortune-telling before, but doing a fortune reading together isn't unusual. We've been here before. Because of me. Because of Toffee. Because of who knows what else.

And then my spontaneous act somehow turned into *our* tradition. So here we are in another fortune teller's booth. Again.

Mel explains to us that Chinese fortune sticks, or kau chim, is one of the oldest fortune-telling methods. Inside the tube are sticks with numbers on them. We're supposed to ask a question and then shake the tube until one of the sticks falls out. The number on the stick corresponds to our fortune in a booklet, which she holds up for us both to see.

"It's based on numbers?" I ask.

Mel nods. "This is also known as lottery poetry."

I cast my eyes over to Logan. There's a hint of amusement dancing across his teal irises.

I can't help but laugh. Because of course it's called that. And

THE FORTUNE FLIP

nothing feels more poetic than the two of us playing a lottery together, yet again.

"What if we ask a joint question?" I propose to Logan.

He rubs his chin, nodding. "Minimize the chances of any flipping."

"Exactly. Toffee's already with Mrs. Walker today so we can rest easy there."

"Okay, let's do it," he says.

"Same question?" I ask.

"As always."

Mel pops the lid off the tube and hands it to me.

The sticks inside look like long Popsicle sticks, their wood faded with red painted on the ends. Chinese numbers are printed along the sides of each one.

Did our luck actually flip? I do wonder about it every now and then. I've learned to accept that we may never really know what happened that day in September. In life, you don't always get concrete answers any more than you get answers about the future.

Even when you hold on tight and try to take control, nothing is certain. Nothing is guaranteed.

Maybe it's when we resist trying to solve life's mysteries that we get to enjoy our present, welcome the future, and reflect contentedly on the past.

Maybe, by letting go of what we *think* we know, we actually change the prophecy.

"What does our future look like?" I ask.

And then, without a second thought, I begin shaking the tube.

The wood knocks against the canister, the sticks slowly inching forward with each movement.

Logan leans closer as one stick becomes a clear front-runner.

I lift the tube and give one last shake. As I do, there's a blur of white, orange, and black. I duck toward Logan, holding my arm over our faces. I peer at the table before glancing over at him. At the same time, we burst out laughing.

Because right there in front of us are Doc and Marty, one of them holding our stick between his orange beak. They look directly at us with their beady eyes for one long breath.

And then they fly away, our fortune disappearing with them.

ACKNOWLEDGMENTS

I've only ever won a lottery once, and that was for tickets to a Taylor Swift concert at the college I went to. And while I've technically lost the Powerball (played as research for this book) and the Great Smoky Mountains Firefly Viewing Lottery (twice, despite having written that experience into my last book), that's okay. Because I won the people jackpot. To have as many wonderful people as I do in my corner, that's the real win.

To Ann Leslie Tuttle, thank you for your endless support. I'm so appreciative that you embrace the ideas I casually toss your way. Thank you also to my film agent, Mary Pender, and the team at WME.

Alex Logan, getting to work with you is such a joy. I'm grateful for you and your sharp insights, humor, and keen eye.

Estelle Hallick and Caroline Green, you're a power duo. Thanks for your passion and excitement and for being such passionate cheerleaders for my books. Thanks also to Rylee Warner, Hanna Lindsley, and Crystal Patriarche at BookSparks for all your efforts on getting this book to readers.

Acknowledgments

What good fortune it is to have a team with amazing folks at Grand Central/Forever, including Beth de Guzman, Leah Hultenschmidt, Dana Cuadrado, Carolina Martin, Daniela Medina, Grace Fischetti, Marie Mundaca, and Melissa Mathlin, Maisa Nammari, Mari C. Okuda, Kristin Errico, and the production team, the sales reps, Mary Urban and the digital sales team, Susan Moon and the entire audiobook team, and Francesca Begos, Joelle Dieu, and the subrights team.

Sanny Chiu—thank you for, once again, creating a cover I can't stop admiring. Karen Tseng, thanks for making the most gorgeous Chinese name seals that all my personalized books get stamped with.

Big hugs and thanks to the booksellers, librarians, Bookstagrammers, BookTokers, BookStackers, book bloggers, reviewers, journalists, book clubs, festival and event organizers, and podcasters. What you all do is important and needed.

A big thanks to Hank Hale, Katie Garaby, and Kevin Thomas Garcia. Hank, thank you for your kindness and for taking the time to chat all things Broadway carpentry. Your knowledge and passion for the craft helped paint a more vibrant picture of what it's like to be a head carpenter.

As luck would have it, I have incredible parents, the best sister, the smartest nieces, and the most loving aunties. Thanks for the love and support. To the dear friends I've made on this writing and publishing journey—from authors to readers to booksellers—thank you for all the soul-filling coffee hangouts, words of encouragement, and group chats that keep me afloat and laughing through it all.

Patrick, we may never pick the winning combination of numbers, but with you, every day feels like winning the lottery. I'm the luckiest to love you, and to be loved by you.

Acknowledgments

My sweet readers—thank you, thank you, thank you. Where to even begin with trying to convey how much your support and excitement have meant to me? If I had lottery money and could rent out a giant carousel or re-create a life-size crane machine to celebrate you, I would do it in a heartbeat. I really lucked out with you all.

YOUR BOOK CLUB RESOURCE

Visit **GCPClubCar.com** to sign up for the GCP Club Car newsletter, featuring exclusive promotions, info on other Club Car titles, and more.

Find us on social media: **@ReadForeverPub**

THE FORTUNE FLIP

READING GROUP GUIDE

DISCUSSION QUESTIONS

1. Do you consider yourself to be lucky or unlucky? Do you have any lucky charms or rituals?
2. Do you think you can make your own luck? Or are you born lucky or unlucky?
3. Would you go to a fortune teller? Which method (cards, tea leaf reading, palm reading, lottery sticks) would you try?
4. Do you think it's helpful or harmful to hear someone's prediction of your future?
5. If you won the lottery, would you go in disguise? If so, what would you disguise yourself as?
6. If you won the lottery, what would you do with the money? Would you tell your family?
7. If you promised to split a lottery ticket with someone and you ended up winning, would you keep that promise?
8. What's your favorite kind of candy and why?
9. Do you enjoy Broadway shows? What's a show that you have seen or want to see?

10. Hazel superstitiously eats longevity noodles on her birthday and believes candy helps sweeten up life. Do you have any cultural superstitions around food or meals? What are they?

11. Logan struggles with a positive mindset. How do you think positivity can help—or hurt?

12. After Logan's accident, the course of his life went in a different direction. Have you ever had a life incident occur that changed the trajectory of your life? What was it?

13. Hazel and Logan both have people in their lives who look out for them in ways they never expected or had to ask for. Are there people in your life who are like that?

14. What do you think of Hazel's decision with her father and brother? Do you agree with how she handled the situation?

15. What do you think Hazel and Logan's fortune stick said before it got carried away by Doc and Marty? Were they haunting or protecting them?

VISIT **GCPClubCar.com** to sign up for the **GCP Club Car** newsletter, featuring exclusive promotions, info on other **Club Car** titles, and more.

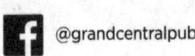 @grandcentralpub   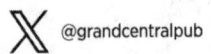 @grandcentralpub   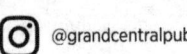 @grandcentralpub

ABOUT THE AUTHOR

Lauren Kung Jessen is a mixed-race Chinese American writer with a fondness for witty, flirtatious dialogue and making meals with too many steps but lots of flavor. She is fascinated by myths and superstitions and how ideas, beliefs, traditions, and stories evolve over time. She lives in New York City with her husband, two cats, and a dog.

You can learn more at:
  Website: LaurenKungJessen.com
  Substack: @LaurenKJessen.Substack
  Instagram: @LaurenKJessen
  Threads: @LaurenKJessen

RAISING READERS
Books Build Bright Futures

Thank you for reading this book and for being a reader of books in general. We are so grateful to share being part of a community of readers with you, and we hope you will join us in passing our love of books on to the next generation of readers.

Did you know that reading for enjoyment is the single biggest predictor of a child's future happiness and success?

More than family circumstances, parents' educational background, or income, reading impacts a child's future academic performance, emotional well-being, communication skills, economic security, ambition, and happiness.

Studies show that kids reading for enjoyment in the US is in rapid decline:

- In 2012, 53% of 9-year-olds read almost every day. Just 10 years later, in 2022, the number had fallen to 39%.
- In 2012, 27% of 13-year-olds read for fun daily. By 2023, that number was just 14%.

Together, we can commit to **Raising Readers** and change this trend. How?

- Read to children in your life daily.
- Model reading as a fun activity.
- Reduce screen time.
- Start a family, school, or community book club.
- Visit bookstores and libraries regularly.
- Listen to audiobooks.
- Read the book before you see the movie.
- Encourage your child to read aloud to a pet or stuffed animal.
- Give books as gifts.
- Donate books to families and communities in need.

Books build bright futures, and **Raising Readers** is our shared responsibility.

For more information, visit **JoinRaisingReaders.com**

Sources: National Endowment for the Arts, National Assessment of Educational Progress, WorldBookDay.com, Nielsen BookData's 2023 "Understanding the Children's Book Consumer"